From Cornwall with Love

Cressy grew up in South-East London surrounded by books and with a cat named after Lawrence of Arabia. She studied English at the University of East Anglia and now lives in Norwich with her husband David. *From Cornwall with Love* is her fourteenth novel and her books have sold over three quarters of a million copies worldwide. When she isn't writing, Cressy spends her spare time reading, returning to London, or exploring the beautiful Norfolk coastline.

If you'd like to find out more about Cressy, visit her on her social media channels. She'd love to hear from you!

🔲 /CressidaMcLaughlinAuthor
🔲 @CressMcLaughlin
🔲 @cressmclaughlin

Also by Cressida McLaughlin

'A wonderful ray of reading sunshine'
Heidi Swain

'I fell completely and utterly in love . . . it had me
glued to the pages'
Holly Martin

'A total hands-down treat. A book you'll want to
cancel plans and stay in with'
Pernille Hughes

'Sizzlingly romantic and utterly compelling, I couldn't put it down'
Alex Brown

'Bursting with [Cressida's] trademark warmth and wit'
Kirsty Greenwood

'Funny, sexy and sweep-you-off-your-feet-romantic'
Zara Stoneley

'Perfectly pitched between funny, sexy, tender and
downright heartbreaking. I loved it'
Jane Casey

'As hot & steamy as a freshly made hot chocolate, and as sweet
& comforting as the whipped cream & sprinkles that go on top'
Helen Fields

'Just brilliant. Sweet, sexy and sizzzzling. It was a pure joy to read'
Lisa Hall

'A little slice of a Cornish cream tea but without the calories'
Bella Osborne

'Perfect escapism, deliciously romantic. I was utterly transported'
Emily Kerr

'Utter perfection . . . a total gem'
Katy Colins

'Sexy, sweet and simmering with sunshine'
Lynsey James

From Cornwall with Love

Cressida McLaughlin

HarperCollins*Publishers*

HarperCollins*Publishers* Ltd
1 London Bridge Street,
London SE1 9GF

www.harpercollins.co.uk

HarperCollins*Publishers*
Macken House, 39/40 Mayor Street Upper
Dublin 1, D01 C9W8

First published by HarperCollins*Publishers* 2023
1

A catalogue record for this book is available from the British Library

ISBN: 978-0-00-850369-7 (PB)

This novel is entirely a work of fiction.
The names, characters and incidents portrayed in it are
the work of the author's imagination. Any resemblance to
actual persons, living or dead, events or localities is
entirely coincidental.

Typeset in Birka by Palimpsest Book Production Limited, Falkirk, Stirlingshire

Printed and bound in the UK using 100% Renewable Electricity by CPI Group (UK) Ltd

This book is produced from independently certified FSC™ paper
to ensure responsible forest management.

For more information visit: www.harpercollins.co.uk/green

To all the readers who have fallen for this series,
and who sometimes think about Charlie, Daniel and
all the other characters living their best lives down
in Cornwall, just as I do.

Prologue

Ten Years Ago

Maisie Winters wanted to be as bright as the summer sun, to sparkle just like the light did on the water on these sultry evenings when she walked along Port Karadow beach, the glittering surface of the ocean taking her breath away. She was off to spend a night at the pub with her friends, and she wasn't going to tell anyone how much hope she held in her heart for this casual occasion, simply because *he* would be there.

'Maisie, we need to get going! If you're coming, still?' Her older sister Heather was calling up the stairs, unable to keep the impatience out of her voice, which was fair enough, because she was going to see her friend Laura, and didn't need to walk in Maisie's direction at all. Heather was back in Cornwall for a couple of weeks, but Maisie knew that her heart and her head were in London now, thinking about her MA in Event Management, her sights set on a future running glamorous, high-profile events.

Heather, unlike Maisie, couldn't wait to move away from the Cornish town for good.

'Nearly there,' she called down and, satisfied with her blue summer dress and its pattern of silver stars, the way her blonde curls had been tightened by the puff of mousse, her eyelashes glossy with mascara, she dabbed her finger in the shimmering highlighter and swiped it over each cheekbone. That, she thought, taking a deep breath, would have to do.

Heather was waiting for her by the front door. Her hair was darker blonde, her frame taller, but their hazel eyes were the same. She held up Maisie's handbag, smiled and said, 'Let's go.'

They walked through the town, the buildings kissed with the soft orange glow of a slowly setting sun, the seagulls' cries near the harbour competing with the trills of black-birds in gardens, the laughter of people enjoying barbecues, windows open and music drifting out. They enjoyed a companionable silence, until Heather said, 'Where are you meeting Gemma?'

'She's not coming.' Maisie fiddled with the tassel on her handbag. 'Some prelim essay about contract law that she has to do for her university course.'

'On a Friday night?' Heather sounded surprised.

'She's dedicated to it,' Maisie said, trying to keep her voice even. 'It's all she talks about – moving up to Durham, the campus, the degree.'

'And you're happy to stay here, working in the shop?' Heather kept any judgement out of her voice, which was good because their mum was already judging her enough for both of them.

'I love working in the ironmonger's,' Maisie said. 'And it'll keep me busy until I decide what I want to do.'

'Mum says you're thinking about teacher training.'

Maisie tried not to roll her eyes. '*Mum* is thinking about teacher training for me.'

'And you don't want to do it?'

'I haven't decided yet. I like the idea of being a teacher, but it would have to be primary age. Working at Port Karadow Primary, where—'

'Your placement wouldn't be here, though,' Heather said.

'I could ask. There are other schools in Cornwall and, when I'm qualified, I could come back.'

Heather laughed gently and reached over to ruffle her hair. Maisie dipped away. 'Hey! Don't mess it up!'

'Why, because Colm's going to be at the pub?' Her eyes widened. 'Colm and his friends and you . . . and *no* Gemma? Oh my God, Maisie! No wonder you're so tense.'

'I am *not* tense,' she protested lamely.

'You'll be fine,' Heather said.

'Of course I will,' Maisie scoffed. But her palms were hot and prickling, her throat felt tight, and when the Sea Shanty – the traditional, slightly scruffy pub that the teenagers always flocked to – came into view, she almost turned around and walked away.

'Want me to come in with you?' Heather asked. Maisie was close to saying yes, but then she didn't, because he was leaning on the wall outside. Colm Caffrey.

He was tall, and had recently gone from gangly to broad shouldered, all the running he did keeping him fit, the

3

surfing making him stronger. His hair, as always, was a thick mess of light brown threaded through with natural blond highlights, and his skin was tanned, with a spray of freckles over his nose and cheeks, as if the sun couldn't get enough of him, wanted to give him all it had.

He turned in their direction and pushed himself off the wall, his face breaking into a smile.

'Winters,' he said. 'Good to see you. And Heather.' He nodded to her sister.

'Hey, Colm,' Heather said. 'I'm not staying, just on my way to see a friend.' She squeezed Maisie's arm, gave her a subtle wink that Maisie hoped Colm hadn't noticed, then said, 'Be good, both of you.'

Maisie watched her stride off up the cobbled street, and turned back to Colm.

'Hey,' she said. She was always, *always* nervous before seeing him, but as soon as she was in his presence, the nerves melted away. Or, at least, they changed gear, became more pleasurable, and mingled with a contentment that she hadn't ever felt with anyone else. He was an electric blanket: comfort and charge and heat all at once.

'Hi.' His smile had softened, and there was something in his light brown eyes – eyes that, she sometimes thought, glowed like amber – that made a shiver run up her spine. God, he was beautiful. And he was so carefree, untroubled by life. Even recently, when his parents had decided to divorce, he had seemed to take it all in his stride, saying he was about to start living his own life, he just wanted them to be happy. But, even so . . .

'Shall we go in?' he said. 'I think Phil and Dev are already inside.'

'Sure.' She clutched onto the tassel of her bag, and when Colm brushed her shoulder with his fingers, to indicate she should go ahead of him, Maisie felt as if all that shimmering, churning sea was inside her, never still, not even for a moment.

Maisie was on her third – or was it fourth? – rum and Coke, and the pub was a haze of laughter and warm bodies, people standing in the spaces between tables, their own corner table hemmed in on all sides. Phil and Stu were having a heated debate about something that had happened on the beach earlier that day, Dev was chatting to a girl who had just come in, and without Gemma, her partner in crime, Maisie was, predictably, feeling slightly lost: as if she should make a swift exit, leave them all to it.

'Winters.' Colm's voice was low and familiar, and when he slid along the bench next to her, moving a cushion out of the way, she could feel the heat coming off him, couldn't ignore the way his white T-shirt sculpted itself to his torso. 'Sorry, it took ages to get to the bar.'

'No problem.' She smiled and took a sip of her drink. He put another one on the table next to her, then mirrored her movement, drinking from his full pint glass.

'They're setting up the karaoke,' he said, lifting his eyebrows.

Maisie laughed. 'You'll have a big audience tonight. All the regulars are in, and a fair few grockles.'

Colm surveyed the packed pub. When he turned back to her, his smile seemed strained. 'Heather down from London for a few weeks?'

'If she lasts that long. She loves her course, keeps talking about going to New York once she's got her MA. Not even London is big enough, it would seem.'

'New York, huh? That's a . . . long way away.'

Maisie ran her hand up her glass, catching condensation. 'I'm happy for her, of course, but I just . . . Gemma's off to Durham in September, and I feel like . . .'

'Like what?' He leaned closer, rested his arm along the top of the bench, so it was behind her, his fingers millimetres from her shoulder.

'Like what I want isn't ambitious enough,' she admitted. 'I'm taking a year out, working with Dad in the ironmonger's, and Mum's on my case to get this teacher training sorted for next year – *this* year if I'm quick about it. She has no idea how these things work. But I don't . . . Why would anyone want to leave Port Karadow, Colm?'

Somewhere along the line her voice had become urgent, because for her, places like London and New York were all well and good, but they didn't have the beauty, the peace, of the Cornish coastline, or the cobbled streets, the sense of closeness, where everyone knew and helped each other, her dad able to chat to his customers like friends, sort out whatever problem they had. She was a bit drunk now, and she couldn't rein in her passion for the place she'd grown up in.

Colm took another, longer sip of beer, his eyes following his hand as he put the glass back on the table. She got the sense that he was considering his answer carefully. When he looked at her, there was something she didn't often see in his eyes. He looked sad.

'What I think,' he said, 'is that you should follow your dreams. And if that dream is to stay here forever, to spend every day living in Port Karadow, loving it, then that is absolutely enough. Don't listen to anyone else, Mais. You don't have to give a shit what they all say to you about qualifications and ambition and striving for something more. My reckoning is that, a lot of the time, when people go after something bigger, they end up regretting it, missing what they left behind.' He blinked a couple of times, took another sip of beer, and shifted closer to her. She was about to ask him what *he* was doing – he was also taking a year out, she knew, and had talked about looking into an apprenticeship in digital media after that – when he spoke again.

'Maisie.' His tone was gentler, and his gaze roamed her face, drifting to her lips, then back up to her eyes. 'You know what you want, and there is a lot of strength in that. Hold your ground, build a life for yourself here. It's the best, *best* thing. If that's what you want for your forever, then take it.'

She was so overcome by his words, by his faith in her, that she wasn't sure if she was imagining it when his finger drifted into her curls, hooked one behind her ear. She felt herself drawing closer to him, examining the freckles on his cheeks, wondering, for the millionth time, what those lips would feel like against hers.

'Maisie, I need to tell you—'

A voice boomed from the side of the pub, cutting him off. 'First up, with Roy Orbison's "You Got It", we have Colm Caffrey. Come up to the stage, son!'

Colm sat back, grinning, and wiped a hand over his face. 'I am just about drunk enough to do this,' he said to her, and Maisie laughed. She loved his confidence, loved that he seemed so effortlessly cool and yet still wasn't afraid to make a fool of himself at pub karaoke.

7

As he got up from the table, giving her arm a quick squeeze, and wove his way through people to the small stage, she wondered how much time they would spend together over the blissful Cornish summer stretching ahead of them; whether they would see each other without Dev or Stu or Phil, or even Gemma in tow.

Maisie knelt on the bench so she could get a better view of him and, as she always did when he belted out this song, she imagined that he was singing it to her. He had wiped away her worries with a few words, had told her that it was OK for her dreams to stay in this town, to set her sights no further than the horizon. He had validated her, had made her feel important, strong, cared for. She took another sip of her drink, then sang along with Colm, holding tightly onto the feelings for him that were blooming in her heart – had been blooming for a while now, if she was honest. Deep, delicious, sometimes scary feelings. She felt, in that moment, that everything was right in her world.

A week later, Colm Caffrey moved to Australia, and Maisie's world shattered into pieces.

Chapter One

Present Day

The late May sunshine streamed in through the window of Port Karadow Ironmonger's, using the display of sun-catchers to create rainbows on the floor. Maisie sipped from her steaming cup of tea and let out a sigh, tucking a blonde curl behind her ear. She wondered how long her dad would have stood this aesthetic delight if he was still sitting behind the counter. As it was, whenever he came in, he cast a critical eye over the changes she'd made, his brows lowered, and made the occasional, noncommittal grunt. If he thought something was really out of place, then he told her. But it was hers now, this shop – her domain. Mostly, anyway.

Her phone rang on the counter next to her, and she surveyed the shop floor, listening out for footsteps, the rustle of someone examining an item in one of the aisles, but it was as she'd thought: the after-lunch rush had died down and, for almost the first time all day, she was alone. She glanced at the screen, then hit the answer button.

'Hey,' she said, leaning her elbows on the counter.

'Maisie!' Her sister's familiar voice rang through the speaker, her Cornish accent morphed into something that was part transatlantic. She'd been living in America for seven years now, working on elaborate events that Maisie sometimes saw photos of on the Instagram grids of magazines. She was used to having her connection with her sister reduced to screens and speakers, the occasional package in the post, and because of that they spoke often, as if quantity would make up for the loss of quality.

'This isn't your usual number,' Maisie said.

'Hank's got a new plan with international minutes, so he said I could call you.'

'Hank's a sweetie,' Maisie said. 'Is everything good?'

'Better than good.' Heather gave a satisfied sigh. 'What about you? How's life in cutie-pie PK? Still loving the dust of the shop?'

'Of course. I've been working on a garden display for the window with solar dragonfly lights and a stone water feature. I'm thinking of getting some gnomes.'

'Oh my God.' Heather's laugh was almost a cackle. 'Dad will *love* that.'

'And Mum,' Maisie added. 'She'll roll her eyes so hard at what my life has been reduced to – window displays and staple guns – that she'll cause permanent damage, then she'll blame me for that too.'

'Can you imagine Mom wielding a staple gun?'

Maisie laughed. 'I can't believe you say *Mom* now. You're so cosmopolitan.'

10

'And you're so Cornish,' Heather shot back. 'But really, don't let her get to you.'

'I'm OK about it,' Maisie said. 'I'm so used to disappointing *Mom* that I'd be genuinely surprised if she thought I was doing anything right. I saw them on Sunday, and the look on her face when I walked in wearing denim dungarees and a scarf around my head. You'd think I'd walked into their house naked.'

'You should attend all Sunday lunches wearing a business suit,' Heather said, then tutted. 'You should know that by now.'

'But not living up to her low expectations keeps my life exciting,' Maisie protested.

'I bet,' Heather said with a laugh. There was a short pause, and it was as if a switch had been flipped: banter done with, it was time to get serious. 'You really doing OK?' Heather asked. 'It can't be easy, having Dad constantly on your case about the shop, and Mum trying to change your mind all the time.'

'Yeah, but it's not like any of that's new, is it? I've got pretty good at weathering the storm, and sometimes Dad even shows some appreciation for what I'm doing.'

Heather gasped. 'Sorry, I might be having a heart attack! Seriously?'

'The other day he told me my display of light switches wasn't appalling.'

'*Wasn't* appalling? Good god, I bet you were overjoyed.'

'I ordered a takeaway pizza from the Happy Shack in celebration.'

'That fancy beachside restaurant?'

'Yup. They started doing takeaways after Christmas, and the seafood pizza is to die for.'

'And how much did Sprout get?' Heather asked.

'None,' Maisie told her. 'I got him some sausages instead.'

Sprout was the love of her life. Her scruffy rescue dog, whose short fur was a lot softer than it looked. His head and ears were mostly brown, but the majority of his body was white, so he looked like he was wearing a mask. He was fiercely loyal, energetic, and prone to being incredibly stupid. Like yesterday morning, when he'd chased a wood pigeon along the path above Port Karadow beach, and the pigeon had, for some inexplicable reason, decided to chase him back. Sprout had hidden behind Maisie, terrified, and ever since then he'd been clingy, as if he imagined the pigeon was holding a vendetta against him.

'You had nobody else to . . .?' Heather left the sentence hanging, and Maisie huffed out a sigh.

'Nobody else to share my epic seafood pizza with, do you mean?'

'You know I do.'

'And *you* know I would have told you if there was. Texted you the aubergine emoji, or a GIF of Chris Evans – Captain America, not the ginger ex-DJ.'

'That's who you're hoping for, is it, Chris Evans? What about that guy from school, the other teacher, Jeremy?'

Maisie pressed her lips together. The bell above the shop door dinged, and she waved as two middle-aged women, whom she recognized from events at A New Chapter, the bookshop in town, headed towards the back of the shop.

It was typical, really. Heather had moved to New York to be an event planner for the rich and famous, entirely career-focused. She had never talked about love in the way Maisie thought about it, as something all-consuming, life-changing. Heather liked casual flings, nothing too long-term, but then an all-American television producer, Hank, had spied her at one of her galas, and the rest was history. And some of Maisie's friends, here in Cornwall, had stumbled into love without even trying, and were now living in blissed-out coupledom, talking about their twilight years together and holding hands unselfconsciously.

Whereas Maisie, who had long dreamed of the kind of love written about in novels, had left a short but horror-filled trail of relationship disasters in her wake. Disasters, and one very intense crush, which was perhaps the place where her attempts at love had begun to go wrong. That first time, aged eighteen, when her heart felt like it had been wrenched in half and then stomped on by a man who had disappeared to the other side of the world and had never known how she felt about him.

But now Heather was asking about Jeremy, and that was complicated, too. As she worked out how best to explain it without prolonging the conversation, her customers' voices drifted over from the paint section. She thought, for one startling, terrifying second, that she'd heard one of them say the words *Colm Caffrey*, but she must have imagined it, conjuring his name because he'd popped into her head.

'Jeremy and I didn't work out,' Maisie said to her sister, keen to banish the spectre of Colm. 'I told you this. We had a couple of dates, nearly two years ago, and I realized he wasn't as . . . that he was hard work. It fizzled out, I left teaching, end of story.'

There was a moment's pause, then Heather said, 'Didn't you tell me, last time we spoke, that he'd asked for your help with something?'

Maisie groaned. 'He got in touch last week because he wants my *organizational prowess* for the school quiz and chips event. He's got this new role, community coordinator, and it seems that even though Mr Fielding, the head teacher, has trusted him with it, he doesn't trust himself. It's nothing more than that.'

'There you go, then.'

'He wants me for my meticulous to-do lists, that's all.' Maisie dropped her voice as the two women approached the counter, each holding several paint tester pots. 'Can I call you back?'

'Hank has free international minutes,' Heather said. 'Just put the phone down and I'll wait.'

'OK.' Maisie took the tester pots, scanned them and put them in a large paper bag. Beside her, Sprout popped his head up, and the women fawned over him, just as – Maisie was sure – he'd hoped.

'What a sweetie,' the younger woman said.

'He's so well-behaved,' added the older one.

'Sometimes,' Maisie replied. 'Sometimes, he's the most badly behaved dog in the whole of Port Karadow.'

'Oooh, I can't imagine that.' The older woman was cooing now. 'You're too adorable, aren't you?'

Sprout gazed up at them, pretending to be the obedient dog they imagined he was.

Maisie resisted the urge to ask them whether they'd really mentioned Colm, but she knew, *knew* that they hadn't, so instead she gave them a receipt and said a cheery goodbye, the bell above the door pinging as they left, letting in a waft of spring breeze that made the sun-catchers dance and sent rainbows spiralling across the shop.

Maisie picked up her phone. 'Sorry about that.'

'You were telling me about Jeremy,' Heather said.

'I had *finished* telling you about Jeremy,' Maisie corrected. 'He is not a romantic option. Anyway, why are you trying to organize my love life? Can't you be satisfied with your own?'

'I told you, everything's really good with me and Hank. We're going to get a place together.'

'I thought you already lived together.'

'In *his* apartment. We've decided to get somewhere new that's jointly ours, perhaps a little further out of the city, with more space.' Her sister suddenly sounded timid, as if by saying it out loud, she might jinx it.

'More space for . . .?' Maisie grinned.

'A pet,' Heather rushed. 'Maybe.'

'A pet would be lovely,' Maisie said sincerely.

When Heather was ready to talk about what she and Hank really had in mind, then Maisie would be there for her, but she didn't want to pressure her. It made her realize how much people were moving on with their lives.

Her friend Ollie, who had moved to Port Karadow last October, had been living with her boyfriend Max since the new year. Their love had come quickly, and was showing no signs of becoming less intense. Thea and Ben had been happily ensconced in their cottage for a while too, and as for Meredith and Finn, they were living their best lives with a cat and a dog in a cute little terraced house. She wouldn't be surprised if any of her loved-up friends announced engagements, or pregnancies, in the near future.

'Anyway,' Heather said, 'that's why I asked you about Jeremy. I'm so happy, sis, in a way I didn't ever imagine I wanted to be. Hank and I . . . I think . . . just having that one person on your side, something that's both exciting and comfortable – you deserve that. And I know you've always wanted it.'

'But I have a lot of other stuff to focus on,' Maisie said. 'There's the store, and Sprout – who is incredibly high maintenance.' Except that, right now, her dog was sitting quietly, looking up at her with his large brown eyes.

But she also had her cosy house with a view of the sea from the upstairs windows, which she had been able to buy because, when it went up for sale, it was basically falling down. Over the last two years, she had transformed it bit by bit, because when you grew up as the daughter of an ironmonger, you learnt how to use the tools sold in the shop. She had purpose here, and she liked working for the family business much more than being a teacher.

She had the countryside and the coastline – some of the most beautiful in the world – and she and Sprout went on regular walks, where she took photos of the changing land-scape, the sunset and sunrise, on her trusty camera. Her blog displaying the photographs was mostly just for her, though she had a few loyal followers who commented, who liked the snippets she put up on Instagram. Cornwall was her home, she loved it with all her heart, and there was so much to keep her busy in this beautiful, vibrant town.

'You know,' Heather said, the thick quiet in the back-ground changing to the whistle of the wind. It was just after ten a.m. in New York now – Maisie had the time differences sorted in her head – and she imagined her sister stepping onto the balcony of her and Hank's apartment, her job's unusual hours meaning she often went into the office later in the day, 'I sometimes wonder if you're still hung up on *him*, after all these years.'

'No way,' Maisie said immediately.

'You know who I'm talking about, then.'

'I'm not going to insult both of us by pretending I don't. But Heather, I haven't seen him for a decade. We were eighteen, I had a stupid crush, and then he sodded off to Australia.'

'Colm Caffrey,' Heather intoned, as if she was speaking the name of a notorious serial killer.

'If you say he was the one that got away, I will reach in through the phone and tug your hair,' Maisie said.

'He did a number on you, though.'

'*Heather*. He is so far in the past it's not even funny.' Except that, the moment Heather had mentioned her not having anyone to share her pizza with, Maisie had thought about him. She had imagined her customers saying his name, for God's sake! And, even discounting today, he wasn't exactly absent from her daily musings. His granddad, Liam, still lived in Port Karadow, and was well-loved in the community, which didn't help.

Maisie could still remember Colm's cool confidence, the way he made everything seem so straightforward, as if he already had life figured out. There was a light that seemed to shine out of him, and boy, had she been hooked. And they'd had fun, as friends. Towards the end, she had dared to hope that it could be more than that. She had thought that he understood her: her love for Cornwall, her desire to build a life in her home town. She had seen him as a kindred spirit, and then . . . he'd gone to Australia. It had been so sudden, so unexpected. It had wrecked her, if she

17

was honest. But she was over it – she was twenty-eight: not a teenager any more.

'My lack of joy on the love front is not because of a crush I had ten years ago,' she said now. 'Tell me about your latest glamorous event while I drink my tea.'

Heather paused, and Maisie wondered if she was going to protest, but then she said, 'OK, well, even though it's coming up to summer and the optics are all wrong, I am in the midst of organizing an *American Horror Story*-themed bonanza for a company of investment wankers – I mean bankers. Can you believe?'

'Oh my god.' Maisie laughed and clutched her rapidly cooling mug of tea. 'I want *all* the details, please.' She let the ins and outs of Heather's crazy job take up all her attention, squeezing out thoughts of Jeremy and his sudden reappearance in her life, and more importantly, all memories of Colm Caffrey, who was most definitely not, and never had been, the one who got away.

Chapter Two

On Friday morning, the sun was less sure of itself and, as if in sympathy, the morning started off slowly. Maisie found an old orange octopus toy in the back of the shop for Sprout to chew while he looked out at passers-by, and she spent the morning ordering more of their low-stock items, and scribbling down ideas for a barbecue display, another creative window diorama that would hopefully bring in more customers but would probably also piss off her dad.

'What's this?' a voice asked, and Maisie looked up, startled. She hadn't heard the bell ding.

Ollie had her arms folded on the counter. She was wearing a thin but cosy-looking forest-green jumper, and her red hair was piled on top of her head. Her make-up was simple but effective, with a sweep of black eyeliner. Maisie thought she always looked effortlessly elegant, and had the confidence to go with it.

'Hey,' Maisie said to her friend. 'Just some doodles for summer displays. I'm hoping to make everyone in Port

Karadow desperate to buy a new, expensive barbecue and the accompanying paraphernalia.'

'I would love a barbecue at the barn,' Ollie said. 'Liam's idea of outdoor eating probably involves building a fire and burying jacket potatoes in the ground next to it.'

Maisie laughed. 'I bet Max knows what he's talking about when it comes to barbecues, though.' She gestured out of the window. Sea Brew, Max's independent coffee shop, was almost opposite the ironmonger's, and a constant temptation for her with its luxury coffees and homemade sausage rolls.

'I'm going to talk to him about it,' Ollie said. 'See, you've already achieved your aim and it's just a doodle so far.'

'I think you're flattering me,' Maisie said. '*Why* are you flattering me?'

Ollie clasped her hands together. 'Because I have a proposal for you!'

'You do?'

Ollie was a creative whirlwind, always coming up with ideas for events at the bookshop she worked in and, now she was fully settled in the town, for Port Karadow in general. Maisie thought she was a breath of fresh air, and often cited her to her mother as someone who had voluntarily come to the quaint Cornish town from London, who had big ideas and ambitions, but who didn't feel like those were compromised here. Maisie's mum liked Ollie, and yet she couldn't accept that the Cornish lifestyle was fulfilling enough for her own daughter. It was exasperating.

'You are the *perfect* person,' Ollie said now. 'You're always so involved in local initiatives, you got to the semi-finals of the Book Wars tournament—'

'I honestly don't know how my pitch for *The Dead Romantics* didn't beat *The Woman in Black*,' Maisie cut in.

Ollie laughed. 'You convinced *me*, but some Port Karadow residents are very traditionalist. But regardless, you're a joiner, Maisie.'

'I don't see why I wouldn't be,' Maisie said. 'Why not make the most of the opportunities where you live?'

'Exactly.' Ollie bounced on the balls of her feet. 'And I have got the *best* opportunity for you. For us – everyone, really. And it's for a good cause.'

'You're really building up the suspense here.'

Ollie leaned over and ruffled Sprout's fur, and the little dog waggled his behind in pleasure. 'OK,' she said. 'So this is what—'

The bell dinged, and Maisie waved as Garnet came in. He was one of her dad's contemporaries, and lived in a shambolic house on the edge of town, which had three cars, two camper vans and a boat in the garden, all in various states of disrepair. He was in the shop at least once every other day, and Maisie sometimes wondered if he was the reason the ironmonger's stayed afloat. He returned her wave and strolled down one of the aisles.

'Sorry,' she said, focusing on Ollie. 'I am all ears.'

'Good! So here's the thing – I want to organize a charity calendar for next year.'

'Oooh, that sounds fun,' Maisie said. 'What are you thinking? Calendar Girls' style? Tastefully shot nudes with strategically placed objects in the foreground?'

'You have no idea how close you are to the origins of my idea,' Ollie said, her smile turning coy. Maisie would bet everything she owned that the smile had something to

21

do with Max. 'But I don't think we can do that – or not do it *quite* like that,' Ollie continued. 'I want the whole town on board, for everyone to buy at least one copy for themselves and one for a friend, and if it's naked women – or men – then I'm going to get some hate. We can't go round objectifying people like Max and Ben . . .' Ollie sighed.

'That's a shame,' Maisie said.

'Isn't it?' Ollie laughed. 'But we can get away with being playful. Calendars have to be playful, I think, if they're not purely educational – you know, with recipes and whatnot.'

'So what's your plan?'

'A surfing calendar,' Ollie said. 'Or surfing-adjacent, anyway. Men *and* women, set up in various different poses with beautiful Cornish backdrops. There's lots of scope to be creative, to be funny if we want, and a lot of people we can collar into being models. Max is obviously on board, even though he doesn't surf any more, and so are Meredith and Finn, with their sea swimming obsession, and I'm sure I can get Ben to put on a wetsuit. What do you think?'

'It sounds great,' Maisie said slowly. 'But I am *definitely* not a surfer, and I don't know if I'd look that good in a wetsuit. With me, you'd be getting slow seal rather than sexy surfer.'

'You can sod off with that right away,' Ollie said sharply. 'You're beautiful and you'd look amazing, and if you want to be in one of the photos then a month is yours.'

'Isn't . . . isn't that why you're here, though? You want me to be involved?'

Ollie's eyes widened, then she laughed. 'Maisie, I want you to take the photos!'

Maisie sucked in a breath. 'What?'

'You're a brilliant photographer,' Ollie said. 'Don't think I don't read your blog or ogle your Instagram. That's so clever, by the way: showing a tiny snippet of each photo on the 'gram, so if people want to see the whole thing they have to click over to your website.'

Maisie blinked. Her blog, her photos, were an outlet for her creativity, taking photos of the beautiful place where she lived. She hadn't realized that people she knew were interested in her small corner of the internet. 'You never get the full impact of a photo on Instagram,' she told Ollie. 'The local landscape deserves to be viewed on a big screen at the very least, preferably on huge canvases. But I had no idea you read my blog.'

'It's so soothing,' Ollie said. 'I love the snippets you write under each photo, of what you experience on your walks. And the images are stunning. Meredith told me about it, and I've been hooked ever since.'

Maisie felt the blush all the way to her hairline. 'Thank you.'

'I know you specialize in landscapes,' Ollie went on, 'but you could do the surfing shots. You're so talented, Maisie, and I don't want anyone else.'

'Can I think about it?' Maisie said. 'I would love to be involved, but . . .' But it was a lot of responsibility, she wanted to say. If one of the models couldn't make it, then they could get someone else for that month and no biggie. But if she committed to it and then, for some reason, couldn't do it, or if she *did* do it, and when all the photos were downloaded, they weren't good enough, then she'd be letting Ollie down. And no doubt Ollie had told a lot of people about it: Max and Meredith and Finn; Thea who owned

A New Chapter; Becky who they worked with; Liam, who Ollie and Max were close to as well. If Maisie attached herself to this, then she would have to do a good job, or else—

'Of course,' Ollie said. 'You don't have to say yes right away. It would be great if you did say yes at some point, though.' She grinned, and Maisie laughed.

'I just need to consider what—'

The bell dinged again, and Maisie looked past her friend. She sucked in a deep breath when she saw who had walked into the shop.

'Maisie.' His voice was loud and cheerful.

Ollie glanced behind her, then turned back to Maisie, her eyes wide.

'Jeremy,' Maisie said scratchily. 'How are you?'

'Oh you know, moseying along. Just wanted to pick up some glue before work.'

'Not sure you should be letting the children near Super Glue,' she said.

He laughed and pointed to an aisle. 'Down there?'

Maisie nodded.

'It's for a project at home,' he explained, 'but there's a staff meeting after school tonight, so it made sense to come now. You know how it is.'

'I do.' Maisie was very familiar with the afternoon staff meetings at Port Karadow primary school, and a cold shudder of dread worked its way through her, even though she hadn't had to attend one for a long time. Jeremy loped off to get his glue, and Ollie was on her in a flash.

'He's cute.'

'Yup,' Maisie agreed.

24

Jeremy *was* attractive. He kept his chocolate-brown hair short, but it always curled at the ends, his eyes were blue and his frame was slender, but not weedy; he wasn't at risk of blowing away in the wind. He had a silver stud in his right ear, which gave him a piratical air, and Maisie couldn't decide if she liked it or not. He had the confidence that made the children adore him, and he was ambitious. But when she'd finally worked up the courage to ask him to the pub one evening, there had been something slightly unnerving about him, a self-importance that he'd carried out of the classroom, which had made her attraction dim. She'd persevered for a bit, but she still felt a twist of shame when she thought about how she'd let things fizzle out after their third date, not long before she'd given up her teaching job and severed their connection altogether.

'And you worked together?' Ollie pressed.

'He's a teacher at the primary school. We were colleagues, so . . .'

Ollie narrowed her eyes. 'There's something there, isn't there? Something more. I can sense it.' She tapped her lips with a finger.

'It's really not—'

'Found it.' Jeremy put the bottle of Super Glue on the counter, and Ollie slid sideways to give him space, her gaze unashamedly curious. 'Still loving the pupil-free life?' he asked Maisie.

'Still loving it,' she confirmed. 'It's so much calmer here. You don't realize, until it's no longer happening, how many decibels you're subjected to on a daily basis, teaching at that school.'

'Fair point,' Jeremy said easily. 'I do sometimes wonder

if I have the music up too loud in my car. Mostly when I realize the whole vehicle is vibrating.'

Maisie laughed and put the glue through the till.

'Have you thought any more about what I asked you?' Jeremy went on, and Maisie could almost see Ollie's rapt concentration, like a glowing light around her.

'I don't know, Jeremy,' Maisie said. 'I'm out of all that, now. Working here is more straightforward than teaching, but it's still a full-time job.' *And I don't know if I want to spend time with you again.*

'This is *one* quiz and chips night,' he said, 'and it's not until next month. I just need some help with the organization – the tickets, the food, the questions. You were always so good at that, and it's not as if you'll be dragged back into school life, just for helping with this one thing.'

'Won't I?' she asked, too sharply. She didn't want to think of the pressure her mum would pour on her if she got wind of it.

'Course not,' Jeremy said. 'And it's more of a community event anyway – you don't have to have kids at the school to buy a ticket. It won't be much work, just a couple of evenings together, probably.'

Maisie chewed her lip. He was doing all the things that made her remember why she'd asked him out in the first place. The kind look in his eyes, his attention focused wholly on her, when redheaded bombshell Ollie was standing right next to him. Was there a possibility that . . .? But no. *No.* She had moved on.

'Give me a few more days,' she said, and held out the card reader.

He tapped his card against it. 'Call me,' he said, throwing

her a glance that managed to be both nonchalant and entirely too intense as he left.

'Well then,' Ollie said after a moment. 'You're in demand, Maisie Winters. There must be something in the air.'

'Hmmm,' was Maisie's reply. She ran her hands over Sprout's short, fluffy ears. It had already been an eventful morning, and it wasn't even nine o'clock.

On Friday evening, as he so often did, Maisie's dad came to meet her at the shop, carrying a cardboard cup holder with two cups in it and a paper bag containing whatever pastries Max had left at Sea Brew.

Frank Winters was a large man, whose stockiness in his earlier decades had softened over the years, but he was still an imposing presence. Arthritis had taken away the physicality that he so prized, and was the main reason that Maisie had taken it upon herself to enforce the changes in the family business. Her dad couldn't spend days sitting behind the counter any more, couldn't get items off the highest shelf for his customers, and while it had been – and still was, in some ways – a battle, he had finally conceded that Maisie's proposal made a lot of sense.

'All right chuck,' Frank said. Sprout clamoured a greeting, bouncing off his stool and going to say hello. 'All right stupid,' he added, bending slowly to ruffle Sprout's fur.

'He'll get a complex if you keep calling him that,' Maisie said.

'He loves it.' Frank straightened, not quite managing to hide his wince. 'Fancy getting out of here?'

Maisie beamed. It had been such a busy day that she'd had to sneakily eat her lunch at the counter, and even that had been interrupted by a steady stream of customers. Sometimes, her dad would want to go through the takings and check the stock before they left. Other times, like today, he would release her. Maisie might be responsible for the day-to-day running of Port Karadow Ironmonger's, but in some ways her dad was still in charge. Today, he was obviously in a good mood.

'Give me five minutes to lock up,' she said.

They took their tea and pastries to Port Karadow Harbour, the water a glassy blue reflecting the puffy white clouds, the boats swaying gently.

The harbour front was busy with people strolling, taking in the sea air, admiring the view through the telescope, and sitting on the benches that dotted the concrete walkway. A burger stall was gearing up for a busy weekend, and the place had a frisson, Friday evening combined with the warmer weather, only a few days away from June.

They settled on a bench, and Maisie, who had taken the cardboard holder from her dad, handed him a cup of tea. He held open the paper bag and she took out a cinnamon swirl. Max's pastries were made by a local woman called Beryan, their partnership well-loved throughout the town. Even after five o'clock, the swirl had crunch left in it, and was infused with the delicious, spicy sweetness of the cinnamon, which went perfectly with a swig of hot, milky tea.

'Thanks for this,' Maisie said, when she'd finished her mouthful. 'How are the bees?'

Since retiring, her dad had bought three beehives for their garden. Her mum had complained that the constant buzzing would stop her going out there, but Frank pointed out that the end of their long garden was a wilderness, and she never went that far down anyway. Maisie often wondered if Aimee Winters' first instinct was to complain, before she stopped to think whether there was any reason to.

'The bees are grand,' Frank said. 'Quiet, right now, but happy.' Maisie was relieved he'd found a new purpose, because that was the thing she'd been most worried about when she had encouraged him to give up running the shop. A person with no purpose could easily give up on life. 'Looks like you've had a busy week,' he went on, 'but the counter was tidy.' He nodded, more to himself than her, and Maisie remembered that he hadn't actually given up the ironmonger's, and a big part of his purpose was making sure she was doing right by the business he'd started over four decades ago.

'I run a tight ship,' she said, 'whatever you might think.'

'I *think* you're doing a grand job,' he said, and she wanted to ask why, if he really believed that, did he check up on her all the time? But it was a balmy Friday evening, she was lucky to still be able to spend time with her parents, and for the most part she got on with her dad. She didn't want to upset the harmony between them by being petty.

'Thanks, Dad,' she said instead, closing her eyes and letting the warm sun caress her eyelids.

'And you won't mind putting in a shift tomorrow afternoon, will you?'

She opened her eyes. 'I thought Parker was working with Sandy tomorrow. I have the weekend off.'

'Parker's got his nan's eightieth,' Frank said. 'He can't stay past two.'

Maisie chewed the inside of her cheek. 'When did you find out?'

He glanced at her, then turned his scrutiny to the water. 'What do you mean, pet?'

'I mean, he must have known about his nan's eightieth a while ago – it's not like it's a movable event. When did you know he couldn't do tomorrow afternoon?'

'A couple of weeks, maybe,' Frank said. 'But you can fill in, can't you?'

Maisie gritted her teeth. This was one of the problems with him still clinging on to the business. They had agreed that Maisie would cover the main hours from Mondays to Fridays, with help whenever it was likely to be busy. Then there were several part-timers, including Parker and Sandy, who were supposed to take charge at weekends. Why her dad felt he needed to hold the rota so close to his chest, she didn't know, unless it was one way he could still feel in control. But this, telling her the evening before that she needed to work on Saturday afternoon, was just not on.

'I could have plans,' she said, horrified to hear the whine in her voice.

'But you don't, do you, love?'

'You don't know that.'

'You can move 'em, eh?' He patted her knee. 'You'll still have Sunday off.'

'How generous of you,' she murmured.

'What was that?' He looked at her, his grey brows lowered.

'Nothing,' she said. 'I can do tomorrow afternoon.'

She didn't add that, after this, she was going to wrestle control of the rota from him once and for all. She wasn't a child any more – she was running the family business almost single-handedly, for goodness' sake – and she had to let her dad, and her mum, for that matter, know that they could no longer treat her like one.

'Grand, pet. I knew you would. How's that cinnamon swirl?'

'Delicious,' Maisie said grudgingly.

She stared into the distance, thinking of all the plans she'd had for tomorrow. She had been going to take a long walk with Sprout to make the most of the spring sunrise and the soft mist that often brushed the fields and water at that time of year, and which could make for spectacular photographs; she wanted to catch up on her latest read, a spooky novel called *The Toll House* that she was engrossed in; she needed to do some serious thinking about the two opportunities that had been thrust her way, taking photos for Ollie's calendar and helping Jeremy with the quiz and chips. The second one had more emotional weight than the first, but being the Official Calendar Photographer would take up a lot of time, and was the one she cared more about.

She had planned to phone Meredith later, to see if she and Finn fancied going to the pub tomorrow evening, perhaps with Thea and Ben, and Ollie and Max, too. She could still do that, of course – it would give her something to look forward to after an unexpected afternoon spent at work. It wasn't *that* bad, she decided. And, she added silently, it would be the last time.

Adjustments to the weekend made in her mind, she sipped her tea, licked pastry flakes off her fingers, and let the warm Port Karadow breeze whip her irritation away.

Chapter Three

On Saturday, Maisie made it to midday before she decided to go into work early. It was raining steadily, so her plans for a long walk with Sprout were out of the window anyway, and her phone had been buzzing with messages from Jeremy all morning, as if she'd already agreed to help him with the quiz and chips.

She and Sprout left her colourful, cosy house and walked through the rain, Port Karadow looking like a scene from a downbeat film in its cloak of drizzle, the hazy glow of lights from windows suggesting people were staying warm and dry inside. The moment she stepped into the iron-monger's, Sprout shook his robust little body, sending rainwater across the garden display and the stand of picture hooks.

'Awww,' Sandy said from behind the counter. 'He's ador-able.' She was in her early twenties, with long auburn hair and kind blue eyes, and when she wasn't working at the shop she was busy building her fledgling greetings card business. She was also an unconditional Sprout lover, and he loved her right back. While her dog trotted around the counter to greet Sandy, Maisie went to get a cloth to dry the displays.

'Didn't think you were coming till later,' Sandy said, when Maisie emerged from the storeroom.

'It's only a couple of hours until I'm due here,' Maisie said, which sounded lame even to her. 'I could do with sorting out some paperwork anyway.' They both knew that wasn't true because Maisie hated paperwork, wanted it out of the way as quickly as possible, and so always kept rigidly on top of it.

With Sandy's curious gaze on her, and Parker whistling loudly while he restocked the wall of kitchen utensils, Maisie disappeared into the office, which was a lot tidier since she'd been in charge, but still lacked any sort of comfort and smelled distinctly of sawdust. The storeroom was next to it.

She was lost in a deep-dive of some ancient folders she'd found under a cabinet, which she was pretty sure she should simply throw away, the sounds of the shop a gentle background soundtrack, when the ping of the door was followed by a loud, familiar voice. 'I need to speak to the owner, immediately!'

'I-I'll just see if-if I can—' Sandy started, and Maisie knew she had to step in. Perhaps this was fate. Perhaps she was *meant* to be here, so she could deal with this less-than-welcome situation.

She strode into the shop, where Mr Gerald Duffield, aka Port Karadow Ironmonger's Most Troublesome Customer, was leaning forwards on the counter, his hands splayed across it. He was in his early sixties, Maisie guessed, and lived in a large, elegant property in the lush green country-side surrounding the town.

'Mr Duffield.' Maisie approached the counter, where Sandy and Sprout were both doing excellent impressions of rabbits caught in headlights. 'How can I help you today?'

'The contact adhesive I bought from you last Monday doesn't work.' His flinty eyes bored into her, and she could see that he was almost vibrating with fury.

Maisie took a breath of damp, dusty air. 'Tell me what happened.'

She could see the war in his eyes, between staying monosyl-labic and furious, and telling his story. 'It's for my latest . . . acquisition,' he said. 'A very fine white stag's head, procured from a top-notch taxidermist.' The story was winning out. Maisie spared a thought for the poor white stag, obviously a once-majestic creature, then remembered the burgers she and Sprout had wolfed down at the harbour the other day, and decided not to be hypocritical.

'Sounds . . . lovely,' she said, sliding behind the counter. Sandy scampered away, presumably to the furthest corner of the storeroom. 'But there was a problem?'

'Not with my purchase,' Gerald said. 'But I always add a plaque to my wall hangings. The breed, the estimated size, the kill date. Your Evo-Stik was utterly useless.'

Maisie ruffled Sprout's head beneath the counter. 'Did you leave it once you'd spread the glue on it?' This was a common mistake.

'What?' he barked.

'Once you've put the glue on both sides, the back of the plaque and the mount, you need to leave it to touch-dry, usually for about fifteen minutes, *then* stick the two parts together. If you do it sooner, the adhesive isn't stable.'

Gerald blinked. 'Don't be ridiculous. I want another one, free of charge. I'd also like to be compensated for my wasted time and journey, but I don't expect you'll honour that. As it is, I'm very close to taking my business elsewhere.'

Maisie knew he wouldn't do that, and because of that, she wanted to keep her relationship with Gerald as smooth as possible. It would never be harmonious, but she had a part to play here. 'Do you have the . . . defective packet?'

He took it out of his pocket. The cardboard was soggy, on the verge of disintegrating, reminding Maisie that the rain was still coming down hard.

'Great.' She took it from him. 'I'll get you another packet.'

'Not one that's been sitting there for years,' he called after her.

She went to the glue aisle, and found that the space was empty. Parker should have been keeping an eye on low stock, but she didn't have the time to deal with that right now.

'I'll get you a fresh one from the back,' Maisie called. She heard the bell ding, and smiled at Sandy, who was sipping a cup of tea in the office. 'It's OK, I've placated him. Could you go and see to whoever's just come in?'

'Course.' Sandy put her mug down and slid off her chair.

Maisie found the box of Evo-Stik on a high shelf in the storeroom, and moved the small stool over so she could stand on it. She still had to reach her arms right up, and stand on tiptoe, to reach it. She grabbed hold of the box, and pulled. As it tipped, some kind of spider village that had been resting on top, with dust-covered cobwebs and dead, partly devoured insects, slid off and into her blonde curls.

'Ugh.' She wasn't squeamish – renovating a rundown house and having to explore every dark, dingy corner had knocked her fear of spiders out of her – but it wasn't a particularly pleasant feeling.

Eyes squeezed firmly closed to stop any more cobwebs getting in them, she felt her way off the stool, put the box down and tipped her head forward, shaking it.

'Maisie!' Sandy called. 'Maisie, come here!'

'Just a sec,' Maisie replied, wondering how Gerald was terrorizing her now. She didn't have time to look in the mirror, to make herself presentable. She ran a hand quickly over her face and strode out into the shop, towards the counter.

Then she came to a dead halt, as if there was a solid wall of clear polycarbonate in front of her.

'Hello, Winters,' said the man standing next to Gerald.

He was wearing a very sleek, black and grey waterproof jacket, and his damp hair was flattened to his head, but was obviously still thick, and possibly, *probably* untidy. He sounded confident but also slightly incredulous, and even though there were things that were different about him – his frame was more solid; slender, still, but definitely stronger around the shoulders, and there was something about his voice, his deep tone slightly accented – there were also things that were the same. Mostly, the fact that his skin was tanned, freckled – even more than it had been when he was a teenager and spent most of his summers in the Cornish sunshine – and his eyes. Brown, but not dark. In some lights, Maisie remembered, they looked gold.

She knew those eyes, and so did her body, and all kinds of things were happening in that moment – things that she couldn't make sense of. Had talking about him with Heather, thinking about him more than usual, conjured him here? *Had* those customers the other day mentioned him, because they'd seen him around town? She didn't know, but what she did – suddenly – realize was that he'd said her name, and that she should probably reply.

'Colm,' she said, her voice shaky. 'You're . . . How are you here? It's been . . .'

'A while,' he finished for her. 'I know. Surprise!' He laughed, but she could see that, while there was undoubtedly a slight smugness at her stupefied reaction, he was also nervous. Not that that wasn't entirely understandable. He'd been away – on the other side of the world – for a decade. But now, here he was, and Maisie was struggling to take it in.

Colm Caffrey, her intense teenage crush, the man she had at one point thought she was in love with but had resigned herself to the fact that she would never see again, was back in Port Karadow, and looking soggy but also incredibly, hopelessly gorgeous, in her shop.

Chapter Four

'Did you find my Evo-Stik?' Gerald asked, interrupting Maisie's very important, highly momentous moment.

'It looks like she found a whole nest of tarantulas,' Parker piped up from somewhere behind her, and Maisie remembered the box, the cobwebs, and only now wondered what she looked like. Colm pulled off *drenched* with aplomb. No drowned rat for him, more advertising-outdoor-clothing model. She, on the other hand, didn't think she could pull off dust-bunny chic. Who could?

'Are you OK?' Colm asked.

'Just a regular occurrence in the storeroom,' Maisie said, trying to brush it off, metaphorically and literally.

'I had no idea you worked here now,' he said. 'Is your dad all right?'

'He's good. Grumbling, as always, but—'

'That is *not* a surprise to me,' Gerald cut in. 'My adhesive?'

'Sorry – of course,' Maisie said. 'I've got a fresh box out the back.'

'I thought that's what you'd gone out there to get.' Gerald's voice was frayed. She'd just got him to simmering, she didn't want to turn the heat up again.

'It's coming!' She raced back to the storeroom, ripped open the cobwebby box and pulled out a fresh packet of the adhesive. She hurried back behind the counter, suddenly hyper-aware of every movement she made, every hair tuck, every pull of her eyebrows. 'Here we go.'

Gerald splayed his hands on the counter again, making himself as imposing as possible. Sandy and Parker were adjusting the hand tool display nearby, as if they thought there was still some dramatic mileage in the interaction. Colm stood back, waiting his turn, even though Parker or Sandy could help him with whatever he needed. What *did* he need?

'This one will work, will it?' Gerald asked.

Not if you don't follow the instructions, Maisie thought. 'It's a brand-new packet. It should be fine.'

'I don't want another day like yesterday. Hopeless waste of time. Why sell the products if they're defective?'

'If you follow the instructions to the letter, Mr Duffield, you should be successful.'

'Of course I did. *I'm* not defective.'

Maisie quietly processed the exchange, not trusting herself to reply in a way that would be considered excellent customer service.

As he was shoving the new packet of Evo-Stik in his pocket, Colm took a step towards him and said, 'You know with that one, you have to leave it to touch-dry on both surfaces before you hook them up, right?'

Maisie almost choked on her tongue as Gerald's eyes turned

to pure, grey fury, then he pivoted on his heels and yanked open the door, the bell dinging twice as he stormed out.

When he'd gone, only the sound of the pounding rain remained. Maisie took a deep breath and let her gaze meet Colm's. '*Hook them up?*' she repeated. 'You've gone all antipodean.'

He shrugged. 'Unavoidable, I guess.'

'But you're here,' she said, more to ground herself in this new reality than for his sake.

'I am.' He took another step towards the counter. He really was very freckled, and his hair, she knew, while dark now, was a soft brown, the type that got natural highlights in the sun. She wondered how blond it was now; how he would look when she next saw him, less rain-soaked. Silently, she scolded herself. She shouldn't already be imagining a next time.

'When did you get here?' she asked.

'Two days ago,' Colm said. 'The jet lag is killing me.'

'Are you staying with Liam? Is this a holiday? What's . . . what's happening?'

He laughed gently. 'I didn't mean to shock you.'

'You're a blast from the past, that's all.' That might be the understatement of the century.

'Yeah.' It came out as a long, drawn-out sigh. 'This place too. So much has changed, but a lot is the same. You're here, though. I thought you were a teacher.'

'How have you been keeping tabs on me?' She folded her arms, and Sprout, who had been dozing since Gerald's first outburst, raised his head above the counter and barked.

Colm leaned over, holding his hand out to her dog, then turned questioning eyes on her. 'Who's this?'

40

'This is Sprout. He won't bite you.'

'Good to know.' He ruffled Sprout's head, and her dog whined in ecstasy. Maisie couldn't help noticing Colm's long, tanned fingers, his nails white and clean against the golden skin. 'And, for the record, I haven't been keeping tabs on you. Granddad updates Melissa, who's living in Portugal now, did you know?'

Maisie nodded. Melissa was Colm's older sister. She'd lived in London for a long time before moving to Portugal with her new boyfriend, Tiago. 'So Liam updates Melissa, and Lissa updates you?'

'Yup.'

'Are you staying with your granddad now?'

Colm pursed his lips, and kept on stroking Sprout.

'Are things still frosty between you?' Maisie asked.

'It's not so easy to set things straight when you're thousands of miles apart, and one of you isn't the biggest fan of technology. Besides, it was me going to Australia that pissed Granddad off in the first place.' He drew his hand back and Sprout followed it with his nose, whimpering gently.

'It was quite sudden,' Maisie said slowly. But now wasn't the time to rehash this, to open old wounds. She was still reeling from him just . . . *being here*. 'Where are you staying, then?'

Colm ran a hand down his face. 'Granddad's let me have the cottage, you know that yellow one, about ten minutes' walk from Foxglove Farm? And he didn't have to do anything for me, so it makes me think we can maybe patch it up. We've got time, at least.'

Maisie's heart sped up. 'How long are you staying?'

'Indefinite, indeterminate. Not sure.'

Her mind flooded with questions. Why had he left Australia? Why had he come back here? Was he alone? Did he have a girlfriend with him? A wife? *A family?* Did she want to catch up with him? Her immediate instinct was yes, she did. But she didn't want to bombard him, so she took a tiny, physical step backwards, and a larger mental one.

'And can I . . . was there a reason you came here, today?' She laughed awkwardly. 'I mean, is there something I can help you with? House-wise?'

Colm let out a long exhale, as if trying to rid himself of all the complications in his life – it sounded like there were complications, if he wasn't sure how long he'd be in Port Karadow – then gave her a lopsided smile. 'I'm going to need loads of stuff for the cottage, but right now I need a doormat. The flagstones are a deathtrap when it's been raining.' He gestured outside. 'That's as far as I've got, but I think if I make one decision, one tiny improvement, it'll feel like a win.'

Maisie knew exactly what he meant. When she'd bought her house, started work on the renovations, it had seemed like an insurmountable task, but once she'd broken it down, decided which rooms to start on, made that first purchase from her dad, she had felt like she was getting somewhere, like it wasn't so unmanageable after all.

'Come with me,' she said. 'Sandy, can you cover the counter? Parker, don't you need to be heading off to your gran's birthday?'

'Oh shit, yeah! Thanks, Maisie.' He hurried out the back to collect his coat, while Maisie led Colm to the far wall, where their range of doormats was laid out. They had a good selection of coir mats, some plain, some patterned, a couple with silly slogans like: *Guests make me happy: some when they arrive, most when they leave.*

Colm stood next to her, and she could feel his damp sleeve rubbing against the fabric of her dress, but she didn't mind, because already, she was relishing being close to him. It was a mix of heady nostalgia and new, pure attraction. Colm had been a handsome teenager, and he'd only got better with time.

'Maisie Winters,' he said. 'Running Port Karadow Ironmonger's. I never would have picked it. Your dad's really OK?'

'He's got arthritis,' Maisie explained. 'He's adamant he can carry on, but he was getting so tired, and the physical side of this job was becoming too difficult. He's stubborn about it, though. He still insists on being in charge of the rota, even though I'm running the show. I've had to fill in today for Parker like a Saturday girl.' She was suddenly thankful for her dad's reluctance to let go. If she'd had the whole weekend off like she was supposed to, when would she have found out Colm was back?

'Sorry he's got health issues,' Colm said, 'but at least he's the same Frank Winters I remember.'

'You sound nostalgic,' Maisie said.

'This place is thick with nostalgia. Too much, in some cases.'

'Why do you say that?'

He glanced at her, then went back to looking at the mats. 'Oh, you know. A decade is a long time.'

She waited for an explanation, feeling the first wave of frustration, because Colm was – or at least had been – very good at putting anything serious on the back burner.

He liked to give the impression that his life was carefree, and Maisie had often wondered if that was the reason his departure had seemed so sudden: because he hadn't wanted to talk about whatever was going on, was happier to just leave everything behind, giving no proper explanation to his friends. Well, this time, she could try and start them off on a different footing.

'What's happened, Colm?' she asked. 'What's going on?'

'Have you been to Rose Cottage?' he said, instead of answering. 'Granddad's got Foxglove Farm, then there's Foxglove Barn – where Ollie and Max are. Ollie, who lived with Melissa in London for years, but who is here now, with her boyfriend, a dog named after a Jane Austen character and a cat called Oxo . . .' He shook his head, 'And then my quaint yellow cottage, it's out there in the woods, and it is *pitch black* at night.'

Maisie frowned. 'I've walked past it. It is . . . fairly rural.'

Colm turned towards her. 'It's like something out of a sinister fucking fairy tale. I feel like there's a real possibility that a wolf is prowling around outside, and he's going to be seriously annoyed when he discovers I don't have a grandma to feed him.'

'Colm.' Maisie didn't know whether to laugh or comfort him. 'There are no wolves in Cornwall, and I expect you're much safer here than you were in Australia. What about all those creepy-crawlies, like the funnel web spiders that eat your skin? Ugh.' She shuddered, because *those* spiders, she was legitimately scared of.

His gaze drifted up to her hair, and a second later he was reaching up, his fingers tangling with her curls, pulling out a bit of cobweb she hadn't managed to get rid of. 'You'd have faced them all down,' he said. 'Better than me, probably.' Maisie resisted another shudder, this time because his touch, although it was only in her hair, felt delicious and also too much. She wondered how her crush could have done this: lie dormant for an entire decade only to wake up, and – quite possibly – intensify, when the object of her affections waltzed back into town.

'I don't know if I would have,' she scratched out.

He shook his head. 'Sorry. I'm being melodramatic. I'm lucky that I have somewhere to come back to, that Granddad's letting me squat for a bit.'

'Well,' Maisie said, turning back to the display, 'like you said, the little things make a huge difference. We'll start with a mat, and take it from there.'

'You're going to be my personal interior designer?' Colm asked.

'I can provide you with tools, paint, furnishings and fixtures. And, actually, some ideas, too. I spent the last couple of years doing up my own house, so I've got first-hand experience.'

'Where did you buy?'

'Horizon Road,' she said. 'You know, a few roads back from the beach. It's close to the Happy Shack, which is this amazing new restaurant that's opened up. There's a lot to catch you up on.'

'Horizon Road's great,' Colm said, and she could hear that he was impressed.

'It was a total dump when I bought it, which was why I was able to get it in the first place. Then all the planning, renovations, decoration. It was hard work, but it was worth it.'

'You did that on your own, or . . .' He asked it casually enough, and it was a fairly standard question. She shouldn't read anything into it.

'On my own,' she said brightly. 'Sprout wasn't any help at all.'

'He's a cool dog,' Colm said. 'Maybe I should get a dog.'

'Let's stick to a doormat for now.'

He laughed. 'You're right. I don't want to get ahead of myself.'

She risked a sideways glance at him, watched him run a hand through his hair, which was starting to dry out, revealing that, yes, living in Australia had given him a lot of blond highlights.

He was a classic Cornish surfer boy, and in some ways it made sense that he'd levelled up, taken those freckles, his sun-hungry skin and lean limbs to Australia. But now he was back, and he was looking at doormats and clenching his jaw, and there was a story there – a whole decade-worth of stories, in fact – and Maisie had to follow Colm's advice and not get ahead of herself, either.

'You know,' he said, running his fingers over the rough coir of a mat with an orange fox motif on it, 'what I'd really like is a mat that says *Fuck Off*, but I don't suppose you have one of those.'

Maisie sighed, hid her smile and picked up one with the word 'Hello' written on it in a happy, swirling font. 'Why don't you start as you mean to go on?' she said, handing it to him.

Colm took it from her, and for a moment they just looked at each other, his eyes warm and honey and, possibly, a little bit startled. She didn't blame him. *Fucking hell*, she thought, because if any situation was worthy of a few swear words, it was this one. She couldn't wait to speak to Heather later on. Her sister was, she thought – using an expression that Colm had been fond of back in the day – going to *lose her shit*.

She smiled at Colm, trying to keep the maelstrom of emotions reined in, and led him, and his very genial new doormat, back towards the front of the shop.

Chapter Five

The Sea Shanty was still Maisie's favourite pub in town. It was right in the centre, on a cobbled street not too far from the picturesque town hall, and was distinctly unpretentious. There was no over-hyped gastropub menu, just various different versions of things with chips: pie and chips, fish and chips, burger and chips. It had no ideas above its station, and she loved it for that.

When she got there that evening, Meredith and Finn had already commandeered the largest table. It was round, in the corner of the room below the television that only ever seemed to go on when the BBC were showing their programme about Cornish fishing trawlers, and was flanked by a curved bench covered in sagging cushions. A tea light flickered gently in a gold glass holder in the centre of the table.

Meredith, pretty and freckled, with curly brown hair, sat next to her boyfriend Finn who, like Maisie, was naturally blond. He had the look of a rich interloper, with high cheekbones and an endless supply of Barbour coats, but he was effortlessly warm, and one of the funniest people she knew. Their beagle, Crumble, was under the table, and Sprout made a beeline for him, the dogs already firm pals.

'Maisie!' Finn stood up, and she accepted hugs from them both.

'I thought I'd be the last one here,' she said, laying her coat along the top of the bench. 'Do you need drinks?'

'We're good,' Meredith said. 'How was your day?'

Maisie thought of everything that had happened. 'Weird,' she confirmed. 'I'll get a drink and tell you all about it.'

As she was coming back from the bar with a glass of Prosecco (she had earned the bubbles), she saw that the others had arrived: Thea, slender with long dark hair, timid until you got to know her, and her handsome builder boyfriend Ben, who was quiet despite his imposing physical presence, and Ollie and Max. The dog numbers multiplied too, with Ben's Australian Shepherd Scooter, and Ollie's chocolate Lab, Henry Tilney.

Maisie joined in with the round of hellos and flurry of hugs. She tried not to think about the fact that it was three loved-up couples, and then her.

'So,' Ollie said, when they were settled with drinks and several bags of crisps, 'what's up, people?'

After Maisie's initial confession to Meredith and Finn, she felt reluctant to open up about Colm, and stayed quiet while the others traded stories. It was Ben's admission that got all the attention.

'You're fitting Marcus Belrose's new kitchen?' Ollie screeched. 'At his *house*?'

Ben rolled his eyes. 'Yup. We know each other a bit, and

he offered me the contract. He knows exactly what he wants, which is a breath of fresh air in my line of work.'

'I'll bet he does,' Ollie muttered.

Ben laughed gently. 'It's a good thing. So many of my clients expect me to be interior designer as well as builder, but Marcus has every detail planned out.'

'Is he as horrifying as everyone says he is?' Maisie asked.

Marcus Belrose had moved to Cornwall the year before, opening his seafood restaurant, the Happy Shack, to critical acclaim and tables booked months in advance. He was somewhat of a celebrity, with a myriad of TV appearances under his belt, and had a reputation for being haughty and arrogant, something Ollie had experienced first-hand.

'He's OK when his ego's not in play,' Ben said.

'But when is that ever the case?' Ollie asked. 'He's got tickets on himself.'

'He's an award-winning chef,' Max said with a laugh. 'But I agree that he could be nicer about it, less self-important. You don't get anywhere by acting like you're better than everyone else.'

'Exactly.' Ollie planted a kiss on her boyfriend's cheek.

'So,' Finn said, 'Ben's had to spend the day in the company of Marcus Belrose; the painting I'm working on started out half-decent and then turned into a puddle of sludge, and Max . . .'

'. . . Had a good day in the café,' he finished. 'People want coffees and hot sausage rolls when it's wet.'

'Max is the picture of eternal optimism,' Finn finished. 'What about you, Ollie?'

'I had a day off, so I—'

'Planned about fifteen events for the bookshop,' Max cut in, with a grin.

'Hey.' She slapped him playfully on the arm. 'No, I was doing research for our calendar.'

'Ah yes.' Max nodded. 'The extra work you've given yourself. I had forgotten about that for a moment.'

Ollie sighed laboriously. 'The RNLI always needs more money, they do a brilliant job, and it isn't exactly a horrible project: It's going to be a whole lot of fun. I just need to find a few more willing models, and lock down my photographer.' She turned to Maisie.

'You know,' Finn said, 'some might say you were getting off easily, taking the photographs rather than posing for them.'

'I bet you're already planning exactly how you want to look, Finnegan,' Ben said. 'I expect when Ollie asked you to take part, you thought all your Christmases had come at once.'

'Are you saying, Benjamin Senhouse, that you think I'm vain?' Finn asked.

Ben sipped his pint, his wide shoulders rising in a shrug.

'Do you want to be the photographer?' Max asked Maisie, his green eyes serious. 'Just because you're skilled at it, doesn't mean it's the right time, or project, for you.'

'I love being involved in local initiatives,' Maisie said. 'I just don't want to say yes without thinking it through. And it's been a weird day, so I'm all . . . confuddled.'

'Anything we can help with?' Meredith asked, pulling Crumble away from the table when he tried to go for the leftover crisps.

'Is it Jeremy?' Ollie asked. 'Has he been pressuring you about the quiz and chips?'

'No,' Maisie said. 'Though I need to sort that out, too.'

'Who pressures people about quiz and chips?' Finn asked.

'Teachers who want to prey on Maisie's good nature,' Ollie said. She glanced at Max and he raised an eyebrow. 'That's not what I'm doing,' she insisted. 'We're friends, and Maisie is an amazing photographer, but if she wants to say no, then of course that's absolutely fine.'

Maisie sipped her Prosecco. 'It's not either of those things. I had to go into the shop today, and I had a . . . blast from the past.'

'Who was that?' Thea asked, nabbing a salt and vinegar crisp.

'Colm Caffrey,' Maisie said. His name sounded good – important, somehow. She liked the alliteration, the way the words had hard beginnings, softer endings.

'Ooh Colm!' Ollie's eyes widened. 'That's Melissa's younger brother, Liam's grandson. I met him a few times, *years* ago, when I was first living with Melissa in London and he came to visit. We saw him briefly yesterday, but only to say hello. I remember Liam telling me he hadn't seen him since he left Cornwall, and that they'd not parted on the best of terms.'

'You knew him before he went to Australia?' Max asked Maisie.

She nodded. 'We were in the same year at school, and we were friends. You were a few years ahead, weren't you?'

'Yeah,' Max said. 'I'm the ripe old age of thirty-five now, so I was well before your time.'

'So now this Colm person is back, and he came into the ironmonger's?' Thea asked. 'And that's confuddled you?'

'A bit,' Maisie admitted. 'It's complicated.'

'Seems like this Colm guy has complicated relationships with a lot of people,' Ben pointed out.

'He's turned up here after spending a decade on the other side of the world, and he left suddenly, without any real explanation. Not to me, anyway.' Maisie realized, too late, that her voice had risen. She could see that everyone's curiosity had increased a notch. Several notches, perhaps.

'He's staying in Liam's yellow cottage,' Ollie told the others. 'It's a bit rundown, I think, hence the ironmonger's trip. Unless he just wanted to see you?' She turned to Maisie.

'What did he want?' Meredith asked.

'He wanted to buy a doormat that said *Fuck Off*,' Maisie said.

Finn chuckled. 'I like him already.'

'I told him that he should start as he means to go on, and that he shouldn't alienate everyone before he's even been here a week. There's stuff going on there. He was always really laid back.'

'A mystery,' Ollie said, looking positively gleeful. 'Does he surf, do you know?'

Maisie drained her glass of Prosecco, then put it on the table with a little more force than was necessary. 'Colm is the epitome of a Cornish surfer boy. Unless he's had a personality transplant while he's been away – and that's incredibly unlikely since he's been living in Australia – then he loves surfing.'

'Excellent,' Ollie said.

'Oh dear,' Max added quietly.

Thea gave Maisie a compassionate look. 'You can talk to us, if you want to.'

Maisie nodded. 'I just need to sort through it all in my

head. Talking to Dad about the shop, the quiz and chips, your calendar.' She gestured to Ollie, who mouthed back *no pressure*. 'And . . . and Colm. I don't need to *do* anything about him, exactly, it's just strange that he's here again, after all this time.' She exhaled. 'Let me get more drinks.'

'Nope.' Ben put his hand on her arm and stood up. 'I'm getting the next round. Marcus Belrose might not be the warmest guy on the planet, but he's very fair when it comes to business deals.'

'When you come back, will you give us juicy details about his house and how he behaves when you're knocking through his walls and upsetting his equilibrium?' Ollie asked.

'Absolutely not,' Ben said. 'Right, what does everyone want? Another Prosecco, Maisie?'

'Yes please.' She nodded gratefully, and didn't mind one bit when Sprout scrabbled his way up onto the bench beside her. A night with friends and fizz was the perfect way to deal with her current predicament. She could talk it out as much as she wanted and then, when it was all getting too much, let them take her mind off it. Right now, she would just be happy if every train of thought didn't lead her back to Colm Caffrey.

Chapter Six

On Wednesday evening, Maisie joined Thea and Ollie on the beach. The sun was starting to set, its golden hue deepening as it went, turning the landscape the colours of a vintage photograph.

'I'll never get used to this,' Ollie said, as they walked barefoot in the shallows. 'When I lived in London, my after-work wind-down used to be a large glass of wine at the Moon and Sixpence. This is so much better.'

'I don't understand people who don't want to live by the sea,' Maisie said.

'Everyone's different,' Thea replied, diplomatically. 'My best friend Esme loves being in Bristol, having lots of pubs and restaurants on her doorstep. I suppose if you have a wide circle of friends, you're constantly meeting different people and love keeping busy – going to the theatre, the cinema, yoga classes – then a town like Port Karadow doesn't cut it. Also, there's only one primary school, no choice in that respect—'

'Don't I know it,' Maisie muttered.

Ollie glanced at her, then picked up a smooth stone and completely failed to skip it into the sparkling water. 'Has Jeremy been giving you trouble?'

'He's started a text campaign,' Maisie told them. 'It's a bit of a bombardment, but I haven't said yes yet, and he's running out of time, apparently.'

'Because if you don't agree, he'll have to organize it all by himself,' Ollie said.

'Maybe.' Maisie prodded a bit of seaweed with her toe. Sprout was prancing in the water, splashing as much as his little legs could manage. 'I have no good reason to say no.'

'You don't have to say yes to anything you don't want to,' Thea said. 'Ben is big on the whole "saying no is powerful" thing. You don't even have to give a reason.'

'You have to prioritize,' Ollie added. 'What do you *really* want to do? Do you want to talk to the fish and chip shop about a bulk order, spend hours creating quiz questions, when instead you could be helping me pose friendly, happy people wearing wetsuits, and taking photographs of them – something you *love* doing?'

Thea laughed. 'Ollie.'

'Besides,' Ollie went on, unperturbed, 'Jeremy has an earring. I saw it when he came into the ironmonger's that time.'

'Jeremy does have an earring,' Maisie said. 'I thought it was attractive, once.'

'But you've come to your senses, so don't you think—'

'Oh hey,' Thea said brightly, 'did you hear that there's going to be a big summer festival in Porthgolow?'

'There is?' Maisie asked.

56

'Meredith mentioned it. Charlie Harper, who runs the Cornish Cream Tea Bus and organizes those food markets on the beach, is planning a week-long festival at the end of July. I've signed A New Chapter up to have a bookstall, and I know you've had a stand at the lights pageant before.'

'Just selling sets of LED Christmas lights,' Maisie said. 'But I'm ordering some nice new barbecue sets for the summer, and I'm sure I can think of other things we could sell.'

'From the way Meredith described it, it seems like the whole of Porthgolow *and* Port Karadow are going to get involved. It'll be a proper summer celebration.' Thea smiled. 'I'll give you Charlie's number so you can book a slot, and if you're early enough we could try and make it so we're next to each other.'

'I'd love that, thank you.' They walked in silence for a few beats, Maisie enjoying the gentle shush of the waves, the warmth of the sun kissing her face, the calm of the evening.

'Are we still scouting for people for your calendar, Ollie?' Thea asked.

'Always,' Ollie said. 'You know, Maisie, I think being my photographer will be a lot less work than the summer festival, so—'

'That guy would be *great*,' Thea cut in, and Maisie and Ollie turned to look where she was pointing.

The sun had slipped further towards the horizon, the amber orb forcing Maisie to shield her eyes with a hand so she could see who Thea was talking about. He was only a silhouette, but something shifted inside her, a recognition of the way he was moving in the water, his dark wetsuit shiny, his board a cheerful blue, the colour of the sky in a child's painting.

It was Colm, and the sight of him in one of his natural habitats made her breath stall. How many times as a teenager had she sat on the beach with her friends, while the more adventurous among them took their boards into the water? How often had she felt the flutter of attraction as he moved seamlessly, determinedly, in and out of the surf, entirely focused, but not without the ability to be self-deprecating when a bottom turn or cutback went wrong? She wasn't the only one who had fancied him. Who wouldn't, with those looks and that confidence?

She had spoken to Heather on Sunday night, when her sister was recovering from an event she'd organized, and Maisie was recovering from her evening at the pub with her friends, and had told her that Colm was back. After an ear-splitting screech, followed by several moments when she'd tried, and failed, to get a coherent sentence out, Heather had asked if Colm looked good. *Too good,* Maisie had replied. Her sister had then asked why he was back, to which Maisie had had to say she had no clue. When Heather's next question was, *When are you going to see him again?* Maisie hadn't been able to admit, even to her sister, that so far she had been too nervous to pluck up the courage to invite him for a coffee. But there was time, yet. He must still be finding his feet, a bit shellshocked at being in Cornwall again after such a long time away.

Now, watching him in the water, she could tell that he'd surfed in Australia. He was so assured, even though the waves, on this sunny, late-May afternoon, were not that big. Had he spotted them? No, of course not. He was busy tackling the unpredictable swell of the ocean, not focusing on the people strolling along the sand.

At that moment, Sprout ran into the shallows, barking as if there was an emergency. Colm, kneeling on his board, looked back towards the beach. Maisie imagined him squinting, wondering if he recognized the loud dog and the woman walking with two others, if her shorter stature and curls were obvious to him, the way she'd been able to spot him easily. He raised an arm in a wave, and Maisie waved back.

'You know him?' Thea asked.

'That's Colm.'

'Wow. You weren't joking about him being able to surf.'

'Nope.'

'He's on the list,' Ollie said. 'Would you be able to ask him? See what he thinks about being a model in my incredibly worthwhile charity calendar?' She waggled her eyebrows, and Maisie laughed. 'I never really knew him that well,' Ollie went on, 'just as Melissa's little brother, those few times he came to see her in London, whereas you were obviously close.'

'Sure,' Maisie murmured, and they kept walking, Thea and Ollie discussing an upcoming event at the bookshop, their voices eager, because it was easy to love working in a bookshop. Maisie loved the ironmonger's, but it was also dusty and entirely free from glamour, apart from at Christmas when their lights display made one corner of the shop twinkle. She had started to make subtle changes, like setting up the garden display, and she was thinking of incorporating some fairy lights into that as well, to recreate the atmosphere of garden parties and summer nights under the stars, with drinking and music and romance.

'I can ask Colm,' she said, more confidently now. Her stomach flooded with nervous anticipation at the thought of talking to him again.

If she was busy this summer, if she was the embodiment of a social butterfly, involved with school events (surely she and Jeremy could move on from the past?), taking photos for a charity calendar, being a part of the summer festival, what would Colm think? If she was always out and about, flitting between one thing and the next, he would see that she was making the most of her life, that she had done what they had talked about that night at the pub, just before he left for Australia – the night Maisie could remember as clear as day even though it had been ten years ago.

'You know what?' she said, coming to a halt in the sand. Thea and Ollie stopped suddenly, Thea almost tripping over her toes. 'I'll do it.'

'Do what?' Thea asked.

Ollie clapped. 'Yes!'

'You'll ask Colm if he's happy to be a part of the calendar?' Thea said.

'I'll do that, and I'll be your photographer, Ollie, and I'm going to help Jeremy with the quiz and chips, *and* I'm going to book a stall at the summer festival.'

'Brilliant!' Ollie jumped up and down, her red hair catching the sun.

'Are you sure?' Thea asked, always the voice of caution. 'You don't want to say no to at least one of those things?'

'No,' Maisie said, then laughed. 'No, I don't want to say no. I want to be a part of everything this summer, and I want to . . .' *Show Colm what he's been missing.* 'I want to help.' She shrugged, because that sounded lame. 'It's all going to be fun – more fun than convincing my dad to hand over the last bit of control he has at the ironmonger's, anyway – and they're all straightforward things, aren't they?'

'Absolutely,' Ollie said without hesitation.

'They *seem* straightforward,' Thea added, slowly.

'Are you going to ask Colm now?' Ollie gestured towards him.

Maisie glanced back at the water. The sun had deepened to a fiery red, the sea to a silvery slate. Colm was stretched out on his stomach on his surfboard, a picture of easy relaxation.

'Not now,' she said, losing a smidgen of her determination. 'I don't want to shout out to him.'

'Sprout doesn't have any qualms.' Ollie pointed to where Maisie's dog was still barking, this time at a seagull that was bobbing happily on the swell, ignoring him.

Maisie sighed. 'Sprout never has qualms about doing exactly what he wants. I'm going to see if I can stop him spoiling the serenity of the beach.'

She walked back along the shoreline, her heart pounding. She wasn't sure if it was because she was still in Colm's presence – albeit at a distance – or because of what she'd just agreed to.

She couldn't back out now, which was what she'd wanted – accountability with her friends, so she had to be a woman of her word. Was it too much? Could she manage the ironmonger's, organize the quiz and chips, be the photographer for Ollie's charity calendar *and* commit to a whole week of festival busyness in July?

She called to Sprout, who immediately trotted up to her, surprising her with his good behaviour. She crouched to greet him. Maybe she *could* do it: what was there to stop her? She felt a rush of elation just as her dog shook his soaked body, covering her with sea water, and then, before she had a chance to get out of his way, he jumped up, putting his front paws affectionately on her shoulders. She wasn't prepared for it and fell backwards, landing heavily on the sand.

Sprout clambered on top of her and started licking her face. She could hear Thea and Ollie running over to her, and hoped beyond hope that Colm was too far away, busy perfecting some complicated surfing technique, and hadn't noticed. She lifted her dog off her, then held her arms out when her friends reached her, and let them pull her to her feet. Sprout danced in a circle, as if he was the most helpful and adored dog on the planet. He was definitely adored, because Maisie loved the little rascal with all her heart, regardless of what he did. Helpful, though? It wasn't the first word she would have used to describe him.

Chapter Seven

That Friday afternoon, as Maisie hefted a bag of roughly chopped logs out of the boot of her Fiat 500, she wondered if she was a glutton for punishment. It had been two days since the beach, since making all those decisions, and things were already moving at speed. She was meeting Jeremy on Monday to start work on the quiz and chips, and, now that Ollie had her photographer, she had arranged the first calendar photo shoot for Wednesday week.

Maisie locked the car with her fob, then carried the bag of logs up a flagstone driveway that looked like it had recently been pressure-washed. The flower beds in the small front garden were thick with blue, white and purple delphiniums, and she found herself smiling, despite the sweat sliding down her back. She was wearing a summer dress in a blue that wasn't quite as bright as the flowers, and was enjoying the caress of the warm air on her collarbone and bare legs.

Mr and Mrs Arthur had been customers of the ironmonger's

ever since it had opened, and now that they were both in their eighties, her dad had agreed to deliver anything they needed. Maisie couldn't give up on the arrangement now without looking like a monster – not that she would want to.

She set the sack down and knocked on the door, knowing to be patient about how long it took them to answer. Horace opened it with a smile, and his formal outfit of grey trousers, a blue shirt and an oatmeal cardigan gave Maisie a little pang of some emotion she couldn't quite name.

'Thank you, Maisie lass,' he said.

'Where do you want the logs, Mr Arthur?'

'Next to the fireplace as always, that'd be grand. And call me Horace.'

She followed him into the bright, tidy living room, and took the sack to the fireplace, where the log basket was empty save for a couple of slender twigs.

'It's getting warm out there now,' she said, an indirect way of asking why they needed wood for the fire now they'd reached June.

'Not for my Jeannie.' There was something in Horace's voice that made Maisie turn from her task. He lowered himself to the arm of the sofa. 'Cancer,' he said. 'She's lost a lot of weight, feels the cold more than she used to, and in the evenings . . . well, the fire's more about comfort than anything.'

Maisie felt her throat close up, her eyes prickle with tears. 'I'm so sorry,' she said. 'I had no idea.'

Horace nodded. 'It's recent, but quite an invasive type.' He gave her a wry smile. 'Aren't they all, though? Cancer's not got any good varieties, has it?'

'No,' Maisie said. 'No, it hasn't. Is there anything I can do? Is there a—'

He waved her away. 'We were both saying, only the other day, how lucky we are to have got to this age without experiencing anything too terrible. You have to count your blessings, don't you?'

'I guess—'

'And time moves on, Maisie love. It doesn't stand still for any of us.'

'Of course, but—'

'You just keep delivering our logs, anything else we buy from Frank's place. Your smile is as good a help as anything, and I'll tell Jeannie you were here and were so kind, and that'll perk her up once she's awake.'

Maisie nodded and turned back to the logs, unsure what else to say. When she was done, she took the empty sack, made sure she hadn't left any detritus on the carpet, and stood up. Mr Arthur did too, gesturing for her to go ahead of him.

'Do you have people helping you?' she blurted, when she'd reached the front door. 'With food and company and . . . and . . .'

Horace put a hand on her arm. 'We have a small army. You know how Port Karadow is.'

'I'm so glad,' Maisie said. She felt the first tear try and release itself, and willed it to stay put.

'I didn't mean to distress you.'

'Oh, Mr Arthur, it's just – I am so, *so* sorry.'

'I know, lass. The fact that you care makes a big difference.' His smile was gentle, and she just about resisted hugging him.

Once they'd said goodbye and he'd closed the front door, she flew down the path and onto the pavement, and ran straight into something warm and solid. The shock made her breathless, and her eyes were so blurred with tears that, at first, she couldn't see what it was.

'Hey, where's the fire?' Hands gripped her arms, and the voice, managing to combine amusement with concern, added to her chaotic swirl of emotions.

Of course, she thought. Not content with having cobwebs in her hair the first time they were reunited, falling on her bum on the sand when he was surfing, now she was fleeing from a house, a sweaty, teary mess.

But what could she do but look up, into the eyes of Colm who, she noticed, was also sweating. Except on him it just looked ruggedly healthy, especially as he was wearing workout gear: a grey shirt with a subtle Nike swoosh, and navy shorts. His breathing was coming quickly, and she realized she'd crashed into him mid-run.

'I'm good,' she said, but it came out choked.

He frowned. 'Obviously you're not. Come and sit down.' He released one of her arms but wrapped his fingers around the other one, pulling her gently towards the low wall of a house. They couldn't just sit on someone's wall!

'My car's just here.' She pointed the fob at her Fiat, and it bipped unlocked. She'd left Sprout with Sandy at the shop, conscious of not putting her dog in a hot car when there was no need. She just wanted to go back there, send Sandy on her way, and lock up. A walk along the beach, the cool sea breeze, was what she needed.

Instead, Colm opened the passenger door and manoeuvred Maisie into it so she was sitting sideways on the seat, her feet on the pavement. He rested his arm on the open door and unscrewed his bottle of water, handing it to her.

She wanted to fling it in his face, if only so he would remember that rather than her tears, but she couldn't do that, so she took a sip and found that, actually, the cold water was soothing.

'What's happened, Mais?' he asked gently.

She ran a hand through her unruly curls. 'Just a . . . a delivery for the shop,' she said. 'Mr and Mrs Arthur—'

'That couple who used to run a lemonade stall by the harbour?' Colm asked.

Maisie balked. He remembered them? 'Yes, them. They ran the lemonade stall, and Mrs Arthur used to crochet animals and vegetables for all the fairs and school fetes. She started to do it for her grandchildren, and it became this whole thing, where she made loads more, then sold them to raise money for charity. Heather had a cauliflower that she loved.'

'I want to hear how Heather's getting on,' Colm said, 'but what's this with Mr and Mrs Arthur?'

'Mrs Arthur has cancer,' Maisie said. 'Mr Arthur just told me, when I dropped off their logs. And I know they're both in their eighties, but . . .'

'It doesn't make it any easier,' Colm finished. 'I'm sorry. Sorry it's happened to them, and sorry it's such a shock for you.'

'I'm OK,' Maisie said. She sat up straight, took a deep breath. 'I don't know why I'm such a mess.' She laughed, but it was a watery, bubbly sound. She looked away and wiped her eyes.

Colm crouched in front of her. His hair was, as she had guessed the other day, in an untidy cut, which worked because it was thick, and an enviable mix of brown and blond. Everything he did had always just . . . *worked*. 'What are you doing now?' he asked.

'Going back to the shop to lock up, then taking Sprout home.'

'Are you OK being on your own?'

'I'm fine,' she said, 'but thank you.' Was he offering to spend time with her? It was so tempting, but was it a good idea? 'How's the doormat?' she asked, changing the subject.

'It's great. A bit too pleasant for my liking, but it does the trick.'

'And you're running,' she said, 'and surfing.'

'I never stopped either.'

'I bet the surfing was good in Australia,' she went on, trying not to let her eyes linger on his biceps, or his thighs, now that he was crouched in front of her in not so ginormous shorts.

'It was pretty amazing,' he said, and she heard the Aussie twang on the last word. 'Terrifying sometimes.'

'Australian waves are better than Cornish ones?' She gave him a haughty look, and he laughed.

'Not at all. They're just different.'

'I bet everything was different.'

'Yup. Pretty much.' He pulled himself up to standing using her car door. 'Do you want me to drive you back to the shop?'

Maisie laughed. 'I haven't lost the use of my hands, Colm.' Then she added, more gently, 'but thank you for the offer. I'm OK, now. The water helped. And . . . you. I mean, you being here. It stopped me sitting here and sobbing for half an hour.'

'You should have a cup of sweet tea when you get home. That's some kind of universal, feel-better remedy, isn't it?'

'I might do that.' She smiled. 'And if you want to . . . I mean, we could always catch up, sometime? I can tell you about how Heather's taking over New York, and you can tell me about Australia. You know, just like old friends, getting together for a drink.'

He looked down at her, his jaw rigid, her nerves jangling as time stretched between them without him answering. Then he crouched in front of her again.

'That sounds great,' he said. 'A lot has changed, and it'd be good to catch up on what's been happening.'

'Brilliant.' It came out on an exhale.

'But I'm not going to let you hide behind Heather.'

'What do you mean?'

Colm bounced on his haunches. 'You said you'd update me on Heather, who's out in New York doing glamorous things with some guy with an overly American name, Randy or something.'

'It's Hank,' Maisie said with a laugh. 'Another update from Melissa via Liam?'

'Yeah. And I do want to hear how she's getting on, but I'm more interested in you, Winters.'

'Good,' she said, portraying a boldness that she wasn't feeling. 'That's settled, then. We'll go for a drink. I have something I need to ask you, anyway.'

'You're making demands on me already?'

'Of course. You're back in Port Karadow. Don't you remember that you can't get away with living a solitary, quiet little life here? You need to be fully invested.'

He laughed and stood up, lifting his T-shirt up to wipe the sweat from his face, exposing a strip of tanned, toned stomach. He'd done it on purpose, she decided, the absolute asshole. 'I'm not sure I'm prepared for that,' he admitted. 'But I guess . . . we'll see.'

'You just try and escape, Colm Caffrey.' She stood up and closed the passenger door, then glanced at Mr and Mrs Arthur's house, feeling a pang of guilt that she was out here, enjoying herself with a gorgeous man, when there was so much quiet heartbreak behind their solid front door.

Colm tipped his head back and groaned. 'Come on then, get your phone out. I'll give you my number.'

Maisie got it out of her bag, and silently delighted in typing a new contact: *Colm Caffrey*. She put in his number as he read it out to her, then made him repeat it, so she knew she hadn't mistyped it.

'Right,' he said. 'Best be off. My pace is shot to hell.'

'You should have paused your fancy watch, then.' She gestured to his right wrist. He was left-handed; she'd forgotten that nugget of information up until now.

'I should have,' he agreed. 'Catch up with you soon, Winters.'

'See you later, Colm.'

She watched as he turned, loped a couple of long strides and then broke into a jog, which soon turned into a swift run. He was out of sight almost before Maisie realized he'd gone.

She got into her car, saw from the dashboard clock that it was five minutes after closing and that Sandy would be waiting for her. She pulled out of her parking space, sending another silent goodbye to Mr and Mrs Arthur. She wondered if there was anything else she could do for them. Then, her mind choosing to focus on happier things, she thought about what Colm had said.

I'm more interested in you, Winters.

It was a hugely unhelpful thing for him to say. They were two people who hadn't seen each other for a decade – who had been good friends, granted – meeting up to decide if they still had enough in common to reignite that friendship. That depended, of course, on how long Colm was planning on staying in Port Karadow. And yet Maisie's heart was already racing far ahead. She needed to put a stop to it, otherwise she would be adding Colm Caffrey to her list of romantic disasters for a *second* time, and that would be the most depressing, humiliating, love-defeating thing of all.

Chapter Eight

It felt strange walking across the playground of Port Karadow primary school, with its blue chalked hopscotch grid and the other game markings that had once been burned into Maisie's brain as she stood outside in all weathers, watching the children on break duty.

Now, at six o'clock, the children were long gone, and the building was mostly deserted. She tried the glossy red doors and was mildly surprised to find them open. But then, Jeremy had told her to come straight to his classroom – at least he had done, after Maisie had resisted his offer of meeting at his house. She didn't want to rekindle anything beyond their status as ex-colleagues, didn't want to give Jeremy the impression that she was open to it, especially when she had been the one who'd let it peter out last time.

'Maisie, so lovely to see you!' Jeremy sprang up from his desk, and her gaze tracked along the window, where mini gardens in egg boxes decorated the sill. 'Spring challenge,' he said, when he saw her looking. 'Each one has a couple of seeds in. We're going to water them and monitor their progress.'

'But you got them to make cardboard plants, too,' Maisie said, nodding approvingly. 'In case no growth spurt is forthcoming.'

'It seemed wise.' Jeremy tugged the collar of his navy shirt, as if he was too hot. 'I've come to the conclusion that this job is eighty per cent managing disappointment.'

Maisie laughed. '*I* decided that it's at least fifty per cent fielding questions you don't know the answer to, which is galling when you're trying to educate them. *Who designed the patterns on snails' shells? Why hasn't my dad's shed fallen down when my next-door neighbour Mr Harvey's did? Where does shouting come from?* They shine a light on everything.'

'There's some revulsion there despite your affectionate tone,' Jeremy said, gesturing to the seat in front of his desk. She was grateful that he'd got a chair from the staff room, so she didn't have to perch on a child-sized one. 'Do you miss it at all?'

Maisie sat down, checking her white blouse with its bee print, her long maroon skirt. The blouse's tiny buttons had a tendency to pop open when she wasn't paying attention. 'I don't,' she told him. 'Occasionally, if I pass a family in the street or children come into the shop, I think about those times when they actually understood something I was trying to explain, or were delighted by an activity, but I love working in the ironmonger's, and it's a lot less exhausting.'

'I hear you,' Jeremy said. 'I'm spending tomorrow up to my elbows in papier mâché, and the digital whiteboard has got some glitch where it keeps wiping the screen when I'm halfway through writing something out.' He rubbed his forehead. 'But you're not here to listen to my woes or gloat about no longer having them.'

'I'm here for quiz and chips,' she said brightly. She had dropped Sprout off with Thea and Ben on her way here, and they'd promised to walk him along with Scooter. She hoped it wouldn't be too long before she could get back to them all.

'Right.' Jeremy thumbed through a notebook, then pressed the pages flat. 'Here's where I'm up to so far. We have the date confirmed, the numbers of tickets we can sell, and I'm sending out the first notice to parents on Friday. I've locked down a general large order with the Good Plaice, and they've sent over their price list, but I've not narrowed it down to what we're going to offer on the night—'

'You can't let them order anything off the menu, or it'll be chaos,' Maisie said.

'Right. So there's that, and there's the quiz itself.'

'Which you've not even started.'

Jeremy gave her a sheepish smile. 'This is where I need the most help.'

'OK, well I can make a start on that,' Maisie said carefully.

She didn't want to commit to writing the whole thing, because it was no mean feat. The Port Karadow residents who booked tickets for the quiz and chips were fiercely competitive, and they expected a high standard of quiz, with diverse rounds, jokers and tie-breakers where necessary. She couldn't just watch a few episodes of *The Chase* and steal the questions.

She thought of Thea's comment about saying no, about how powerful it was. Maisie wasn't quite ready to do that, but she would think carefully before agreeing to whole swathes of tasks.

'That would be brilliant.' Jeremy's relief was evident. 'Could we go through my list, just to make sure I've not forgotten anything vital, like . . . I don't know, ticket prices or something? I haven't actually thought about those.' His cheeks turned beetroot.

'But now you've reminded yourself.' Maisie slipped easily back into 'encouraging teacher' mode.

'I have!' Jeremy grinned, and Maisie returned it with a smile.

As they went through his to-do list, her thoughts returned to her encounter with Colm, and why it had been such a jolt to have his concern aimed at her. She had lots of people who looked out for her – Heather, who was a lifeline for so many reasons – but his gentle questions, his warm hands on her arms . . . it had been a long time since she'd had that kind of attention from a man. She was determined not to read too much into it: Colm had returned to his childhood town, and she was a familiar face. Even so, it threw things into perspective.

Before her disappointing dates with Jeremy, which were nearly two years ago, her last relationship had been with a gardener called Gavin. It had come to an abrupt halt after less than six months, when she realized that he was unable to contain his bountiful affection, and was sharing it between her and a few other women at the same time.

As Jeremy read out the schedule for the quiz and chips night, told her about the raffle he was proposing to run, to raise money for the wildlife area they wanted to create in the school grounds, Maisie decided that she had been starved of male companionship. No wonder she was hanging onto every moment with Colm like he was some kind of romantic life raft. She would have to stop it immediately.

'So,' Jeremy said, leaning back in his chair, 'I think we're there.'

'We have a solid plan,' Maisie corrected, tapping her phone, where she had written her list of tasks. She had to come up with an abridged version of the fish and chip menu, confirm it with the Good Plaice, and get started on the quiz. But she already knew that, by agreeing to start it, the whole thing would end up as her responsibility.

'Thank you.' Jeremy sounded sincere. 'You know, Maisie, it isn't the same here without you.'

'*Obviously* not.' Her laugh was slightly too loud.

'You brought so much energy to this place. So much *spark*. You're doing what's right for you, and that's great, but I want you to know I haven't forgotten you.'

Maisie hesitated. She had decided to do this to help the school, and because she didn't want there to be any lingering awkwardness between her and Jeremy. But she also didn't want to give him the wrong impression. 'I haven't forgotten any of you either,' she said carefully. 'I'll always feel some loyalty to the school, even though I'm never going to work here again, and I'm happy to help you with this. It's going to be a fun night. Who have you got to compère?'

Jeremy's breath hitched, and Maisie felt a shiver of foreboding. 'I was thinking,' he said, 'as you're coming up with the questions – so you won't be able to take part yourself – that you'd be best placed to compère it, too.'

The foreboding, it seemed, was warranted. 'Oh. Right.

Could you let me think about it? Because it's quite a big thing, being compère.'

'I was there for your Book Wars rounds at A New Chapter. You're a great public speaker.'

Maisie sighed. How had she allowed herself to be trapped like this? 'Let me think about it,' she said again, more firmly. She told Jeremy she'd be in touch when she'd made progress, said goodbye and strode into the evening sunshine.

The sky was an intense blue, and the air smelled of the sea. She gulped in its freshness, relieved after the confines of the cluttered classroom. She had unequivocally failed to say no: to any of it. And now, not only was she going to have to write the quiz, but she had to deliver it, too. She only hoped she'd made it clear that she was doing it for the school, not because of any remaining fondness for Jeremy.

She set off in the direction of Thea and Ben's house, craving her friends' company and her dog's unconditional love. She hoped that, when she explained what had happened, she wouldn't get an *I told you so*. But then Thea wasn't like that.

She was almost at their beautifully renovated cottage, when her phone made a quiet 'uh oh' noise, telling her she had a message. Her heart skipped when she realized it was from Colm. He'd replied to the one she'd sent him earlier, announcing herself and telling him that he could put her number in his phone now, too.

Good to know. Was worried you weren't going to use the gift I'd bestowed upon you. ;)

He hadn't used an emoji, but the semi-colon and bracket that had long ago been considered a winky-face. It felt like the first glimpse of the Colm she had known and . . . well, cared about, his cheekiness on full display. She stood to the side of the path to let a couple go past her, and replied.

I was excited to use it. Shame I've also used it to sign up to some dodgy websites selling male virility products. Oops! :o

She didn't have to wait long for his response.

You know that doormat I was looking for? The phrase I really wanted on it? ;)

Message received. x, she replied, feeling momentarily like the coolest person on the planet, then put her phone away and started walking again. That was the problem with Colm: being near him made her cool by association, and that was a hard drug to wean yourself off, even if you'd only just rediscovered it after a whole decade of abstinence.

Chapter Nine

Ollie and Max lived in the recently converted Foxglove Barn, which was part of Liam Byrne's estate, about a thirty-minute walk from the centre of Port Karadow. Ollie had asked if Maisie, Thea and Meredith, who had somehow become the charity calendar project team, would be happy to get together on Friday evening. Other than watching a *Pretty Little Liars* marathon and eating a Thai takeaway, Maisie had no other plans, and she would feel more settled about being involved in the calendar when she had a better idea of how much time it was likely to take up.

Foxglove Farm was red brick and stately, with a neat lawn in front boasting a very old yew tree. The barn was off to the side, its large windows gleaming, and as Maisie headed for the front door, she couldn't help being reminded that Liam was Colm's granddad. But this evening was *not* about Colm.

'Maisie.' Ollie opened the door before she'd had a

chance to knock. 'Thank you for coming. And you, Sprout,' she added, bending to stroke him. 'Come in. I have wine, beer or Prosecco, tea, coffee, hot chocolate – whatever you fancy.'

Maisie followed Ollie into the open-plan living space. Its decor was soothing, with pistachio green walls and lots of exposed pine, and while it was mostly tidy, there was evidence of it being lived in: a book splayed open on a side table, a sprig of wildflowers in an old Stokes tomato ketchup bottle on the mantelpiece, the air filled with the smell of warm pastry and, beneath that, something smoky, like incense.

'I love your spring bunting,' Maisie said, letting Ollie take her jacket and Sprout's lead. There was a string of yellow, pink and blue bunting hanging along the mezzanine level.

'Thanks.' Ollie beamed. 'I'm a big fan of a garland. Now, I've made mini quiches. Do you want cheese and bacon, feta and spinach or red pepper and sun-dried tomato?'

'Oh, wow.' Ollie had opened the oven door, and heat and delicious aromas filled the space. 'If I'd known helping with the calendar included all this, I would have agreed ages ago.'

As Ollie was arranging quiches on a cooling rack, there was a knock on the door, and Maisie went to let Thea and Meredith in.

Twenty minutes later they were settled at the rustic dining table, plates of pastries and brownies – that Ollie had included in her cooking marathon – tantalizing them from the centre, Prosecco poured into four glasses.

Ollie opened the plan she'd created on her iPad. 'I'd like

to try and get all the shoots done by the end of the summer, depending on the weather and the availability of Maisie and our models. And I want some kind of physical publicity we can give away at the festival, to let people know it's coming and start getting pre-orders in.'

'You mean a teaser?' Thea said.

'Exactly. Perhaps a desktop calendar for the rest of this year, with one of the photos on.'

'Or a mini whiteboard,' Meredith suggested, nabbing a cheese and bacon quiche. 'People love those. You can have a customisable photo at the top, then there's a little white-board and pen below. The whole thing is magnetic, so people can stick them to their fridge and use them for messages.'

'That sounds perfect,' Ollie said. 'It means we'll need to get at least a couple of the shots finalized fairly sharpish – we've got less than two months until the festival, and we'll need to include editing and production time.'

'Who have you got signed up so far?' Maisie asked.

'Right.' Ollie tapped her iPad screen. 'We have Meredith and Finn,' she looked up and Meredith did an elaborate, seated bow. 'And Thea and Ben?'

Thea nodded. 'Ben says as long as he doesn't have to actually go on a surfboard in the water, he'll be a part of it.'

'Excellent! Max has agreed to the same, and then . . .' She bit her lip, her expression impish.

'Oh no,' Thea said. 'You've got some kind of celebrity, haven't you? Marcus Belrose?'

Ollie laughed. 'God no! Not after I hurt his pride with that terrible cooking class in the bookshop. He scowls any time he sees me, and I'd avoid the Happy Shack if it didn't do the best seafood in Port Karadow.'

'It is *great* seafood,' Meredith said, sighing.

'Who have you got as model fodder, then?' Maisie wondered if she'd have the composure to photograph genuine celebrities, or if her hands would be too shaky to adjust the settings on her camera.

'OK,' Ollie said, bouncing in her seat, 'this is *such* a coup, but—'

'I'm home!' Max called from the hallway, and Henry, Sprout and Crumble went racing to greet him.

'Hold your excitement.' Ollie got up and, when Max came into the room, the dogs around his feet, they wrapped their arms around each other and kissed.

'Aw,' Meredith said softly.

'It's almost too adorable,' Maisie added, feeling a swell of happiness for her friend, along with a slight stab of envy.

'Sorry to interrupt,' Max said.

'You're not.' Ollie dragged him to the table. 'Want a beer? I got a crate of zero lagers, let me get you one.'

Max kicked off his shoes and followed Ollie into the kitchen. 'Can I help?'

'You can help by drinking a beer, having some mini quiches and giving us your input. I was just about to tell them my big news.'

'Oh, about Sa—' Ollie pressed a hand to his mouth and he chuckled beneath it. 'I wasn't going to steal your thunder.'

'Come over here,' Maisie said, 'the tension is killing me.'

'And me,' Thea added.

'Not me.' Meredith tore the crust away from her quiche. 'I know everything.'

'How do you know?' Thea asked.

'I know because I know.' Meredith tapped her nose.

Max settled at the table, Ollie refilled the four glasses with Prosecco, then held hers out. Everyone clinked, and waited.

'So,' Ollie said. 'Not only are we having esteemed Porthgolow business owners, Charlie and Daniel Harper as one of our couples, *but* we've also got Charlie's cousin, Delilah Forest, and her boyfriend Sam Magee. The stars of BBC period drama *Estelle* are going to be part of our humble little calendar.'

'Oh my God,' Thea murmured. 'They're so lovely, too.'

'Holy shit,' Maisie said, sounding as dazed as she felt. 'Really?'

'Really! Meredith is friends with Charlie, and gave me the introduction. I have some more people on my list, including Finn's actor aunt, Laurie, and her partner Fern. It's almost like people are clamouring to be a part of this.'

'Are you surprised?' Thea asked, with a gentle laugh. 'You could make the opening of a Quavers packet sound exciting.'

'She's not wrong.' Max leaned back in his chair and took a swig of his zero beer. He'd had a health scare at Christmas, a recurrence of an old illness, and since then he'd been taking his health even more seriously, completely giving up alcohol. Maisie was quietly, incredibly impressed by him – and Ollie – and the way they had stayed so positive in the face of such horror and uncertainty. But, she supposed, when you'd had a close call, it put everything into perspective, reminded you to live your days to the full. Also, they had each other to lean on, which she knew made a huge difference.

'You also have Colm.' She hadn't meant to blurt it out like that.

'Ooh yes, Colm,' Ollie said. 'Have you had a chance to ask him yet?'

Maisie thought of their encounter outside the Arthurs' house, and how she'd teased, in her Colm-infused rush of adrenaline, that she had something she needed to talk to him about. They'd messaged a few times since then, but hadn't arranged a meet-up, and she knew she was stalling because every encounter with him felt both precarious and precious and, if she was honest, a bit too much.

'Not yet,' she admitted. 'But now I can tell him more about the plan, really sell it as a great opportunity alongside the other models you've got.'

'If he's been living in Australia, he's not likely to know what *Estelle* is,' Thea pointed out.

'BBC shows get everywhere,' Meredith said, 'and he's had Liam to catch him up on all the news while he's been abroad.'

'I'm not so sure about that,' Ollie said. 'Liam hasn't told me the whole story, but they weren't in touch much while Colm was away. Melissa, his sister, was, though: they talked a lot via Skype and FaceTime, and I know she went to visit him a couple of times.'

'He adores surfing,' Maisie said, 'which is a big thing in our favour.'

'He'll be one of the few genuine surfers in it,' Max said, with a grin.

'You know what?' Ollie took a pepper and tomato quiche off the plate. 'We could go and ask him right now. His cottage is so close – we pass it quite often when we're walking Henry.'

At his name and the word 'walking', Henry bounded over to the table, followed by Crumble and Sprout, their small white and brown bodies dwarfed by the chocolate Lab.

'That sounds a bit like an ambush to me,' Max said gently.

Ollie stood up. 'Henry needs a walk, and it's not dark yet. I know we bumped into Colm when he first got here, but we haven't gone and asked him for a bag of sugar or anything.'

'Shouldn't he be asking *you* for a bag of sugar?' Thea said.

'Let's change things up, then. Let's go and say hello!'

'*All* of us?' Meredith asked, but she was already standing, her bright eyes twinkling with the possibility of this new adventure.

Maisie felt a hot flash of panic. She had *not* imagined the evening including an impromptu visit to see Colm. She was still in her work outfit, a pale yellow top and a long blue skirt with daisies on it. It was pretty, but not exactly glamorous, and she had no clue what state her curls were in. 'What if he's not at home?' she said.

'Have you got his number?' Ollie asked.

She nodded, but she was even reluctant to call him. Her body had turned into a bundle of nerves, hot wires in a computer server room that someone should have turned off, but had been abandoned to get warmer and warmer until . . . BANG.

'Do you *want* to call him?' Thea asked. Her dark eyes were serious, as if she could see beneath Maisie's skin to the fiery tangle beneath.

'We could tick off another month on our calendar,' Ollie said.

Maisie looked between them, and suddenly, where a moment ago she'd been sure she wanted to avoid it at all costs, now the possibility of seeing Colm, of speaking to him, was so tantalizing that she couldn't imagine not doing it.

She scrolled to his number and hit the 'call' button. It rang and rang, and then there was his voice, deep and casual, with that new twang that made it unmistakably his. *This is Colm Caffrey, leave me a message if that's your thing.* The beep came quickly, sneaking up on her, and she ended the call abruptly.

'He's not picking up,' she told the assembled group. But now all the dogs had their harnesses on, Meredith putting on Sprout's as well as Crumble's, and it would be cruel not to walk them after getting them excited.

'No harm in swinging by the cottage,' Ollie said. She grabbed the tray of brownies, took them into the kitchen, pulled a Tupperware box out of a low cupboard and put them inside. She closed the lid with a satisfying click. 'And, we have goodies to bring.'

'What about some wine?' Max pointed to two bottles standing on the counter.

'Good idea.' Ollie grabbed a bottle of red.

Maisie took Sprout's lead from Meredith with a smile. She realized she was more intrigued about seeing where Colm was staying, the fabled Rose Cottage, than she was nervous about having a spontaneous meeting with him.

Max gestured for them all to go ahead of him, and Maisie followed the others out into the calm, quiet evening, where the only sounds were a robin serenading them from the yew tree, and the distant, gentle shush of the waves. As they started walking, she took a surreptitious – but very necessary – deep breath.

Chapter Ten

The party of five people and three dogs walked through the woods surrounding Liam's farmhouse. The air was scented with the gentle sweetness of the wildflowers that bloomed in patches where the canopy was thinner, and the evening light cut through the leaves in slivers, alighting on vibrant bluebells. Maisie thought the bright, concentrated rays looked like fairies, with flies and motes dancing in the beams like stardust. There were a lot of legends around this area, as with all of Cornwall, and being in the subdued, green-hued glow of the forest was slightly otherworldly.

'Have you been on any photography courses?' Meredith asked her.

'No, nothing like that,' Maisie admitted. 'I read photography magazines for composition tips, but I'm mostly self-taught. Up until now, my photos have just been for my own pleasure and my blog, so I've never bothered to get legitimately good at it.'

'You *are* legitimately good,' Ollie said. 'You don't need a certificate to tell you that.'

Maisie was warmed by the compliment. 'I've done hardly any portraits, apart from Sprout.' At his name, her dog looked up at her, a leaf roguishly sticking out of his mouth.

'Sprout counts,' Ollie said. 'I wouldn't have asked you to do this if I didn't think you were perfect for it.'

'That's very kind,' Maisie said, and didn't add that she was also a more appealing prospect than paying a professional photographer. But it was for charity, everyone was doing it voluntarily, and now she'd committed, she was genuinely excited about being involved.

'This is it,' Max said, as the yellow cottage, nestled amongst a cluster of silver birch and willow trees, came into view. It was beautiful, with rose bushes sprawling up the walls, their blood-red and pure-white blooms standing out against the yellow painted stone. Maisie wondered who Liam had employed to keep it looking so nice when, up until Colm had moved into it, it had presumably been standing empty.

'God, how dark is it here at night?' Thea sounded genuinely horrified. She had moved to Port Karadow from Bristol, and her and Ben's sea-facing cottage, while on the outskirts of town, wasn't nestled in a valley or enclosed by trees.

'Very dark,' Maisie murmured, remembering how Colm had complained about it when they were choosing him a doormat. She didn't know where he'd lived in Australia, but thought it might have been Sydney, and she couldn't picture him in a dusty outback town, far from the city lights or the surf he loved so much.

'Do you want to knock?' Ollie asked, holding back Henry.

'Sure.' Maisie surreptitiously ran her hands down her skirt, then went ahead, taking the winding path that led from the woods to the cottage. There was a gravel driveway with a gleaming Citroën hybrid parked in front, telling her that there was, at least, a road up to the house, even if it was one of those narrow Cornish tracks that made you think the satnav was messing with you.

The cottage had a white front door with a shiny brass knocker in the shape of a fox's head, the window next to it made up of small panes of glass, the interior dark beyond. A budding jasmine crept over the door frame, and a wren trilled from a nearby tree. It was, Maisie thought, utterly beautiful.

'Wow,' Meredith said. 'Liam's hidden cottage is a full-on stunner.'

'It's magical,' Thea murmured.

Maisie imagined walking up to this postcard-pretty dwelling, the front door opening, and being greeted by a doormat that told her to fuck off. She bit her lip and lifted the fox-shaped knocker, then brought it down twice. The wren took off pipping into the undergrowth.

She didn't have to wait long for the door to swing inward, and suddenly Colm was there, wearing an oversized navy dressing gown, his hair damp and messy, as if he'd just run a towel through it. He went from frowning to surprised in a split second, Maisie only noticing because she'd managed to drag her gaze away from the triangle of tanned, hair-smattered chest she could see in the V-shaped opening of his soft-looking robe. Her inner wire-tangle was about to burst into flames.

'Hello,' he said. 'I wasn't expecting a welcoming party. OK, Winters?'

'Good thanks,' Maisie chirped.

'Hi . . . Ollie and . . . Max, isn't it? And Henry Tilney?'

'Hey,' Max said.

'And this is Meredith and Thea,' Ollie added. 'The beagle is Crumble, and Maisie's dog is Sprout.'

'I know Sprout,' Colm said. 'Good to see you all. Is this . . . early carol singing? An intervention because I parked on a grass verge by the town hall? My granddad's decided he's had enough and you've come to kick me out?' His gaze flitted between them, but kept landing on Maisie.

'It's part welcoming party, part something else,' she said.

'You parked on a *grass verge*?' Meredith exclaimed.

'I know.' Colm sighed. 'I got shouted at as I was pulling away. No idea who she was, but she was furious. I didn't even see a sign.'

'That's the thing about Port Karadow,' Thea said cheerfully. 'You're just meant to *know* these things.'

'I'd somehow managed to forget that,' he admitted. 'Come in, if you want? There's just about room for all of you.'

'These are for you.' Ollie thrust the wine bottle and Tupperware box at him, and Colm took them, surprised.

'Thank you. You really didn't need to do that. Come on in.' He turned and led the way into the house.

Maisie felt a tiny prod in her lower back, and followed him. Sprout stayed close to her heels, sniffing the air suspiciously, while Colm led them down a narrow corridor and into a spacious room with a generous-sized fireplace, wooden beams dissecting the low ceiling, and a pale green suite that looked comfortable but had seen better days. Maisie's gaze alighted on the personal touches: a Kindle with the case folded back on the arm of the sofa, next to a pair of black-framed glasses that she couldn't imagine Colm wearing; empty beer bottles, the labels from various Cornish breweries, lined up on the mantelpiece. The scent of beach filled the air, and it made her wonder where his surfboard was.

'Take a seat.' He gestured around the room, and they all perched on sofa arms or sank onto cushions. Henry lay in the middle of the floor, while Crumble and Sprout stayed close to their owners. 'Can I get any of you a drink?' he asked. 'I've got beer, fruit juice, coffee. I might have some tea bags somewhere, if you're lucky. Or we could open the wine, start on whatever delicious thing is inside this box?' He went to take the lid off, but Ollie held a hand out.

'Those are for you,' she said.

'I'm fine thanks,' Thea added, and everyone else agreed.

'Sure, but let me know if you change your mind.' Colm put the bottle and box on a side table, then sat on the floor in front of the fireplace and stretched his legs out, the dressing gown reaching halfway down his calves. Henry crawled along the carpet and put his head in Colm's lap, and Colm stroked him between the ears, the movement almost unconscious.

'So this is part welcoming party, part something else,' he said. 'Something that required a personal visit? Have you been speaking to my granddad about me?' His tone was light, but Maisie thought there was something blunter beneath it: nervousness, or uncertainty.

'No,' Ollie said, 'but why would Liam—'

'You know I said, the other day, that I needed to ask you a question?' Maisie cut in. 'It involves all of us, really.'

Colm leaned back, his hands flat on the carpet behind him. 'Shoot.'

'Maisie?' Ollie prodded.

It made sense that she was the one to ask him, but she had already been planning on doing it, though in a much less performative way than them all descending on his cottage when he'd clearly just come out of the shower.

She sat up straighter. 'Ollie's organizing a charity calendar,' she explained. 'Photos of surfing and beach scenes, surfers and their pets, amusing tableaus, all to raise money for the RNLI. We thought, because you're such a keen surfer, that you might want to be involved.' She exhaled. Apart from the wren, who'd gone back to singing outside, and the dogs' gentle snuffles, the room was quiet, Colm's gaze trained unwaveringly on her. 'We've come to ask if you'd like to be one of the models,' she clarified.

His lips parted, and she saw a flash of surprise in his eyes. There were roses clustered at the window, the small panes and shrubbery filtering the light so that his brown eyes almost seemed to glow. 'You want me to be Mr December?'

'If you're particularly wedded to Christmas,' Ollie said. 'But I thought you'd be more of a July or August.'

'Is that a compliment?' He smiled at her, then turned his attention back to Maisie. 'Was this your idea?'

'The calendar is Ollie's idea,' Maisie said. 'But I know how much you love surfing. You seemed like an obvious choice.'

'I can't pay you, I'm afraid,' Ollie added, 'but it should only be a couple of hours of your time, with your own surfboard and wetsuit, somewhere scenic. And then obviously your details will go in the calendar, your name and what you do.'

'What *do* you do?' Meredith asked, unabashed.

'You mean other than surf and hide in my granddad's dated cottage?'

'This place is *lovely*,' Maisie protested, and Colm shot her a look.

'I'm a web designer,' he told Meredith. 'Freelance since getting back, so the going's predictably slow, but I'm hoping it'll pick up.'

'Well that's good,' Ollie said.

'Which bit? That I'm a web designer or that it's not working out so well?' His smile seemed genuine, but Maisie wondered how practised it was.

'What I mean,' Ollie went on, 'is that we can include the details of your business, so anyone who buys the calendar will be able to get in touch with you.'

'Free advertising in return for getting my kit off for the camera?'

'It's not a nude calendar,' Thea said hurriedly.

'I wouldn't have minded, necessarily.' Colm shrugged. 'Who's taking the photos?'

'That would be me.' It came out sounding unbelievably prim, and Maisie wanted to rewind time, to pretend that she was unaffected by the image he'd planted in her head, of him posing nude in front of her, forcing her to look at every golden-hued inch of his body in order to get the best photos.

His easy amusement flickered out, and the air in the room seemed to thicken. 'You're a photographer, on top of everything else?'

'It's a hobby,' she said, 'but I'm good at it, so I'm the official calendar photographer.'

He nodded. 'That makes it easy, then. Of course I'll do it.'

'Yes!' Ollie said, and Meredith squealed in delight.

'That was straightforward,' Max said.

'It was a straightforward request,' Colm replied. 'Just tell me when and where you need me, what you need me to bring. Oh, I don't have a pet, though, unless you count the tiny black and white cat I keep seeing round here. He doesn't have a name tag, but he must belong to someone.'

'If you've started feeding him,' Meredith said, 'then he belongs to you.'

Two points of colour appeared on Colm's cheeks, and Maisie knew, without a shadow of a doubt, that he was feeding the stray.

He had always been a sucker for a fluffy, defenceless animal. She remembered once, when they'd found a hurt seagull on the beach, and even though there was little chance of it recovering from the shock or its injuries, Colm had cupped it gently in his hands, walked all the way home with it, and kept it in a large cardboard box, giving it food and water. He'd taken the box into the garden every morning, giving it the chance to fly away, and then one day, it had – its thank you a trail of poo, splattered all over a fresh lot of washing that his mum, Bryony, had just put on the line.

Maisie had only heard about the triumphant resolution, Colm sitting on a table in the sixth-form common room, telling everyone who was in there. He'd been full of pride, not remotely bothered that his mum had been furious, making him do all the washing and ironing for a month afterwards as punishment.

'You can borrow Sprout,' Ollie said now. 'Can't he, Maisie? He'd look great with your dog in his arms. What do you think of that?' She booped Sprout's nose, and he yipped happily.

'Is that OK, Winters?' Colm gave her a steady look.

'Of course!' she said it automatically, though she wasn't sure how she felt about it. Colm and her dog, cuddling up together with the Cornish sea behind them; so many of her favourite things in a single photo frame.

'Why do you call her Winters?' Thea asked.

'It's my surname,' Maisie said, with a laugh.

Colm folded his arms across his chest, which pushed his dressing gown further open, revealing more of his tanned chest. 'A couple of years before I moved to Australia, *Game of Thrones* came out.'

'Is it really that old?' Thea shook her head, incredulous.

'The first ever episode is called "Winter Is Coming", did you know that?' He didn't wait for anyone to reply. 'And obviously the catchphrase was everywhere, so every time I saw Mais, it was unavoidable. I'd say, "Winters is coming", and she'd scowl at me in that adorable way of hers, where she tries to look angry but isn't remotely capable of it.'

Maisie frowned, because she had entirely forgotten he used to say that to her, and also because she was very capable of looking, and being, angry.

'Winters is coming,' Meredith repeated. 'I'll have to remember that.'

'*Game of Thrones* is over now, though,' Ollie said, but she was giving Maisie a curious look.

'I don't remember you doing that,' Maisie admitted. 'Unless you didn't do it to my face?'

'Oh no, I said it to your face,' Colm told her. 'Trying to get you to wrinkle that perfect nose was my number one goal in life. Probably why I didn't do so well in my exams.' His grin was entirely disarming, and Maisie's wires almost short-circuited.

'Shut up,' she said. 'You got amazing results.'

'They didn't mean a whole lot in Australia,' he said. 'But anyway.' In a second, he had jumped to his feet and pulled the dressing gown firmly closed. 'Never mind all that. The important thing is that I'm up for this calendar. Just let me know when you need me. Maisie, you've got my number.'

She stood along with everyone else. 'I tried to call you, but . . .'

'So it wasn't supposed to be an ambush? I must have been in the shower, washing all the seaweed off.' He'd stepped closer to her, and she was struggling to focus on anything beyond his proximity.

'Do you surf a lot?' Max asked.

'Every day, if I can. How about you?'

Max shook his head. 'I'm more about yoga and walking these days.'

Colm opened his mouth to reply, and a frown flickered on his face. 'Granddad told me about your myocarditis. I'm sorry – that can't have been easy.'

'Thanks,' Max said, sounding surprised. 'It's all good now. I just need to be careful.'

'I'm always up for a hike, especially when the country-side's this great.' Colm gestured out of the window. 'Give me a shout if you fancy a tagalong.'

'I'll do that,' Max said, and the two men shook hands. Ollie grinned, clearly delighted that they had managed to befriend the new guy, despite their rather aggressive tactics.

They filed back down the corridor and out into the sweet-smelling garden. Maisie was the last to leave, and as she reached the front door, she felt a hand squeeze her waist. She turned around.

'You do want this, don't you?' Colm asked, his voice low, just for her. 'Me being involved?'

'I suggested it,' she said. 'And of course I do. A Port Karadow surfing calendar wouldn't make any sense without you, now that you're here.'

'Great.' His smile was gentle, but there was a lightness to his expression, a spark that hadn't been there before. 'I'm looking forward to you taking pictures of me.'

'Why's that?' Her pulse was thrumming. Did he realize how flirtatious he was being?

'Because your gaze is always so steady,' he said. 'It must be a special thing to be the sole focus of it, even if it's only for a little while.'

Maisie couldn't find the right words to reply. In her head, she was saying, *If only you knew how long you were the sole focus of my gaze.* But if she told him that, a can of ancient worms would be opened, and Maisie wasn't ready for that.

'I'm looking forward to it too,' she said instead. 'Thanks for letting us impose on you.'

'No imposition.' He pointed to the welcome mat, the word *Hello!* in its cheery, swirly font. 'I'm always happy to receive visitors.' He grinned at her, and Maisie couldn't help but grin back. How was she going to survive having Colm, wetsuit clad and possibly cuddling her mischievous dog, as her photography subject? If her internal wires were blaring DANGER now, then God knows what the alert level would be when it came to that particular scenario.

'Bye, Colm,' she said.

'See you, Winters.'

She raced to catch up with her friends, hearing the gentle click of his door closing behind her. She wasn't surprised when Ollie put an arm around her shoulders and pulled her close, then said, 'I need to know all about "Winters is coming".'

Maisie waited for Thea or Meredith to rescue her, force a change of subject, but from the curious looks they were giving her, that even Max was levelling at her, she knew she wasn't going to avoid the conversation.

As they reached the green-hued light of the woodland, she made herself a promise. She would tell them about her teenage crush, but she would not, under any circumstances, admit that it had returned with a vengeance; that whenever she was in Colm's presence, she felt as giddy as the school-girl she used to be. That way lay disaster, especially with Ollie and all her good-intentioned interventions, and Maisie wanted to have a long, blissful summer, filled with laughter and sunshine, and absolutely zero disasters.

Chapter Eleven

Frank and Aimee Winters lived to the east of the town, their road of semi-detached houses in a slightly elevated position, so from the attic room, which had been converted when Maisie and Heather were teenagers and the place suddenly felt too small, you could see down to the harbour, the sea stretching into the distance beyond.

Right now, Frank, Aimee and Maisie were in the dining room at the back of the house, where the walls were painted a pinkish-red, and it was only the French doors into the garden that stopped it from being like a horror film set. But Aimee Winters was bold in all aspects of her life, from colours to conversation starters.

'Is grown-up Colm Caffrey as sexy as everyone's saying he is?' she asked as she carried a bowl of roast potatoes to the table, their crunchy surfaces flecked with rosemary, 'or is that just the view of a gaggle of menopausal women who haven't had any action in years?'

Maisie almost dropped the wine bottle she was holding.

'God, Mum,' she said, glancing at her dad. But Frank was absorbed in the Sunday paper, and Maisie knew he had decided a long time ago to be selective about which of his wife's conversations he got involved with.

'Well, is he?' her mum pressed. 'I've cooked a whole roast dinner, so the very least you can do is give me some good gossip. And you used to know him – used to moon over him, at least – so I refuse to believe that you haven't seen him since he got back. It's not like running that place is a full-time job.'

That place was how she often referred to the ironmonger's, and Maisie felt a familiar stab of protectiveness. Her dad looked at her mum over the top of his paper, then glanced at the roast lamb, and Maisie wondered if he was weighing up what it would cost him to start an argument.

'We're always busy at work,' Maisie said brightly. 'And, as you know, it's not just about serving customers. There are orders to arrange and restocking to do, accounts to tally. I had more free time when I was a teacher.'

'That you earned because your job was important,' Aimee said.

'On Friday, I helped a customer who needed to build a ramp so his disabled son could get into and out of their new house easily,' Maisie said. 'Don't you think that's important?'

'They should have got in touch with the council,' her mum said, striding into the kitchen. 'We have a service for installing necessary equipment, or providing grants so the resident can organize the work themselves. If they've just moved to the area, you should point them in our direction.'

Maisie felt her dad's hand on top of her own. 'One of

the reasons she loves having you round is so she has a sparring partner,' he said quietly. 'I gave up the fight a long time ago.'

Maisie exchanged a conspiratorial smile with him, and resolved to be as sweet as the lemon meringue pie she'd seen in the fridge. 'Work's going well, then?' She followed her mum into the kitchen. There was enough food to feed all the covers at the Happy Shack, and Maisie knew she would have leftovers to last her the next couple of days, parcelled up in neat tinfoil packages by her mum.

'There's a consultation into the management structure kicking off,' she said, her shoulders straightening. After being a stay-at-home mum until Heather and Maisie were settled in secondary school, Aimee Winters was now PA to the head of Social Care at the local council. It was an important job, and not remotely easy, but her mum did sometimes make it sound like she was in charge of a small army.

'Oh God, is there?' Maisie said. 'Are you at risk?'

'I have been assured that my job is safe.' She gave Maisie a warm smile. 'And Phillip needs my help formulating the new support staff structure. We're working on it together.' Phillip Houghton was head of Social Care, a man Maisie's mum revered. Whenever his name came up, Maisie felt hurt on behalf of her dad, though she didn't think her mum would ever betray him. For all their sniping and differences, she was sure her parents still truly loved each other.

'That's great, Mum.' She accepted the bowl of purple-sprouting broccoli, and led the way back into the dining room. There was a blue tit on the feeder outside, and Maisie watched it flit back and forth between the seeds and the bush it was using as shelter. It made her think of the verdant paradise surrounding Rose Cottage, full of sound and colour and wildlife, if not wolves.

'What about you?' her mum asked, as Frank discarded his paper in favour of the electric carving knife. Sprout hated that thing, but he had long ago been banished into the front room during Sunday lunches, since he always found a way of sneaking onto the table, regardless of how watchful everyone was.

'What about me?' Maisie asked.

'Aside from working at that place, I understand you're helping out with a school event?' Aimee raised a perfectly groomed eyebrow. Her hair was naturally blonde, like Maisie's, but last year she'd dyed it a rich, chocolate brown and had her eyebrows done to match. She had told Maisie it made her look more serious, which Maisie had tried not to take as an affront.

'The quiz and chips next Friday,' Maisie said.

She had spent most of yesterday in her courtyard garden, with her laptop and a pen and notepad, coming up with quiz questions, then verifying each one using at least two different sources, because Jeremy had told her there could be no doubt about the answers. It had been a total mind-fuck, and when she'd finally stopped she had blurred vision and at least fifty tabs open on her laptop – and she still had three rounds to come up with.

'What are you doing for the quiz and chips?' her mum asked, doling out Yorkshire puddings.

'I've arranged the menu, and I'm writing the quiz.'

Her mum sat back. 'You're writing the whole quiz?'

'Jeremy's got to sort out the tickets and make sure there

are enough teams, and he's doing a raffle. So he asked me to write, and compère, the quiz.'

'Goodness.' Her mum exchanged a look with Frank, and Maisie knew what was coming next. 'How did it feel, being back in the school? I assume that's where you were?'

Maisie cut a slice of lamb, then chewed and swallowed it slowly before she replied. 'I went there to meet Jeremy. It felt like somewhere I'd moved on from.'

'You know,' her mum said, 'I'm sure if you told them that you'd had a change of heart, they'd have you back in a flash. Jeremy clearly misses you.' He'd said as much, but Maisie didn't quite know what that meant, and wasn't inclined to investigate. His WhatsApp messages had been frequent, checking in with her about how the quiz was coming on, when the reason he'd asked for her help in the first place was that he knew how organized she was, and that she wouldn't let him down.

'I don't miss being there, though,' she said. 'I'm happy at the ironmonger's, which is our family business, in case you'd forgotten. If I wasn't working there, we'd have to sell it.' She looked to her dad for support.

'As much as I hate to agree with that statement,' he said with a gentle smile, 'Maisie's right. I can't run it the way I used to, and we're lucky – luckier than we realize, sometimes – that Maisie was willing to take it on.'

'It might be better to sell it,' Aimee said. 'Have a fresh start, Frank. You'd be fully retired, instead of this halfway house where you're still organizing rotas and dropping in on your customers all the time. And you'd have some money in the bank.'

'The ironmonger's isn't struggling,' Maisie said firmly.

It had been, before she took over, but that was because her dad was trying to do everything when he was no longer capable of it, and pride had stopped him asking for help. Maisie had brought the shop back to full health, and it was making a good profit again. 'And what would I do if we sold it?'

'Anything you wanted.' Her mum gave a frustrated laugh. 'Honestly, Maisie! Why is this so hard for you?'

'Why is *what* so hard? Living my own life? Having my own ideas about what success and happiness look like? Why is *that* so hard for *you*?'

'Come on now,' Frank said quietly, which was about as much intervening as he ever did.

'You know Heather has been invited to be on the Met Gala team for next year?' her mum said.

A lump lodged in Maisie's throat. She *hadn't* know that, but that was only because Heather had been busy with an event yesterday, and they hadn't had their usual catch-up.

'I thought that would make you sit up.' Her mum pointed her fork at her, a tiny potato on the end.

'I don't want to organize the Met Gala, Mum. It's amazing that Heather is, because that's what *she* wants to do. I've got the shop, the quiz and chips, this calendar I'm helping with, and my blog. I'm busy, and happy, and I don't ever want to be a teacher again, to go backwards with my life.'

'What about Colm? Isn't seeing him also going backwards?' She said it gently enough, but when the water was calm in Aimee Winters' world, it usually meant there were sharks gathering under the surface.

'He's a friend,' Maisie said carefully. 'It makes sense that, while he's here, he would want to catch up with people he knows. I think he's a bit isolated, because he's been gone for such a long time, and it's been good to see him.'

Aimee nodded and went back to her roast dinner, the lack of a comeback making Maisie nervous. She felt as if her phone was burning a hole in the pocket of her dress, because she and Colm had been exchanging messages since Friday. Nothing overly dramatic, just her apologizing for the bombardment at his cottage, him reassuring her that he didn't mind, and after that they'd slipped into an easy back-and-forth. It was friend stuff: communication that didn't require her to picture the slice of chest she'd seen when he was wearing his dressing gown, and certainly not as frequently as she had been doing.

After lunch, Aimee went to meet friends at the Happy Shack for their customary Sunday drink, and Maisie and her dad settled down to look at the ironmonger's accounts. Having survived her mother's inquisition, she decided to broach the sensitive subject she'd been wanting to talk to her dad about.

Sprout had his head on her lap as they sat on the sofa, happy to be reunited with her, especially as she'd sneaked him a roast potato.

'Dad,' she said, once they'd been through everything they needed to. 'What do you think about me taking over the shop's rota?'

He stared at her. 'Why on earth would you want to do that? You've enough to be dealing with. This is the one bit I *can* do.'

All Maisie's thoughts of him trying to control her evaporated, and she found herself shrugging. 'It's just that . . . I was blindsided, the other Saturday, when Parker had to leave early and I had to cover.' She pictured Colm standing in the doorway, hair dripping, like a mirage of her desolate love life and a tantalizing treat all wrapped up in one.

'I'm sorry about that, love. It was short notice for me, too. But I'd like to help, wherever I still can. I've got my bees, but I still want a part in the shop.'

'I get it,' Maisie said. 'If you want to keep doing it, then I don't want to take it away from you. But could you let me have the rota sooner? Just so I'm prepared.'

Her dad patted her knee. 'Of course, pet. You're doing grand there, you know.' He was unusually quiet, some of his trademark bolshiness – which came out once Aimee had gone to meet her friends – missing. Then he added, 'I went to see Horace and Jeannie yesterday,' and she knew why.

'How are they doing? How's Jeannie?'

Frank let out a long breath. 'I didn't see her, but Horace said she's doing as well as can be expected. He said you'd given him some comfort with your latest visit.'

Maisie stared at her hands. 'I only delivered the logs. I'm so sorry for them.'

'Me and all,' Frank said. 'But we're doing what we can, and that's all I want from our place. To serve the community, look after the loyal customers and anyone else who needs it. Your mother . . .' He paused for a moment. 'Your mother gets caught up in the flashier accomplishments, and I know I'm partly to blame, working all hours at the shop while she brought you and your sister up. When I met her she was glamorous, fiercely independent, and that all changed – well, she's still glamorous, of course. But she measures her happiness in different ways to you and me, and I understand that.'

'I get it, too.'

Her dad smiled. 'You're stronger than you realize, Maisie. And what you're doing with the ironmonger's, it's all I could have asked for. To me, success is helping, giving kindness and support where we can, people knowing they have somewhere they can rely on. I know you feel the same.' He held out a plate of chocolate digestives, and she took one. They dipped their biscuits in their tea, then both took a bite.

'I just want to make a difference *here*,' Maisie said, when she'd finished her mouthful. 'I can't imagine loving anywhere as much as I love Port Karadow, and it's enough for me.'

Was it enough? Having a close group of friends, her dog, the countryside and the sea, her house and the shop, where they looked after people and knew their customers by name? Despite all her mum's pressurizing, Maisie had stayed firm. But now she thought of Colm, of all his years in Australia, and she wondered if staying in the same place she'd been born in, settling for her one little corner of the planet and not exploring the world, was the right thing to do. And then she wondered if she was looking at herself through her own eyes, or if she was suddenly trying to see herself through someone else's.

Chapter Twelve

On Monday morning, after Maisie had put the 'Open' sign outside the ironmonger's on the Main Street cobbles and given the counter a clean, she made a list of everything she needed to do that week, so she could organize it all in her thoughts.

She had been up until after midnight finishing the quiz questions, so that Jeremy wouldn't panic when she saw him that evening. She didn't mind helping people; she just didn't quite know how she'd gone from *helping* to being the lynchpin of the whole event.

'All right?' Parker stepped through the door and took down the hood of his hoody.

'Good thanks, Parker. What about you? Nice weekend?'

'Yeah. I mean, I was here, wasn't I? But it was OK.'

'Great. And thanks for doing a couple of hours this morning.'

'No worries. Extra time, isn't it?' He sauntered to the office, presumably to make a coffee.

Maisie had a delivery coming and needed an extra pair of hands, because delivery lorries parking on Main Street were frowned upon, so she needed to get everything inside as quickly as possible. She arranged a vase of artificial wildflowers on the counter, and went to help Parker clear space in the storeroom, keeping an ear out for the bell.

Half an hour later, there was enough room for everything they were expecting, and the driver had phoned to tell her he was ten minutes out.

'Ready, Parker?' She pushed her curls off her forehead, trying to instil some get-up-and-go into him, to get him moving more like an Olympic athlete than a young man who'd dropped out of his A-levels to pursue a career in video game testing.

Instead of her colleague, it was Sprout who answered, barking in a way that put her on high alert. She peered towards the front of the shop and saw the reason for his excitement standing next to the counter: Colm, and his granddad, Liam.

She left Parker in the storeroom and went to meet them. 'Hello,' she said.

'Hey.' Was it her imagination, or did Colm look faintly embarrassed?

'Hello Maisie,' Liam said warmly, and Maisie returned his greeting.

Liam Byrne was in his eighties, and was a tall, proud man, his posture always impeccable. He was well known in Port Karadow, for owning the beautiful Foxglove Farm Estate, and, much more recently, resurrecting his career as an author of Cornish-set mystery books, which was something Ollie, Max and A New Chapter had had a big hand in. Knowing that Colm and Liam hadn't parted on the best of terms, and even though Liam was letting Colm stay in Rose Cottage, she was both pleased and curious to see them out together.

Colm was as tall as Liam, and she could see other similarities between the two men: the sharpness of their cheekbones; the long, straight nose; the warm eyes, though Liam's were darker than the striking golden-brown Colm had been blessed with. She wondered how many hearts Liam had broken in his younger years.

'It's lovely to see you both,' she said.

'We've come to trouble you for the items needed for a garden trellis,' Liam said. 'If that's something you can help with?'

'Of course. We have made-up trellis panels out the back, or a variety of wooden planks if you want to make it yourself, which I can cut to the right length. Obviously then there are fixings – let me show you everything, and you can decide what would work best.'

She led the way to the back of the shop, aware of the imminent delivery, more aware that Colm was right behind her. 'Is the trellis for Rose Cottage?' she asked.

'Yup.' Colm popped the 'p' at the end, so she knew there was a story there. Luckily, Liam loved stories.

'The roses around Rose Cottage are, seemingly, an inconvenience,' Liam told her, 'so I suggested we put up a trellis to tame them.' Maisie could hear the amusement in his voice.

'I just don't love running the gauntlet of having my clothes or skin ripped to shreds every time I enter or leave the house,' Colm said. 'I get enough of that with Thor.'

Maisie turned around. 'Who's Thor?'

'Thor's the stray cat,' Colm said. 'The one I mentioned the other day. The name's ironic.'

'Because he's as soft as his adopted owner?'

'He comes to see me every day.' There was something like pride in Colm's voice. Their eyes held for a second, then Maisie gave him an indulgent smile and he looked away. 'And I'm not soft,' he added quietly.

'Or prone to exaggeration,' Liam said. 'Though the phrases *running the gauntlet* and *ripped to shreds* are very emotive.'

Colm narrowed his eyes. 'You are enjoying this far too much.'

Liam chuckled. 'I'm very much enjoying having you back here, young man. I'm sure I'm not the only one.'

Maisie was very close to telling Liam he wasn't the only one. Instead she said, 'Here are the trellis panels, and the wood is just in that room there. Think about what you want to do, then come and find me. We've got a delivery arriving, so I need to go and get that sorted, but I'm around.'

'Thanks Mais,' Colm called as she hurried back to the front of the shop, where Parker was talking to a tall man in a red T-shirt and grey shorts, holding a tablet.

'Here I am!' She glanced at the huge lorry taking up the whole of Main Street. 'Shall we get going?'

The three of them made an efficient tag team, the driver bringing the boxes to the wedged-open front door, Parker passing them to Maisie, who piled them in their newly cleared space. She was settling one box of paint tester pots on top of another when a voice startled her.

'Need any help?' Colm asked from the doorway.

She spun around. 'Oh! We're OK, thank you. You're a customer.'

'A friend,' he corrected, and when Parker appeared with another box, Colm took it and brought it over to the pile. He was wearing a pistachio-green T-shirt and ripped jeans, and he looked delicious. Pistachio ice-cream had always been her favourite.

With his help, it only took another ten minutes until the storeroom was full, Parker had begun to sort through the items, and the huge lorry had beeped in goodbye – or reverse – and trundled up Main Street, leaving the cobbled road tourist-friendly once more.

'Thank you so much for that,' Maisie said, when Colm and Liam returned to the counter with three trellis panels and some fixtures.

'No worries,' Colm replied. 'Seems we timed it right.'

'You were perfect,' Maisie said without thinking. She cleared her throat. 'Just these?'

'These will work a treat.' Liam patted the panels.

'I'll give you a discount for all your help. No quibbling,' she added, when she saw Colm was about to protest.

'Thank you,' he said instead. 'I wanted to get some planks, just so I'd get to see you using the saw, but then I realized I'd have to build the bloody thing myself, so I went with the easy option.'

Liam tutted.

'I hate using the saw,' Maisie admitted. 'I'm not allowed to say that to customers, because it's a service we provide, but I'm relieved not to have to do it.'

'Grand decisions all round then,' Liam said. 'Though don't let him fool you, Maisie.'

'About what?'

'About him always taking the easy option. I expect he's told you that—'

'Time to go, Granddad.' Colm picked up the trestle panels and nudged Liam's shoulder, so he was forced towards the door.

'Told me what?' Maisie asked.

'Nothing,' Colm said.

'This is elder abuse!' Liam called at the same time.

'I'll buy you a coffee and a sausage roll in Sea Brew,' Colm said to him.

Maisie was about to follow them out of the door – she couldn't leave it like that – when Parker appeared. A quick glance told her that he'd had a fuchsia-pink, paint-related disaster, and she needed to deal with it. She turned back to the open door, wondering how she could delay the two men, when Colm gave her a quick, utterly flirtatious wink, then led his granddad across the street to the café, leaving Maisie flustered and mute, and struggling to remember what she was supposed to be doing for a good ten seconds.

After the paint spill was cleared up as much as possible (the storeroom floor might have the faintest pink stain forever), the work day passed normally, or as normally as possible after Colm and Liam's visit, the questions it had left Maisie with along with the memory of that wink.

After work she walked to the primary school, dropping Sprout off with her parents on the way. She told them she was running late, so her dad wouldn't quiz her about the delivery, and her mum couldn't surreptitiously stick an 'I want to come back' badge to her dress – she wouldn't have put it past her.

'Come in,' Jeremy said, gesturing expansively at his classroom. 'I can't believe we're only a few days from the quiz and chips. How are you?' He stepped towards her, and Maisie thought that he was going to shake her hand, but he hugged her, instead. She was too shocked to relax into it, and after a couple of awkward seconds he stepped back. He dropped into the seat behind his desk, and she took the one opposite.

'Did you get on OK with the questions?' he asked.

'It wasn't easy.' She didn't want him to think she'd breezed her way through it. 'But I'm happy with the result.'

She'd emailed him the finished quiz the night before, hoping he would have had a chance to look at it so they didn't have to go through it now, or – worse – she had to sit in silence while he read the entire thing.

'It's actually brilliant,' Jeremy said, sliding some printed sheets out of his desk drawer. 'Creative, hard but not impossible, a lot of good talking points. I love that you've included a question related to Port Karadow in every round. Very clever.' He beamed at her, his silver stud winking in the evening sunshine. Maisie wanted to accept the praise, but his exaggerated enthusiasm, along with the hug, had put her on edge.

'I'm glad,' she said. 'I worked hard on it.'

'I can tell, and I'm beyond grateful – for that and for the menu, which is ideal. And you'll be the perfect host on Friday night.'

'It should be fun,' she said. Now that she'd created a quiz that she was proud of, she was looking forward to delivering it.

They stared at each other over Jeremy's desk, which was

cluttered in a cheery way, an apple standing on a stack of books, a pen pot with at least three forks in it. There was a glasses case, and Maisie wondered if it was his, because she'd never seen him wear them. It sent her thoughts back to the living room of Rose Cottage, her surprise at seeing a pair of glasses lying next to Colm's Kindle. His wink replayed in her mind again – it had been on repeat since that morning – and what was it that Liam had said? *Don't let him fool you, Maisie.*

'Maisie? Maisie.' This time it was Jeremy saying her name.

'Sorry, what was that?'

'Want to run through the timings with me?'

'Sure.' She sat up, trying to look attentive, and was surprised when he dragged his chair around to her side of the desk. He sat close to her, and she caught the scent of his citrussy aftershave.

'We need to give everyone long enough to answer, but not too long that we're still there after midnight,' he said, as if Maisie had no concept of how quizzes worked. 'It's all about the timing. And, of course, the break for fish and chips is key. We also need enough time to draw the raffle prizes – we've got some good ones: a three-course meal for two at the Happy Shack, even a night's stay plus spa treatment at Crystal Waters in Porthgolow.'

'Ooh, I love it there,' Maisie said, 'though I've only been for afternoon tea.'

'It's a beautiful setting,' Jeremy agreed. 'Very romantic.' There was something in his expression that made Maisie want to run away.

'So timing is key,' she said, turning back to the papers in front of them. 'I think I'll be fine. I spent four years running lessons, after all.' Her laugh sounded as forced as it felt.

'I could give you a refresher.' He pressed down on the paper, his fingers millimetres from hers, then cleared his throat. 'And . . . Maisie?'

'Yes, Jeremy?'

'I just wanted to say, about what happened between us, before you left. I know it was a couple of years ago now, but I have to tell you that—'

'Please don't,' she rushed.

'I *have* to,' he said. 'I've thought about almost nothing else these last couple of weeks.' He turned towards her, his knee brushing against hers. 'Look at me, Maisie.'

God, did she have to? She turned slowly, and then, as if all her wishes were being granted by a benevolent Cornish piskie, she saw a small, fair-haired boy standing in the doorway, a pretty blonde woman behind him.

Seeing Maisie's attention drift, Jeremy turned around.

'Go on, Oscar.' The woman gently nudged the boy forward.

'Mr Shoreham,' Oscar said. 'I left my glasses behind, and Mummy says I can't see without them.'

'He really can't,' Oscar's mum added, giving Jeremy an apologetic look. 'I'm so sorry to interrupt.'

'Not at all,' Jeremy said smoothly. 'I did wonder if you needed these.' He picked up the glasses case from his desk, walked over and crouched in front of the boy. 'I was going to give them back to you tomorrow. We'll have to make sure you don't forget them in future.'

Maisie used the distraction to gather up her things and hurry to the door.

Jeremy looked up. 'Wait, Maisie.'

'I think we've been through all we need to,' she said. 'You

117

have important teacher business to attend to. I'll get here for five thirty on Friday, OK? I've got someone else locking up for me.'

Before Jeremy had a chance to reply, she gave them all a quick wave, flashed Oscar's mum a grateful smile that must have confused her, and slipped into the empty corridor. Her steps echoed against the walls as she hot-footed it out of there.

By the time Maisie had picked up Sprout, mostly avoided scrutiny from either parent, and got home and made herself kedgeree, one of her favourite comfort foods, she was feeling less frazzled about the parallel dimension she seemed to have stepped into: Liam's mysterious comment, Colm's flirtatious wink, Jeremy's sudden closeness.

She took her food out to her tiny courtyard garden, where the sun was setting. The evening light had softened everything, and if she closed her eyes and let the sound of the waves and the warm breeze wash over her, she could almost empty her mind of confusing thoughts.

Then her phone made a gentle 'uh oh' sound, telling her she had a message. Her brief meditation forgotten, she picked it up. It was Colm.

Thanks for the trellis bits and the discount. This building malarkey is harder than it looks. :)

Then, a few seconds later:

Good day, after I left?

There was definitely something strange going on. Had a mermaid swum close to shore and cast a love spell on all the men in town? Whatever it was, Maisie was going to take advantage of it.

What did your granddad mean when he said I shouldn't be fooled by you?

Granddad is going senile. Ignore him.

He is NOT. Don't be so rude! Good day thanks, though I had to meet with an ex-colleague to finalize plans for the school quiz and chips on Friday night.

I'm going to that! Me, Granddad, Marion his housekeeper (secret bit on the side), Ollie and Max are a team. You organized it?

Maisie stared at her phone. He was *going?*

She typed frantically. *You don't have any children! None of you do – apart from Liam, and your mum's a bit beyond school age.*

Mum also lives in Edinburgh, so it's prob too far for her to come. But I don't know the rules – Granddad sorted the tickets. I'm trying to be nice to him, build bridges etc. So I'll see you then, and on Wednesday.

Maisie was confused. *What's happening Weds?*

The first photo shoot for the calendar. I asked Ollie if I could come and see how it all worked. She said yes, so I get to see you doing your thing.

Maisie groaned, and Sprout looked up from his spot next to her chair, where he was waiting for her to drop a bit of haddock. Colm was going to be at the quiz, and he'd inveigled himself into the calendar shoots too. It was going to be hard enough when he was the wetsuit-clad subject, but if he was going to be hanging around at other times, charming everyone and throwing her the occasional, flirty wink, what was she supposed to do?

She wanted to do a good job for Jeremy – despite their history, and the strange way he'd been acting today – and for Ollie. She prided herself on being organized and calm, and not the distracted, fluttery teenager she turned back into whenever she was with Colm – at least on the inside. She was sure some of that behaviour had slipped through to the outside, too.

She took a sip of lemonade and picked up her fork, unprepared for the newly concerning situation to get in the way of the delicious dinner she'd cooked herself. But afterwards, she only had one option: she needed an emergency call with her sister.

Chapter Thirteen

The day of the first RNLI calendar photo shoot was the most blissful day of the year so far. The light was perfect and the air was warmer than it had been, but with a freshness that Maisie wanted to bottle and keep in every room in her house. As the clock ticked around to five thirty, and with Sandy at the ironmonger's to lock up for her, she checked her camera equipment again.

Everything was there, as it had been the last five times she'd checked, and she set off, walking through Port Karadow, surrounded by the seagulls' cries, and with the smell of chips, already deliciously pungent, enticing the evening crowd into pubs. A beat-infused pop song played from an open window somewhere nearby, and sprays of wildflowers crept out of gaps in crumbling walls. It felt like summer.

The beach was busy with groups of teenagers playing frisbee, children building sandcastles, a couple strolling in the shallows and one brave man or woman – she couldn't tell which – swimming, their pale hat skintight against their head. Maisie walked along the path above the sand, avoiding the busiest part that, at this time of year, was off limits to dogs.

Ollie was waiting for her at the south end of the beach, next to where clusters of rocks encroached on the golden sand. She waved madly as Maisie approached. 'Hello!' she called. 'You're the first – after me, I mean.'

'Hey.' They hugged, Maisie briefly wrapped in Ollie's arms and her expensive, subtle perfume. 'The weather's turned up for us.'

'I know!' Ollie glanced out to sea, a hand shielding her eyes. 'It's perfect.'

Maisie slipped her camera bag off her shoulder and got out her equipment: tripod, camera, the different lenses she would need. 'Do you have any ideas for the shots today?'

'Other than that it's going to be Meredith and Finn in their wetsuits, I don't,' Ollie admitted.

'No surfboards?'

'They're swimmers, which I think is fine. We don't *need* to have surfing paraphernalia in every shot, and this adds variety.'

'OK.' Maisie glanced around her, at the expanse of sand, the water and the glistening rocks, which, when the tide was out, would harbour pools full of watery treasure. 'What about some shots on the rocks? They'll add structural interest, and we can arrange Meredith and Finn in various poses, try a few things out.'

'We're going to be arranged, are we?' Finn's bright voice cut in. The couple were already in black and navy wetsuits, and had colourful beach towels under their arms. Maisie waited to hug them both, the soft, grippy material brushing her arm as she embraced Meredith.

'You have to be arranged,' she said. 'I can't have you going rogue – not on my first shoot.'

'Have you met my boyfriend?' Meredith asked, and they all laughed.

'You will do as you're told.' Maisie realized that she still had the perfect schoolteacher's voice; it had just been waiting in the wings to be used.

'Yes ma'am.' Finn stood to attention.

She finished setting up her equipment, then walked to where the rocks reached all the way down to the sea. She wanted to make the most of the soft, evening sun, and thought this would be the best place to do it. 'Why don't you come around here? Bring the towels, and Crumble.'

The beagle bounded down to meet her, and Maisie crouched to stroke his nose and ruffle his ears. Sprout joined them, never one to miss out on attention.

'Where do you want us?' Finn put one foot up on a rock, then leaned his elbow on his knee and put his chin in his hand, assuming an overly serious pose. 'About here?' He squinted, looking out to sea as if he was an admiral over-seeing a fleet of ships.

'Not *quite* like that,' Maisie said, grinning. 'But we want different height levels, for sure. More than anything, people have to be drawn into the photo, so I need elements that will lead them into the shot.' She realized she would need to be in the shallows to get the angle she wanted, and kicked off her sandals, walking into the sea with the camera around her neck.

'Hey!' Meredith said. 'We're the ones in the wetsuits.'

'This is where I need to be,' Maisie told her. 'Right, this is what I want.'

As she manoeuvred Meredith and Finn into place, and as they coaxed Crumble to where she wanted him and Ollie held Sprout back, she instinctively knew what she was doing. She could see the composition of the image in her mind, could picture exactly how it would look, large and glossy above a month-view calendar. She wasn't used to photographing people, but she knew how to set up a shot, and in a lot of respects Finn and Meredith were no different to the huge oak tree in the woods surrounding Foxglove Farm, or the standing stone near Stone Cove that looked magical with the morning mist swirling around it.

She moved her subjects around, an arm raised here, a leg straightened there. She put them behind the rocks, in front of them, on top of them. She liked how Meredith was tentative but committed, a shade of hesitation in her warm eyes, while Finn was completely at ease, a born performer. They complemented each other perfectly, and Maisie got lost in her task, excitement thrumming through her veins as she took photo after photo, and knew that at least some of them were good enough for the calendar.

She spent a long time crouching, angling her camera up to take shots of Meredith and Finn from below, unbothered by the sand and seawater seeping into her black, floral-print dress. When she stood up, she saw that Ollie and Sprout weren't the only ones watching, and sucked in a breath.

Colm was standing next to Ollie, wearing a blue T-shirt, grey board shorts and scuffed trainers. The gold strands in his hair shone in the evening sun, and he had his arms folded, his tanned skin and defined muscles drawing her attention.

'You look like a professional photographer,' he said, and she forced her gaze up.

'Hardly,' she replied. 'But I've got good instincts, and it's fun.'

'Can I look at the shots?' Ollie bounced on her toes.

'Sure. I have a whole bunch now, so you can see if you think we've got enough. Models, take a break,' she said loftily to Meredith and Finn, and they laughed.

'I want to see too,' Meredith said.

'Me three,' Finn added.

They clustered behind Maisie while she lifted the camera so they could all see the screen, and scrolled through the photos to the beginning. There were noises of assent, comments of, 'This one's great,' and 'I love that one,' and Ollie, an unusually whispery voice in the background saying, 'Oh my God.' Colm, she noticed, stayed mostly quiet, but she *also* noticed – how could she not? – that he was directly behind her, his warm breath tickling the back of her neck.

She tried to focus, tried to fight the way her body was reacting to him being so close; the caress of his exhaled air against her skin, the way it was extra warmth on this already warm day, but also somehow refreshing: a sensation she wanted to lean into. She clicked through the shots, proud of how she was keeping her composure, until she realized she wasn't.

'Maisie. Maisie!' She had been pressing the button, scrolling through the photos robotically, not paying attention. 'You've gone about fifty frames past it!'

'Sorry. Which one was it?'

'Back back back,' Ollie said, and Maisie clicked through them again. 'I think we've found the one. The sun is right and Meredith and Finn look great. Here – it's perfect!'

Maisie stopped clicking and looked at the shot. Meredith was sitting sideways on a rock draped with a beach towel, the pink, yellow and blue a pop of unnatural colour against the glistening grey slate. Finn was standing half behind her, looking down, and Crumble sat proudly beside her, his nose angled up as he gave Finn an adoring look. The sun was hitting the sides of their faces, the waves frothing at the base of the rock, the movement there somehow, despite the fact that it was a single moment in time.

'Yes.' Meredith sounded awed.

'Amazing,' Finn murmured, and Maisie felt a spark of pleasure, because Finn was a painter, so if he thought it was good, then it must be.

She waited for Colm's verdict, but it was Ollie who spoke next. 'I can't believe we have our first photo in the bag. Maisie, you're brilliant, thank you.'

'Oh no – no problem.' She turned around, caught Colm's eye, then gave her attention to Ollie. 'I'm glad it's working out.'

Ollie scoffed. '*Working out* is the understatement of the year. I knew you were the right person for this. I can't wait for the next shoot – we've got Charlie and Daniel booked in.'

'And Sam and Delilah,' Meredith added. 'You can decide whether you want them in one month, or split across two. But you could do that one in Porthgolow, with the bus or the hotel – both would be good backdrops.' She glanced at Maisie. 'I mean, if you think that would work.'

'I am open to any and all ideas for composition,' Maisie said.

'I already know what I want.'

Everyone turned to look at Colm, and when he smiled, Maisie felt as if he was in competition with the sun. They'd better get out of here before golden hour arrived, she thought, because in that ethereal glow she had a feeling he'd look positively godlike.

'What do you want?' Ollie asked. 'Although, bear in mind that Maisie and I, as creative director and producer, have the final say.'

'Oh, I think you'll like this one. Just picture it.' He stretched his arms out in front of him, hands moving as if he was framing a scene. 'Me, wetsuit pulled down to the waist, walking out of the sea. No other props needed.'

There was a heavy silence, and Maisie hoped that someone – *anyone else* – would fill it.

'Sounds all right,' Meredith said nonchalantly.

'It sounds very Ursula Andress,' Finn added, shooting his girlfriend a look.

Colm laughed. 'Yeah well, that went down OK, didn't it?'

Ollie narrowed her eyes. 'Are you going to be trouble? Because I'm on a quiz team with you on Friday night, and I don't want to be thrown out.'

It was another reminder of what else Maisie had to look forward to this week.

'I really hope I'll be trouble,' Colm said. 'Life gets boring otherwise. But I will try my best to be a good model.' He turned to Maisie. 'What do you think of my idea?'

Something about him was off. He was standing with his legs apart, arms folded, unabashedly cocky, but there was

127

a rawness in his expression, subtle enough that she thought only she would notice it, knowing him better than the others did. It made her think his suggestion was a kind of defence mechanism: that he was being deliberately over the top to hide what was going on inside. She still knew so little about why he'd left Australia, about the man he'd become since he'd moved away from Cornwall a decade before.

'It sounds perfect,' she said, because now wasn't the time to delve. 'Just the kind of fun thing we want. We could find you a scallop shell to hold, or a rainbow parasol to twirl.'

'Yes,' Ollie said. 'Yes, that! Take it from salacious to silly, while also keeping the goods.' She gestured at Colm, and Maisie marvelled at how unselfconscious she was.

'Great,' Colm said, but he was looking at her, not Ollie.

Maisie wanted to ask him if he was OK. Had he had some bad news? He'd been so quiet throughout the shoot, the photo flick-through, then this outlandish suggestion.

'Hey, Colm,' she said, but had no idea how to finish the sentence.

He looked at her a moment longer, then said, 'I need to head off. Thanks for letting me come today, Ollie. Catch you all soon?'

The others said goodbye, then turned back to the rocks to collect their beach towels and retrieve Crumble from the water.

'See you Friday,' Maisie said.

Colm took a step towards her, reached out and squeezed her hand, his skin warm against hers. 'See you, Winters.' Then he turned and walked away across the sand, the sunlight kissing his shoulders and his hair and every other part of him it could reach, and Maisie didn't blame it at all.

Colm had always been carefree, but right now there were some troubling thoughts happening behind his expressive amber eyes. And what was troubling for Maisie, was that she was desperate to find out what they were, and see if she could help soothe them away. But she did also want to see him walking out of the sea half-naked, like a male version of Ursula Andress, and that, she decided, was an equally worrying realization.

Chapter Fourteen

The back of the school hall was adorned with a display of jellyfish in a variety of mediums: drawings where the creatures bobbed below a line of blue pencil sea; papier mâché models, one of them leaning at a drunken angle on its stand; 3D paintings, their rainbow tentacles made of tissue paper. Maisie stared at them, using their vibrant imperfection to calm her. Tonight was the night: she was compère for the quiz and chips.

She walked across the hall and up the few steps onto the stage. Jeremy had given her a high stool with a back, and a tall table with two copies of the quiz questions on it. The answers, he had told her when she arrived, were locked away in his desk drawer, as if this was the Oscars and not a school quiz on a Friday night.

'Would you like a glass of wine?' he asked her now. He was wearing a vibrant blue shirt and dark trousers, his dark hair gently styled, his earring glinting. He looked good, Maisie thought, and even more nervous than she felt.

'I'd love one, thank you.' It was a bring-your-own, as it was taking place in a school, and Maisie had a couple of cans of gin and tonic in her bag. But if Jeremy was offering her wine, she wasn't going to say no.

He disappeared and returned with a large glass of white wine. She took it, realizing with a happy jolt that it was crisply cold.

'Thank you,' she said. 'Are you OK?'

'This is my first one being in charge,' he admitted. 'Mrs Phelps usually does them, but now I'm community co-ordinator, it's all up to me.'

Mrs Phelps was the dragon-like deputy head, who Maisie had always secretly thought ruled the school, the much milder Mr Fielding merely a figurehead principal.

'You must be going up in the world, if Mrs Phelps has let go of this and given it to you.' She smiled.

'Given it to us,' he corrected. 'You're missed here, Maisie.'

He said it as if he was speaking on behalf of the entire teaching staff, and that settled her nerves slightly. And she could see Mr Fielding now, coming in with his wife and teenage daughters, wearing a tweed jacket even though it was a Friday night in the middle of June. He was deeply loyal to the school, and had seemed quite upset when she'd decided to leave. Mrs Phelps, as ever, had remained inscrutable.

'Don't bring me into this,' she said jokily. 'Unless tonight goes really well, in which case then of *course* I had a huge hand in it.'

He looked at her, his blue-eyed gaze intense, his brows creasing as if he was about to say something serious. Maisie glanced away, over his shoulder, and something – some*one* – caught her eye.

131

Colm was a steady figure in a sea of movement. Liam and Marion, Liam's housekeeper, were putting ketchup and mayonnaise, as well as bottles of wine, on a table at the back of the hall, while Max and Ollie pulled out chairs. Colm was like the still point in one of those hyper-lapse videos, and he was looking at her. Or, more accurately, he was looking at Jeremy's back, because Jeremy was shielding her from his view.

'Do I get a microphone?' she asked, dragging her gaze away.

'Oh shit, of course.' Jeremy hurried off the stage, his long strides eating up the wooden floor.

Colm had sat down at his team's table, in the position facing the stage. He raised his hand in a brief wave, and she waved enthusiastically back, wondering why she felt as if she'd just been found around the back of the bike sheds.

'Good evening, ladies and gentlemen, boys and girls,' she said. The room was full of the great and good of Port Karadow – the youngest competitor looked about fourteen – and there were lots of faces she knew well, some she knew a little, and all of them were smiling, chatting and laughing, looking forward to their evening of entertainment.

One team was made up of Mr Fielding and his family, and a couple that Maisie didn't know; another was Liam, Marion, Max, Ollie and Colm. Thea, Ben, Meredith and Finn – plus Finn's aunt Laurie and her partner Fern – made up another team. Maisie recognized Lizzy – who she often saw in town and who also came to the book club – and her husband with some other people, and there was another table made up of several teachers from the school.

Her parents knew about it, of course, but she wasn't remotely surprised that they weren't here. Helping out at the quiz was not the same as resurrecting her teaching career, so her mum wasn't interested. Her dad was probably in the garden with his bees.

She explained how it would work – ten rounds, all different subjects, and each team had a chance to play their joker, which they needed to announce before their chosen round started. There was lively debate on the tables about which round they wanted to use it on, then Maisie told them the fish and chip menu would be circulating, and that they needed to choose their food now. When the orders were collected, Jeremy would phone them in, while Maisie started the quiz.

She helped him collect the menu slips, saying hello to everyone as she did so, and soon found herself at the Foxglove Estate table.

'Hello, Maisie love,' Marion said, smiling warmly. She was a small, lithe woman with dyed blonde hair, who helped Liam with various tasks around the farmhouse, and was always abreast of any gossip in the Cornish town. 'You're looking well.'

'Excellent introduction,' Liam added. He seemed relaxed, sitting next to his grandson, and she thought they must have completely cleared the air after their decade-long alienation. 'You're an expert at this.'

'Just helping out,' she said breezily. 'Have you all made your food choices?'

'I don't think you need anything other than cod and chips on here, to be honest,' Max said. 'Apart from the halloumi burger for the veggies.'

'But their chips will be done in dripping,' Marion said.

'They're not,' Maisie told her. 'They're cooked in vegetable oil, I checked.'

'Well, well.' Marion folded her arms. 'Everyone's buying into it these days.'

Max laughed. 'Vegetarianism? I think it's been around for a while.'

'You know what I mean,' Marion said, but she was smiling.

'What about you, Colm?' Maisie asked, aware that he'd been quiet up to this point.

'We've tasked him with coming up with a team name.' Liam patted Colm on the shoulder. 'So his brain is currently occupied.'

'Team names are bloody impossible,' he said, looking up at her. He was wearing a cream cotton shirt, and he'd rolled the sleeves up, showing off his tanned forearms. 'What do you think?'

'I have to be impartial, because I'm quiz master.' She stood up a little straighter.

'Helping with a team name is hardly collusion,' Ollie said.

Maisie tapped her fingers against her lips. 'Universally challenged.'

'That's a bit old hat,' Marion said.

Maisie shrugged. 'The Foxglove Farm Massive.'

Ollie winced, and Max grinned.

'OK, that was terrible – I don't know!' She flung her arms up in defeat.

'I told you,' Colm said. 'It's impossible.'

'We'll come up with something,' Ollie assured him.

Maisie glanced around the hall. 'Do you have your orders? I should be getting back.'

Liam handed her their completed menu sheet.

'Was that young Jeremy I saw you with earlier?' Marion asked.

Maisie caught Ollie's eye before replying. 'He's in charge tonight. He just asked me for a bit of help.'

'With devising the *entire* quiz,' Ollie said.

'You and he were sweet on each other, weren't you?' Marion's gaze was steely, and Maisie could easily picture her as a bird of prey: soaring up high, so she could see the whole town, finding a mouse far below in the grass and – whoosh – swooping so suddenly it didn't have time to get away. At this moment, Maisie was the mouse.

'Not – I mean, not really,' she managed, feeling her cheeks heat. 'Not at all now, anyway.'

She could sense Colm watching her, but she refused to meet his eye.

'I'd best get back,' she added. 'We're about to kick off. Get that team name ready, please.'

'Yes boss.' Colm gave her a quick salute.

She returned to the stage, where a microphone was now resting on the table, next to her glass of wine. She sat down, took a large, grateful swig, and looked over her question sheet.

Everything went smoothly for the first half, even when Maisie went around the room, asking everyone to announce their team names. There were the usual puns – Les Quiserables, Smarty Pints and Quiz Tarrant, but she was blindsided when she asked Liam for his team's name, and he said, 'Winters Is Coming.' It was inexplicable to everyone else, but – of course – not to her. She tried not to roll her eyes, tried to ignore the flutter low in her stomach, and got on with asking the questions.

At half time, she read the scores out. In first place was Meredith and Thea's team, The Smeg Heads, which Maisie thought was mostly due to Fern and Laurie. Winters Is Coming were in fifth. There was good-natured grumbling, as there always was, and when the smell of fish and chips hit the hall, everyone's attention turned to the food.

Maisie didn't want to be seen to be favouring any of the teams, so she accepted her cod and chips and went back to her stool, wishing that Sprout had been allowed to come. But then she heard the clunk of another stool being placed next to hers, and turned to find Jeremy sitting down, with his own paper package and his pint.

'It's going well, I think,' he said, and there was a hint of schoolteacher in the way he nodded at her, as if she'd successfully put tissue paper legs on a jellyfish.

'I think so too,' she said. 'Everyone's super competitive, as always.'

'I do have a couple of tips, for the second half.'

'Oh?'

'You're sometimes a little too fast reading out the questions,' he told her, spearing a chip with his wooden fork. From the smell, it seemed as if he'd put an offensive amount of vinegar on his dinner.

'Right,' she said lightly. He was *critiquing* her?

'Mrs Knox, at the back of the room, is struggling to hear.'

Mrs Knox was eighty-five, and lived three doors down from her parents.

'She would have done better sitting closer to the front,' Maisie pointed out, and Jeremy shot her a look.

'And you have too much . . .' he paused, as if searching for the right word. Maisie decided he would make an excellent headteacher, because his condescension in that moment was all-consuming. 'Emotion,' he settled on. 'When you read them out.'

Now she was entirely baffled. 'Emotion?' she repeated. 'I'm too *emotional* reading out the questions?'

'You're very bright and bubbly, which is generally a good thing, but you need more consistency. Keep the humour out of your voice. The dramatics.' He wasn't looking at her, but tearing a piece of batter away from the fish with his fork.

Maisie didn't feel truly angry very often, but right then she could have happily dumped her glass of wine over his head, then proceeded to remove his earring just by pulling it, as hard as she could. Any lingering affection she might have had for him disappeared, and when she replied, it came out clipped.

'I get that this is your thing, Jeremy. Your gig. But you did ask me to compère, and I don't think I'm doing a bad job. I'm clear, and I'm repeating anything anyone asks me to, but I'm not a robot. I am a person, and I have emotions, and I don't think these people *want* me to say everything in a toneless dirge. That's not how this works. If you feel like I'm threatening your position at the school—'

'Of course not,' he scoffed, but his cheeks had gone pink.

'Then that's your problem, not mine. I am never going to work here again, so you don't need to worry. And, as you asked me to do this, you have to accept *how* I do it. In case you'd forgotten, I wrote the entire quiz.'

Jeremy chuckled uncomfortably. 'Maisie, come on—'

'No,' she said. 'You don't get to—'

'Hey.'

They both turned, and her already pounding heart kicked up a gear. Colm was standing on the stage, not that far away, holding a half-full pint glass. She noticed that his cheeks were slightly flushed.

'I didn't mean to interrupt,' he went on. 'Just thought I'd come and say hello.'

'We're busy,' Jeremy said.

Maisie squeezed her fingers into fists. 'We're just eating our chips. Come over.'

He sauntered over and put his glass on the table. 'I'm Colm,' he said, holding his hand out to Jeremy.

Jeremy's pause seemed to last for infinity, but he eventually shook Colm's hand. 'Jeremy.'

'I'm guessing you were telling her how she's killing it with her quiz,' Colm said casually, and Maisie knew, then, that he'd overheard some of their conversation.

Jeremy sat up straighter. 'There haven't been any complaints.'

'You told me Mrs Knox was struggling to hear,' Maisie reminded him.

'The old lady on the table next to ours?' Colm asked. 'If that's her, the only reason she can't hear is because she's talking nonstop. Marion's told her off twice already.' He gave them a rueful smile, which seemed to fluster Jeremy even more.

'It's imperative that this event goes well for me,' he said.

'Aiming for principal, are you?' Colm asked.

Jeremy glared at his fish and chips. 'Was there anything specific you came over for?'

Colm shrugged. 'I wanted to see if Winters was doing OK up here.'

'I think you can see that she is.'

'I am here, you know!' Maisie's anger turned swiftly to exasperation. 'And there *were* complaints, Jeremy, but mostly from you.'

'I was simply giving you some friendly guidance.'

Colm laughed quietly. 'Is he for real?'

Slowly, Jeremy stood up, the legs of his stool screeching against the floor as he pushed it back. 'I'm really sorry,' he said tightly, 'but I don't think this is any of your business.'

Colm's eyes widened, and Maisie watched as he folded his arms across his chest. It had the effect of emphasizing his biceps beneath his shirt, and she wondered if he had done it on purpose.

'I just came to talk to Maisie,' he said, his tone placatory. 'I didn't mean to get in between anything.'

Jeremy sagged slightly.

'But,' Colm went on, his voice still deceptively light, 'if you do anything to offend her, or upset her, then – as long as she's given me permission – I will have to do something about it.'

Jeremy sucked in a breath. 'Only if she gives you permission?'

Colm nodded. 'Yep. As much as I would like to do something about it right now, I've learnt a couple of really good lessons about how thinking before you act is always the better choice. So, if I did decide to act, in a way that would interrupt Maisie's quiz, I'd make sure I had her consent first.'

'That sounds a bit weak,' Jeremy muttered.

'Come on you two,' Maisie said. She wanted to defuse this ridiculous argument, but she had to concede that Colm talking about her and consent in the same sentence was doing all kinds of things to her insides.

'See now,' Colm said, his eyes still fixed on Jeremy, 'that sounded like you were offending *me*. And I've already given myself permission.'

'Enough!' Maisie stepped between them, her arms up, palms out. While her right hand stayed inches from Jeremy's chest, her left somehow found its way against Colm's shirt, where she was met with warm cotton and the promise of firm skin beneath. 'Do not have a stupid, pointless punch-up in the middle of this quiz!'

'Christ.' Jeremy took a large step backwards and ran a hand through his hair. He looked out across the hall where, when Maisie followed his gaze, it turned out most people were chatting and eating their fish and chips, and paying no attention to the stage. But she noticed Finn and Ben standing up at the back of the room, staring in their direction. Ben mouthed 'OK?' at her, and she smiled and nodded, just as Jeremy edged around her to pick up his fish and chips, then strode off the stage.

Maisie turned to Colm, realized she still had her hand pressed against his chest, and was about to take it away when he lifted it and placed a kiss against her palm, turning her thoughts to mush.

He let go and gave her a sheepish grin. 'I hadn't meant to do any of that,' he said. 'Doesn't he wind you up?'

'He has never wound me up more than he has tonight,' she admitted. 'But what on *earth* was all that about?' She flung her arms at him. Her palm was still tingling.

Colm ran a hand over his face. 'He was being a dick. I just wanted to come and say hello to you. I've had a few beers.'

'A whole trio of excuses,' she mused.

'Reasons,' he shot back. 'Not excuses.'

'Would you really have punched him in a primary school hall, with tissue-paper jellyfish on the walls?' She gestured, and Colm turned to look at the display.

He looked back at her and shrugged. 'I don't know. If you'd let me, maybe.'

She shook her head. 'You, Colm Caffrey, are ridiculous. But thank you for defending me.'

'Any time. You are doing brilliantly, though. Everyone's saying so. Where does he get off?'

'He's ambitious,' Maisie explained. 'He wants to move up the ranks here, which sounds stupid for a small-town primary school, but he does. He wanted this event to be a success, and didn't think he could do it on his own, so he got me to do the quiz, the food, and then—'

'When it turned out you'd exceeded his expectations and were getting all the praise, he had to take you down a peg.'

'Yup.' Now Thea, Meredith and Ollie were waving enthusiastically at her. She laughed and waved back. 'At least I know not to say yes when he asks for help next time.'

'Did you two really have a thing?' Colm asked.

She took a large sip of wine before replying. 'We went on a few dates, a couple of years ago, when I was still working here. But it . . . didn't turn into anything.'

141

'It seems to me like he hasn't quite got the message that you're no longer interested: that that particular ship has sailed.'

'The beer's making you bold, huh?'

He tipped his head back, closed his eyes briefly. 'It's Friday night. There's nothing wrong with a few beers.'

'So let me ask you something.' Movement caught her eye, and she saw Jeremy tapping his watch face pointedly. Ugh. 'Quickly.'

'Anything,' he said.

'What's wrong?'

He frowned. 'Nothing. I'm only mildly drunk, I didn't punch Jeremy, I—'

'No, I mean, on a bigger scale.' She was running out of time. Everyone was returning to their seats, putting their empty cartons in the rubbish bags that were circulating. 'The other day, at the beach, you were so quiet. And then you just . . . what's going on, Colm? Why did you come back to Port Karadow?'

'You don't like me being here?'

'I didn't say that, and I do – I *do* like you being here, but I want to know why you've come back. What happened in Australia? Are you . . . are you OK?' The last words seemed to come out into silence, and she realized everyone was waiting for her to start again, watching this scene play out with curiosity – and in some cases, impatience.

Colm glanced towards the hall, then leaned in and kissed her on the cheek. His hand brushed her arm, just below the sleeve of her dress, and she felt it like an electric current, all the way to her fingers. 'I'd better go,' he said. 'Everyone's waiting. Knock it out of the park, Winters.' Then, without attempting to answer any of her questions, he picked up his glass and strode down the steps and through the hall, to his table at the back.

Maisie had no other choice but to return to her stool and pick up her question sheet. She decided that she was going to be more bubbly, more emotional and – if it called for it – even more dramatic, than she had been in the first half.

Chapter Fifteen

The day after the pub quiz was the warmest of the year so far, feeling more like August than June. Maisie had taken Sprout for an early walk, and as the sun rose higher and the heat increased, she was glad that she had.

When Ollie phoned to ask if she wanted to spend the afternoon on the beach, she didn't hesitate. She dropped Sprout off with her dad, who, as soon as the rescue dog had come to live with Maisie, had created a cool spot for him in their kitchen, complete with basket, food and water bowl, then took herself and her woven tote bag to Port Karadow beach.

Ollie had told her that they would be near the place where they'd done the first photo shoot, and that's where she found them: Ollie, Thea and Meredith, all boyfriend- and dog-free, their colourful beach towels laid out in a row.

Ollie was wearing a lime green bikini, Meredith's was black and more conservatively cut, and Thea had on a blue one-piece. The high sun was gauzy and the water glittered, its depths ranging from pale azure to turquoise. The generous wind threw waves against the sand, the white froth bubbling, and Maisie could see the dark shapes of surfers out where the swell was bigger.

'Maisie,' Ollie called, leaning up on an elbow. 'We're so glad you could come. We've only just got settled. There's lemonade and fizzy water in the cool box, and we've all brought suncream.'

Maisie pulled a bottle out of her bag. 'Me too.'

Thea shuffled to the side. 'Come and put your towel in here. There's room.'

'This is more like Crete than Cornwall,' Meredith added.

Maisie spread her towel out, kicked off her sandals, and lifted her dress over her head. Her swimsuit was a one-piece, in a shade of red a little darker than crimson. Heather said reds worked well with her pale colouring, bringing a rosiness to her cheeks.

'That is super cute,' Ollie said. 'We look like a row of Fifties pin-ups. This should be one of the calendar photographs.'

'What?' Thea said. 'No way. I am not appearing in your charity calendar in a swimsuit. I'll put on a wetsuit and pretend that I do surfy things, but that's it.'

Ollie laughed. 'Surfy things! You sound like such a pro. Ben's definitely on-board too, isn't he? I need his buff-builder physique in my calendar.'

'Of course,' Thea said.

'Where are they all, anyway?' Maisie took a bottle of lemonade out of the cooler, and started to apply suncream to her shoulders.

'Max is working at the café,' Ollie said. 'Liam's got Henry Tilney.'

'And Ben's helping Finn build an extension to his studio at Laurie's house,' Meredith explained. Finn was a painter, creating atmospheric seascapes in oils and acrylics, and, though he lived with Meredith, he still had a studio at his aunt's cottage, which overlooked one of the coastline's more secluded coves.

'They're doing buildery stuff today?' Maisie asked. 'But it's so hot!'

'*Buildery stuff*,' Ollie repeated. 'Loving the technical terms we're coming up with.'

'Ben doesn't mind working when it's hot,' Thea said. 'He'll probably be doing it shirtless.' Her expression turned dreamy.

'Whoa there, tiger,' Meredith said, then burst into a fit of giggles. It set Ollie off, then Maisie, and then Thea, and soon they were all laughing, Maisie's suncream going on wonky.

Once their laughter had died out, Maisie settled on her towel and closed her eyes, letting the sun warm her skin. She didn't have to think about anything today. The quiz was done, and it had been a success – if you ignored the standoff between Colm and Jeremy – and that was a big item off her to-do list.

'Ooh Maisie,' Meredith said, 'have you booked a stand for the summer festival?'

Maisie opened her eyes. 'Crap.'

'It's OK,' Meredith went on. 'I mean . . . did you still *want* to have a stand? You sell so many summer-festival-appropriate things, so I'm sure you'd be popular.'

'I do still want to, I just haven't got round to it. There was all the organizing for last night, but now I can focus on other things.'

'I'm so glad.' Meredith sounded relieved.

'You are?'

'I was speaking to Charlie the other day, and I might have . . . uhm . . . reserved you a space. Please don't be mad with me! I didn't want you to miss out, and I wanted us all to be together.'

'I'm not at all mad,' Maisie said. 'Honestly. I want to be part of it – thank you.' She flopped back on the sand. 'As long as we can do this at least once every couple of weeks. The summer festival will be amazing, but it's going to be hard work, too. We know that from the lights pageant.'

'The Christmas lights pageant is incredibly well organized.' Meredith sounded slightly defensive.

'Of course it is.' Ollie took a bottle of fizzy water from the cooler. 'But these things are always a combination of fun and exhausting, so I agree with Maisie – work hard, play hard, sunbathe hard. That should be our mantra for the summer.' She held up her bottle, and they all leaned in and clinked. The moment was infused with warm skin and the tang of lemonade, the gentle shush of the waves. Maisie felt utterly content, soaking up their friendship like her skin absorbed the suncream. She let out a satisfied sigh, watching a seagull circling high above her, making the most of the air currents.

'Now we need all the gossip from last night,' Ollie said.

Maisie's shoulders tensed. 'What do you mean?'

'All we need to remember about last night,' Meredith said, 'is that Thea and I won.'

'Laurie and Fern won,' Ollie countered, 'if you're talking about the division of knowledge.'

'You'd be surprised how much Finn knew about obscure old films,' Thea said.

'And Ben was pretty good at the sports round,' Meredith added.

'Anyway,' Ollie said pointedly. 'I'm not talking about your win. I'm talking about what happened on stage in the break.' She pinned Maisie with her gaze.

'Oooh yes!' Meredith grabbed a bottle of lemonade and opened it in one swift movement, which resulted in it fizzing all over her hands. 'Eek!'

Thea handed her a clump of tissues, and Maisie pulled her sunglasses over her eyes and lay back down, hoping the distraction would work, but Ollie said, 'Not so fast.'

'What I was going to say,' Meredith added, 'before I covered myself in lemonade, is that Finn and Ben noticed: it was like some kind of caveman thing, they instinctively knew that other men were about to fight. I swear I saw the hairs go up on the back of Finn's neck.'

'There wasn't going to be a fight,' Maisie said.

Ollie raised her eyebrows. 'I didn't realize that Jeremy and Colm knew each other.'

'They don't.' Maisie rolled onto her front.

'So what was happening?' Thea asked.

Maisie knew that she was in trouble then, because Thea was the least gossipy amongst all of them. She groaned.

'Come *on*, Maisie,' Ollie said. 'Were those two incredibly sexy men fighting over you?'

Maisie sighed, sat up and lifted her sunglasses onto the top of her head. 'Jeremy came over in the break to give me some . . . pointers about my quiz delivery.'

'He *what?*' Meredith said.

Ollie shook her head. 'What an *utter* tool.'

'You delivered it perfectly,' Thea said, frowning.

Having close friends, Maisie thought, made such a difference. 'Thank you,' she said, then proceeded to tell them everything that had happened: every stupid, posturing moment from Jeremy and Colm, the way it had turned hostile so quickly. When she told them how Colm had defended her – *If you do anything to offend her, or upset her, then as long as she's given me permission, I will have to do something about it* – and even though it had been utterly over the top, her friends' response was universal.

'Ooooh,' Meredith said.

'Wow,' Thea added quietly.

'Consent is sexy whatever the context,' Ollie said. 'And I wouldn't mind Max punching someone on my behalf, as long as they really, properly deserved it.'

'Max catches flies in a jar and lets them out of the café window,' Meredith pointed out. 'I can't see him punching anyone.'

'I think Colm would have,' Maisie said, doodling in the sand by her foot.

'He likes you,' Ollie stated, waggling her toes. 'He dropped you into the conversation a few times last night, especially towards the end, after he'd had a few beers.'

'Because,' Maisie said, hating how Ollie's interpretation of events was making her heart flutter, 'I was doing the quiz, and because, other than Liam, he is just getting to know everyone here. Most of his friends from school have moved away.'

'Why would *anyone* move away?' Thea asked. 'Port Karadow is the best.'

'You don't need to tell me that,' Maisie said. 'I never want to leave.'

'And now Colm's here,' Ollie mused. 'I haven't been able to get much out of Liam or Melissa about why he's come back all of a sudden. Not their story to tell, apparently, so it's all a bit mysterious, and you know how much I love a mystery.' Her smile was cat-like.

'I do want to know what's happened,' Maisie admitted. When she looked down, she realized that the shape she'd drawn in the sand was a large, slightly wonky, heart.

She picked Sprout up from her parents' house at just after seven, in that slightly dreamy haze that came from spending a long time in the hot sun doing nothing much at all. Ollie had made sure they all stayed fed and hydrated, and Maisie had worn her hat, but she still felt sun-tired, and wanted a large glass of water and to watch a film she didn't have to think too hard about.

She strolled down her road, her legs still peppered with grains of sand, humming a Maddie & Tae song. The sun was dipping below the rooftops, turning window panes golden. Her house came into view and she smiled, thinking of her bright, cosy living room and the evening ahead of her, then frowned. She tried to make sense of what she was seeing, because there was something wrong, out of place, about it.

The out of place thing got up from her doorstep and walked towards her, down her own path.

'Hello.' She looked Colm up and down, then glanced at the sky. She had spent a perfect, sun-speckled day on the beach, so where had *he* been?

'Maisie,' he said. 'I'm sorry to come and find you at home, but I went to the ironmonger's and it was shut.'

'It would be, by now. Are you OK? Because you look . . .' He was drenched, his dusky blue T-shirt clinging to his body as if he'd been in a wet T-shirt competition, his hair plastered to his forehead. Did he do this to her on purpose? Upping his sex appeal by turning himself into a *Baywatch* extra at least 50 per cent of the time? She wouldn't be surprised if, the next time she saw him, he was in nothing but a pair of tight boxers. Pushing that potent image aside, she managed to finish the sentence. 'You're soaked.' Talk about stating the obvious.

'My kitchen tap has sprung a leak,' he said, 'in quite a dramatic fashion. I've switched the water off, but I don't know what I need to do to fix it. Can you help me fix it?' His eyes were wide, slightly panicked, and her heart squeezed. This, she was sure, was not something Colm would usually get stressed about. But she was also sure that he wasn't quite himself at the moment; that he had his own, personal thundercloud hanging above him.

Maisie's plans of a quiet night slipped away, leaving a much more desirable prospect in its place. How much had the sun got to her, that she was secretly elated about spending the evening helping Colm fix his broken tap?

'Give me five minutes,' she said, unable to stop herself squeezing his damp, muscled arm. 'I'll go and get my tool box.'

Chapter Sixteen

Colm drove them to Rose Cottage in his hybrid, the ride smooth and almost too quiet, so that when they weren't speaking, it felt painfully awkward. Was that because of last night? Maisie was reluctant to bring it up, so she focused on what she felt comfortable with.

'If the tap hasn't been used for years, then suddenly gets a lot of use, weaknesses will make themselves known very quickly.'

Colm glanced at her. She wondered if he was bothered about dripping all over the new-smelling car.

'So it's not used to being used,' he said, 'and now that it is, it doesn't like it?'

'Exactly that. Not how you were hoping to spend your Saturday night, I guess.'

'It's more excitement than I was anticipating, that's for sure.'

How did he spend his evenings when he wasn't accompanying Liam to a school quiz? 'Hopefully we can fix it quickly, then you can get back to whatever you were doing.'

'Working, mostly.'

'On a Saturday night?'

He turned onto the track that wended its way through the woods towards his cottage. The low sun sent spectacular amber rays through the sturdy tree trunks.

'I've got a new client,' he told her. 'My only client, in fact. A financial services company in Truro. I'm building them a website, and in the absence of any social plans, and the need to get myself up and running, that's my night.'

'Right,' Maisie said, as he swung into the cottage driveway, which was, if possible, even more alive than it had been a couple of weeks ago. The wren sung melodiously from the bushes, and as she lifted Sprout and got out of the car, a number of sweet, floral scents washed over her. 'It's like a sensory garden,' she murmured, turning in a circle. There was something different about it, something . . . 'You put the trellis up!' It was secured to the wall next to the front door, the chaotic rose bushes tied to it, so they had more structure.

'Yeah,' he said. 'Looks OK, doesn't it?'

'It looks lovely,' she gushed.

Colm got her tool bag out of the boot and led the way to the door. 'It's quite . . . claustrophobic,' he said, after a moment. 'Everything's just crowding in.'

Maisie followed him inside, where the flowery scent was replaced by the comforting smell of toast. Her stomach rumbled. The small windows filtered the sun, the amber hue even more intense than it had been outside, alighting on every metallic surface, adding touches of shimmer. Claustrophobic wasn't the word Maisie would have used, but then she wasn't Colm.

'You must have had a lot of space in Australia,' she said carefully.

He put her tool bag down and gestured to the kitchen. 'Everything's on a bigger scale there. And it's a lot more modern – or it seems to be, compared to here.'

Maisie looked through the doorway into the kitchen. The tiled floor was under half an inch of water. 'Yikes.'

'I didn't know whether to clean up, or leave it until it was fixed.'

Maisie nodded. 'Always wait until the end to clean up. You don't know what's going to happen in the course of mending something.' She grabbed her tool box and went to the threshold, then slipped off her sandals.

'I can get a towel, or—'

'It's fine. I have some new taps with me, so we can replace the old one. We'll keep the water off until we're ready to test it, but hopefully this will solve the problem.' She peered at the offending item, a mixer tap that looked at least a decade old. Its seal had clearly given up the ghost. She turned to get the tools she needed, and jumped at a flash of unexpected movement. 'Shit!'

'OK?' Colm asked from the doorway. 'Ah. This is Thor.'

The cat was tiny, not much more than a kitten. He was black, with a white tummy and white paws, which he was placing delicately in the puddles, heading towards her. Colm had crouched down, holding Sprout by his collar, but her dog just looked curious – he only ever chased birds and leaves.

'Sprout should be fine,' she told Colm. 'And Thor is indecently cute.' When the kitten was close enough, she stroked him, and he angled his head up, closed his eyes

154

and let out a loud purr. 'You still don't know where he came from?'

Colm tiptoed into the kitchen, and she saw he'd taken his shoes off, too. Sprout stayed in the doorway, probably confused by the flooded floor.

'He just started showing up here, a couple of days after I moved in. I asked Granddad, Ollie and Max, but none of them know anyone around here with a cat. There aren't that many people around here at all.'

'He turned up here, you fell for his cuteness and started feeding him, and now he knows he's on to a good thing.' Maisie smiled up at him, and Colm put on a hurt expression.

'You try ignoring him when he's meowing and prancing all over you. It's impossible.'

'I can see that,' she said. 'Do you want to take him? I have a feeling he's not going to make this job a whole lot easier.'

'Sure.' He scooped the kitten up, and Maisie wondered if Colm and Thor would be a better calendar photo than him doing his best Bond Girl impression. They could keep the damp T-shirt, in concession to the whole surfing aspect, but . . . She shook her head.

'Can I do anything to help?' he asked.

'Just watch what I'm doing, then when we need to turn the water back on, you can go and do that.'

She set about dismantling the broken tap; the work was damp and grubby, but the actions were soothing in their familiarity. She talked Colm through it, keeping her voice gentle, almost as if she was reminding herself of the steps. It was a tone she used with some of her customers, usually the older ones, the ones who called her *girl* – or occasionally a horrendous *girlie* – who didn't believe she could be more competent at DIY than them. She didn't know if Colm would feel as if his pride was being dented, but when she glanced behind her, he was leaning against the doorframe, a purring Thor hanging over his arm and Sprout pressed against his leg, looking entirely at ease.

'Did you do web design in Australia?' She turned back to the broken seal, which was being a bugger to remove, because it had somehow welded itself to the base of the tap.

'Among other things,' Colm said. The silence stretched, then he added, 'I worked for a marketing and PR company, so we did all sorts for our clients: websites, social media accounts, marketing campaigns. Sometimes PR stunts. It was fun, always varied.'

'It sounds great.' She had always thought of Australia as a fun country, and his job sounded exciting. 'Did it turn out to be *too* fun?'

'What? Ah, no.' He laughed softly. 'You think I grew up, wanted something less pressured as I got nearer to thirty?'

'It's getting close.'

'So close,' he agreed. 'Can you believe it?'

'Not really,' she admitted. 'Sometimes I feel as if I'm still sixteen.'

'Sweet sixteen,' Colm murmured, then coughed. 'Sorry, that sounds creepy, doesn't it?'

Sweet? Maisie thought. 'So you didn't grow up too much?' She wouldn't let him distract her, not now she was getting close to the answers she was craving.

'I can't believe you'd accuse me of that. No, I didn't. Not intentionally, anyway. I had it sort of . . . thrust upon me.'

'In what way?'

'In that I put a lot of myself – time, effort, money – into this company, and it didn't work out.'

'You're so good at being vague,' she said, finally releasing the seal which, now it was detached from the tap, disintegrated in her hands. She took the shiny new tap and all its components out of her toolbox.

'It's not something I love talking about.'

Maisie glanced at him. Thor was nudging Colm's chin with his furry head, over and over. 'So let's talk about last night instead. Your weird, not-quite-alpha-male attack on Jeremy.'

Colm groaned, his eyes fluttering closed. 'Can we not?'

Maisie turned back to the sink, smiling to herself. 'A few of the others noticed.'

'Max and Ollie?'

'Ben and Finn, Thea and Meredith's boyfriends. They went on high alert, like they knew a drunken male hissy fit was in the offing.'

'You know,' Colm said, 'one thing I really missed about you, Winters, is the way you endlessly flatter me.'

'Hissy fit is accurate,' she said. 'But Jeremy's more the type to throw one of those.'

'Exactly.' There was something like pride in his voice. 'He was being an idiot.'

'And I was dealing with him. But I didn't totally hate what you said.' She got closer to the tap, her nose almost pressed against the chrome, as if she could hide from that admission.

'Good,' Colm said. He sounded relieved.

They were quiet after that, Maisie working on the tap,

Colm moving about behind her. When she glanced around, she saw that he was using a couple of towels to soak up the water.

'I thought I told you to wait until I'd finished.'

Colm shrugged, Thor draped across his shoulders like some kind of fur stole. 'There's no way you don't know what you're doing.'

Maisie sighed and tightened up the screws on the tap. 'Right then. Moment of truth. Can you turn the water back on?'

Colm saluted and went out the back door, and she heard him crunching on gravel, walking around the side of the house. 'Done!' he called, and she turned on the tap.

A steady stream of water came out of the appropriate place, no sprays or leaks or unwanted water spouts.

'All good,' she called, and a moment later Colm was grinning beside her.

'Thank you,' he said. 'Thank you so much for rescuing me.'

'You could have done this yourself,' she replied, as a way of hiding how pleased she felt.

'Yeah, I really couldn't. I had no clue what I was doing. What can I do for you? Anything, Mais.'

She glanced around at the detritus, the floor still partly sodden. 'Why don't we clear up, and then, if you've got any bread, and cheese, a toastie wouldn't go amiss.'

He looked surprised, then pleased. 'Deal. Go and sit down if you like, leave the clearing up to me.' Before she could protest, he lifted Thor off his shoulders and pressed the warm, purring bundle into her arms. 'He needs constant affection,' he said seriously. 'That's your job right now.'

Maisie let him push her gently towards the living room, drying her feet on one of the towels he'd laid out before walking, barefoot, onto the carpet.

She was drawn to the corner of the room, beyond the sofas and the fireplace, where a snug alcove with a heavy beam above it created a cubbyhole. There was a small desk set into it, with a silver laptop on top, the screensaver a bouncing ball that danced across the screen. If she nudged the trackpad, what would she see? He had started to open up about Australia, about his job there not working out. What had happened, exactly? She touched the black-framed glasses that lay next to the laptop, still unable to imagine him wearing them. Thor chirruped, as if warning her off, and she turned around, about to head for one of the sofas, when she saw that Colm was standing in the doorway, looking at her.

'I didn't peek at the screen,' she rushed out. She thought she saw a flicker of amusement in his eyes, but he didn't reply. 'I promise, Colm.'

'You know what?' he said. 'I've hardly enough cheese to make a toastie worthwhile.'

'Oh.' Her spirits sank. She'd pissed him off, and he wanted to get rid of her.

'Besides,' he went on, 'it's a great evening. You know where does an epic cheese toastie – with chips?'

'Where?'

'The Sea Shanty.'

'Really?'

'Let me buy you dinner, such as it is, and a couple of drinks.'

Maisie smiled. Although she was sure that he was partly doing this, changing his mind about making her food here, because she was invading his living space, she couldn't feel too sad. An evening with Colm at the pub felt like a great way to finish the day. He abandoned the mop – the kitchen looked back in order anyway, no more puddles on the floor – and walked towards her.

He lifted Thor out of her arms, his fingers grazing her skin. 'Sorry, buddy,' he murmured to the cat, as he settled him on the sofa. 'You can't come, but there's food and water in the kitchen, and I'll put on a film for you.'

'You put on a film for the cat that isn't yours?' She couldn't help laughing.

'He gets anxious when it's too quiet. Music's OK, but films are better.' Colm pressed a few buttons on the remote, and she saw the title flash up on the TV. He was putting on *Pretty Woman* for a stray cat. 'Let me get a jacket.' He walked out of the room, entirely unembarrassed. Maisie heard his feet on the staircase, the echo of his steps vibrating through the small cottage.

'Looks like we're going to the pub,' she said to Sprout, crouching down to stroke him. It didn't just feel like a good way to finish the day, she realized. It felt like old times.

Chapter Seventeen

They walked through the woods in the glowing evening light, insects and bees buzzing around them, every step bringing with it a new smell of something floral or earthy. Sprout was in his element, snuffling in the undergrowth.

Colm had changed out of his sodden T-shirt into a white cotton shirt, open at the neck, and dark jeans. Maisie was still in her dress from the beach, still with salt water in her hair, sand between her toes, and – despite washing them thoroughly – possibly still grime under her fingernails from replacing the tap. Usually, she would insist on going home to shower and change, but she had the feeling that, if she did, the evening ahead would dissolve like a mirage.

They talked about the quiz, though not the interval; about Thor and Sprout, the calendar and Colm's upcoming photo shoot. She loved how he spoke about Thor as if the small cat was already a firm part of his life, and the needy part of her wondered if, now he had a pet to care about, he would be more likely to stay.

'Do you have more clients on the horizon?' she asked as they left the woods behind, their footfalls echoing on the pavement as they reached the roads at the edge of town.

'I've had a couple of enquiries,' he said. 'Firms I've been recommended to by this finance company. I've not got the deals done yet, though.'

'You sound thrilled,' she said.

He laughed. 'They're not the most inspiring businesses. Essential, but not . . . fun.'

'And you said that what you were doing in Australia – Sydney, wasn't it – was fun?'

'Yeah.' He crouched and took a bit of plastic out of Sprout's mouth, and Maisie felt a flash of guilt because she hadn't even noticed her dog was chewing something he shouldn't. 'We worked with big events companies, sports teams, a couple of magazines. They were always colourful, interesting projects. Stunts that got people's attention because they were totally out there. Floating a giant inflatable apple down the Parramatta River for a wellness company.'

'Like the rubber duck that sailed down the Thames.'

'Exactly like that. We had big budgets, clients who wanted to make a splash. Today I've been creating a website page listing the credentials of staff members. And their photos – it's like a row of passport shots, as if they've been told not to smile. White shirts, black jackets, flat blue backgrounds.'

'So,' Maisie said, as they neared the Sea Shanty, its sign – depicting a group of singing sailors – swaying gently in the breeze, a string of golden lights trained along the tops of the windows, 'you need to go after the clients you want.'

Colm pushed open the door and gestured for her to go ahead of him.

She walked over the threshold, Sprout at her side, and breathed in the smells of beer and chips, the waft of unpretentious, welcoming pub.

'Oh shit,' Colm said, as he came up behind her.

'Shit what?'

He pointed at the small stage, the microphone set up on it. 'Karaoke.'

Maisie laughed. 'You used to love karaoke!'

'When I was eighteen and had the unwavering confidence of someone who has never taken a good, long look at himself.'

'Let's find a table,' she said. 'You promised me a Sea Shanty toastie.'

'I did,' he admitted. 'Let's do it.'

There was an empty table left in the corner, the furthest they could be from the karaoke set-up. They sat on the bench that ran along both walls, at right angles to each other.

'I didn't even know this place *did* toasties,' Maisie said, looking at the menu.

Colm plucked it out of her hands. 'They don't, officially. I was in here a fortnight ago, and saw Des, the barman, eating one. I convinced him to make me one, too.'

'But he's not going to do that on a Saturday night when it's heaving and there's karaoke.'

Colm's smile made her entire body feel as if it was made of water, liquid and unstable. 'He will for me.'

'What was that you were saying about unwavering confidence?'

He laughed as he went to the bar. He hadn't even asked her what she wanted to drink.

'What is going on here, Sprout?' Her dog had settled beneath the table, his head on his paws, as if he was content to watch whatever this was play out.

Colm returned with a bottle of Prosecco in a bucket, two flutes, two full shot glasses, and a smug expression.

Maisie took the shot glasses, allowing him to extract the flutes from where he had them tucked between his arm and his torso. 'What's this?'

'The good tequila. We don't need any of that salt and lime nonsense.'

'And *why* are we starting the evening with tequila?' But when she glanced at her watch; they'd been at Rose Cottage for longer than she'd thought.

'Why not?' He shrugged. 'And Prosecco's your favourite, right? I wanted to say thank you, for fixing my tap. For dropping everything to rescue me. And two of Des's cheese toasties are on their way.'

'This is all very kind, and you are far too pleased with yourself.'

Colm laughed, tipping his head back. 'I love that your gratitude comes with a side of putting me in my place.' He held his shot glass up.

Maisie clinked hers against it. 'You always benefited from being put in your place now and then.'

'Cheers to that,' he murmured, and they sank their tequila.

It burned all the way down Maisie's throat, and she was suddenly very conscious that she hadn't eaten a whole lot, and nothing since Ollie had gone to buy sausage rolls and pastries from Sea Brew for them to eat on the beach earlier.

The toasties didn't take long to arrive, and they were as amazing as Colm had promised: doorstops of toasted bread with at least two different types of cheese inside, onion and tomato relish, plus a portion of crispy, skin-on fries, along with a dollop of garlic mayonnaise.

'Are you a barman whisperer?' Maisie asked, after she'd demolished half of hers. 'Is that what you were really doing in Australia?'

'Come on, Winters. You know that all you need to do is be nice to people, respect them, and you can usually get what you want.'

'That is crazy cynical,' she said, around a mouthful of mayonnaise-covered chip.

'I'm not cynical,' he protested. 'I'm not fabricating being nice.'

'You just admitted you used it as a tactic to get what you want.'

'I didn't. I said if you *are* nice, you can often get what you want. They're two different things. Kindness makes the world go around, doesn't it?'

Maisie rubbed her forehead. Despite the carb load, she was already feeling the effects of the bubbles on top of tequila, and that was on top of her senses being scrambled by an evening spent with Colm. 'What went wrong with your company in Australia?'

Colm's smile slipped. 'I told you, it didn't work out.'

'And why did you leave so suddenly in the first place?'

'What?' She saw his shoulders stiffen.

'You left, to go to the *other side of the world*. It was so sudden, Colm. Everyone was surprised, and I . . .'

'You . . .?' He leaned closer just as Des turned on

165

the mic, squealing feedback adding to the already noisy pub.

She huffed. This was too much like the night she'd spent, in this very pub with him, the week before he went. He'd been so kind to her then, so reassuring, and she had thought that they understood each other. Then he'd left Port Karadow, been gone from her life in an instant.

Her thoughts must have shown on her face, because he leaned even closer, his fingers brushing her arm, and said, 'What's wrong, Mais? Why are you pissed off with me?'

'I'm not.' She took a swig of Prosecco.

'You are,' he said. 'Somewhere deep down, in here.' He placed his hand, palm flat, over her collarbone. It was warm, but it felt incendiary, and when their gazes snagged, she saw that he was as surprised as she was that he'd done it. He whipped his hand back.

Maisie was incredibly grateful when, on the other side of the pub, the singing started in earnest, bringing a necessary halt to their conversation.

'You should go up there,' Maisie heard herself say, an indeterminate amount of time later.

'Nope.' Colm shook his head and ran a hand through his hair. It was unruly, slightly fluffy, and looked incredibly soft. When would *she* get to run her fingers through it?

'You used to do it all the time,' she said instead. 'Didn't you do it in Australia?'

'Lainey didn't—' he started, then came to a thudding halt.

Envy curdled in Maisie's gut. 'Who's Lainey?'

Colm sighed, then propped his elbows on the table. 'She was my girlfriend, in Sydney. The one I was with longest, anyway.'

'How long?'

'Six years. A big chunk of my twenties.'

'Wow.' Maisie swallowed. 'You must have . . . I mean, she must have been . . .'

'Yeah. But like so many things, it didn't work out.' He kept his gaze on his glass, his brows furrowed. 'It's all in the past, anyway. And I realized, recently, that it was actually meant to—' He cut himself off again. 'But she didn't like me doing karaoke. She thought it made us both look bad.'

Maisie's laugh was confused. 'But it's *meant* to make you look bad – unless you're a budding Ed Sheeran—'

'Who wants to be a budding Ed Sheeran?' Colm shuddered, and Maisie whacked him on the shoulder.

'You know what I mean. Lainey wasn't . . . she didn't like *fun*?'

He held her gaze, his eyes almost golden under the pub's lighting, someone's rendition of 'Danger Zone' filling the cracks in their conversation. 'She was very particular,' he admitted. 'Cared a lot about appearances, perceptions. She always looked good, but then she was . . .'

'Always looked good, huh?' Maisie blamed that comment on the alcohol.

Colm continued as if he hadn't heard her. 'But actually, when it came to it, she wasn't who I thought she was.'

'I bet you made such a gorgeous couple.'

Colm scoffed. 'So much bitterness for someone so sparkly.'

Maisie sat up straighter. 'I'm not bitter about anything.'

'You look like you've chewed an entire lemon. What's that all about?'

'*Shush*, Colm.' Her maturity when she was drunk was astounding.

He gave her an amused grin. 'If it'll cheer you up, I'll do it.'

'Do what?'

'Karaoke.'

'You *will*?' Her heart was back to sprinting. 'What song?'

'Come on, Winters,' he said. 'Is there really any other choice?'

Maisie thought back to all the times when he'd got up and sung, entirely unselfconsciously, and wondered if she'd be able to take it. 'No,' she scratched out. 'No, there isn't.'

He looked glorious, standing on the tiny stage, jean-clad and with his white shirt slightly rumpled, extra relaxed and confident after a few drinks. Maisie steeled herself. She wanted to focus on every single moment, so of course someone slid onto the bench alongside her. It was Lizzy, who she knew from the book club, and when they passed each other on the coastal path, walking their respective dogs.

'He cuts a pretty picture, doesn't he?' Lizzy said.

'Too pretty,' Maisie replied, and Lizzy laughed.

'So many rumours going around about why he's back.'

'Things didn't work out,' Maisie told her. 'That's all he'll admit to.'

'Get a few more drinks in him, and he'll open up like a flower in the sun. Word is, Des is doing a lock-in tonight.'

'Seriously?' It had been a long time since Maisie had

been to a lock-in. 'Golly, then I think . . .' But she didn't finish her sentence, because the opening bars of 'You Got It' by Roy Orbison thrummed through the pub. Except it sounded more upbeat, like the Welshly Arms cover. When they were teenagers, every time he'd performed it, Maisie had imagined he was singing it to her. As he sang the first line now, mostly in key but with a few inevitable wobbles, she went right back there.

It was a great song, a crowd-pleaser, people joining in and swaying along, and Maisie felt a surge of pride – that he was her friend, that she was there with him, and he was holding this pub full of grizzly fishermen and couples on dates, groups of friends on holiday – in the palm of his hand.

As he came to the end, everyone was singing along, following the words on the screen if they didn't know them off-by-heart like she did, and as the last chord sounded, Colm flung his arms in the air and then bent forwards in a bow. The pub filled with cheers and applause, and Maisie watched as he stood up straight, his cheeks flushed, his eyes sparkling and, a second later, focused entirely on her.

As he handed the mic back to Des and hopped off the stage, she went to meet him. They reached each other in the middle of the crowd of tables, people sitting back down and turning their attention to the next singer or their conver- sations.

Maisie held her arms out to hug him. 'You were—' she started, but Colm closed the gap and, instead of wrapping his arms around her, he kissed her. His lips pressed against hers for one beat, then two, and the maelstrom of chatter, the twang of the new song, disappeared. He pulled back, and she pressed her fingers to her lips as he looked down at her, a horrified expression on his face.

'Mais, I'm so sorry—'

She slid her hand behind his neck and brought him back down to meet her, their lips connecting again. *This*. They had never done this before, despite all the times she'd wanted to, the hours she'd spent imagining how it would feel. They were finally, finally kissing each other, and despite the haze of alcohol, it was as if every millimetre of her skin was exposed to the brightest, sparkliest sun, the most beautiful day on her favourite Cornish beach. It was a rush of sensation so pure, so right, that she never wanted it to stop. She could feel his warm hands on her waist, could feel every grain of sand that still clung to her feet. She was nothing but feeling.

She imagined what it would be like to kiss him when they were both sober. She wanted that, more than anything.

Eventually he pulled back, looking down at her with an intensity that made her want to step into him again.

Someone shouted, 'Get a room!' and Colm chuckled, the sound deep and rusty.

'Do you want a glass of water?' he asked, and she nodded. 'Go back to the table, I'll join you.'

As she sat down, her legs decidedly shaky, Lizzy nudged her side. 'I see you got him to open up, then.'

Maisie laughed, pressing her hands against her hot cheeks. 'Not in the way I imagined.'

'In a better way?'

Maisie looked Lizzy straight in the eye. 'I still want to know what's going on with him.'

The older woman nodded. 'That's my girl. Don't let him distract you with kisses.'

'I'd quite like both,' she said, and it was Lizzy's turn to laugh. She clinked her glass against Maisie's and went back to her husband, leaving Maisie alone at the table, wondering whether her heart would ever beat normally again.

Colm returned with two pints of water, and slid onto the bench next to her. Maisie wondered if he'd had the same thought as her: that he wanted to kiss her sober. She accepted the water and took a long, cooling sip.

'You were great,' she said, when she'd put her glass down.

'I kind of got that you felt that way, considering your reaction.' His smile was pure cheek.

'Unbelievable.' Maisie shook her head. 'You kissed *me* first.'

'Not like *that*. That second one – that was all you.' His Adam's apple bobbed. 'If that's the response I get, then I'm going to have to be—' he stopped himself.

'You're going to have to be what?'

He held her gaze. 'I'm going to have to be a budding Ed Sheeran.'

His meaning thumped through her. He liked it: he wanted to do it again. She couldn't think about that now, so she asked him what it was like to surf in Australia, if he'd ever encountered any sharks, and soon she was listening to his stories, his movements relaxed, his laughter close to the surface, and she was drinking it all in.

How was it easier between them now they'd kissed? Had he been thinking about it too? Had they broken through some barrier, a tension that had always been between them? When it was her turn, she told him about teaching at the primary school, the way the kids tested her every day, then about her dad and her decision to go back to the ironmonger's.

The pub emptied, the tourists leaving, group by group, after last orders. The locals remained, the lock-in happening without ever being mentioned, neither Maisie nor Colm making a move to leave. She went to the bar and got more water, then he got them both coffees, laughing at Des's reaction when he'd asked for them.

Time didn't exist, Maisie decided. It was just a construct, anyway, and she wanted this night to last forever.

'Do you remember coming in here that last summer?' Colm asked, returning to their table with two bags of Scampi Fries. Now Maisie *did* glance at her watch, and saw it was just after three in the morning.

'With all our friends?' she asked.

'That was one of the things I missed the most,' he admitted. 'After I went.'

'Why did you go? It was so unexpected. And I know . . .' She took a deep breath, 'I know your mum and dad were getting divorced, and it can't have been easy, but . . .'

Colm huffed out a breath. 'Dad gave me an ultimatum.'

Maisie blinked. 'What?'

'Their divorce was as far from amicable as it could get, and Dad had got this job in Sydney, as if he couldn't wait to be as far away as possible, leave Mum behind. Melissa was already in London, but she came back here often – you probably remember – but Dad said I wouldn't see him, that he'd be gone for years.

'He spun this line about how great it would be in Australia. I wanted time to think, said I could join him later, maybe, but he . . . I guess he was scared I wouldn't follow through with it. So he said now or never, basically.' He shrugged, but Maisie could see that his shoulders were tight with tension at the memory. 'He sold it to me as this amazing adventure, and I said it sounded cool, and the next thing . . . I was on the plane.'

'Wow,' Maisie said. 'You never . . . never really explained.'

'I thought if I did, if I told you and Phil and Dev and Stu, then you'd try and talk me out of it.'

Maisie nodded. 'I think we all would have. Is that why you and Liam didn't speak for so long?'

Colm rubbed his cheek. 'Granddad sided with Mum, of course – she's his daughter – so he thought I was betraying her by going. And then I was so far away, in this new life that Dad was so focused on. It felt right that I'd gone in some ways: Melissa was still in England, closer to Mum, and I went with Dad, but then it seemed way too hard to bridge all the gaps I'd created, on the phone or via email. I didn't . . . I wanted to give my new life a chance, and it was just . . . it felt impossible.'

'I'm sorry.'

'No, I'm sorry.' It was almost a whisper. 'Australia was great, in some ways. But I missed you all, and this place, so much.'

'You hurt me,' she blurted, then slapped a hand over her mouth. She was feeling a lot more sober now, and she hadn't meant to say that.

Colm looked startled. 'What? You mean, I—'

'That night, in here. The one you mentioned. You really hurt me.'

His surprise turned to confusion. 'Do you mean you thought . . .'

173

Maisie shook her head. 'It wasn't that I thought you fancied me, that you wanted something to happen between us. You were too handsome, too popular, for me.'

He held her eyes for a beat, and the look he gave her took her straight back to their kiss. 'Maisie, that is so wro—'

'It was what you said to me,' she cut in.

Colm swallowed. 'What did I say?'

'You told me that staying in Cornwall was the right thing to do, that I wasn't small minded – or silly – to want to live in Port Karadow my whole life. Mum had been going on at me about my choices, as always. She was pleased that I was considering teacher training, but she didn't want me to stay here, and I just . . . I have never wanted to be anywhere else.'

'I told you it was great that you knew what you wanted,' Colm said, frowning. 'I remember that. We were drunk, I know, but I haven't forgotten it. I said you should stick to your guns: I thought you were brave for doing it.'

'Exactly,' Maisie said. '*Exactly.*'

'I don't understand. Wasn't that a good thing?'

Maisie nodded, feeling nothing but relief now that she was getting it out, telling him the thing that had made her resent him all this time, her hurt mingling with the desire that hadn't ever gone away. 'It was. And then, suddenly, you were gone, leaving Cornwall and going as far away as you possibly could, and not looking back. It felt like you were mocking me, and I've never forgotten it. Not for a single day.'

Chapter Eighteen

Ten Years Ago – Colm

It should have been a straightforward Friday night in the pub with his mates – a bit more reckless, perhaps, now that anything resembling school was over and they were looking forward to spending summer on the beach. But nothing about his life felt straightforward any more, and he didn't know what to do with that. He didn't know how to deal with the realization that, in less than a week, he would be thousands of miles away from here. From Mum and Granddad. His friends. *Maisie.*

Even the bold evening sun, the weekend sounds revving up, shouts and music and the always-on soundtrack of the waves, couldn't bring his mood up.

He kept replaying the moment his dad had walked into his room and told him. He had been thumbing through a prospectus, looking at apprenticeships he might be able to start after Christmas – he wasn't sure about taking a whole year out – and wondering idly about his future.

Then his dad had blown his future out of the water. He'd asked him to go to Sydney with him, to start over in a place that was like Cornwall on steroids, the surfing unbeatable, the days long and hot. He had felt a surge of excitement at the prospect of a sun-drenched holiday, a reason to delay his decisions further.

But then his dad had clarified. It wasn't a holiday. He wanted Colm to move out there with him, or else they wouldn't see each other for years; the air fare was so expensive, his new job was going to be full-on. Melissa, his sister, was in London now, but still came back to Port Karadow regularly. Mum had her, he reminded Colm, and he didn't want to lose his son, too. And Colm was done with school now – there would be opportunities for him; so many possibilities. He'd already, he'd told him, got Colm's initial visa sorted out.

A hundred questions had flooded into his mind, but his dad had said, *I'm going at the end of next week, son. A few more days and I won't be able to get you a ticket. You'd be mad to turn this chance down.*

And so he'd said yes, not really understanding what it meant, what his life would look like out there. But who else got the chance, at eighteen, to go and live in Australia?

He reached the Sea Shanty, Port Karadow's premium scuzzy pub, the streetlights outside starting to wink on as the sun faded, bringing out the deep blue of twilight. He had a tightness in his chest at the thought of telling everyone – Phil, Stu and Dev – that he was leaving so soon. And what about Maisie? The vice around his ribs squeezed, so he waited outside, breathing in the sea-fresh air, trying to banish the hundred questions he hadn't had an answer to. He wanted to see his friends, have some drinks, forget about it all for a few hours.

His breath stalled when she appeared, wearing a dress almost the same shade as the sky. Her blonde curls were bunched around her face, with those quiet, assessing eyes that he loved looking into, the small nose that she wrinkled when he teased her. She seemed nervous, her shoulders tense, even as she spoke with her sister, Heather, and he wondered for a crazy second if someone had told her he was leaving.

He pushed off the wall and said, 'Winters, good to see you. And Heather.' He was proud of how calm he sounded, when seeing her here, knowing he would be gone next week, that he wouldn't see her again – for how fucking long? years, maybe – felt like a huge mistake.

Heather spoke first. 'Hey Colm. I'm not staying, just on my way to see a friend.' Then she added, 'Be good, both of you.' Her throwaway line made Colm think of all the things he wanted to say to Maisie about how he felt, what an idiot he'd been for staying quiet all this time. But he'd left it too late.

'Hey,' Maisie said, and Colm felt some of the tightness around his chest release as she smiled at him.

'Hi.' He returned her smile. 'Shall we go in? I think Phil and Dev are already inside.'

'Sure.' He allowed himself the gentlest of touches, his fingertips brushing her shoulder, and wondered, desperately, if that was all he would ever get.

*   *   *

177

He was drinking too quickly, he knew that. Laughing too loudly, squeezing everything he could out of the night. But the thoughts never quietened down. What would his dad do if he changed his mind now? He'd already bought Colm's plane ticket, sorted his visa, and they'd been making plans, Colm trying to match his enthusiasm and eagerness. If he said that he wasn't going, then not only would his dad be gone, but they'd part on bad terms.

His mum, his granddad were already heartbroken, disappointed at his choice, and he knew he was in a lose–lose situation. Only Lissa, his sister, had been calm about it. She'd told him on the phone that it *was* a great opportunity, and that he didn't have to stay forever – why not go and see what happened? He could always come back if it didn't work out. She was the only one, at the moment, who was able to make him feel even remotely chilled. She and Maisie. Maisie had been quiet this evening, he thought, and as he went to the bar to replenish their drinks *again*, he wondered how he was going to tell her.

'Winters.' He slid along the bench to sit next to her. 'Sorry, it took ages to get to the bar.'

She looked so beautiful, smiling and telling him it wasn't a problem. Part of him wished she'd be angry with him; that they could have an argument and make it somehow not matter that he was leaving. Except that was never going to be the case, was it? He was a coward, so he took the cowardly option: he avoided the subject altogether.

'They're setting up the karaoke,' he told her.

Maisie laughed. 'You'll have a big audience tonight. All the regulars are in, and a fair few grockles.'

Regulars. He wouldn't be a regular here much longer.

'Heather down from London for a few weeks?' he asked.

'If she lasts that long. She loves her course, keeps talking about going to New York once she's got her MA. Not even London is big enough, it would seem.'

The band tightened around his chest. He knew how close Maisie and Heather were, how much she missed her sister not being here any more. 'New York, huh? That's a . . . long way away.'

'I'm happy for her, of course, but I just . . . Gemma's off to Durham in September, and I feel like . . .'

'Like what?' She'd wrinkled her nose in the way he loved so much, and he couldn't help leaning closer.

'Like what I want isn't ambitious enough. I'm taking a year out, working with Dad in the ironmonger's, and Mum's on my case to get this teacher training sorted for next year – *this* year, if I'm quick about it. She has *no idea* how these things work. But I don't . . . why would anyone want to leave Port Karadow, Colm?'

The words were like a punch in his solar plexus. Not only because *he* was leaving, going so, so far away, but because people were judging her, hurting her so casually with their biased assessments. He had always thought she was so strong, so clear-eyed when it came to her future, how much she loved the town they grew up in. It was one of the things – the many, many things – he admired about her. He had to tell her this, at least. He took a long glug of beer, trying to assemble his thoughts into words.

'What I think,' he said, 'is that you should follow your dreams. And if that dream is to stay here forever, to spend every day living in Port Karadow, loving it, then that is absolutely enough. Don't listen to anyone else, Mais.

179

You don't have to give a shit what they all say to you about qualifications and ambition and striving for something more. My reckoning is that, a lot of the time, when people go after something bigger, they end up regretting it: missing what they left behind.' Would he regret it? A part of him already was. Leaving her behind, especially. But he couldn't disappoint his dad, not now he'd agreed to it.

'Maisie,' he went on, trying to take some of the heat out of his words, leave only conviction behind, so that she'd listen to him. 'You know what you want, and there is a lot of strength in that. Hold your ground, build a life for yourself here. It's the best, *best* thing. If that's what you want for your forever, then take it.'

He watched her eyes widen, her lips purse, and he wanted to kiss her then, so badly, but he settled for sliding his fingers into the curls at the side of her face. He couldn't start anything now. Not when he was leaving. He had to explain it all to her, hope she'd understand.

'Maisie, I need to tell you—'

The booming voice startled him, and then released him. His get-out-of-jail-free card. His you-are-the-biggest-fucking-coward-on-the-planet card. 'First up, with Roy Orbison's "You Got It", we have Colm Caffrey. Come up to the stage, son!'

He forced a grin, told Maisie he was just about drunk enough to perform his usual party trick. He gave her arm a squeeze, tried to hold on to the sensations, how warm her skin felt against his palm, as he made his way to the stage.

This song was for her: it was always for her, and he needed to put extra effort in tonight, so that, somewhere, deep down, she would know how he felt. Because next week he would be gone, and surely it would be more heart-breaking for both of them if he admitted it to her? It would be the worst possible thing he could do, so instead he had told her that she was right, and brave, for staying true to herself, for following her *own* dreams rather than someone else's. He could do that for her, at least.

Then he got up on stage, sang his song, and didn't tell her that he was moving to the other side of the world. He thought it was the best way to save their hearts a whole lot of pain. Only part of him believed that his excuse made sense.

Chapter Nineteen

Present Day

'Maisie, I'm so sorry,' Colm said. 'It was such a crazy time—'

'God, it was,' she said, because how could she be cross with him now? He'd been ripped away from everything he knew, faced with a choice that was so, so unfair. Her anger should have been aimed at his dad. 'But at the time, I didn't know that. I just knew that you'd left.'

He dropped his head, almost to the table. 'I wanted you to know that I thought what you were doing, standing your ground, was the right thing. I felt so . . . out of control myself. I'd agreed to go with Dad, and I was already regretting it, but I knew how upset – how angry – he'd be if I changed my mind. He'd bought me a plane ticket, arranged a visa for me, had all these plans for the two of us. I felt like I'd messed things up for everyone, by being unsure of my own decisions. I had to suck it up, but you

'. . . you knew exactly what you wanted. I admired you so much.'

'Colm,' she said softly. She wished she'd known, at the time, how he was feeling; that there was this war going on in his head. 'You didn't even tell me you were leaving.'

He looked up, swallowed. 'I tried to, that night. So many times. But in the end I was too much of a coward.'

She shook her head. 'What you were dealing with . . . I'm sorry. I shouldn't have brought it up tonight. It's all so far in the past.'

'Of course you should have,' he said. 'Do you feel better, now you have?'

She nodded.

'Well, then.' He trailed his fingers lightly down her face. 'I never, ever meant to hurt you,' he murmured, then he pressed his lips gently against hers. Maisie closed her eyes, leaning into it, and decided that, even though she wasn't entirely sober, the water and coffee and Scampi Fries had helped, and this delicate, tentative kiss felt even better than their first.

As they drew closer to each other, she sent a silent thanks to the old, faulty tap that had brought them together on this summer's evening – or yesterday, she realized, because this was a brand-new day, and she was kissing her teenage crush in her favourite Port Karadow pub as the sun came up. Life, she thought, couldn't get much better than this.

They walked out of the Sea Shanty into a hazy dawn. It had been years since Maisie had gone to a lock-in, and this one would surely stay in her memories forever. The light was pearlescent, making everything it touched look soft and tinged with gold. She drew in a deep breath, and Colm tipped his head back, groaning quietly.

'I hadn't meant for that to happen,' he said, then added, 'the whole lock-in thing. Staying until morning.' He looked down at her. 'But I'm not saying that I regret it, that I didn't want—'

'It's OK.' She pressed her fingers to his lips, and he smiled against them. 'I got what you meant. It isn't exactly how I thought my weekend would turn out, either.'

'But you're glad it did?' His voice was gentle.

'Very.'

Their houses were in opposite directions, and Maisie didn't want to let him go. From the way he hovered, hands in his pockets, she thought he might feel the same.

'You should go and check on Thor,' she said.

He shrugged. 'He's not even my cat.'

'But you already see him as yours.'

Colm's smile was lopsided. 'You know me too well.'

'There is so much I don't know about you,' she protested.

'Let's see each other again soon, then. Change that.'

Despite the weariness making her limbs heavy, the headache pulsing behind her eyes, she felt a flicker of electric excitement. 'I'd love to.'

He leaned in, gave her a soft, quick kiss, then they said goodbye and turned away from eachother, Sprout padding happily at Maisie's side. After a few steps she glanced back, meeting Colm's gaze as he did the same. They smiled, waved, and went their separate ways.

Giddiness carried Maisie through the town's empty streets, past the dawn chorus from robins and blackbirds in burgeoning front gardens, the sea shimmering like a blanket of misty gemstones, the sunlight falling on her shoulders like confetti. She made it back to her little house without seeing another soul, and fell into bed with a smile on her lips.

'I heard there was a lock-in at the Sea Shanty on Saturday night.'

These were the first words Maisie's mum said to her on Monday, standing on the other side of the counter in the ironmonger's. Maisie still felt tired and off-kilter after sleeping most of yesterday morning. Her mum rarely came into the shop, but of course, today, she was here.

'Did you?' she said, because her mum hadn't asked a question.

Aimee raised a neat eyebrow and folded her arms. She was wearing a grey skirt-suit and a pale green blouse, obviously on her way to work.

Maisie straightened her shoulders. 'What do you want me to say?'

Her mum made an exasperated noise. 'I want to know what happened.'

'Why don't you ask the person who told you about the lock-in, then?'

'Maisie Winters.'

'I need to get on, Mum. And, in case you'd forgotten, I'm twenty-eight. I have my own life, and I know you don't approve of a lot of it, but . . .' the bell pinged, and Maisie lowered her voice as Elmer, one of their regulars, came in, though he didn't even look in their direction. '. . . I don't have to tell you anything,' she finished.

'So you *did* stay in the pub, singing and cavorting with Colm Caffrey until the small hours?'

The words ignited the memory, and Maisie felt herself flush. 'So what if I did? It was the weekend, I fixed his tap for him, and—'

'And now you look terrible, at work on a Monday morning. You really think your customers will put up with this?'

Maisie closed her eyes. 'They won't even notice. And if they do, they'll probably just wish they'd had as good a time as I did.'

'It's irresponsible. If you were still at the school, you wouldn't be being led astray like this.'

'Excuse me, Maisie love?' Elmer was hovering.

Maisie turned to him. 'Yes, Elmer? How can I help?'

'Do you have cable ties?'

'We have a whole section. Let me show you.'

'That's ever so kind.'

'It's not a problem.' She left Sprout behind the counter and led Elmer to the aisle where the cable ties lived. She didn't add that it was also a huge relief to get away from the laser eyes and almost Victorian disapproval being aimed at her. She showed him the different options, praying that her mum would have left by the time she'd finished, but no such luck.

She stepped back behind the counter. 'Did you want anything, or are you just here to get the gossip about an event you think I shouldn't have been at?'

Aimee sighed. 'You should be thinking about your future. What you want to do with it.'

'I want to do what I'm doing now,' Maisie said. 'Why is that so hard for you to believe?'

'And Colm? Is he in your future?'

Maisie thought of the message he'd sent her yesterday evening. A photo of him wearing his glasses – he looked great in them, despite his obvious tiredness – with Thor draped around his shoulders. Underneath, it read:

He was still here when I got back. Looks like I have a cat! :)

He hadn't mentioned anything about the pub or their kisses, and in a way she was glad. She was happy just to see what happened next.

'Colm is in my present, and the present is all we have,' she said.

Her mum glanced at her sleek silver watch. 'Sometimes, you are impossible to talk to. I need to get to work.'

'Have a lovely day,' Maisie said brightly.

She watched as her mum aggressively pushed the door open, then disappeared up the hill. She wanted a good relationship with her, wanted them to – possibly, one day – do things together, like walks on the beach, coffee dates, maybe even spa days. But how could she, when her mum had made it her mission to attack every one of her choices? Maisie felt she was happy with the life she had, the choices she'd made. But every time her mum confronted her, there was always a small voice that questioned everything. Was this life too small? Should she be trying to achieve more?

She rubbed her eyes, started reorganizing the already tidy display of LED torches and screen cleaning cloths on the counter. But she realized – since Saturday night, when Colm had given her his version of that evening in the pub; what he'd meant and how he'd been struggling – some of that incessant questioning had quietened. He hadn't meant to mock her: he *admired* her.

It was Monday morning and she was still recovering from the weekend, but after that revelation, after their kiss, after getting to spend so much time with him, she couldn't regret it, not even for a second.

Chapter Twenty

Porthgolow was smaller than Port Karadow, with a perfect curved bay, golden sand and ruffling, foam-topped waves. It looked like a giant had taken a dainty bite out of the coastline, and Maisie loved it. She and Ollie had driven there together, and as they got out of the car, Maisie hefting her camera gear onto her shoulder, she could see the red, polished Routemaster on the sand – the Cornish Cream Tea Bus. It was Sunday morning, a week after the lock-in, and the late June sun had burned off the early morning mist, leaving a clear, bright sky.

'I think we should set up the shots on the beach, with the bus in the background,' Ollie said. 'Then, if we've time, we can do some by the outdoor hot tub at Crystal Waters. What do you think?'

'I think you've got creative director genes,' Maisie said.

Ollie laughed. 'I just have strong ideas about what I think looks good, and we're spoiled for choice here.'

They walked across the sand, and a couple came to meet

them from the bus, already wearing wetsuits. The woman was tall, with red hair cut in a short bob, and looked vaguely familiar. The man's thick, dark hair was being ruffled by the breeze, his wide shoulders giving him a good silhouette in the skintight black wetsuit.

'Ollie!' The woman waved.

'Charlie! Daniel!' Ollie called back. 'This is our photographer, Maisie,' she said when they reached each other. 'Maisie, say hello to Charlie and Daniel Harper.'

'It's lovely to meet you.' Maisie held out her hand, but the other woman stepped in close and hugged her.

'The suit isn't damp, I promise,' Charlie said.

'I don't mind,' Maisie replied. 'Photo shoots on the beach are never pristine.'

'Good to meet you.' Daniel had an easy smile and radiated confidence, but Maisie got the impression he was always on high alert, as if he might have to run off and solve a hotel-related crisis at any moment.

'I really appreciate you doing this,' Ollie said, as they walked towards the bus. 'I have such high hopes for this calendar.'

'It's a wonderful idea,' Charlie said. 'And in this area, the RNLI is one of the most deserving charities.'

'People don't always know what to do with the Cornish currents,' Daniel added. 'They watch a few episodes of *Baywatch* and think they can start surfing without any issues, that the water will behave as they want it to.'

'*Baywatch*?' Charlie laughed. 'How old are you?'

'There was that film not long ago, with The Rock and Zack pretty-boy whatsisname.'

Charlie ruffled his hair. 'You're so cute.'

Daniel turned to Ollie and Maisie. 'See what I have to put up with?'

'We're never going to side with you,' Ollie said cheerfully. 'You realize that, right?'

'Of course.' Daniel grinned. 'Where do you want us in these sealskins? Down by the water?'

'With the bus behind you, if that's OK,' Maisie said. 'And I was thinking that . . . You mentioned that your cousin, Delilah—'

'Lila and Sam are on their way,' Charlie said. 'They were filming at the crack of dawn, so they're just getting sorted on the bus.'

'Perfect!' Maisie felt a flash of excitement at the word 'filming', followed by a squeeze of apprehension, because she was going to be taking photos of actors who were captured by professional photographers and camera operators every day, and she was a long way from that. 'I'll set my stuff up,' she added, more quietly.

Maisie had secured her camera to her tripod, and was looking through the viewfinder, trying out different angles, when two figures hopped off the bus.

Delilah and Sam were both undeniably attractive, and there was a confidence about the way they moved, even just striding across the sand. Lila was petite with long dark hair, big eyes and a fizzing energy, and Sam was tall and lean, his locks dark blond, his smile gentle.

Charlie made the introductions, and Maisie tried to be professional rather than starstruck.

'It's so lovely to meet you,' she said to Lila. Her wetsuit was teal with pink swirls, a welcome burst of colour in contrast to the others' more sombre designs.

'And you,' Lila said, smiling. 'I hope this won't be too hard for you . . . I'm worried I don't have a good side, but Sam has two, so he'll make up for me.'

Sam held out a hand for Maisie to shake. 'Ignore her.'

'She can't ignore me,' Lila protested, 'or I'll be left out of the photo.'

'I'll get you in, don't worry,' Maisie said. 'And I would suggest that you *also* have two good sides, but I won't know for sure until we get started.'

Lila laughed. 'I like you already. Right! Put us where you want us. We're used to that.'

Maisie directed the shoot, feeling slightly out of her depth the whole time. These weren't people she knew, like Meredith and Finn, and they were all scarily successful in their different fields. Lila was a whirlwind, laughing and joking constantly, and Daniel had a surly set to his jaw, as if he was doing this under sufferance, but whenever she spoke to him he smiled, and was as compliant as she needed him to be.

She set the shot up close to the water, tried a number of different arrangements, but nothing was working. One moment Ollie was clasping her hands anxiously, the next folding her arms. The whole thing felt awkward and unsettled, and Maisie was worried that her nerves were getting the better of her.

'We're missing something,' she admitted to the others. 'There's something that's just not . . . Could we do some shots directly in front of the bus? I know Routemasters and wetsuits don't exactly go together, but—'

'We could drive the bus down to the water,' Lila suggested.

'Or not.' Charlie laughed nervously.

'Don't you have dogs?' Ollie said. 'I'm sure we spoke about that on the phone. We're including as many pets as possible, because they always add some fun to the images.'

'You let Marmite anywhere near here,' Sam said, 'and . . . well, you know that saying about never working with animals and children?'

'Is he a complete horror?' Ollie asked.

Four voices chorused, 'Yes.'

'Excellent.' Ollie grinned. 'Is he close by?'

Charlie nodded. 'My friend Juliet has got him – and Jasper, actually – on the bus with her while she covers for me.'

'Not too far to go, then,' Ollie said. 'Dogs would make this better, right, Maisie?'

'I think so. And maybe . . .' She chewed her lip. 'I just don't know.'

'We'll start with the dogs and take it from there.' Ollie was adamant.

'You're making a mistake,' Daniel said smoothly. 'Marmite is going to scar you for life.'

'What kind of dog is he?' Maisie asked.

'A Yorkipoo.'

'How much trouble can a Yorkipoo be?' Maisie said, as Charlie strode up the sand towards the bus. Daniel and Sam exchanged winces. Lila squeezed Maisie's shoulder in a way that seemed worryingly sympathetic.

'OK, so Marmite doesn't want to sit still,' Ollie said twenty minutes later, as the Yorkipoo, who was undeniably,

193

outwardly adorable, bounced out of Daniel's arms and ran in a circle around their patch of beach.

'We told you,' Lila said. 'He has more energy than everyone else put together.'

'Whereas Jasper . . .' Daniel stroked the ears of his German shepherd, who had been sitting placidly, doing exactly what was asked of him. Maisie was tempted to fling her arms around the dog's furry neck and cling on until this was all over.

'I don't think these wetsuits will be much good after this,' Sam said, running his hand down his arm. 'Mine's got as many holes as a sieve.'

'I should have clipped his claws.' Charlie tipped her head back and closed her eyes.

Maisie stared at the sand. She had to *think*. Marmite was a cute dog, and if they could get one shot – even if he was mid-action – where it all came together, they would be fine.

'Is there anything that will . . .' she started, but Marmite took off up the beach, barking loudly, and everyone turned to follow his progress.

'He doesn't usually chase other dogs,' Charlie said. 'That's his one saving grace.'

'But that's not a dog,' Daniel pointed out.

Maisie's stomach swooped.

'Look who's here,' Ollie said brightly, as Marmite threw himself at Colm's legs, bare below knee-length shorts, and he crouched just in time, scooping the dog into his arms. Even from a distance, Maisie could see that he was laughing.

'Why is Colm here?' she asked. They had been messaging each other since last weekend, but they hadn't made good on their plans to get together again. Had it been a one-off, drunken kiss, or were they both just nervous about what came next?

'He wanted to come again today,' Ollie said. 'He seems quite invested in the whole calendar. That's OK, isn't it?'

'Of course it is.'

'Hey.' Colm reached them, Marmite's head tucked snugly under his chin. 'Is he yours?'

'He's ours,' Charlie said. 'He's Marmite, and I'm Charlie Harper.'

'Colm Caffrey.' He held out his hand, and introductions were made, more hands shaken. 'Is it going well?' he asked, his gaze landing on Maisie.

'Marmite isn't exactly behaving himself,' Charlie admitted. 'Maybe we could leave him out of the shot?'

'We can't sacrifice cuteness,' Ollie said. 'We can *do* this!'

'You're having the bus in the background?' Colm strolled over to Maisie.

She gestured to the viewfinder. 'This is the set-up so far, but Marmite won't hold still for even a second, so it ends up looking like Charlie and Daniel are kidnapping him and he's trying desperately to get free.' Now he was close, she could smell his aftershave, something sweet and nutty, like pecans and vanilla.

'What about a cream tea on the sand?' he said, bending down to peer through the viewfinder.

His suggestion was met with silence, and he stood up straight, his cheeks going slightly pink.

'What I mean is,' he went on, 'you've got those ornate chairs and tables outside the bus. You could put them in the shallows, sit on them with a few props, a teapot and cups, look like you were having a cream tea in your wetsuits

– a mash-up of the surfing theme and your café. Then one of you could have Marmite on your lap, and it would look a lot less like he was struggling, even if he still was.'

There was a beat of silence, then Ollie said, 'Holy shit.'

'What is it you said you did again?' Daniel asked.

'Right now I build websites, but I've spent some time doing PR. Stunts, events and marketing – the whole shebang.'

'It's a great idea,' Maisie said. She was slightly awed, and a little bit cross that she hadn't thought of it.

'You think?' Colm asked, and she could see that he was pleased.

'I really do. Shall we go and get the chairs and tables?'

'I'll go,' Charlie volunteered. Daniel, Sam and Ollie went with her.

'It does mean I'll have to go in the water, if we still want the bus in the background of the shot.' Maisie rolled up the legs of her cropped trousers.

'Everyone has to suffer for their art,' Colm said, stroking Marmite under the chin.

'Did you train puppies in Australia, too?' she asked.

Colm's expression was amused and intense all at once. 'Just my natural charm and magnetism.'

Maisie laughed. 'Of course.'

'You know,' he murmured, stepping closer, 'I could always—'

'Uh-oh.' Lila's exclamation cut him off.

'What is it?' Maisie turned away from Colm to look up the beach.

Lila gestured to where the others were walking back towards them, carrying a table and several chairs. 'Charlie doesn't look happy.'

At first, Maisie wondered how she could tell, but then she noticed that the other woman wasn't quite as poised as she had been before, and that Daniel was walking close to her, their chairs occasionally clunking together, glancing sideways as he spoke, as if he was giving her a pep talk. Charlie was nodding, but her eyes were on the ground.

'What's wrong?' Lila asked, as soon as they'd put the furniture down.

Marmite yipped, scrabbling in Colm's arms, and he handed the dog to Charlie.

'I just had a call from the meteorologist I've been in touch with,' Charlie said, holding Marmite tightly.

'The one you were talking to about the tides?' Lila said.

Charlie nodded. 'And it's not good news.'

'What's the not good news?' Lila asked.

'The *not good news*,' Charlie said, 'is that they're expecting storms and unnaturally high tides at the end of July, during the week of the festival. Obviously they can't say for sure, but it's looking like a strong possibility. He said that the storm conditions were likely to be, and I quote, "unusually intense for this time of year".'

'So . . .' Lila drew a question mark in the sand with her toe. 'What does that mean?'

'It means we're fucked,' Charlie said.

'Hey.' Daniel rubbed her shoulder. 'Don't say that. We'll just have to adjust our plans.'

'How do we adjust things, when our summer festival – ninety per cent of which was going to take place on or around Porthgolow beach, with food trucks and flimsy market stalls, bands on a temporary stage, a surfing competition – is now likely to be underwater: rained down on from above, and flooded out by high tides?' She gestured to the sea, currently shimmering in a cheerful, inviting way.

'We'll do it somewhere else,' Daniel said. 'There's room at Crystal Waters for some of the stalls, and—'

'Not enough of them,' Charlie replied. 'And if the tides are high and the storms are wild, we can't just move everything else to the seafront and hope it stays dry. Porthgolow isn't big enough. And all these small businesses arrange their summers long in advance, so I can't change the date, because they'll have booked slots at other fairs and festivals, so we'll end up with hardly any of them being able to make it.'

Maisie fiddled with the settings on her camera. The photo shoot had turned bleak and sad and entirely un-summery, despite the golden hue of the day and the sounds of other people enjoying themselves. There was a cloud hanging over them, because of the literal clouds that were, apparently, going to descend on the Cornish coastline.

'You could move it to Port Karadow.' She hadn't realized she'd said it aloud until six pairs of eyes turned towards her.

'What?' Lila said.

Maisie swallowed. 'Port Karadow is bigger than Porthgolow. The harbour front is protected from the water, with a wall and railings, and there are lots of places we could commandeer. There's the town hall, and there's the bookshop – A New Chapter has an upstairs events space. There are pubs and the Happy Shack, and we've had the lights pageant for the last couple of years, with stalls and parades and music. You could move everything there. We couldn't stop the rain, of course, but there would be less chance of the whole thing being flooded out.'

Charlie hugged Marmite tighter. 'Would everyone be OK with that? It would probably mean taking over the whole town, and it would need a lot of coordination – I can do that, of course, but I don't know the people, the business owners, the spaces we'd want to use.'

'I do,' Maisie said, as if the Off switch inside her brain had stopped working. 'I know everyone in Port Karadow. I could ask them all, be joint coordinator, speak to the planning team at the council. There's the primary school, too, with a hall and classrooms we could use as spaces for the stallholders, and—'

'Maisie.' Colm's laugh was gentle. 'This is a huge thing.'

She nodded. She could see the glimmer of hope on Charlie's face, Lila with her hands pressed to her cheeks, Daniel's expression calm but assessing. Sam, like Colm, was frowning slightly. 'I'm sure everyone would be willing to help,' she said. 'After all, quite a lot of us were going to have stalls here anyway.'

'Thea will be so happy,' Ollie said. 'And Meredith – it makes all kinds of sense.'

'Mais.' Colm stepped towards her, as if he wanted to take her into a secluded corner and have a private word. But beaches didn't have corners, and anyway, she was the best person to do this. And, she thought, if she pulled it off, it would be a huge achievement: moving an entire festival from Porthgolow to Port Karadow; getting everyone on board and rescuing Charlie's big summer event. Her mum couldn't tell her she wasn't doing anything with her life if she did this, could she? 'Maisie,' Colm said again.

'Don't you think it's a great idea?'

'Absolutely. For someone else.'

'Why?'

He gestured in the vague direction of Port Karadow, then at the aborted photo shoot. 'You're running the ironmonger's full time, you're taking the photos for the calendar, you're . . . you're offering up the whole town! Are you sure you can get everyone on side?'

'Of course I can.' She folded her arms.

'The *school*, Maisie?'

'Jeremy owes me.'

Colm suddenly looked entirely frustrated, all that calm indifference wiped away. 'You don't have to do this. You don't have to prove yourself to anyone.'

Maisie pulled herself up straight and turned away from Colm. How did he know that was at the heart of her blurted offer? How could he see inside her, to where her heart was thump-thumping a warning inside her ribcage?

'Let's move the summer festival to Port Karadow,' she said. As Charlie squealed and reached in for a hug, Marmite's small, soft body between them, the warning thump got louder. 'It's the perfect solution,' she added, trying to drown it out. But she didn't miss the way Colm ran his hands down his face, looked tired and worried and pissed off all at once.

She hoped the other Port Karadow residents would be a lot more positive about the plan she'd just come up with. She couldn't really afford for them to say no.

Chapter Twenty-One

There was no time to lose, and Maisie was already in a panic.

The summer festival was basically a month away, and she knew the length of the to-do list needed to run a successful event, especially one with multiple businesses and stallholders involved. And that was when it was straightforward, and didn't include moving the entire thing from one location to another.

'Let's do this, Sprout,' she said, hoping it would fire her up, too. She could feel sweat pooling at the base of her spine as she walked from the ironmonger's towards the primary school.

It was Friday afternoon, and she'd left Sandy in the shop, wanting to catch Jeremy now that the school day was over.

Since Monday, the day after the photo shoot with Charlie that had kicked this whole thing off, she had been doing the groundwork. Anisha was high up in the planning team at the council, and Maisie had gone straight to her because, without her buy-in, the entire plan would come to nothing. Anisha had been calm and practical, and had called an emergency meeting with her team.

She had come back to Maisie on Wednesday, saying the plan had been approved, and that she and her colleagues would arrange the necessary permits for temporary trading, the permissions needed, as long as Maisie could find locations for all the food and craft businesses, the events and performances that were due to move a little way up the coast.

Maisie had assured her she could, and had immediately tackled the most straightforward places, the ones where she knew she would get a yes. Thea was fully on board with A New Chapter, and Meredith had spoken to her boss Adrian, who was happy for anything to happen in Cornish Keepsakes as long as Meredith was in charge of it. But there would be a lot of businesses coming from out of town, who didn't have shops to trade from, and Maisie needed to secure enough undercover space for them all.

She said hello to an older couple who regularly came into the shop to buy bird seed, and it made her think of Mr and Mrs Arthur. She hadn't been to see them for a few weeks, and her dad hadn't given her an update. She made a mental note to add it to her to-do list. First, however, she had to get this out of the way. The school was her secret, all-weather weapon for the festival, and standing between her and success was Jeremy.

She thought about how, when they'd finally got the right shots in Porthgolow, Colm had tried to talk to her, and she had batted his concerns away. When, the day after the shoot, he'd resorted to texting her, she had told him she was talking to Anisha, that everything was fine, and then changed the subject. Since then their messages had been constant and easy, as if Colm's frustration on the beach had been a temporary glitch. But it still felt a long way from their night at the Sea Shanty, and the plans they'd made to spend more time together.

The school was quiet when she arrived, and she waved at Clarence, the caretaker, who was mowing the small lawn behind the staff room. She pulled open the door and walked towards the classrooms, her wedged sandals echoing in the empty corridor. She was wearing one of her favourite dresses, ocean blue with a pink and orange flower pattern, and she hoped it would give her the confidence boost she needed.

Jeremy's door was open, and she had to fight the urge to turn and walk away when she saw him sitting at his desk, tie undone, doing some marking. She squeezed her eyes shut and then, before she could talk herself out of it, knocked on the door.

Jeremy looked up, his surprised expression shuttering when he saw her.

'Hi Jeremy,' she said. 'Can I come in?'

He beckoned her forward, every inch the teacher, turning her into a naughty schoolgirl.

'Maisie.' He gestured to the chair opposite him, then leaned back and clasped his hands over his stomach. 'What can I do for you?'

'I have a favour to ask you,' she said, then silently chided herself. 'An opportunity to talk about, actually.'

'Well, which is it?' His smile was tight.

'Charlie Harper, who runs the Cornish Cream Tea Bus in Porthgolow, has been arranging a summer festival.'

'Good for her.'

'And she's just found out that there are likely to be some pretty rough storms, some unusually high tides, the week it's due to go ahead. It's the last week of July, just after term ends.' Jeremy stared at her impassively. She took a deep breath. 'I've suggested she can move the event to Port Karadow. We have more room, more indoor spaces if the rain is torrential. Obviously, the school is one of the best buildings we have.'

'That won't work,' Jeremy said. Beside her, Sprout snuffled. 'And you shouldn't have brought your dog in here.'

'My parents couldn't look after him, and I promise I won't stay long. But why can't we use the school for some of the craft stalls?'

'Because we can't just loan it out like that.'

'Why not? It's a community space, and it's been used for all manner of things in the past.'

'It won't work, Maisie.'

'Because of what happened at the quiz?'

'It's not about that.'

'Are you sure? Because you've been acting like a brick wall since the moment you saw me. I think, whatever I was going to say, you were ready to turn me down. What about if I go to Mr Fielding?'

'I'm responsible for all events now,' Jeremy said. 'I told you that. And this will be too much, too soon after the end of the school term.'

Maisie sat forward. 'You won't have to do anything except let us use the space. We'll be in charge of all the logistics. This is a *good* thing, Jeremy. It will show the school in a positive light, and you can have stalls too, to promote the summer club and raise more money for the wildlife area. You'll be seen as a generous, kind-hearted teacher, willing to help the wider Cornish community. And there are so many people on board already. The whole town's getting involved, and you'll be part of it. There are no downsides for you.'

'What if I just don't want to do it?'

Maisie stroked Sprout's head, the action soothing. 'I worked so hard on that quiz,' she told him. 'I did it for the good of the school and Port Karadow, and to help you out. I don't see why you can't do the same.'

'Your boyfriend *threatened* me.' Jeremy leaned over the desk towards her, almost startling her off her chair. 'At *my* event. Do you have any idea how that made me feel?'

Maisie tried not to focus on the label Jeremy had given Colm. 'So this *is* about quiz night? Could I remind you that, actually, you left most of it up to me: getting me to do the grunt work and the hosting and . . . and everything, basically. It might have been your event, but it wouldn't have happened without me.'

'That is not—'

'*And,*' she went on, 'then you had the nerve to tell me I was doing it wrong. Don't you realize how crappy that was? I know Colm could have behaved better, but what he said to you – he wasn't wrong, either.'

'It was a threat.'

'You were so rude to me.'

'You rejected me!'

She sat back, breathing heavily. 'What?'

If Maisie's cheeks were as red as Jeremy's, then they were both doing impressive clown impersonations. And that was what she felt like, suddenly: a total clown.

'Our dates, before you gave up your job here,' Jeremy said. 'You didn't – you never called me back, you started avoiding me in the staff room. And then you quit your teaching role, and I thought . . . it made no sense, Maisie.'

'I didn't want to get into this,' she said, much more calmly.

'Then you shouldn't have come here.'

Maisie let out a long, slow exhale. 'I'm sorry if I hurt you,' she said. 'It was never my intention, but I . . .' She thought of what Colm had told her, about their night in the pub before he left for Australia. 'I didn't think it was working between us, and I didn't want to go on any more dates with you, but I was a coward about it. I'm sorry.'

She waited for him to say something, to respond to her apology.

'Jeremy?'

'You need to go.'

'So the answer's no, then?'

He nodded, and for a moment she thought he might relent, but then he said, 'It's not going to happen.'

Maisie didn't know whether she felt despair, anger or hopelessness, or a combination of all three. She stood up and smoothed down her dress. 'Please think about it. Take me out of the equation, think of the good it would do for the town, the school, the well-being of the community.'

He didn't reply, and she stepped into the cool corridor, then strode towards the exit, Sprout close by her side. He always knew when she was upset, and got in on the action by being extra needy, as if that would take her mind off her troubles. Clarence was still mowing the lawn, and Maisie wanted to scream into the still, hot air.

This had been her first big challenge, the first time her

efforts to move the festival might go either way, and it turned out she was still paying for her cowardice, her failure to be clear with Jeremy two years ago.

She reached the school gate feeling like a total failure, which wasn't remotely helpful when the next thing she had to do was try and convince Marcus Belrose to let them take over part of his restaurant. She flashed back to Porthgolow beach, Colm's face when he'd said, 'The *school*, Maisie?'

She had wanted so badly to prove him wrong, to show him – her mum, too – that she was right at the heart of Port Karadow, and that everyone there loved and respected her as much as she loved the town. But she'd just been turned down, and she was going to meet her second challenge weakened by the defeat.

There was nothing for it but to square her shoulders, press the reset button, and try again.

Maybe Marcus Belrose and the Happy Shack would be a pleasant surprise? After all, it couldn't get much worse than her altercation with Jeremy. As she walked through the town, the sunshine in contrast to the dark clouds gathering in her thoughts, she decided there wasn't a moment in her life to date that she regretted as much as she regretted inviting Jeremy on that first date.

Chapter Twenty-Two

The Happy Shack was Port Karadow's premier eating location, opened the year before by Marcus Belrose, who had moved from the north of England to get a piece of the Cornish culinary pie. It was colourful and vibrant, mixing the elements of a fisherman's hut with sleek metal furniture and a wrap-around veranda. It was a quirky mash-up of nets and wood, brass and gloss that was somehow effortlessly stylish, and it was booked out most nights.

At just before five on a Friday evening, the place was already buzzing, the veranda filling up with people having pre-dinner drinks and making the most of the lingering sun, which was draped over the coastline like a golden cloak.

Maisie felt her palms prickle with sweat. She looked down at Sprout, and he looked up at her, a companion in nervous solidarity.

A couple came up behind her, the man clearing his throat. 'Are you going in?' he asked.

'Oh! Yes – but you go first.' She ended up holding the door open for them, and then another couple. She followed them in, and was met by the enticing smells of fried garlic and butter.

She stood in the short queue, waiting her turn, and when the smartly dressed front-of-house manager, whose long dark hair was pulled back in a neat ponytail, smiled and asked if she had a reservation, she shook her head like a nodding dog that had gone wrong.

'I need to see Marcus Belrose,' she said.

The woman frowned. 'Does he know you're coming? He's busy with prep right now.'

'He doesn't,' Maisie admitted, 'but it'll only take five minutes. I have a proposition for him.' Her choice of words didn't seem to allay the fears of his staff member. 'I'd like to ask him about the Happy Shack's role in an upcoming summer festival.'

'Oh! He would usually look at those sorts of requests via email.'

'Well, I'm here, so I'm saving him some paperwork.' She beamed, and saw a returning flicker on the woman's face.

'Let me see if he has a few minutes.'

'Thank you.' Once the woman had gone, Maisie took in her surroundings. The inside of the restaurant was still quiet, the gleaming tables laid out ready for the evening service, sunlight pooling in through the glass walls, alighting on the shiny cutlery and the bottles behind the bar. It was like a room that had been scattered with diamonds.

'Hello?' The voice was deep and brimming with impatience, and Maisie turned, finding herself face-to-face with Marcus Belrose. He was handsome in a haughty sort of way, with dark hair slicked back from his forehead, and a beard that was almost too neat to be real. He wore chefs' whites on his lean frame, a black apron over the top, and his dark eyes glittered.

'I'm Maisie.' She held her hand out.

He left a deliberate pause, then reached out and shook it. 'I know who you are: you run the ironmonger's. I don't have long.'

'I appreciate that,' she said. 'I wanted to talk about a summer festival that's coming up at the end of July. It's being organized by Charlie Harper, who runs the Cornish Cream Tea Bus—'

'I know about the bus too,' he said.

'It's Charlie's festival,' she went on, 'but with summer storms and high tides expected in July, we're moving it to Port Karadow. Porthgolow is smaller, you see, and the beach, where she was going to have all the stalls, is clearly a no-go, so—'

'What does this have to do with the Happy Shack?'

'Right.' Maisie swallowed. 'We were wondering if you wanted to be a part of it: run a special menu for festival week, and also, if you'd be happy to host a few other, smaller, food-related businesses in your function room.' She gestured beyond the bar, where she knew there was a sizeable space that could be booked out for parties.

He seemed to consider it for a few seconds, his eyes narrowing. Then he said, 'No. Next question.'

Maisie's mouth fell open. 'I . . . uh . . . Why not?'

'Because we don't "host" other food companies.' He made quotation marks in the air when he said 'host'.

'You could, though.'

Marcus folded his arms. 'Imagine if a travelling hardware company meandered into Port Karadow in their van, and asked if they could set up their shop, selling exactly the same things as you, in that back room where you store all the wood. What would you say?'

He'd been in her shop? 'This is different,' she tried.

'Of course it is.' He chuckled. 'How?'

'Because if we don't find room for everyone, we'll have to scale down the festival, or risk a whole load of small businesses being flooded out. I'm not proposing that we set up seafood or burger companies here, but there are local chocolatiers, brownie-makers, old-fashioned sweet sellers. They're not direct competitors, so—'

'It's too complicated.'

'We could have some non-food stalls here instead, if that would make you feel better? Jewellery makers, local crafts-people. I just thought keeping the foody theme inside these walls would—'

'You know what would make me feel better?' Marcus said.

'What's that?' She already knew what was coming.

'If you and your charming little dog went and asked somebody else about their hosting availability. What about the school? They've got endless rooms that'll be empty during the holidays. Can't you accommodate all your stall-holders there?'

'I've already asked,' Maisie said. She hoped Marcus would leave it at that, but he suddenly seemed interested.

'And?'

'And it turns out today is a day of knock-backs.'

His brows came together. 'Well, I'm sorry.' He sounded

slightly softer. 'It's not something I can accommodate, not for an entire week, but I will think about a special menu. Will you email me the dates?'

Maisie nodded. 'Of course.'

Marcus glanced at his front-of-house manager. 'Kim, get Maisie a drink of whatever she'd like. There's a table on the veranda that's reserved from six, so you've got half an hour, OK?' He squeezed her shoulder.

'Thank you.' Maisie was too frustrated to say anything else.

Marcus gave her a curt nod and went back to the kitchen.

'What would you like?' Kim asked. 'We have a lovely Aperol Spritz, if you fancy something summery.'

'That would be great.' Maisie let the woman lead her through the double doors onto the veranda, to a small table in the corner.

'I'll be back,' Kim said, and left her to it.

Maisie slumped onto a chair and let the gentle breeze caress her face while she soaked up the sight of Port Karadow beach, with its golden sand and shimmering water, the small waves lapping at the shore, and bigger ones further out, perfect for surfers. She thought, for a moment, that she had done it: that Marcus had seen the light, right at the end. It was great that he was keen to be a part of the festival, but her biggest problem, her main role, was to find space for everyone. If it was going to be a week of torrential rain and strong winds, the stallholders needed to be undercover.

She took out her phone and sent a message to Charlie. *Having a mixed response here today, but we've already got a lot of people on board, and I'm determined. :) I'll update you with progress in a couple of days. xx*

Kim came back with a tray on which was a huge goblet, the orange liquid inside adorned with lemon slices and mint leaves, and a sparkly blue straw. She put it on the table, along with a bowl of what looked like mini arancini balls, and another of dog biscuits.

'Wow,' Maisie said. 'Thank you.'

'You got further than most people do,' Kim said with a wry smile.

'What do you mean?' Maisie took a sip of the drink, and her mouth flooded with the sweet, summery flavour.

'He usually dismisses people before they get a sentence out. He listened to you.'

'He didn't agree, though.'

Kim nodded. 'He was burned a bit last year – almost literally. He agreed to do a cooking class at the bookshop, and it didn't go well.'

'I know all about that,' Maisie said.

'So he's cautious, but he's not . . .' She tapped her fingers against her lips. 'He's very fair, even if he's not the most patient person. It might not be game over quite yet.' With that, she gave Maisie a quick smile and walked away.

Maisie picked up an arancini ball and popped it in her mouth, closing her eyes at the herby richness, the soft, comforting squish of melting mozzarella in the middle.

It might not be game over quite yet. It was those words, more than anything, that gave her a glimmer of hope. Maybe, once she'd gathered up a bit more courage, she could go back to the beginning and start again. She took another sip of her perfect drink, bent down to stroke Sprout, and thought how much better this moment would be if there was a scruffy-haired, suntanned surfer sitting opposite her, sharing her arancini balls.

Chapter Twenty-Three

By Saturday morning, all Maisie wanted to do was lie on the beach and read a book. She had found a few locations with willing owners who would take on some of their stallholders, and Anisha had confirmed that the permits were being rushed through, and was working with her planning team on promotion for the festival. Maisie had put her directly in touch with Charlie so there would be no communication errors.

The possibility of a summer festival had thrilled most of the community-minded Port Karadow residents – something she hoped would eventually rub off on Jeremy and Marcus – and a lot of the businesses on Main Street had agreed to be involved. Thea and Ollie were planning events for the bookshop, and had agreed to have three craft stalls inside A New Chapter, saying they could move shelves to accommodate them.

She had also secured the use of Port Karadow's beautiful town hall, which had been number three on her list of

Useful Undercover Spaces. It was bigger than the Happy Shack, but it was also an ideal venue for concerts and performances, so couldn't be entirely full of stallholders for the whole week. She had to try again with the school and the restaurant, but she needed time to regroup.

'Where do you want to set up?' Ollie asked her now. 'Are you going to get him to hold Sprout? Is he really going to be happy to walk out of the water, à la Ursula Andress?'

The reason Maisie couldn't read on Port Karadow beach today was because she was at Stone Cove, a picturesque, secluded bay not far from Liam's estate. It was much smaller and quieter than the main strip of sand, and this morning the light was perfect: crisp and clear and burning off the last of the overnight cloud. It was the day of Colm's photo shoot, and a whole kaleidoscope of butterflies was fluttering inside her.

'I'm sure he'll do whatever we suggest,' she said to her friend. 'And come up with a few more ideas of his own.'

'Is it fun, spending time with him again?'

Ollie had Henry with her today, and he and Sprout were frolicking in the shallows. The cove was speckled with rock formations that framed the water, and the waves here were much rougher than on Port Karadow beach, tumbling in from the wide blue ocean, boisterous and brimming with photographic potential. Maisie could picture how Colm would look emerging from it, a still, strong figure, surrounded by the unrelenting Cornish sea.

'Maisie?' Ollie prompted.

'Yeah? Oh, yes! It's been good to catch up.' She got out her tripod, began extending the legs.

'That, Maisie Winters, is the blandest answer anyone has given to any question, ever.'

Maisie laughed. 'You have a point.' She thought for a moment. 'I love spending time with him, but it's confusing, too. I don't know what he wants.'

'Have you asked him, or snogged him, or . . .?'

She tried so hard to keep the truth from her face. Clearly, she failed.

'You *didn't!*' Ollie stepped closer.

'There was a lock-in at the Sea Shanty. I thought everyone would have known about it by now: my mum certainly did.'

'Mums know things by osmosis, so they don't count. You and Colm kissed? Seriously?'

'We were a bit drunk, there was karaoke.'

Ollie nodded. 'A perfect storm.'

'And since then, it's been good between us. Flirty and fun. But we haven't spent any more real time together, and I don't know what he thinks about it, if—'

'I'm ready for my close-up.' Colm stood at the point where bushy scrubland turned to sand, wearing a dark grey wetsuit, his sky-blue surfboard tucked under his arm. He had the wetsuit slightly unzipped, showing off a slice of tanned collarbone, and Maisie's brain shut down for at least three seconds. He walked towards them, his brows lowering when she didn't respond.

'Hey Colm,' Ollie said. 'We were just talking about you.'

'Deciding how to maximize my potential?' His gaze flicked between Ollie and Maisie. 'I tried to bring Thor, but when I mentioned all these big waves, he opted for the sun spot on the sofa instead.'

'Wise kitten,' Maisie said.

'She speaks! Everything OK, Winters?'

'Fine.'

'How's the festival wrangling coming along?'

'Yeah. It's so-so.'

His smile softened. 'Want to talk about it?'

'Later, maybe. Right now, we need to immortalize you in pixels.'

'Righto!' He rubbed his hands together. 'Do I get Sprout and the Austen dog?'

'The Austen dog, as if you've forgotten, is called Henry Tilney,' Ollie said.

At the mention of his name, the chocolate Lab bounded out of the water and raced at his owner, and Ollie squealed as a huge lump of excited, wet dog zoned in on her. Just before he reached her, Colm deftly stepped in and crouched, and Henry barrelled into him, knocking him onto the sand and licking his face.

Maisie grabbed her camera and took shot after shot. Colm was laughing, lost in the moment, and she wanted to capture it. When she finally looked up, she saw that Ollie was watching her with an eyebrow raised.

'Come on then, Honey Ryder,' Maisie said. 'Stop canoodling with the dog and let's get to it.'

Colm extracted himself from Henry and stood up, still laughing. His wetsuit was dusted with sand and his hair was a total mess, and he looked utterly perfect. 'Where do you want me?'

'Here.' It was out before her brain had time to catch up.

His laughter died, and his gaze turned serious.

'Over here,' she clarified, swallowing. 'I want to take some photos on the rocks, with Sprout, before we get you sauntering out of the water with a conch shell. Leave your surfboard for now.'

'You're the boss.' As he walked past her to get to the rocks, he trailed his finger along her arm, leaving fiery sensations in his wake.

Colm, Maisie soon discovered, was an ideal model. He was undeniably good to look at, he was entirely pliable and he knew, somehow, exactly what she meant when she said things like, 'Be a bit softer,' or 'Look like you're contemplating which topping to have on your dirty fries,' or 'You look too handsome right now.'

In between her prompts, he and Ollie kept up a steady stream of conversation, Maisie joining in when she wasn't focusing on composition or her aperture settings. They talked about Liam and the Foxglove Estate, about Max's plans to do a charity walk along the Cornish coastal path sometime next year, about the events Ollie was planning for the bookshop.

'That's brilliant, Colm,' Maisie said, when she had far more shots than she could ever need.

'You think the rocks are going to work?' Ollie asked.

'We've got some great photos, but we're going to have to do the Bond Girl thing, too.'

Ollie raised her arms in a silent cheer. 'I thought you'd decided it was too ridiculous.'

'It *is* ridiculous,' Maisie said. 'But if anyone can pull it off, then it's Colm.'

He grinned. 'OK, just . . .' He picked Sprout up. They had finished on quite a high rock, and with the tide going out, it was slick with water and seaweed. Ollie hurried forward and took Sprout from Colm, and the dog wriggled against her, his muddy paws on her dress.

'Sorry!' Maisie called.

'Don't worry,' Ollie said. 'Nothing a washing machine won't fix.'

Now dog-free, Colm held out his hand, and Maisie rested her camera in its bag and went to help him. He wrapped his warm fingers around hers and then, bracing against the rock, lowered himself down. He landed, *thump*, in the sand, and he was so close, standing right in front of her. She was at eye level with that enviable portion of tanned, firm collarbone.

'Hey.' His voice was soft.

She looked up. 'Hi.'

'You went to the school?'

'I crashed and burned.'

Anger flickered across his face. 'That prick. I—'

'Here's your seashell.' She pushed the large conch shell into his hand, and he looked at it, confused. Then he smiled.

'Not now, huh?'

'Not now, Caffrey. Unzip your wetsuit and get in the sea.' She pointed to where she wanted him, aiming for stern.

He grinned and said, 'I love it when you're bossy.' Then he walked into the water. She wasn't sure if it was his words, or the look he'd given her, that made her feel as if someone had dropped a whole tray of ice cubes down her back.

'Oh my God, this will have to be the cover.'

Ollie was standing next to Maisie and her camera, which was mounted on the tripod, aimed at where Colm was, for the fifth time, walking towards them out of the waves, his wetsuit unzipped to the waist.

'Don't let Max hear you say that,' Maisie murmured.

It was an effort to get the words out, because at least 90 per cent of her brain was focused on not missing a moment of this, the eighth wonder of the world. Colm, topless and tanned, water droplets caressing his skin, striding purposefully out of the water with his eyes locked on her – actually the viewfinder, she reminded herself – was now her ultimate fantasy. What would he do when he reached her? Would he sweep her into his arms and kiss her, or carry her back into the sea with him, where they could live out a watery existence together?

'I can appreciate the aesthetic qualities of this sight without being disloyal to the man I love,' Ollie said. 'But I also think you should ask him what he wants, or just kiss him again, because Maisie—' She grabbed Maisie's arm and spun her around to face her, 'are you *seeing* this?'

'I *was* seeing it, until you pulled me away.' Maisie gestured in Colm's direction.

'He kissed you, right? And it wasn't a peck?'

'Not a peck,' Maisie confirmed.

'And he's *lovely*,' Ollie continued. 'He agreed to help out with the calendar, and he's considerate and funny, and it seems as if he really cares about you. He defended you against twat-face Jeremy.'

'I know all this,' Maisie said. 'I know it, and it's torture.'

'Why on earth?'

'Because he's my teenage crush, Ollie. I'm twenty-eight now.'

'Your teenage self was wiser than I was at that age. And it's

221

not like you're salivating over an ageing teen actor or a boyband member who's outgrown his songs and his haircut. Look at the guy!'

'What's next?' Colm called from the shallows.

'Maisie is going to come over there and ravage you,' Ollie said quietly, so only Maisie could hear. 'Stop overthinking things, please.'

'I'm trying to.'

'If you don't tell him how you feel, if you don't see where this could go, he will be snapped up by someone else in half a heartbeat.'

'OK,' Maisie said, because she knew Ollie was right. She just didn't have her certainty.

'Can I come out now?' Colm called. 'I think there's some kind of shark . . .'

'Oh God, get out!' Maisie screeched, and Colm laughed and walked out of the water, his hands up in front of him.

'It's seaweed,' he said. 'Got all you need?'

'More than.' Maisie tucked a curl behind her ear. 'You were great, Colm.'

He shrugged. 'It wasn't exactly a hard gig.'

'That was amazing,' Ollie added. 'Thank you so much for doing this. I need to go now, but Maisie will be in touch to show you the shots.' She hugged him, gave him a quick kiss on the cheek, then did the same with Maisie. 'And think about what I said, OK?'

'Sure,' Maisie replied.

Ollie collected her dog and hurried up the beach, towards the scrubland and the standing stone that gave the cove its name.

'Sit for a minute?' Colm said, when she'd gone.

Maisie packed up her camera and followed him back to the rocks. She sat next to him, spreading out the skirt of her dress so it wasn't bunched up. She could feel the warmth of his body, the way it sheltered her from the wind coming in off the sea. He still had his wetsuit pulled down to the waist, and she was conscious of all that sun-kissed skin so close to her. He rested his elbows on his knees, and she looked straight ahead, where Sprout still hadn't tired of chasing waves.

'What happened at the school?' he asked gently.

Maisie sighed. 'Jeremy and I got into a fight. I tried to stop it happening, but he was obstinate, and . . . he's annoyed about how I ended things with him.' Out of the corner of her eye, she saw Colm turn to face her. She didn't dare look at him. 'I didn't really explain myself. I let things fizzle out between us, and then I left the school – not because of him,' she hastened to add. 'But the timing . . . It wasn't my proudest moment, and now he's holding it against me.'

There was a pause before Colm replied. 'And you really need the school for the festival?'

'It's the biggest building in Port Karadow, and it'll be empty. It could accommodate so many stallholders if the weather's as bad as they're predicting.'

'Shit.' He sighed. 'Who else?'

'Who else what?'

'Who else has been a total wanker to you?'

'Nobody,' Maisie said, laughing.

'Come on. This isn't just about Jeremy, is it?'

'No,' she admitted, 'it's not.' She told him about her week – about the argument with Jeremy, Marcus Belrose's dismissal of her suggestion, Anisha's support and the town hall triumph. Colm listened, sometimes nudging her shoulder, occasionally cursing under his breath. 'So there you go,' she said, when she'd finished. 'That's where I'm at.'

Colm nodded. 'OK, the first thing to know is that all is not lost.'

'How can you be so sure?'

'Because I spent the best part of a decade working for a business that relied on the art of persuasion. Whether we wanted people to buy things, attend events, believe in a concept – whether we were subtle or brash about it, speaking to one person at a time or thousands, it was all about getting them on our side.'

Maisie turned towards him, her knee nudging his, and let her gaze linger for a moment on his chest before meeting his eyes. 'So what's the secret?'

His smile was tentative, which surprised her. 'You need them to see what they're missing. Make them realize that what you're offering is the best they're going to get. Make it impossible for them to turn you down.'

'I . . . don't know how,' she said.

'I don't believe that.'

'Flattering me is not going to convince me I can do this.'

'What about kissing you?'

'That's not—' she started, but he cupped her cheek and brushed his lips softly against hers.

'This OK?' he whispered. 'If it's not, then—'

'It's OK,' she assured him. She closed the gap again, her touch bolder than his, so that he knew there was no ambiguity.

This kiss, with the sea breeze tangling in her hair, the rock cold beneath her, Colm's warm arm around her waist

224

and the firm, sandy skin of his chest pressed against hers, was the best kiss of her life. There was no tequila haze, the air was crisp and perfect, and Colm felt, and tasted, like nothing she'd experienced before. The night in the pub had given her a hint, but this was the real thing, and it made every inch of her come alive, as if she'd woken up from a hundred-year sleep.

When they pulled apart, he trailed his fingers down the side of her face, tucked a couple of wayward curls behind her ear. 'Can I help you?'

'Help me with what?' Maisie was slightly dazed. 'I mean, what we just did—'

He grinned. 'Let's do more of that, but . . .'

'But?'

'I think you should go back to Jeremy, and Marcus, and get them both on side.'

'I can't.'

'You can,' Colm said firmly. 'And I'm going to tell you how to do it.'

'You could do it for me?' She gave him her brightest smile.

Colm laughed and pressed another kiss to her lips. 'Don't do that.'

'What?'

'Don't bewitch me into doing this for you.'

'Colm, I have never bewitched anyone in my life.'

'That you *know* of.'

She sighed, pretending to be disgruntled, but it was hard when she felt as if she was floating on clouds. Part of her wanted to invite Colm back to hers, but just kissing him was so good, and she didn't want to rush it. 'OK then,' she said. 'How do I win them over?'

'This is like opening the box to the meaning of life, so you need to pay attention.'

'I would say I'm entirely focused, but you're sitting there all topless and sun-blushed, so it would be a lie.'

Colm sighed and shook his head, as if he was disappointed in her. 'Right then.' He turned away from her, back towards the sea, and held out his arm. Maisie tucked herself into him, and his arm came around her, pulling her close. 'Here it is, Maisie. The secret to getting those idiots eating out of the palm of your hand.'

'I'm ready,' she said. Having Colm in her corner, her lips still tingling from his kisses, and his arm anchoring her to him and to the ground, she suddenly felt as if she could do anything she set her mind to.

Chapter Twenty-Four

Find their pain points and their personal goals.

This was the mantra Maisie walked to the Happy Shack with on Monday afternoon. It was what Colm had told her to do, sitting on the rock at Stone Cove on Saturday, and now she felt infused with his confidence and his kisses. She took a deep breath and pushed open the door.

There was a different front-of-house manager working today, a slightly older man with neat, silver-fox hair, whose smile was solicitous but a little bit aloof.

'I'd like to see Marcus Belrose please.'

'I'm afraid that's not possible,' the man said. 'I can show you to your table, if you have a booking.'

Maisie matched his smile. 'Can you tell him it's Maisie, and that I have a new proposition for him?'

The man hesitated, then gave a sharp nod and disappeared. It was a repeat of last week, but this time everything *felt* different. She had sent Marcus an email first thing that morning, asking to see him again, but she hadn't had a reply and she couldn't afford to wait. She hoped that, at the very least, he would have seen her name in his inbox and was prepared for her reappearance.

A few minutes later, he walked out of the kitchen wearing the same chefs' whites, black apron and etched-in scowl. Maisie imagined that his face brightened slightly when he saw her, but that could have been her new confidence working its magic.

'Maisie Winters,' he said, sauntering up to her.

'Hello, Marcus. Today, I am also your fairy godmother.' She wrinkled her nose. 'Sort of, anyway. I'm here to make all your dreams come true.'

He raised an eyebrow, then gestured towards the bar. 'Let's sit for a moment.'

The manager was still hovering, and Marcus said, 'A couple of coffees please, Devon.'

Devon nodded and slipped away, and Maisie hoisted herself onto a bar stool.

'So,' Marcus said, 'you're going to make my dreams come true?'

'If you agree to host several of the confectionary stalls in your function room, then we'll give the Happy Shack space on all the festival promo. Your logo, your name; you alongside the Cornish Cream Tea Bus.'

'What would that look like?'

Maisie took a deep breath, then said, '*The Cornish Cream Tea Bus and the Happy Shack present the Summer Indulgence Festival. All your favourite things in one place.*'.

Maisie had talked to Charlie about her idea, and had discovered that she wasn't remotely precious. She just wanted a successful festival, making vendors and customers as happy as possible, especially considering the expected challenging weather. She didn't care about status the way Marcus did, but no way was Maisie relinquishing it all to the celebrity chef. She kept going.

'Your central location and the space you have, not to mention your reputation, means we want you to be part of this, but you need to get on board with the issues we're facing, too. And just think what this will do for your profile. You're helping to make it possible. If we don't have space for stalls indoors, then the whole thing might have to be called off.'

Marcus drummed his fingers on the polished bar as Devon put two tiny cups of espresso down. The chef downed his in a second, as if it had been a shot of tequila. Maisie did the same, and almost choked on the hot, bitter liquid.

'Are you in?' she asked, once she'd got her throat under control. 'Or do you need time to think?'

'And if I say no?'

'If you say no, then it's the Sea Shanty.'

Marcus scoffed. 'No way.'

'They don't have as much space as you do, but they have a small function room upstairs, and they make the best cheese toasties you could ever hope to find.' *Pain point*, Maisie recited in her head. Marcus wants to be at the top of the culinary tree.

'Have you tasted *my* cheese toasties?' Marcus asked.

It was Maisie's turn to scoff. 'You don't have a hope.'

His expression turned to steel. 'I'm in. But I want to see the promo material before it goes out.'

'Of course. You and Charlie will have equal sign-off.' Maisie hoped her frantic heart-hammering was well hidden. 'And I'll need your festival menu for the website. I'll be in touch about the details.' She slid off her stool, more elegantly than she'd thought possible, and Marcus stood up.

'Good to work with you, Maisie.'

'You too.' When they shook hands, she matched his grip for firmness.

A light drizzle had started to fall, the weather so different to the last few weeks of blissful sunshine. It felt fitting, though, because now she had to go and see Jeremy. Marcus, despite his status and his hard edges, had always been the warm-up. At least now she had a win under her belt.

As she walked from the seafront restaurant through the winding, picturesque streets of Port Karadow to the primary school, she took out her phone and typed a quick message to Colm.

Marcus is on board. One down, one to go! x

The reply came moments later.

See! You can do this. Let me know how it goes with J. And Thor says if all else fails, get your hammer out. ;)

Grinning, she put her phone back in her bag.

As she approached the school she saw Jeremy, messenger bag slung over his shoulder, leaving the building. It put her slightly off-kilter, because she'd been imagining doing this in the calm solitude of his classroom.

'Jeremy,' she called, before he could get in his car.

He glanced in her direction, and even from a distance she could see his sigh. 'What is it?' he called. 'I have to get home.'

'Two minutes of your time.' Maisie hurried over to him, aware that the rain was making her hair frizz.

'What do you want now?'

Pain points and personal goals, she repeated to herself. 'How much does Mr Fielding care about being a part of this community?'

Jeremy opened the passenger door and slung his bag onto the seat. 'He's involved in stuff.'

'Right.' Maisie nodded. 'The quiz and chips, regular exhibitions of the children's work. It's the only primary school in Port Karadow, after all.'

'Where are you going with this?'

'What would Mr Fielding think if he knew the school had had the chance to be at the centre of a week-long summer festival, one which most of the town have already signed up to be involved in, and you'd turned down the opportunity?'

'It's not practical.' Maisie could see a pulse ticking below his ear.

'What about the lights pageant? You had a craft fair in the school, food stalls selling mulled wine, a display of your pupils' Advent calendars. That was only a couple of days after the end of term, and it was still manageable.'

'It's less than a month away.'

'I know,' Maisie said. 'But I'm in charge of organizing it, and I've got sign-off from the planning team at the council. You will barely have to lift a finger – we'll get everything sorted.'

'You're not going to change my mind.'

Maisie took a deep breath. She had hoped he would say yes – she hadn't wanted to take this next step, but she thought of what Colm had told her. *Sometimes you need to be ruthless. It's not a bad thing, Mais, as long as you don't go for all-out blackmail.*

'I need to get home,' Jeremy said.

'So if I was to make an appointment with Mr Fielding tomorrow,' Maisie said, before he could leave, 'and talk through my plans with him, would he say the same as you? I know you're community coordinator, but I can still ask him.'

'You can't be serious.'

'Just imagine the whole of Port Karadow, bursting with summer spirit and sparkle, and then this place with cold, empty rooms of . . . *nothing*, right in the middle of the action.'

'Mr Fielding trusts me to make the calls.' He sounded as if he was speaking through gritted teeth, and Maisie thought this was probably her final chance.

'But does he know you're not always basing your decisions on the facts?'

'Maisie—'

'That you hold personal grudges, and let them impact your choices?'

Jeremy opened his car door, stood for a moment, then slammed it closed again. 'I'll talk to Mr Fielding tomorrow.'

Maisie exhaled, shock mingling with relief, and not a small amount of guilt. 'Great. I'll email you the proposal when I get home, so you have all the information to take to him. If he, or you, need anything else, then just call me.'

'Why are you doing this?'

'What do you mean?'

'*This*. This . . . harassment.'

She sucked in a breath. 'Harassment? Jeremy, this has nothing to do with you, except that you coordinate events for the school. I would have much preferred to go straight to Mr Fielding, but I knew you'd love that even less. I just want the festival to be a success. I hate that things have turned sour between us . . . I never meant for that to happen.'

Jeremy glared at her, then his shoulders slumped, all the irritation falling out of him. 'I really liked you.'

'I liked you too,' she said quietly. 'And I know I could have communicated better when I . . . ended things. I *know* that it wasn't fair of me, that I behaved really badly. But you haven't been that great to me recently, either. So we could put it behind us, couldn't we?'

'We don't have to,' he said. 'I could apologize. We could start over—'

'I'm really sorry, Jeremy,' she cut in. 'I don't want to try again. Can we just move on?'

He ran a hand through his hair, then nodded. 'Sure. Friends, then?'

She held out her hand. 'Friends. And thank you, for speaking to Mr Fielding. I really think this festival is going to be a huge triumph for everyone.'

'Yeah. I mean, probably.'

She didn't think she'd ever heard anyone sound so begrudging in her life, but she smiled, and felt something loosen in her chest when he returned it.

She walked out of the school car park feeling almost giddy, the rush of success, of relief, like a fresh wind gusting through her. She took out her phone and was about to text Colm, when she saw she already had a message from him.

Call me when you're done. x

He picked up on the second ring. 'How did it go?'

'It's done,' she said. 'It was hard, but he said he'd talk to Mr Fielding tomorrow.'

233

'Brilliant! I knew you could do it.' There was a pause, then he said, 'Any personal stuff?'

'A bit,' she admitted. 'He knows, now, that I'm not interested in rekindling anything. I think we might have made a tentative truce, even if I went in a bit strong to get him to agree.'

'You did what you needed to,' Colm said. 'Don't feel guilty about that. Are you OK?'

'I'm good. Happy. Relieved.'

'You've persuaded the two most obstinate men in Port Karadow – if you don't count my granddad. That's no mean feat.'

'It felt a bit dirty, doing that to Jeremy.' She chewed her lip as she walked, the rain fading and a sparkle of sunshine peeking through the clouds.

'He wasn't playing by the rules to begin with,' Colm said. He sounded so certain about it, a little of Maisie's guilt slipped away. 'And, when you think about it, you were saving him. The principal would have found out he'd turned you down, and he would have got a bollocking. You've done nothing wrong, and we need to celebrate.'

'We do?'

'Come to mine on Saturday.'

'Saturday?'

She couldn't keep the disappointment out of her voice, and he laughed gently. 'I've picked up another client, so I'm snowed under right now. By Saturday you'll probably need to prise my fingers off the keyboard.'

'I can do that. I'm pretty unstoppable these days.'

'You always were,' he said. 'Keep me up to date with festival stuff, OK? If there's anything I can help with, you know I will.'

'I thought you were snowed under.'

'I'll always keep a bit of time aside for you, Winters. But if I open the gates too much and let you come round tonight, my carefully constructed schedule will come crashing down around me.'

As Maisie walked past a front garden fragrant with yellow roses, she couldn't keep the grin off her face. Saturday couldn't come soon enough.

Chapter Twenty-Five

Over the next few days, Maisie felt as if she didn't have enough space in her brain, let alone time, to cope with everything. She leaned on Sandy and Parker more than usual, giving them extra shifts, letting them serve customers and stock shelves while she created spreadsheets on her tablet to document which stallholders would be set up where, and talked to Charlie about the requirements for each vendor. Fitting everyone into place was like doing a huge, 3D jigsaw puzzle.

She was touched that Charlie kept her up to date with the marketing, sharing initial designs of the logo and banner with her, asking for her opinion. She treated her like a genuine organizer, and not just a runner, dealing with the logistics. Anisha was also a calming influence. She had a wealth of experience, a seemingly endless knowledge bank and an unflappable approach that always put Maisie at ease.

Still, with the shop to run, the approaching festival to organize, as well as fitting in the calendar photo shoots, she had an awful lot to juggle. She was viewing Saturday as a shimmering point on the horizon, even though it was nowhere near the end of all her additional responsibilities. It would be a welcome respite, one that would involve Colm, his charming cottage and his cat, and hopefully more of his kisses.

She had been inspired by his pep-talk, his PR knowledge giving her the tools she needed to sell the festival to Jeremy and Marcus, after her dismal first attempts. She had also seen it as a gift, his way of opening up to her, telling her more about his time in Australia, even if he'd kept it firmly within the boundaries of what she needed to know to get ahead. But since then, her curiosity had only increased, and she was struggling to shush the internal voice that told her there were other ways of finding out about him.

It was Thursday afternoon, she had forty-five minutes before she needed to leave for the next photo shoot, and Sandy was here already, even though Maisie had only asked her to lock up. The ironmonger's was quiet and, sitting at the counter with her tablet in front of her, Maisie's willpower finally deserted her.

She pulled up Google, typed *Colm Caffrey + Sydney* into the search bar, and waited for his barely touched Facebook profile to land at the top. Instead, up popped a news article. It was from an Australian newspaper, and Maisie frowned as she read the headline, her pulse ratcheting up. What the . . .? A message alert slid onto the top of her screen, and she felt a hot rush of guilt. It was as if he knew what she was doing.

Do you still eat seafood?

Swallowing, she replied to Colm's message. *You're planning ahead – I'm impressed! I'm a lifelong Port Karadowan, of course I do. xx*

Then she went back to the article, her stomach twisting into knots, her guilt mingling with heartbreak for Colm, and hurt that he hadn't confided in her. She had found the reason things hadn't *worked out* for him in Australia, his casual flippancy hiding such a horrible, soul-destroying story that she wondered how he had managed to keep it from her – from everyone – for all this time.

Charmed Cove wasn't the official name of the little cut-out beach close to Port Karadow, but it was what Meredith and Finn called the place where, most mornings, they came to swim. Secluded, like Stone Cove, it had much steeper cliffs surrounding it, and Finn's aunt's house sat nestled into the hill, his part-built studio extension visible on the side. The swell here was strong, perfect for surfing shots.

When Maisie reached the gravel space at the top of the cliff, Ollie's car was already there, along with a Land Rover that, on closer inspection, she saw was a hybrid. She took her dog and her camera bag, and made her way carefully down the steps cut into the cliff.

Ollie waved up at her, then pointed to the man and woman alongside her, who were both in wetsuits and, this time, had surfboards. This, Maisie knew, would test her photography skills to their limits, even if she was a 100 per cent focused. But, after stupidly looking Colm up on the internet, she knew that focusing would be a struggle.

'This,' Ollie said, gesturing to Maisie as she reached the sand, 'is our photographer, Maisie. Maisie, meet our victims for this evening, Hannah and Noah.'

'Hi.' Maisie put her bag down on the sand.

'Hello!' Hannah had long blonde hair tied up in a pony-tail, and a wide, friendly smile. 'It's so lovely to meet you.'

'You too. And you're Noah?'

'That's right.' He was tall, his dark curls cut slightly long, and his eyes were incredibly blue, especially standing next to the sea. 'Good to meet you, Maisie.'

'Hannah and Noah are friends of Charlie and Daniel's,' Ollie explained. 'Hannah's the chef at the Seven Stars in Porthgolow, and Noah's a freelance eco-consultant.'

'Oh wow,' Maisie said. 'So you're all about sustainability, then? Guess you're not a fan of all the fishermen around here.'

'My dad's a fisherman,' Noah told her. 'And Hannah's fish pie is the best, so . . .'

'It's a very conflicting job,' Hannah said, with a grin.

Noah shrugged. 'I can only do what I can do.'

'Do you live in Porthgolow?' Maisie asked, trying to move onto easier topics.

'We're buying a house there,' Hannah said, her voice full of excitement. 'At the moment I'm above the pub, and Noah has a place in Mousehole.'

'But I can work from anywhere,' he added. 'The pub can't do without Hannah.'

'And then, next summer . . .' she bounded over to Maisie, holding out her hand. The sparkling engagement ring caught the light, the square-cut sapphire a deeper blue than the sea. 'I'm sorry, I know we don't know each other, but I can't stop telling everyone!' She looked at her fiancé, and he returned her smile. Maisie could see the depth of feeling in his eyes, even while the rest of him stayed calm.

'Congratulations! That's so lovely. I expect you didn't imagine having this set-up for your engagement shoot.'

Hannah laughed. 'Noah and I have been learning to surf together, so in some ways this is perfect – not that it's actually an engagement shoot, of course.'

'I could take some photos for you, if you want? Another time, I mean.' She was getting used to portraits, and would be happy to do a shoot for the loved-up couple.

'Oh! You don't have to,' Hannah said.

'I'm not sure an engagement photo shoot is really our thing,' Noah added. 'Is it?' He looked at his fiancée, tentative. 'If you'd like to, then we could?'

'Let's have a think. Maisie, could you look after this?' Hannah took her ring off and handed it to her. 'I should have left it at home, but I don't like taking it off unless I have to.'

Maisie took it carefully, and put it in the small, zipped compartment of her camera bag.

'You want us to actually do some surfing for this, right?' Noah smiled, his whole face softening.

'If you can,' Ollie said, 'then that would be amazing.'

'Action shots aren't exactly my forte,' Maisie added, 'so let's all go easy on each other. Start by getting in the water with your boards, doing what you usually do, and we'll take it from there.'

'Right.' Noah nodded and took Hannah's hand. 'Ready?'

'Always,' she said, and together they walked into the water.

Maisie watched them, her heart squeezing. 'They're such a lovely couple.'

'Aren't they?' Ollie said. 'They have an adorable dog, too, but I thought we should have at least a couple of genuine surfing shots in our calendar, and Charlie said they were the most experienced out of her group of friends.'

'They certainly look the part.' Maisie crouched and peered through the viewfinder, taking a photo of them walking into the tumultuous waves, surfboards under their arms, holding hands.

'OK, that one is perfect,' Ollie said. 'I honestly don't know how I'm going to choose the final photographs.'

'We can sit down when we've finished the shoots and work it out together.' Maisie watched as Hannah and Noah got onto their boards, starting on their stomachs.

'Do you ever rest?' Ollie asked.

Maisie glanced at her. 'That's rich, coming from you.'

Ollie laughed. 'I know, but this is my natural state. When I met you, you were so chilled out, happy at the ironmonger's, coming to bookshop events, taking long walks on the beach with your dog.' She blew a kiss at Sprout, who had just returned from a foray into the shallows.

'Things have just got busy.'

'Because of me,' Ollie said.

'Because of *me*,' Maisie corrected. 'And – so many other reasons. Trying to prove my mum wrong, not wanting to say no to anyone, Colm . . .'

'So you're getting busy with Colm, too?'

Maisie managed a laugh. 'Not like *that*.' *Why* had she Googled him? It was one of the stupidest things she'd ever done. 'Not yet, anyway,' she added, trying to keep things light. She waited while Noah got to his feet on his board, crouching in a typical surfer stance. She snapped quickly, getting in as many photos as she could. 'He's invited me for dinner on Saturday.'

Ollie squealed, and for a moment Maisie thought Hannah had fallen off her board. 'Shit, Ollie!'

'Sorry.' Ollie grinned. 'It's just exciting.'

Maisie's stomach did a matching somersault. 'I keep imagining what my teenage self would think if I told her that one day I would be having dinner at Colm Caffrey's cottage, with him and his cute kitten, and that there was so much more to him than that cool confidence . . .' *So* much more. Why hadn't he told her? She shook her head.

'You have got it so bad,' Ollie said gleefully. 'Can I get a debrief afterwards?'

Maisie looked away from the water to give her a firm stare.

'I'll let you pick the next book-club read,' Ollie tried.

'I picked in November,' Maisie said.

'I'll convince Max to get Beryan to make you a whole tray of those peanut butter blondies you like so much.'

'Blondies in exchange for date details?'

'Exactly. And if you don't agree, I'll ask Liam to get the details from Colm instead.'

Maisie grinned. 'I'm almost tempted to let that happen. Can you imagine Liam asking Colm for details of date night? I'm glad they're getting on better now.'

'Liam is *thrilled*. He's so much more cheerful than he was.' She sighed. 'I don't think he'd be happy if Colm's stay turned out to be temporary.'

Maisie's throat tightened. 'He hasn't told me what he's planning long term. I don't think he knows himself, or if he does, he's keeping it close to his chest. He's good at that.'

'Has he told you what happened in Australia?' Ollie asked, as Maisie took photos of Hannah and Noah following the same wave, amazed that she was getting some decent photos. 'I think Liam knows, but he's not telling me or Max – not that I'd expect him to. It's not his story to tell.'

Maisie thought of what was – had always been – readily available on the internet, for anyone to look up. But she didn't think it was fair to give Ollie that version: she wanted to hear it directly from Colm, because newspapers made money by exploiting the most salacious details, and she knew she couldn't trust everything they said: the suspicion, the accusations. How much of it had Colm really had to suffer through? She aimed for neutral as she replied to her friend.

'Something went wrong with his job, but he hasn't told me about it.' There. None of that was a lie. She hoped, on Saturday, he'd be more forthcoming. She tried to dissolve all her thoughts of Colm, gave Ollie a quick smile, then turned back to the sea, and the happily engaged couple surfing their hearts out in the beautiful Cornish waters.

Chapter Twenty-Six

Maisie was reminded exactly what she was doing all the festival work for, when Saturday dawned with the rain pounding against her bedroom window. Sprout was more enthusiastic about their soggy walk than she'd expected, and they took the path down to the beach, the sea roaring as if it had stubbed its toe, rainwater pelting the surface. It was wild and raw, and so unlike a traditional July morning. But it helped calm Maisie's nerves, and silence the narratives about that evening that had been playing on an endless loop through her head, including what Colm would say when she told him what she'd found out.

She arrived at his cottage just after seven, the rain still a steady thrum, his lush garden dripping, the roses and marigolds vibrant beneath the strange yellow hue of the sky. A robin sang unabashedly, and Maisie thought that Thor must be tucked up inside, away from it all.

She took the bottle of wine and packet of luxury nougat

off the passenger seat. She'd remembered, a couple of days ago, that he used to love it, that he'd often had some with him in school, and that it had made his breath smell sweet.

She hurried to the door and knocked loudly. It opened almost instantly, Colm grabbing her arm and dragging her inside.

'Quick,' he said, and she fell, breathless, into the tiny corridor.

'What's wrong?'

He blinked at her, and she decided it should be illegal for someone to look so hot in glasses. 'It's hammering down,' he said.

'Oh.' She laughed. 'I noticed that. I thought we were hiding from someone, or . . .'

He grinned at her. 'You're nuts, Winters. But also, you look great.'

'Thank you.' She gave him a twirl. She was wearing one of her newer dresses, black with little cartoon foxes on it. It fell just below the knee, its neckline not too daring, but showing off her collarbone and a hint of cleavage.

He reached up and wiped a raindrop off her forehead, the pad of his thumb slightly rough against her skin. He was wearing a loose turquoise shirt with exaggerated stitching, the sleeves rolled up to his elbows, and dark jeans.

'Come through,' he said. As she followed him, Maisie was aware of a delicious smell, creamy and peppery and unmistakably of the seaside. 'I'm doing seafood linguine.'

'Wow. You're giving Marcus Belrose a run for his money.'

'I was taught a great recipe in Australia, and it sort of became my thing. Whenever we had people for dinner, or . . .' He shut the lid of his laptop, then bent in front of a discreet silver sound system Maisie hadn't noticed before. It looked old-school, somehow, now that most people played music through their phones or TVs.

'You and Lainey?' she prompted. She didn't want anything to be off limits tonight.

'Yup. This OK?' He pressed play, and the melodious, Aussie tones of Vance Joy drifted into the room.

'Oh, I love him,' Maisie said. She didn't add that whenever she'd heard 'Riptide' or 'Lay It All on Me', she'd thought of Colm, all the way on the other side of the world.

'Good. Can I get you a drink?'

Maisie held out her bottle of wine, which was white and already chilled, and the nougat.

Colm's eyes widened as he took them. 'I can't believe you remembered. Thank you.' He held up the wine. 'I'll put this in the fridge for later. No Sprout?'

'I left him with Dad. Where's Thor? I thought he'd be sheltering from the rain.'

'He must be doing it with someone else.'

Maisie laughed.

'What's funny?'

'You look so sad. You miss him.'

Colm gave her a rueful smile. 'He's a great cat.'

Maisie followed him into the kitchen, leaning against the counter while he poured them both generous glasses of wine from a bottle he took out of the fridge. A pot bubbled on the stove, emitting all the delicious smells she'd been enticed by when she walked in.

Colm handed her a glass, then held his out. 'To old friendships.'

Maisie touched her glass to his. 'To old friendships and

new beginnings.' Their eyes held, and she watched his Adam's apple bob above the open collar of his shirt.

They sat on the sofa, angled towards each other, the background a soft mix of thrumming rain and gentle music. Maisie tried to focus on that, instead of the way her whole body was tingling in Colm's presence, and all the things she wanted to say to him.

'How's the festival prep going?' he asked.

'It's good. I have my prime locations now, and Charlie's treating me like joint organizer, which in some ways is really flattering, but also feels a bit . . . pressuring.'

'You're doing a lot of work for it. You should get the appropriate credit.'

'And you,' she said. 'You should get credit for being my negotiation coach. I wouldn't have the primary school or the Happy Shack without you.'

'That's not true,' he said, touching her knee. 'A few more days, and you would have gone back there with all the resolve and kick-assery you needed.'

'Kick-assery?' Maisie said, laughing.

Colm glanced towards the kitchen, as if the gently simmering pot might be about to boil over. 'It was what my boss used to say whenever we pulled off a big success,' he admitted. 'That we'd achieved peak kick-assery.'

Maisie sipped her wine, then said, as nonchalantly as she could, 'You liked working with him?'

'I need to check on dinner.' He moved to get up, but Maisie grabbed his sleeve, keeping him in place.

He looked at her, surprised.

'Tell me about Australia,' she said softly.

He shook his head. 'That's all in the past, and it's—'

'I Googled you,' she blurted, then felt her cheeks flame. She took a large sip of wine, watching as Colm's expression went from surprised to hurt. He was rigid, a trapped animal, then he leaned back against the sofa and ran a hand through his hair.

'What did you see?' he asked.

'I didn't look at much,' she rushed. 'There was this article, in the *Sydney Morning Herald*, but I . . . I would rather hear it from you. Who knows how much of the truth they actually include in those pieces?'

Colm's laugh was humourless.

'I'm so sorry, Colm. I . . .'

'It's OK.' He squeezed her knee, his hand hot through the flimsy fabric of her dress. 'It's out there for everyone to see, I guess.'

'But you didn't tell me.' She tried to keep any accusation out of her voice.

'Why would I want to tell you about it? Admit all of that to you? I'm trying so hard to put it behind me, to start again.'

'You can't just erase it, though,' she said gently. 'And wouldn't it help, to talk about it?'

Colm stood up and went into the kitchen, and Maisie felt a surge of frustration, anger at him for holding things back from her after they'd kissed, after their closeness at the beach, sitting on that rock together. He turned the gas down under the saucepan, the simmering bubble fading to nothing against the raindrops, the music, then he came and sat down, turning his whole body towards her.

He took a long sip of wine, then nodded, as if preparing himself.

'There was something pretty magical about Anders, my boss,' Colm told her. 'He was always full of energy and ideas: I don't know how he managed it, being that switched on every day. It was his company – First Bite. I started there not long after I moved out with Dad, as an assistant to begin with, but then I moved up the ranks, and Anders sponsored my residency. I ended up being made a partner – the article must have said?'

'It did,' she whispered.

'I was one of their first employees, when they were starting out. After I'd been there a few years and we were doing well, getting a good reputation, I invested some of my savings to help them grow – expand the staff base, reach new clients. It was . . .' He glanced towards the window, where a rose bud was tapping against the glass. 'I was pretty passionate about it. I thought, for a little while, that I'd found the place I was meant to be.'

Maisie understood, because that was how she felt about Port Karadow. But the look in Colm's eyes reminded her that he had been relieved of his assumption in quite a dramatic way. 'The scenery and sunshine,' she said. 'A job you loved. Lainey.'

He shook his head. 'She wasn't . . . I mean . . .' He broke off to drink more wine, the music track changing to 'Snaggletooth', one of her favourites.

Maisie stayed quiet, both dreading what was coming and yet desperate to hear him tell her, in his own words.

Colm exhaled, his shoulders dropping. 'It turned out that Anders was good at other things besides PR wizardry and charming clients. He was good at siphoning off money, too. We suddenly had gaps in our finances, our clients' accounts, and we got investigated by the fraud division. He'd just been . . . he'd been *taking* it all, leaving the company with nothing, confident that as we got more successful, he could put it all back. But gamblers never can, can they? They take more and more and . . .' He wiped a hand over his mouth.

Maisie winced. It was as bad as the article had suggested, then. 'All the money you'd invested?' she asked quietly.

'It was gone. And so was the company's reputation, and my job. I was lucky, really. It could have been a lot worse. I got hauled in under caution as one of the partners – I bet the article focused on that bit – and I could have ended up in prison, like Anders. He could have faked paperwork, implicated me in any number of ways. As it was, it took a long time for the Fraud Division to believe I hadn't had a clue what he was doing.'

'I can't imagine what that was like.' Maisie's hand found its way to his forearm, and she squeezed tightly. 'How scary it must have been.'

'Pretty scary,' he admitted. 'And then, it turned out Lainey wasn't OK being with someone who'd been investigated like that, whose job and reputation were gone.'

'What?' Maisie whispered harshly, because the article hadn't mentioned that part. 'That is *not* fair.' How dare she leave him like that, at his lowest moment?

'I was tainted by association, couldn't get another job in PR out there, so . . .'

'Home,' Maisie said, surprised by how firm she sounded. 'You came home.'

'It was the only thing that made any kind of sense,' he admitted, 'that gave me a glimmer of hope. Nothing else felt right.'

She slid her hand down his arm and entwined their fingers together, and Colm let her. 'It sounds horrendous,' she said. 'To be so happy, to think that it's all going so well, then to have everything turned upside down like that, to lose so much.'

'It was a shock, that's for sure. But you know me – I bounce back. Nothing ever goes that deep with Colm Caffrey, right?'

His bitterness surprised her. 'Who said that?'

'Nobody. Forget it. Ready for me to put the pasta on?'

'No.'

He raised an eyebrow. 'Why not?'

'Who said that about you? That nothing ever goes that deep?'

'Mais, don't worry.'

'I *do*, though. Because it upset you.'

He pressed his lips together hard, so all the blood went out of them. 'Anders,' he said eventually. 'When I confronted him about what he'd done. But he was – I mean, he was looking at a prison sentence. He wasn't exactly in the best place.'

'He was a dangerous, self-centred fool, letting you, and everyone else there, suffer so much.'

'He thought he'd get away with it, that nobody would ever find out.'

'It's not true, what he said about you.'

'I know that.' Colm's tone was warmer, reassuring, as if the dark moment had passed. '*Now* can I put the pasta on?'

'You are one of the most generous, most thoughtful people I know,' Maisie said. 'And I understand that you're generally an optimist, that you take what the world wants to offer you and focus on the best bits, leave the negativity behind if you can. But I've seen it, since you've been back. I knew there was something really wrong.'

He looked down at her hand resting on his knee. 'I'm sorry I didn't tell you about it. I was ashamed, because I didn't have a clue what Anders was doing. Sometimes I thought it would have been better if I *had*. If I'd been labelled a criminal, rather than a blinkered idiot.'

'Colm, come on,' she said. 'Have you talked to *anyone* about it?'

'Dad wasn't much help. He told me to move on, try something new. He wasn't pleased I was coming back here. But I spoke to Mum, on the phone. A lot of long-distance calls between Sydney and Edinburgh when it was all kicking off, and since I've been back, Granddad. He's a wise old dog. Once he forgave me for following Dad out there, he's been . . . he's really looked after me.'

'I'm glad. And how are you . . . are you OK? As much as you want to, I can't imagine it's something you can just leave behind.'

'I'm getting on with moving on.' He gave her a hint of a smile. 'I've got these new clients, a couple of opportunities on the horizon. The hardest part is being alone here; that's when my thoughts and memories get the better of me. But Thor's great to have around, and Granddad's close by, and there's the surf. I've also been distracted by this pretty amazing woman who runs the ironmonger's, so . . . I'm doing OK.'

She squeezed his knee. 'I'm glad. And you know that I'm always here, if you ever need to talk. You shouldn't feel ashamed about what happened, and I'm a good listener. I want you to let me in.'

Colm put his hand over hers. 'You were supposed to circle back to the *pretty amazing* part of that statement.'

Her heart thudded. 'I didn't want to make it all about me.'

He laughed, his eyes brightening, all traces of sadness gone as he leaned towards her. 'You hardly ever do, Winters. And because of that, I'm going to kiss you now, OK?' He paused, his face inches from hers.

'Don't you want to put the pasta on? You seemed pretty insistent, before.'

'The pasta can wait.'

She chewed her lip, pretending to think about it. 'Oh, go on, then.'

When Colm pressed his lips against hers, shifting closer and bringing his hands to her waist, she fully expected a battle: that he was going to tickle her or grab her, do something to pay her back for her teasing. But it soon became clear he was intent on teasing *her*, but in a very different way. She shivered as his hands drifted up her arms, as one came to rest on the back of her neck. Every pulse point in her body clamoured for attention.

'Colm.' It came out as a gasp, and he pulled back to look at her.

'This OK?'

'It's very OK, only I . . .'

'What?' He pressed a kiss to the soft skin of her neck, and she had to resist the urge to hold his head just there, to experience his warm lips in that exact spot, possibly forever.

'It's just that I . . .' She couldn't say it out loud, could she?

He sat back, his hand still lingering on her arm, as if he didn't want to break the connection completely. 'We don't have to do anything,' he said. 'This can just be dinner and talking. There's no pressure, no expectations.'

She shook her head. 'I want to. Really. All I was going to say, was that . . . that I have wanted this for so long.' She let out a breathless laugh. 'You have no idea.'

'I might do,' he murmured. Then he smiled, bright and confident, and added, 'I'd better make it worth the wait, then.'

He leaned back in to kiss her, and Maisie wrapped her arms around his neck, surrendering herself to the perfect, dizzying, addictive feel of him, and wondered if any of her younger selves, aged eighteen right up to twenty-eight, would have believed anyone if they'd told her she would finally have Colm in her arms like this. She thought – even though it was hard to think, with him murmuring her name into her ear, as if he couldn't quite get his head around it either, then brushing his lips over her earlobe, her throat, her collarbone, and then lower – that the answer was quite probably: *no fucking way*.

Maisie Winters was a total cliché.

She sat cross-legged on the sofa, wearing Colm's turquoise shirt, cradling a big bowl of seafood pasta that smelled better than anything she'd ever sniffed at the Happy Shack. Colm was next to her, her knee resting on his thigh, while he wound strings of tagliatelle around his fork, back in his jeans and a grey T-shirt he'd found from somewhere.

As soon as they'd untangled themselves from each other, she'd realized she was ravenous, and Colm must have felt

the same because he'd said, '*Now* shall I put the pasta on?'
She'd finally agreed, sliding his shirt on while he pulled on
his jeans and went into the kitchen.

'This is delicious,' she said.

'I'm glad. I wanted to do something special when you
came round.'

'You've certainly done that,' she said, and he laughed.

'You have always surprised me, Maisie, did you know that?'

'In a good way, or . . .'

'Always good,' he said. '*Always*. And right now, I just . . .'
He looked down at his bowl, moved the pasta and mussels
around with his fork. 'This is the first time, since I got back
to Cornwall, when everything feels OK. And not . . .' He
put his hand on her knee. 'If you make some joke right
now about me just needing to get laid, then I don't know
what I'll do.'

'It's tempting.' Maisie gave him a soft smile. 'But I know
that's not what you mean.' If he felt anywhere close to how
she was feeling, then she got it. She didn't know quite how to
explain it, but it was as if some constantly chattering voice
inside her had calmed. Everything about being with Colm
had felt right, and now that rightness, that sense of being
exactly where she needed to be, was overwhelming.

When they'd finished eating, Colm put their bowls in
the sink, collected the half-empty bottle of wine, and
gestured for her to bring their glasses.

'Come on.'

'Where?'

'Upstairs.' He held out his hand, and Maisie took it.

She followed him up the narrow staircase, to a tiny landing
with three doors coming off it. He turned right, and Maisie

was suddenly in his room, the ceiling steeply angled above the bed, the dusky-blue covers pulled neatly across. Two windows along the far wall looked out on the thicket of trees. Colm opened one of them, letting in the fresh scent of rain, the sound of drops falling through leaves, the trill of birdsong.

Maisie noticed the small pile of books as she put the glasses on his bedside table. A Mick Herron spy thriller, a non-fiction book about ocean life around the world, and *The It Girl* by Ruth Ware.

'Ollie lent that to me,' he said, wrapping his arms around her waist. 'I've not read her books before, but I'm always willing to try new things.'

'It's a great attitude to have,' she said, her voice dropping as he kissed her neck. 'What do you suggest we try now?' She turned in his arms, and he moved his kisses to her cheek, her nose, and then, finally, her lips.

'I have a few ideas.' He blinked, and let out a low huff of a laugh.

'What is it?' Maisie asked as he undid the buttons on his shirt, the one she was still wearing.

'I never thought this would happen. You, here, in my room. Obviously, when I first imagined it, it wasn't *this* room. It was—'

'Wait.' She put her hand on his chest. 'You didn't . . . you never imagined this – us, together; not all those years ago, before you went away?'

His brows drew together, and he looked pained all of a sudden. 'I cared about you a lot more than I think you ever realized. But let's not talk about the past, or the future. I don't want to be in either of those places right now. I just want to be here, with you.'

'Me too,' Maisie said, but she got caught up on his words.

She knew, now, why his past was an uncomfortable subject, but what was wrong with the future? But then he was kissing her again, and she was sitting back, then lying on top of his bed. She let him overwhelm her, the way he kissed her, the warmth and safety, the all-consuming pleasure of being with him, and everything they'd said fell away, replaced by touch and feel, and the sound of the birds singing outside Rose Cottage, enjoying the sunshine after the rain.

Chapter Twenty-Seven

Maisie got home on Sunday evening, and wasn't sure whether she'd driven there, or simply floated. She fed Sprout, had a shower and changed into summer pyjamas, then she dialled her sister's number.

Heather answered on the third ring with, 'Yo sis, what's up?'

'I had dinner with Colm last night.'

There was a long pause, then Heather said, '*Dinner* dinner, or working on the calendar dinner, or big dinner party dinner where Colm just happened to be there?'

'Dinner at his cottage, just the two of us. He made seafood pasta, but we didn't end up eating it until much later than he intended.'

'Oh my God,' Heather gasped.

'I've only just got home,' Maisie said, and knew that she sounded a little incredulous.

'Holy hell! So it – so you . . . you and he . . .'

Maisie hardly ever heard her sister flustered, and it made her laugh. 'He likes me, Heather.'

'Obviously.'

'I wonder if he did back then, too. There were a couple of things he said . . .'

'This is amazing. Was it amazing? Was he all you ever dreamed of?'

Maisie nodded, even though her sister couldn't see. She felt a bit choked up. 'He is. He's kind and attentive and funny, and he's so – he's gorgeous, in every way. He had such a shit time in Australia. Some really awful things happened.'

'Like what?'

Maisie took a sip of water, and told her sister all of it: about the company, his girlfriend, everything he lost. The way his confidence had been shattered, and it was clear he was still trying to rebuild it, even though he sometimes came across as cocky. That, she reasoned, was why he hadn't told her about it to begin with, why she'd had to force his hand.

'But now he's in Port Karadow,' Heather said. 'He's got his granddad, and you, and all these new people you're introducing him to.'

'He has.' Maisie looked out of her window at the dusk settling over her street. 'I hope it's what he needs.'

'I think,' Heather said, 'that Colm is very lucky to have come back home to you.'

Maisie grinned, feeling warm and content, and when she finally hung up the phone, there was a message waiting for her.

Thank you for a great weekend. Can't wait to see you again – when are you free? Cx.

* * *

259

When Maisie got to Sea Brew on Monday, planning on treating herself to a flat white and a sausage roll, Lizzy was there, talking to Max.

'Hey Maisie,' Max said. 'Good weekend?'

'Lovely thanks.' She willed her cheeks not to go pink. 'You?'

'It was a quiet one, but sometimes they're the best.'

'I was just telling Max about your hotshot Colm,' Lizzy said.

'Oh?' She must be the colour of beetroot, now. 'He's not really *my* Colm. He's just . . . we know each other.' She cleared her throat when Lizzy raised an eyebrow, and Max gave her a sympathetic look. Had Ollie told him that she had kissed Colm? She couldn't imagine them having secrets from each other. 'Why is he a hotshot?'

'Martin – my husband – was in Truro the other day, at his accountant's offices. They're getting a shiny new website, courtesy of Colm.'

'Oh, yes, he's doing freelance web design.'

'And it's not stopping there, apparently,' Lizzy went on. 'Whispers abound, Maisie love.'

'What whispers?'

'That he's in high demand, has big ambitions about starting his own PR company.'

Maisie frowned. He hadn't said anything about it at the weekend. Granted, they had got rather distracted, but when he'd told her what had happened in Australia, he hadn't mentioned that he was hoping to go back to that: recreate what he'd been doing over there but with him in control.

'In Cornwall?' she asked.

'It's not very likely, is it?' Lizzy dug in her bag and pulled

260

out her purse. 'You need to be somewhere more central if you're running whole client accounts. Companies don't just want little local campaigns in Cornwall, they want to go wherever the customers are.'

'I don't think Colm wants to move to London,' Maisie said, though she didn't actually *know* that.

'How much of this is conjecture?' Max asked. 'Are you taking a couple of gossipy comments and running with them, Lizzy?'

'How dare you accuse me of that?' But Lizzy was smiling. 'From what Martin said, Colm's talents and ambitions are too big for Port Karadow. This is surely just a stopgap for a man like him.'

Maisie crossed her arms. 'What does *that* mean?'

'He's got the charisma, the confidence. Experience of working on large-scale projects, according to Liam. This isn't where he's going to end up. No offence, Max.'

'None taken,' Max said. 'Everyone's ambitions are different. But maybe we should speak to Colm, before letting the whole town know he's already on his way out.'

'You mark my words.' Lizzy took her coffee cup from him. 'Get in as many kisses as you can,' she said to Maisie. 'He'll be gone before you know it.' She said goodbye to them both and waltzed out of the door.

'Don't listen to her,' Max said. 'She loves stirring every pot going. What can I get you?'

'A flat white and a sausage roll, please,' Maisie said, but her earlier giddiness had faded. Lizzy might be a huge gossip, but she was also shrewd. She understood people, and situations, and although Maisie didn't want to agree with her, a lot of what she'd said made sense.

Colm had spent time running glossy campaigns and devising PR stunts, hosting events for magazines and sports teams. According to the *Sydney Morning Herald* article she'd read, before the fraud, his company had had a glowing reputation. Was building a few websites from his desk at Rose Cottage really going to sustain him? As Max had said, assumptions were always a bad idea, but Maisie couldn't help thinking that she already knew what Colm would say, if asked that exact question.

Around – and also during – her day job, in between serving customers, Maisie worked on the festival. Anisha had helped her plan how many stalls could fit into each location, but Maisie had been in charge of assigning everyone a spot. Moving it to Port Karadow had allowed Charlie's original blueprint to increase in size, especially since Maisie had secured the school, the town hall and the Happy Shack as locations. It was turning into a summer extravaganza, and she hoped the predicted bad weather wouldn't put visitors off from all the delights they would be offering.

On top of that, Ollie had found a company that produced mini whiteboards, and had suggested they use one of the shots of Colm to promote the calendar at the festival. Maisie didn't mind spending hours looking at photos of him, but spending time with him was even better.

On Thursday night, she was back at Rose Cottage, discovering that, far from the weekend getting any pent-up attraction out of their systems, it had been the ignition for a fire that looked set to keep burning.

Within seconds of her stepping through the doorway, Colm was pressing his lips against hers, then helping her pull his T-shirt over his head. After kissing her for what felt like hours in the cottage's narrow hallway, he managed to ask her about her day while also leading her upstairs and removing all her clothes. They fell into bed, laughing, and Maisie said, 'This is the sexiest interrogation I've ever had.'

'It's not an interrogation.' Colm pulled the duvet over them. 'It felt rude not to ask how your day was.'

'Very solicitous of you,' she murmured, as he kissed her collarbone. 'How was *your* day?'

'Entirely dull and pointless until you got here,' he said, then he proceeded to show her just how much he'd missed having her there, until Maisie's laughter was gone, and she gave herself up to other sensations instead.

'I didn't even offer you any food,' Colm said, later, when she was lying in his arms. The sun had sunk towards the horizon, and through the gaps in the trees outside his window, Maisie watched the sky turn the ethereal blue of dusk.

'I really didn't mind,' she said. 'But I am hungry now.'

'Me too. What do you fancy?'

'Let me make it. Have you got the ingredients for a toastie?'

'I should do,' Colm said, 'but you don't have to do it.'

'I want to see if I can make you forget Sea Shanty Des's toasties.'

'There are many ways that you make me forget Des, and the Sea Shanty, and pretty much everything else.'

'I'd still like to cook for you.'

'I'll come down.' He went to pull the covers off, but Maisie leaned over the bed and stilled him with a kiss.

'Stay there. I'll bring them up.' She smiled and pulled on the dressing gown hanging on the back of his door; the navy one he'd been wearing when they'd ambushed him to ask about the calendar. She remembered how nervous she'd been then, how much of a stranger he'd still seemed. She left Colm in bed and went to find the ingredients for a cheese toastie. She wanted him to know that she would look after him – if he let her – and this seemed like a simple but effective way to do it.

She had mixed grated cheddar with red onion, added tomato chutney that she'd found in the fridge, and was putting the sandwiches under the grill – hatless first, to melt the filling – when a clatter made her jump. She turned to find Thor on the counter, having slunk in through the open kitchen window.

'Everything OK?' Colm called.

She went to the bottom of the stairs. 'Thor making a grand entrance,' she shouted up. 'Everything's fine.'

She checked the grill, then watched as the cat pranced along the back of the sofa and hopped onto Colm's desk. He'd left his laptop open, and Maisie envisaged little white paws pressing some combination of keys that would do irreparable damage.

'Oh no you don't,' she murmured. She hurried over and picked the kitten up, and his paw nudged the trackpad, waking up the screen, then sent a pile of papers scattering to the floor. Maisie put the kitten next to his food bowl, and filled it with the remains of a tin of cat food she found in the fridge. 'Dinner time,' she said, and Thor started eating.

She went to pick the papers up, averting her eyes because

she didn't want to pry. But then she felt the glossy coating of a leaflet, and glanced at the title.

Rehoming Stray Cats: Advice from the RSPCA.

Maisie swallowed. He was going to give Thor to the RSPCA? She supposed it made sense, if nobody had claimed him, but . . . She put the papers in a neat pile on Colm's desk, and her eyes fell on the screen.

The name blared across the top of the webpage he had open.

Swagger and Style, PR Professionals.

There was a series of images under the heading: a giant coffee cup on the fourth plinth in Trafalgar Square; a packed event in what looked like the glass-domed splendour of Alexandra Palace; a meeting space surrounded by potted plants, with a view of the Thames beyond.

Maisie scrolled down, reading the company's mission statement, a sick feeling settling inside her. Was this where Colm was going? She felt a scratchy prickle on her back, and then Thor was on her shoulder, kneading his paws into the soft fabric of Colm's robe, his head nuzzling her cheek.

'Is he leaving again already?' Maisie whispered. 'Is he going to London and leaving us all behind, just like he did before?'

Thor purred and nudged, and she tried to take comfort from it. But then her eyes fell on the top sheet of the papers she'd just rescued. There were notes, written in Colm's looping handwriting:

Their requirements. Where I fit. Experience, knowledge, new ideas. Competition?

It looked like the jottings of someone thinking about a job application, or an interview.

Lizzy had been right, she realized, as the smell of charred toast hit her and she went to rescue the food, Thor still draped around her shoulders.

They had only given in to the simmering tension between them five days ago, but already Maisie had begun to think that Colm was back for good, that he wanted something that was more than just fun and flirtatious. It had been both those things, but it also felt to her as if it went deeper than that.

But he was looking at London PR firms, trying to find Thor a new home, so the kitten wouldn't feel abandoned when he'd gone. What about her, though? What about the fact that he'd be abandoning her for a second time? She told herself that he didn't owe her anything: they hadn't talked about what this was between them, what either of them wanted it to become.

He didn't share Maisie's values, her deep love of Port Karadow. He'd only been back for a couple of months, so it was stupid to think he'd return, after all this time, and immediately decide it was where he wanted to stay. His horizons had always been more distant than hers.

She put the toasties on plates, squirted mayonnaise on the side, and added glasses and the bottle of Prosecco she'd brought with her to the tray. Could she bear to keep spending time with him, knowing that he was on a count-down and hadn't told her? Should she leave now, start the horrible process of separating herself from him, aware that the longer she let it continue, the worse it would be when he went?

It didn't take her long to decide that she wanted as much of Colm as she could get, for as long as possible.

After all, he hadn't entirely kept his intentions from her. What had he said on Saturday? *Let's not talk about the past, or the future. I don't want to be in either of those places right now. I just want to be here, with you.*

The more time she spent worrying about how temporary it was, the less she would enjoy it. Denial, she decided, was the best course of action. She put a smile on her face, pushed open the door with her knee, and tried to ignore the horrible, uncertain ache in her stomach as she went to join him in bed.

Chapter Twenty-Eight

'Are you sure you're OK?' Colm asked her the next morning. He was drying his hair with a towel, and had another wrapped low around his waist, showing off all that delicious tanned skin that Maisie had only recently got to explore. 'If you ask Ollie to do the shoot later, then we could spend the morning together.'

Maisie sat up on her elbows. She had been hoping to keep her worries from him, to act like nothing was wrong, but she was obviously failing. 'I've got Sandy covering in the shop today, specifically so I can go and shoot Thea and Ben for the calendar.'

'But that's not going to take all day, is it?' Colm sat on the end of the bed and leaned towards her. He wrapped a hand around her ankle, and started drawing circles on the sole of her foot with a finger.

'Colm!' Maisie tried to pull her leg away, but he held firm. 'After the shoot I need to meet with Anisha, go through the final set-ups for the school and town hall. We're only ten days away from the festival.'

Colm groaned and slumped, face down, on the bed. 'Why did this have to be your busiest summer?' His voice came out muffled. 'I haven't even seen inside your house yet, all the renovation work you've done. It's your domain, and I want to explore it.'

Maisie's chest squeezed. 'When I agreed to all this, I had no idea that we'd . . .' That wasn't entirely true. She'd agreed to the projects partly to impress him, but now all it meant was that they couldn't spend much time together.

'I know.' He looked up at her. 'But it's going to get easier, right?'

'By August, I'll only have the ironmonger's.'

'Right.' He laughed. 'You'll *only* have your full-time job.'

'You're working hard too, by the sounds of things,' Maisie said. 'All those new clients.'

'Yeah.' It came out as a huff. 'Not sure this website building is going to be a long-term thing, though.'

The ache in Maisie's chest intensified. 'Oh? Why not?'

'I miss the other side of it,' he said. 'The events, the PR stunts. Getting in the thick of it with clients. I liked helping you get those venues for the festival, even though I wasn't actually doing the getting.'

Maisie nodded slowly. 'So what do you think you'll do?'

Colm sat up, and her foot felt cold without his hand wrapped around it. 'I'm not sure yet,' he admitted. 'Something will come to me, though. It always does.' He crawled up the bed, up her body, so she had to lie back

269

down. He loomed over her, his impossibly handsome, smiling face blocking out the morning sun. Maisie didn't mind: to her, Colm felt like sunlight, and she didn't want to think about how dark it would be when he wasn't there any more.

'Maisie, do you think we should have the pile of books over by that rock, or over here? Which works best?'

'Hmm?' The sea was dazzling today, the sun bright and high, washing everything with a perfect summer glaze, so Maisie knew on some level that these would be the best photos yet. On the other hand, they could be her worst, because she couldn't stop thinking about what she'd found on Colm's desk, or that he'd brushed her off when she'd asked about his plans, or the fact that he hadn't told her about the devastating thing he'd gone through in Australia, until she'd admitted to him that she'd sought answers online instead.

'Oi, Winters!' The shout was followed by a loud thump, and Maisie jumped as a book landed at her feet, sand spraying up her legs. 'What is *with* you today?'

Ollie seemed curious rather than angry, and Thea and Ben were waiting alongside her, wetsuit-clad and with surfboards in their arms, though Thea had a horrified look on her face.

'Nothing,' Maisie said. 'I'm good. What was the question?'

'I can't believe you threw a book!' Thea squealed.

'I told you.' Ollie turned to her. 'These were all in the bin at the charity shop. The actual *bin*. They're all damaged to the point of being unreadable, and they were either going to end up as salty, sandy props for this shoot, or I was going to turn the salvageable pages into paper roses I could sell at the festival, to raise more money for the RNLI.'

'It's just hard to watch,' Thea murmured.

Maisie looked at the open book at her feet, the pages reminding her of Colm's looping handwriting on the note-paper on his desk, then turned her attention to the viewfinder.

'How about if the pile of books goes here?' Ollie called over. 'We'll have them this side, the tool box on the other, then Thea and Ben in the middle with their surfboards.'

'Sure,' Maisie said.

'Or how about we just wait until the massive shark I can see circles closer, get a great shot of it munching through Ben's torso, then put that on the cover?'

'Sounds good.' Maisie adjusted the depth focus, shifting to the side so she could get better light on Ben's face.

'Right, that's it!' Suddenly, Ollie sounded cross, and Maisie looked up. Thea gave Ben her surfboard and hurried over, and a second later her two friends were standing in front of her, Ben hovering in the background, a neat crease between his eyes.

'Maisie Winters.' Ollie put her hands on Maisie's shoulders. 'What is up with you?'

'I told you,' Maisie said. 'I'm fine.'

'So you were totally paying attention when I suggested Ben should be sacrificed to a shark for the good of the calendar?'

'Oh.' Maisie felt her cheeks heat. 'No. I didn't – I'm sorry, Ben.'

He waved her away. 'Are you all right?' He looked so concerned – they all did – that a lump solidified in Maisie's throat. She tried to clear it, and an utterly mortifying half-sob came out.

'Oh, Maisie,' Thea said. 'What's happened?'

'I don't want to . . .' She kept her eyes on the imprints of Ollie's sandals, where she'd walked backwards and forwards across the sand.

'I think I only need half a guess,' Ollie said.

'What's your half a guess?' Ben asked.

'His initials are CC.'

Maisie looked up. 'Colm Caffrey. Sometimes I wonder if he's actually Liam's grandson, or one of the legends he created – a cautionary tale for anyone thinking of giving their heart away.'

Thea squeezed Maisie's arm. 'What's he done?'

'Don't we need to get on with the shoot? I have a meeting with Anisha in a couple of hours.'

'We'll have the pictures we need in no time,' Ollie said. 'But you're suffering, and I am already furious with Colm. Tell us what he's done.'

'He's been amazing and attentive, sexy and funny and sweet.'

Thea frowned, and Ollie rolled her hand. 'And . . .?'

Maisie closed her eyes. 'And I don't think he's staying in Cornwall.'

There was a pause, then Ollie said, 'Have you asked him?'

She thought of their conversation that morning, Colm's easy deflection. *Something will come to me, though. It always does.* 'I did,' she said, 'in a roundabout sort of way. He avoided the question, so I think maybe . . . he doesn't want to admit it, so he can keep seeing me for as long as possible.'

'You need to talk to him,' Thea said. 'It might not be

what you think, or it might be that he doesn't know *how* to talk to you. If he had a hard time in Australia, then perhaps he's being extra cautious.'

'I agree,' Ollie said. 'There could be all sorts of reasons why he hasn't told you what he's planning. He could be exploring any number of things.'

'He's been in touch with the RSPCA about Thor,' Maisie said. 'He wants to make sure he's looked after when he's not at Rose Cottage any more.'

Ben stepped towards their little group, easily carrying both surfboards. 'It might be that, as Ollie says, he's putting some feelers out, seeing what opportunities are available. Just ask him, flat out, what he's planning.'

Maisie gave Ben a grateful smile. 'That is the best thing, isn't it?'

'It can't hurt,' Ollie said. 'But you know we're here, OK? Whatever you need.'

'You're amazing.' Maisie hugged Ollie and Thea, then gave Ben a quick embrace too, though she couldn't get her arms all the way around the surfboards. 'Now, let's decide where to put these books and tools, and get the sexiest, weirdest shot for our calendar.'

'Sure?' Ollie's gaze was direct.

'Sure,' she said firmly.

She didn't want to admit that the thought of speaking to Colm terrified her. What if he told her he was going, and that they only had a couple of weeks left? Or the conversation forced them to have a frank discussion about what this thing was between them, and Colm told her it was just a bit of fun; that Maisie had been willing, and she'd never managed to hide her attraction to him, so he'd

273

made the most of it. That, she decided, would be worse than him leaving: him staying, but not being a part of her life in the way she wanted him to be.

Her meeting with Anisha was fun and productive, the woman the perfect combination of friendly and no-nonsense. She was happy with all Maisie's layouts, had secured the necessary permits, and saw no disasters on the horizon. With the festival planning on track, and Anisha's confidence rubbing off on her, Maisie felt better than she had done all day.

She went to pick Sprout up from her parents' house, and her mum opened the front door. She was in her dressing gown, and her hair was a mass of voluminous waves, as if she had been hanging upside-down for two hours.

'Hello Maisie.'

'Oh. Hi, Mum. I didn't realize you'd be home.'

'I do live here,' Aimee said, barking a laugh. 'There's a regional awards ceremony in Truro tonight, so I came home to get ready. Our department is up for three awards.'

'That's great.' Maisie slipped past her into the living room, and found her dad watching an old episode of *Police Interceptors*, Sprout asleep on his lap.

'Hey love,' he said. 'How did it go with the planning people?'

'Really good, thanks.' Maisie sat on the arm of the sofa. 'It looks like moving the festival here was the right thing to do.'

'You're organizing it, are you?' Her mum had moved to stand in front of the mirror, and was threading a dangly earring into her lobe.

'I'm helping,' Maisie said. 'Charlie can't have it in Porthgolow, because there are these summer storms and high tides forecast, and it was supposed to be on the beach.'

'Glorious right now, though,' her dad pointed out.

'Yes, but the festival's still ten days away, and it's better to plan for the worst-possible scenario.'

'You know,' her mum said, 'you should be in charge of the whole event. You flit here and there, divide your attention between a hundred different things, but if you put your mind to it, I expect you'd be able to achieve rather a lot.'

Maisie tried to take it as a compliment. 'Thank you, but I just like to—'

'Otherwise, you're never going to hold onto a man.'

Maisie blinked. 'What?'

Aimee looked at her in the mirror, her lips glossy red, her eyes hard. 'Colm Caffrey. He's not going to be here long, by all accounts: going for some high-powered job in London. I suppose, when it came to it, there wasn't enough to keep him here.'

Maisie could feel her dad looking at her, but she didn't want to turn her head. She thought that, if she moved a single muscle, it would break the dam holding in her emotions. 'Why are you so cruel?' It came out as a whisper.

Her mum turned around. 'What did you say?'

'Why do you have to be so cruel?' She stood up. 'Why does it make you so happy? You're my mum, you're supposed to be supportive.'

'I *am* supporting you.' Aimee folded her arms. 'You need tough love. The softly softly approach doesn't work with you.'

'The softly softly approach doesn't work for *what*, Mum? What is it you think I need?' She held a hand up in front of her. 'Oh, I know. You think I should be a human rights lawyer or living in New York, doing something you can tell your friends about without feeling embarrassed, because running the family business, looking after the people in this town, isn't worthwhile.

'I know you think I'm not reaching my potential, but what I would really like is for you to listen to me, understand what *my* goals are, rather than yours. I am happy with my life, and I don't think it's too much to ask that you respect that!'

'Love . . .' her dad started.

'Look at the evidence, Maisie,' Aimee said. 'Gemma, your best friend, moved away the first chance she got. Heather is in America. Colm came back for ten minutes and, surprise surprise, he's off again. Sometimes, you have to realize that what you're doing isn't enough. The smart thing is to recognize it, then do something about it.'

Maisie swallowed. 'The only person I'm not good enough for is you. I never have been, so now – you're right – I'm going to do something about it. I'm going to stop even *thinking* about your warped expectations, let alone try to live up to them!' She pulled her sleeping dog off her dad's lap, her back tweaking as she lifted him. 'Come on, Sprout.'

'Maisie love,' her dad called after her, but she couldn't stay there another second.

She yanked the front door open and stepped outside, her breath coming in bursts, tears pricking her eyes. As she put her sleepy, befuddled dog on the pavement, attached his lead to his harness and strode away, she thought it was telling that her mum hadn't chased after her. She cared more about being late for her sparkling awards ceremony than she did about her own daughter.

The only problem was, Maisie realized, as she walked towards the warm embrace of her house, some of what Aimee Winters had said might actually be true.

Chapter Twenty-Nine

The fight with her mum sat, like clotted cream, in Maisie's stomach for the rest of the day. That evening she had a text from her dad, apologizing on Aimee's behalf, saying that the restructure at work wasn't as clear cut as it first seemed, and there was some question about her role in the department.

Through her anger and disquiet, Maisie felt a pang of sympathy. That job, and the status it afforded her, meant a lot to her mum, and if that was being threatened, it made sense that she would turn a spotlight on Maisie. But, she told herself, as she walked to the Happy Shack the next morning, it only made sense because it was her mum, who was already primed to tell her how much of a disappointment she was.

Saturday in Port Karadow was busy, as it should be when the sun was warm and bright. People had always flocked to the beautiful seaside town, with its harbour and beaches, pubs and shops and idyllic cobbled streets. They came to it in droves; they didn't abandon it like rats from a sinking ship.

Marcus had asked to meet Maisie to discuss his final menu and the stalls he would be hosting. He'd been surprisingly positive about the festival branding, so she had high hopes for this meeting. Of course, he'd called it on a Saturday morning, which she thought was a power play, but she wasn't going to question it.

Her phone vibrated in her bag, and she pulled it out.

Let me know when you're done with MB. We could spend the day on the beach? Cx

Maisie's stomach twisted. It sounded perfect – sunbathing and swimming, or surfing, if you were Colm, eating ice cream, letting the sun warm their skin. She knew she should start distancing herself from him, to try and make it easier when he left, but she couldn't. She was about to reply when the door of the Happy Shack swung open.

'Are you coming in or not?' Marcus barked.

'I've only just got here.'

'I don't have all day.' He stepped back and she walked past him into the restaurant, dread settling in her stomach at his sharp tone.

'Here.' Marcus gestured to a table. He was wearing a black polo neck and jeans, and his expression was just as dark.

Maisie sat down and took out her iPad, opening the plan she'd emailed him the day before. Marcus sat opposite her.

'You've put the doughnut stand in our function room,' he said, without preamble. She noticed there had been no offer of a drink this time: no Aperol Spritz or tiny, potent espresso.

'That's right,' she said. 'It's a new company, over in Porthmellow. Their flavours are to die for.'

'We have a doughnut dessert on our menu.'

Maisie scrolled through her plan. 'Not on your festival menu. I have it here. It doesn't say—'

'No, on our *regular* menu.'

Maisie pressed her lips together. 'OK. But that week you'll mainly be running the festival menu. If it's just one dessert, and it's bound to be different from—'

'I stated that I wanted *no* conflicts. No crossover between my restaurant and the businesses we're looking after.' He jabbed a finger against the table.

'I really don't think that one pudding option—'

'It's a very popular dessert. Warm, crispy doughnuts filled with hazelnut cream, dusted with vanilla frosting and drizzled with a salted caramel sauce.'

'It sounds delicious,' Maisie said. 'But also—'

'How many people will choose something else if they can get a doughnut from the function room? In fact, how many people will leave dessert off their order altogether, if they know they have options so close by, options where the flavours are "to die for"?'

'Marcus.' She tried to keep her tone gentle. 'If the doughnuts aren't here, they'll be in the school, which is a ten-minute walk away. And if people are coming here for lunch or dinner, they'll want the whole experience. Also, it's just one week: a week which will bring more people to your restaurant anyway.' She knew, as the words left her mouth, it was the wrong thing to say.

'My restaurant has bookings all the way to November.' He leaned forward. 'There is *nothing* wrong with my popularity.'

'Then you shouldn't feel threatened by a tiny doughnut stall run by a brother and sister. We want to support everyone: the big fish and the little fish.'

Marcus shook his head. 'Who else can I speak to?'

'What do you mean?'

'Someone more senior on the festival team.'

Maisie straightened her spine. There was a burst of laughter from outside, a group of friends taking the path down to the beach. 'I'm your contact,' she said. 'I can make all the necessary decisions. I—'

'What about that Colm bloke?'

Maisie stilled. 'Sorry?'

'Colm. I'm sure that's his name. Said he was part of it, that he could help if I needed it. I'd like to talk to him.'

'Colm has nothing to do with this.' Maisie's mind was racing. 'Are you telling me you're not happy with Dainty Doughnuts being in the Happy Shack? If so, I'll get them moved to the school.'

'You can't remove them from the bill altogether?'

'Marcus!' Maisie could feel anger rising inside her, at his selfishness, and at whatever Colm had done to take away her authority. 'You are the *biggest* fish, a big barracuda, and I would really appreciate it, and so would Charlie and Anisha, and everyone else in this town, if you could be a barracuda who *supports* the minnows instead of eating them.'

He gave her a steely look. 'No doughnuts in the Happy Shack. Move that, and we'll be OK.'

'*Will* we now?' Maisie shot back, her patience frayed. 'Fine. I'll get Dainty Doughnuts moved, and let you know who we're putting in their place. I'll be in touch.' She stood up.

'Good to see you, as always.' Marcus offered her a smile that was chillingly genuine. He really was a sociopath, she thought, as she pushed open the door of the restaurant, grateful for the sunshine and the familiar cry of the seagulls, and walked straight into Colm.

'Hey.' He squeezed her arms. 'Where's the fire?'

It was an exact replay of when she'd come flying out of the Arthurs' house and he'd been running past. Then, she'd been trying not to give into the feelings that had resurfaced the moment he'd returned. Now, she had him, and yet there was so much uncertainty, so much confusion, that she felt as if he was slipping through her fingers.

'Did you tell Marcus Belrose that he could go to you about festival decisions?'

'What?' Colm frowned. He was wearing navy shorts and a grey T-shirt with a Sydney motif, the city name in bright blue with a yellow and peach sunset image below it.

'Marcus said he wanted to speak to you,' she told him. 'We're doing something he doesn't like, and he wanted to go over my head – to you!' She laughed, because it was ridiculous.

Colm shook his head. 'I didn't . . .' Then his eyes widened. 'I bumped into him, when I was on a run. He was overseeing that banner being put up.' He pointed to where a long banner hung over the veranda railings, advertising the Summer Indulgence Festival and the Happy Shack's prominent role in it. 'I said everything looked good for the festival, he asked if I was involved, and I said I knew you and could get a message passed on if he needed me to. That is *all* I said, I swear.'

Maisie huffed. 'Unsurprising that he would interpret that as you being senior to me. I don't think, in his world, women are capable of being in charge.'

'Are you OK?' he asked. 'You seem . . .'

'Frazzled? Upset?'

'Both of those things. Let's go and get a coffee.'

'I can't. I need to let Anisha know we're moving things around, then I need to tell Dainty Doughnuts and the honey stall that they'll have to swap places. Marcus can't moan about having a honey stall under his roof, can he? Unless he has some kind of Cornish honeycomb delicacy on his menu that I don't know about.'

'Hey.' Colm slid his hand up her arm. 'Let's go and get a drink.' His fingers drifted to the base of her neck, and he massaged it in a way that made her want to melt.

'I have stuff to do.'

'It can wait thirty minutes.'

'But it can't though, can it? I have to get everything done *now*. I have to sort out the festival and finish Ollie's photo shoots, and I somehow have to do all that around my real job *and* fit in time with you, before you go off to wherever it is you're going next and leave me behind.' She turned away from him.

'What are you talking about?' Colm tugged her shoulder but she resisted, hugging herself instead. She hadn't meant to blurt it out like that.

'Maisie?' When she didn't turn around he walked around her, so he was standing in front of her on the path. 'What do you mean, *before I leave you behind*?'

'You told me that you miss your old job, that designing websites isn't what you want to do. That . . . all this,' she gestured at the beach below them, the restaurant, the town spread out behind them, 'that it's not enough.'

Colm swallowed. 'It's not . . . I don't want to design

283

websites forever, but why do you think that means I'm leaving you behind? That I'm leaving?'

'Because *everyone* has said so, and because—'

'Everyone who?'

'Lizzy, and my mum, and—'

'No offence, Maisie, but do you really trust them over me? I know Aimee's your mum, but do you really think she'd know more about my life than I do?'

'So why didn't you tell me, then?'

'Tell you what?'

She shook her head. 'You mean you have absolutely nothing to tell me, about your house or your cat or your career prospects?'

Colm's expression softened. 'Don't you trust me, Winters?'

'That's not an answer, Colm.'

He looked away, squinting down at the beach.

'Colm?'

When he turned back, his jaw was tight. 'I can't . . . I need a bit more time.'

Maisie's hands started tingling. 'A bit more time to pluck up the courage to tell me you're leaving? Just like you left me to go digging online to discover this huge, horrible thing that happened to you, rather than telling me yourself?'

'Maisie—'

'Now you need a bit more time with me before you start your new life somewhere else? Are you going to go without telling me again? Leave me in the dark, so you can keep things uncomplicated?'

'Of course not!' His gaze hardened. 'It's not like that, and I'm *not* leaving, but I'm also – I need to sort a few things out before I know if it will work.'

'If *what* will work?' She stepped towards him. 'Why can't you tell me? Don't you trust *me*?'

'I trust you,' he said, 'but I need things to be right first, OK? After everything that went down with Anders . . .' He ran a hand through his hair, huffed out a breath. 'I have to be sure that this is what I want.' He squeezed her hand, his fingers warm around hers.

'I knew this was too good to be true,' she said, her mum's words rising to the front of her mind. 'People warned me. But I thought that you really liked me, that you wanted to be with me, and that maybe we could . . .' She stopped herself. She didn't want him to know just how far she'd let her fantasies run away with her.

'I *do* really like you,' Colm said. 'I always have – more than you know. Before I left, before Dad gave me that ultimatum, I was working up the courage to ask you out.'

Her laugh was watery. 'Oh *sure*. Then I didn't hear from you for a whole decade? It must have been a serious attraction.'

Irritation sparked in his eyes. 'My parents had just got divorced, I wasn't in the best place – and I was thousands of miles away! I thought it would be pointless, more painful for both of us if I got in touch. I had to look forwards, not backwards.'

'Why do you think you need to lie to me? It's not like this has been a thing between us for more than half a second!'

'I'm not lying, Maisie.' He tightened his hold on her hand. 'I wouldn't do that to you.'

'But you haven't been fully honest with me. You didn't trust me with what happened in Australia.' She stared at the floor. Her eyes and nose were burning, the tears threatening. 'Mum was right.'

'What did she say?'

She looked up, surprised at the anger in Colm's voice. 'She said . . .' It hurt to repeat it, but she felt like she had to. 'She said I wasn't enough for you to stay.'

'Maisie!' He laughed. 'That couldn't be further from the truth.'

'But you won't tell me what's going on.' She shook her head. 'I just don't think that . . . I don't think this is working.'

She felt him stiffen, saw the stillness fall across his broad shoulders, while his cheery T-shirt rippled in the breeze. 'We've just started getting to know each other again. And I promise, I *promise* you,' he pressed his palms together, as if he was praying, 'I will talk to you as soon as I can. But you know that things haven't been easy for me. I need to show myself, let alone everyone else, that I can do this. That I can make something of myself and not completely fuck it up.'

She nodded, even though the swell in her throat felt almost too big to breathe past. 'I get it, Colm. I understand that Port Karadow isn't big enough for you.'

'That's not what I mean. It's important for me to . . . I don't want to let you down.' He dropped his hands to his sides, and his expression was so sad, so lost, that she had to fight the urge to pull him against her and hold on tight. But she couldn't ignore what he was doing, what had happened in the past. She had to protect herself.

'It makes sense,' she said. 'You need to sort yourself out, and I have loads to do, too. We just aren't in the right place for this.'

'You can't mean that. When we're together – I'm not imagining that you've been as happy as I am. Can you just trust me, please?'

Maisie thought of that night in the pub, all those years ago, when he'd said what she wanted to hear and then left the country for a decade. She thought of the newspaper article she'd read, the shock of seeing his name associated with a major fraud. The things she'd found in his cottage: the plans he was making to get rid of Thor, to start a new life in London, and the fact that he couldn't even admit it to her.

'I'm sorry.'

He took her hand. 'Don't do this, Maisie.'

She squeezed once, then let go. 'I need to get going. I need to sort out this festival mess.'

'You can't—'

'See you around, Colm. Don't leave again without saying goodbye.' She was surprised at how bitter she sounded.

She strode up the hill, away from the beach and the shimmering sea, and her own, personal sunshine that was Colm Caffrey. She could feel the storm clouds gathering, could sense someone watching her from inside the Happy Shack. Well, what did it matter? If Marcus Belrose had witnessed it all, then honestly, why should she care?

She'd almost reached the top of the hill when she heard Colm call out.

'I'll prove it to you, Winters! I'm going to make you see just how much you mean to me!'

She didn't turn around, didn't pause for even a second.

'I'm not giving up on us!' he shouted.

As Maisie stomped through the town, past happy families

and sunburnt groups of friends enjoying a blissful Saturday, she wished that she had the faith to believe him. The problem was, she was all out of belief in him and, more importantly, in herself.

Chapter Thirty

With every step away from Colm, Maisie felt like she was losing more oxygen. She could turn around right now and go back to him – she'd heard what he'd shouted up to her. But she knew that if she did that, it wouldn't feel right. Nothing, at this moment, felt right.

She couldn't fall head over heels for Colm if he wasn't planning on sticking around, if Port Karadow wasn't where he wanted to end up, if he didn't want to let her in. The only problem was, she realized, she already had.

She walked on towards the town hall, trying to turn her attention to Marcus Belrose and his aversion to Dainty Doughnuts. The hall was holding an exhibition of work by local painters and, as Maisie stepped inside, she was captivated by a large canvas showing an intense summer sunset, the sea so vivid that she could imagine stepping into it. The painting was of one of the smaller coves, rock-clustered and secluded. Doughnuts, annoying chefs – and even, for a few seconds, Colm – slipped from her mind as she stared at it.

'Crumble did that bit in the corner,' a voice said behind her.

Maisie spun to find Finn smiling at her. 'This is yours?'

He rubbed his hand across his neck in a rare moment of uncertainty. 'What do you think?'

'It's magnificent. Crumble didn't really help, did he?'

Finn pointed at the bottom corner, the texture of the dark rock impressively realistic. 'I held him up, pressed his paw against it. If you look closely, you can see.'

Maisie peered at the canvas, spotted the doggy pads, and laughed. 'I can't believe you did that!'

Finn shrugged. 'My art's for me, first and foremost, though selling it has its perks.' He smiled gently. 'I write the name Red somewhere on every painting, too.'

Red, Maisie knew, was his nickname for Meredith. 'Like a secret message,' she murmured.

'Exactly. They make them more complete, somehow. It's good to see you,' Finn went on. 'I didn't realize you knew about the exhibition.'

'I didn't, actually. I'm on a festival mission.' She held up her iPad. 'But I'm stalling, really. I need to call Anisha and then this poor doughnut company, then I need to go and placate Marcus Belrose.'

'Sounds like a tough schedule. Are you OK, other than that?' He glanced behind her, to where a group of people were jostling to look at his painting and the ones next to it. He gently took her arm and pulled her to the side.

Maisie puffed errant curls off her forehead. She hadn't realized how hot it was inside the town hall. She'd need to make sure it was properly ventilated during the festival, unless the bad weather also came with sub-zero temperatures.

'I'm fine,' she said.

Finn raised an eyebrow.

'I've had a bit of a day,' she admitted. 'A few crappy days, actually. Family stuff, work stuff, man stuff.'

'Would the *man stuff* have to do with a certain estate owner's grandson, by any chance?'

'It would.'

'I've heard he's not staying around for long.' Finn's tone was gentle.

'I've heard that, too. That's the problem.'

'What does Colm say?'

'Colm says that he needs to "sort stuff out".' She put air quotes around the last three words.

Finn winced. 'Ah.'

'He hasn't actually said that he's moving away, but he won't *talk* to me. And I get that he's had a rough time, but I can't let myself feel things, imagine that it's all going to work out, and then just be . . . left behind.'

Finn squeezed her arm. 'I'm sorry. He seems like a good guy, from the little I've seen of him, but it's not fair of him to mess you about.'

Maisie rubbed her cheek. 'I don't even know if he is. But he needs to figure out what he wants, and while he's doing that, I don't think he can focus on a relationship, too.' She felt disloyal saying it, because he'd been attentive, wholly with her whenever they were together. But he was still keeping things from her, and that told her he wasn't ready for whatever they'd set in motion to turn serious.

'Give him a bit of time, maybe? He might figure things out and realize you're at the top of his list of priorities.'

'He might,' Maisie said with a sigh. 'I just have a feeling

that, by the time that happens, he'll be a long way from Cornwall.'

'I'm sorry.'

'You're lovely. Thank you, Finn.'

'Anything I can do – me or Meredith – you know where we are.'

She nodded. 'I hope you sell your painting.' She waved goodbye and stepped out into the sunshine. There was no point in delaying it any longer; she had some phone calls to make.

Anisha stayed calm while Maisie explained the situation, but there was a tightness in her voice that suggested she wasn't exactly delighted at Marcus Belrose's behaviour. Penny at Dainty Doughnuts said she didn't mind where they were, they were just happy to be part of the festival, and Maisie wished she'd recorded the conversation so she could play it back to Marcus as an example of how to behave.

Afterwards, with the sun at its highest point, she sat on a bench by the harbour and updated the plan on her iPad, then made the other calls she needed to make. She was dreading going home, because it would only remind her that she could have been on the beach with Colm, and thinking about Colm at all made her feel guilty and confused.

There was only one thing left on her agenda for today, and that was to go back to the Happy Shack, and tell Marcus Belrose that he'd got his way. She got up, sighing as if she was eighty-two rather than twenty-eight, and walked along the beachfront path.

Lunch service was about to begin, and there were people hovering near the restaurant entrance like bees, waiting for friends or looking at the framed menu by the door. Devon was on front-of-house duty, and Maisie gave him her brightest smile.

'I need to see Marcus.'

'He's busy in the kitchen.'

'This will only take two seconds of his time, and I promise he'll be pleased.'

'Tell me what it is, and I'll pass the message on.'

'I'm afraid—'

'Maisie, what are you doing here?'

She closed her eyes for a beat, then turned to greet her mother, who was sitting at a table near the bar with four other women, wearing a sleek cream sundress. There was a bottle of champagne in a bucket on the table.

'Hi Mum,' she said. 'I'm here to see Marcus.'

'I just heard that man tell you he wasn't available.'

'It's fine. I'm just sorting out a few things for the festival.'

'Liaising with the cake and jumble sale stalls?'

'No.' Maisie took a deep breath. 'I'm setting up the vendors, making sure everything fits, and that they all have what they need.'

Her mum frowned. 'I thought Anisha was doing that? She's ever so capable.'

The lump bobbed back into Maisie's throat. This was not the day for her mum to go on the attack: she couldn't deal with it on top of what had happened with Colm.

'Have a nice lunch, Mum.' Devon was talking to a young couple who were about to be seated. Maisie waited until he was free, then said, 'Can you please tell Marcus I'm here?'

Devon looked at her, glanced at her mum, then disappeared in the direction of the kitchen.

Maisie prayed that he would hurry up, but she heard her mum clear her throat behind her. She'd come to stand next to her at the bar.

'Maisie?'

'What is it?'

'What I said to you, yesterday.'

'Which bit?'

'About Colm, and him not wanting to stay here.'

'You mean when you said I wasn't enough for him, and that wasn't a surprise?'

Aimee's eyes widened. 'I didn't put it like that.'

'That's pretty close to the words you used. It's not something I'm likely to forget.'

Aimee squeezed Maisie's arm. It didn't feel as comforting as when Finn had done it. 'I'm sorry,' she said. 'I was stressed. We'd just had a difficult meeting at work.'

Maisie relented slightly. 'I'm sorry your job is under threat.'

Her mum took her hand away. 'Of course it's not. Who said that? No, it's just got a smidge more complicated. These restructures can be tricky to navigate, and I have to support Phillip. But I shouldn't have said that about Colm. If he really *does* like you, then I'm glad.'

Maisie looked at the floor. She wanted to get this meeting over with, take Sprout home, not have to talk to another human being for a good few hours.

'Unless—' Aimee started.

'Make this quick,' Marcus said.

Maisie had never been so happy to see the chef in her life.

'I have moved Dainty Doughnuts to the school,' she told him. 'They were more than happy to accommodate your demand, and I've put the Cornish Honey Farm in their place. I've also confirmed with Charlie and Anisha that the Happy Shack and its festival menu will be mentioned whenever we make an announcement using the loudspeaker – within reason – and Thea has ordered extra stock of your cookbooks, and would love to arrange a time with you to get them signed.

'I'll let you know as soon as we've confirmed Charlie's plug on local radio, and I've asked if you can have your own slot. We'd also love you to open the surfing competition on the Saturday, if you're available.' She took a deep breath. 'How does that sound?'

Marcus scratched his bearded jaw. 'You've been busy.'

'We don't want any disgruntled participants,' she said smoothly. 'Especially not when they're as important as you: you're a key part of this event. The Cornish Honey Farm was over the moon to be relocated to your function room.'

'That all sounds excellent. Thank you, Maisie, for going into bat for me.' There was a gleam in his eyes she hadn't seen before.

'You went into bat for yourself,' she reminded him. 'I just took your demands and made them happen.'

'The sign of an excellent team player.' He grinned. 'Can I get you a drink?'

'No, thank you.' Did Marcus have any idea what a team player was? 'But I'm glad I was able to help.'

'You've worked wonders,' he told her, then turned on his heel and went back to the kitchen, hot steam and enticing smells wafting out in his wake.

'Marcus seemed impressed.' Her mum was still standing by the bar.

'I did what he wanted.'

'He's not an easy man to convince, by all accounts.'

'Don't I know it.'

Aimee sipped her champagne. 'You're not with Colm any more, are you?'

And there it was. Half a second to focus on her success, then back to the failures. 'Bye, Mum.'

'I'll see you tomorrow for Sunday lunch!' Aimee called as Maisie yanked open the restaurant door and stepped into the sunshine. The prospect of Sunday lunch with her parents was about as appealing as being locked in an oubliette for a week.

She walked quickly away from the Happy Shack, Marcus Belrose, her mum and the place where, a few hours earlier, she had flung all her fear and uncertainty at Colm. She had to get home, so she could try and make sense of it all. She was halfway there when she realized Sprout was with her dad. For a moment, she'd forgotten about her little dog, but now he was all she wanted: his warm, soft fur, his non-judgemental gazes, his unconditional love.

Maisie changed course, heading for the comfort of her beloved pet. It wasn't until she'd collected him and was safely on her way home that she started to cry.

Chapter Thirty-One

When Maisie woke on Sunday, her eyes were gritty from lack of sleep, and she felt hollowed out by sadness. At least, this morning, she was heading somewhere lovely. She still had a to-do list (as she always did, these days), but she could try and put her glum thoughts aside for a couple of hours, stop hovering over Colm's number on her phone.

She drove along the coast road, and it wasn't long before the curve of Porthgolow beach appeared below her, the sea a deep, enticing blue, the waves white-tipped and frothy.

She parked in the car park, put Sprout's lead on, and walked across the sand to the Cornish Cream Tea Bus. It was still early, and Charlie had said they'd have the bus to themselves before she opened. Maisie marvelled at how shiny it was, its red paintwork glowing, colourful bunting tied to the upper windows and looped around the large wing mirrors. Its name was emblazoned on the side in gold, glittery paint, the sparkles catching the sun.

The door was already open, the most tantalizing smells wafting out. 'Hello!' She knocked on the open door, then climbed aboard.

'Maisie!' Charlie pulled her into a hug. 'Thank you so much for coming – we could have met in Port Karadow on Tuesday, when I've arranged to walk through the main locations with Anisha.'

'I wanted to come,' Maisie assured her. 'To go through the plan, and to see this.' She gestured at the compact café, with its serving area, oven and coffee machine near the front, the tables adorned with vases full of wildflowers, fairy lights strung up around the walls. 'It's so beautiful.'

'Thank you.' Charlie beamed. 'What can I get you to drink?'

'A flat white would be lovely.'

'Coming right up. And I've got some chicken and ham rolls cooling. Are you up for being my guinea pig? It's the first time I've made them.'

'I am totally up for that. I don't think I've ever had a chicken and ham roll.'

'Like little pies, but with a sausage roll shape and pastry. They might be awful.'

'They don't smell awful.'

'Which means I've passed the first test, at least.'

Charlie busied herself making the drinks, and as Maisie sat down, Marmite, the badly behaved Yorkipoo, came running down the aisle.

'Sprout,' Maisie warned, but the two dogs sniffed each other, circled in the tight space, then hopped up onto a bench together. 'Wow.'

'What's that?' Charlie said.

Maisie pointed. 'It looks like they've made friends.'

298

'I did not expect that,' Charlie grinned. 'I have to show Daniel.'

Maisie thought she would get her phone out to take a photo, but instead Charlie called his name, and a moment later there were footsteps on the stairs.

'He's been doing paperwork,' Charlie told her. 'He said he wanted to do it here because a colleague's using his office at the hotel, but I think it's because he wants one of my new pastries.'

'It's because I don't want to be away from you,' Daniel said. 'Hi, Maisie.' She stood up and he gave her a tight hug. He was all muscle, and smelled of something spicy and expensive.

'Hello.' She decided she wouldn't be intimidated by his cool handsomeness, and an image of freckled, smiling Colm flashed into her mind. 'Our dogs are getting on.' She gestured to the bench.

Daniel laughed and shook his head. 'Charlie says you've done a great job with the festival.'

'I've just moved a few people around.'

'Maisie,' Charlie said sternly. 'You have moved everyone from this beach to somewhere in Port Karadow, ensured most of them have cover if the weather's bad, and got the entire town excited about it. That's a whole lot of effort.'

'Anisha's been brilliant,' Maisie pointed out.

'Anisha's organized the licences and permits,' Daniel said. 'She would never have had the time to relocate every vendor, and she hasn't been dealing with Marcus Belrose, either.' He gave her a knowing look.

Maisie wrinkled her nose. 'I just wish he'd use his confidence for good, instead of evil.'

'He's just really . . . pleased with himself,' Charlie said, bringing the drinks and a plate of chicken and ham rolls to the table. 'But he's a huge asset to have, so I really appreciate you dealing with him.' She sat down opposite Maisie.

'Are these ready?' Daniel asked.

'Do you think I would have brought them over if they were still raw?'

'Great.' He ignored her sarcasm and sat next to Maisie. 'Can I stay?'

'Why? To keep an eye on me?' Charlie asked.

He shrugged. 'Maybe.'

Charlie glared at him, then pushed the plate towards Maisie. 'Have one.'

She did as she was asked. As she bit into the crunchy, buttery pastry, then a juicy, delicious filling of generous-sized pieces of chicken and ham, she saw the couple exchange pointed looks.

'I can step outside if you need a minute,' she said.

Charlie shook her head. 'It's fine. Daniel's just being . . .'

'A caring husband?' he suggested.

'Are you OK?' Maisie asked.

'I'm absolutely fine,' Charlie said firmly. 'But I am so grateful to have your help. When I heard about the weather, I thought I'd have to cancel the whole thing. Everyone's so busy – Lila and Sam have got long days of filming this summer, Hannah and Noah have just got engaged, but then – you're doing so much, too. You've got this, and Ollie's photo shoots, all squeezed in around your day job, haven't you?'

'But they're fun things,' Maisie said, 'and I have reliable staff I can call on at the ironmonger's. And I know Port

Karadow like the back of my hand, so I'm well placed to help out.'

'You've lived there your whole life?' Daniel asked.

'I have, and I don't want to be anywhere else, so anything I can do to help it thrive, then I'm all in.' She took out her iPad, scrolling to her plan. 'There's still time to change the locations of things if you want to, so I thought we could go through it.'

'Perfect,' Charlie said. 'Though I can't see why I'd want to change anything.'

After talking Charlie and Daniel through what she'd done, where everyone was placed, they discussed the surfing competition that would happen on the Saturday if the weather played ball. The summer storms, and especially the predicted tidal swell, could work in their favour, but if the rain was torrential it could still be a washout.

Charlie sipped her tea, the scent of peppermint wafting across the table. 'I'm so relieved, about all of it. You've saved this for us, Maisie.'

'A week-long festival was always going to be ambitious,' Daniel said, 'but don't forget you've got Port Karadow *and* Porthgolow behind you, now.'

'You have,' Maisie agreed. 'Aside from Anisha and the planning team, there's me and Ollie, Meredith and Thea – they'll rope their menfolk in, too. We've got a small army of helpers if we need them.'

Charlie smiled. 'And what about your manfolk?'

'Is that what we are now, *manfolk*?' Daniel said.

'Who do you mean?' Maisie reached for another chicken roll. Comfort food was the order of the day, and this was too good to leave on the plate.

'That guy who came to the photo shoot, who had the idea for our cream tea in the sea set-up – Colm, wasn't it? From the way you were talking, I thought you were together.'

'Oh no,' Maisie said. 'I mean . . . we were. For about five minutes.' She laughed awkwardly. 'It hasn't worked out how I'd hoped.'

'I'm so sorry.' Charlie squeezed her hand. 'I'm sorry that you're going through that, on top of everything else.'

'This is great for taking my mind off it,' Maisie said. She thought of the words Colm had shouted as she'd hurried away from him. 'We couldn't be what we wanted for each other – not right now, anyway.'

Charlie gave her a gentle smile. 'Maybe, once the festival is over, when things have calmed down for you, that might change. I mean,' she glanced at Daniel, 'things aren't always what they seem. A man might give you mixed signals, make out that he dislikes you and everything you're doing, so that whenever you see him you get totally enraged . . .' Daniel rolled his eyes, '. . . then it actually turns out he's been pining for you ever since he met you.'

'I wouldn't say *pining*, exactly,' Daniel said.

'I would.' The smile Charlie gave him was so full of love and mischief that Maisie got a bit choked up.

'Fine,' Daniel muttered. 'I was sick over you: I could hardly think about anything else. But it worked out in the end.'

'I'll say. Anyway.' Charlie turned her attention to Maisie. 'Things might not be right with Colm at the moment, but if you care about each other enough, then you'll find your way back to each other.'

'Maybe,' Maisie said, mustering up a smile.

Charlie seemed to have everything together, with her

302

thriving business, her caring and handsome husband, her idyllic life. Before this summer, Maisie had thought her own existence was fairly idyllic, but now she'd had a taste of being with Colm – the man who, if she was honest with herself, she had never managed to forget – she felt as if, without him, her life would be lacking.

But she couldn't let her relationship with Colm be all on his terms, waiting like a puppet to find out what he was planning to do with his future, then slotting neatly in to whatever that happened to be.

She smiled at Charlie, then Daniel. 'Thank you both, so much.'

Charlie laughed. 'What for? You're the one who deserves all the thanks. I feel a bit pathetic, I should be doing more, but—'

'But you need to look after yourself,' Daniel said firmly.

Maisie glanced between them. 'Are you really OK? You haven't had one of your own pastries yet. Is it—'

'I'm fine,' Charlie reassured her. 'Just coping with a bit of sickness at the moment, not feeling as on top of things as I usually am.'

'Oh.' Maisie frowned. 'Have you had it checked out? I mean—'

But then she stopped, seeing Charlie and Daniel's twin smiles, the way he slid his hand over the table and held hers.

'Oh my God!' Maisie said. 'You're adding a little baby Harper to your Porthgolow dynasty?'

Daniel laughed, and suddenly his happiness was unconfined, all that cool restraint vanishing. 'We are,' he said. 'A little baby Harper.'

'Things are about to get even busier,' Charlie added, her smile wider than Maisie had ever seen it. 'So you can see why we're so grateful for all your help. You really are saving this summer for us – we don't know what we would have done if you hadn't stepped in.'

Chapter Thirty-Two

Maisie left the Cornish Cream Tea Bus full of purpose. She was doing a really good thing by helping Charlie with her festival, considering her and Daniel's news. It also hadn't hurt that Charlie had been so complimentary. It made her feel able to frame her part in the festival in a different way, as something worthwhile, rather than consisting of little more than a hastily drawn-up plan and a few conversations with local businesses.

She needed to stop viewing her actions through her mum's eyes, she acknowledged, and see them through her own. She would also, until the festival was over, have to shut Colm away in a locked box in her mind. Her sadness was just below the surface, and it felt like it was affecting everything, seeping into her bloodstream like a slow-release poison. But she couldn't let it. There was one week left until the festival opened its doors, and there was a whole lot to get done.

*   *   *

The next few days felt oppressive, both because Maisie's to-do list stretched from early in the morning until late each evening, and because the crisp summer days had been replaced by thick humidity and squally showers, the two alternating like a tag-team. It seemed the storms that Charlie's meteorologist had predicted were really on their way.

She was gazing out of the rain-splattered window of Thea and Ben's house, at the cliff tops and the tumultuous sea beyond, trying to order her thoughts, when Scooter, their Australian Shepherd, put his head in her lap. She stroked the dog's nose.

'You look worn out,' Thea said, from the sofa opposite.

'I'm OK,' Maisie replied. 'Everyone's places are fixed, and all the permits are sorted, so the next few days are about fielding problems and answering questions. There are going to be a lot of people coming into Port Karadow with a whole lot of stuff, and even though Anisha's made sure the school car park is available, it's still going to be chaos.'

When Anisha had mentioned the use of the school car park, Maisie had gently asked if she would be happy to talk to Jeremy about it. She didn't want him to backtrack on their agreement at the last minute, leaving them in dire straits.

'I know from the bookshop that organizing a single event involves a huge amount of work,' Thea said. 'Ollie is a whirlwind, but a lot of the time she has to be, to get everything done.'

'Looking effortless takes a lot of effort,' Ben said, from beside Maisie. He was looking at the Screwfix website and jotting things down in a notebook. She wondered if it was more supplies for Marcus Belrose's kitchen.

'Is everything else OK?' Thea pressed, her dark eyes concerned.

Maisie smiled. 'Has the grapevine been working overtime?'

Thea blushed. 'I know that you and Colm had got close, that at the beach that day you were worried about what he was doing, and then Finn mentioned—'

'That I'd ended it?' Maisie finished.

Thea nodded.

Maisie sipped her lemonade, giving herself time to think before she replied. 'It's all too uncertain,' she said. 'I don't think he's got himself properly settled, which is understandable since he's only been here a couple of months, and coming off the back of a really tough time in Australia. We rushed into things, that's all.'

'But you like him a lot,' Thea said. 'It was more than just a rekindled flirtation.'

Maisie swallowed. 'What makes you say that?'

'Ollie, mostly.' Thea shrugged. 'And it was noticeable, how . . . happy you've seemed, over the last few weeks, since he's been here. And how you're not as happy any more.'

'I don't want to get hurt,' Maisie admitted. 'I do like him a lot, of course I do.' She thought it was more than 'like', but she wasn't prepared to admit that to anyone right now, not even herself. 'But if Colm isn't going to stick around, if he's going to be miles away again, then it can't possibly work between us.'

'Colm's really not staying?' Ben sounded surprised.

'I don't think so,' she said. 'He's in his granddad's dated cottage, and he's muddling along with a business he's not enthusiastic about. There's surfing, the countryside and beaches, which I know he loves, but it's not like Port Karadow is the only place he has access to those things.'

'But there are some things that are *only* in Port Karadow,' Thea said. 'Family. Friends. *You.*'

Maisie shrugged. 'Shall we go through your programme for the bookshop? I just need the schedule for now, to make sure there won't be any loud music clashing with your events, and that you've got everything you need.'

Thea smiled. 'You sound so professional. You should do this for a job.'

Maisie laughed. 'I'm actually looking forward to being plain old Maisie Winters of Port Karadow Ironmonger's, after this and the photo shoots are over.'

'You're not enjoying it?'

'It's been fun, but so hectic, too. It does feel good to be contributing to something that's going to bring enjoyment to the town, and revenue and exposure to our businesses.'

'Meredith was saying that Charlie's so relieved, that she wouldn't have been able to juggle everything in Porthgolow with the bus, as well as getting the town ready. Apparently there's going to be a surfing competition, if the weather's OK?'

'There's a big swell forecast for the final Saturday, which will make for some spectacular surfing, according to the people who know about these things.'

'Won't that be dangerous?' Ben asked.

'Surfers love it, don't they?' Maisie said. 'If the waves are small and harmless, then there's no point in them going in.'

She felt a flutter of unease when she thought about Colm and the dramatic weather supposedly on its way. He was unfazed by the water, but she didn't like to think of him out in Australian seas for all those years, where sharks, stingrays and other deadly things lurked below the surface. At least he was here now, where it was marginally safer.

'They're all idiots,' Ben said.

'Says the man who posed as a surfer for Ollie's calendar.' Thea grinned at him.

'I don't think anyone's going to check our credentials,' Ben argued. 'That's not really the point of it, is it?'

'Oooh.' Thea turned back to Maisie. 'Has Ollie got the mini whiteboard sorted?'

'Yup.' Ollie had emailed her the day before, forwarding her the dispatch confirmation, which included the photo she'd chosen to encourage people to pre-order the charity calendar.

'And . . .?' Thea drew the word out.

Maisie got out her phone, opened the email and held it out. 'Here it is.'

Thea took it, her eyes widening. 'Woah.'

Ben leaned forward to look at it too. 'I mean, that is definitely going to prove popular with some people.' He shot Maisie a look.

'Yeah,' she said, sounding as defeated as she felt.

Of course she'd seen the photo. She had seen all the photos, because she'd *taken* them all, had spent hours poring over them, editing the ones with potential, ensuring they got the most out of the lighting, the dramatic backdrops, the figures in the foreground.

The one that Ollie had chosen was of Colm walking out of the sea, wetsuit tugged down to his waist, exposing his strong, tanned torso and all those kissable freckles. He had a half-smile on his face, but was glancing off to the side, as if he didn't realize he was being snapped. He looked incredible.

'Colm Caffrey wetsuit model,' Thea said quietly. 'Who knew, huh?'

Maisie scoffed. 'He certainly did. He set up this whole scene.'

When Thea replied, she sounded sad. 'He's really not staying in that beautiful cottage? Not building a life here, with his runaway kitten and the ocean so close to his front door?'

Maisie was about to give another vague reply, when Ben answered for her.

'Either he's staying for longer than you think, or he's paying Liam back for his generosity by making Rose Cottage more appealing to a new tenant.'

'Why's that?' Thea asked, and Maisie turned towards him.

Ben looked up from his iPad. 'He's asked me to quote him for a kitchen extension. Whether it's for him or someone else, he's helping Liam bring his secluded cottage into the twenty-first century.'

Chapter Thirty-Three

A brand-new kitchen, Maisie couldn't help thinking, as she walked through town over the next couple of days, checking the stall locations, ensuring the guardians of each building were still on board with the plans she'd emailed through. And not just a kitchen, but a kitchen *extension*, she mused, as she sat at the counter in the ironmonger's, going through her list of festival attendees in the quieter moments, phoning them to confirm they had all the supplies and information they needed; that they knew where to come, where to park, what the timings were for every day the festival was running.

Colm Caffrey had asked Ben Senhouse, one of Port Karadow's premier builders and current contractor for Marcus my-kitchen-is-my-temple Belrose, for a quote on a kitchen extension at Rose I'm-going-to-get-eaten-by-wolves Cottage.

Was he planning on staying and turning the cosy cottage into a home? But no, she thought. No way. She could picture him in a stylish bachelor pad, all granite worktops and glass walls, but not that snug, characterful cottage. Every time she'd been there with him, it had felt temporary. Or had she just felt that way about their relationship, because she couldn't get her head around the fact that it was more than a long-held fantasy?

She'd pressed Ben for more details, but he'd had little to tell her, beyond the fact that it was likely to be a complicated job due to the cottage's age and probable restrictions, but that the barn conversion where Ollie and Max lived might have set a precedent.

Maisie had even more questions than she'd had before her trip to Thea and Ben's house, and the only way she could find out for sure was to speak to Colm. She couldn't do that, however, because she had so much to focus on right now, and what if she asked him, and he told her that he was acting as project manager for his granddad, but wasn't staying beyond that? It would crumble the emotional brick wall she'd built for herself, and then she would let Charlie and Daniel – everyone – down, by being a wreck instead of a calm, collected festival organizer.

She already had a voice in her head telling her she'd given up the best thing she'd ever had: her chance at a future with the only man who'd made her truly happy. If she spent any more of her time and energy on Colm-related reflections, she wouldn't be fit for anything.

By the time Monday morning, and the first day of the festival came around, her thoughts were as unstable as the weather, which was veering between bright sunshine, high winds and short, forceful downpours, the forecast over the next few days suggesting that things were only going to get worse.

Her task for the first morning was to visit the school, town hall and Happy Shack, to make sure that the stall-holders had settled in OK. Her ringtone was set to ear-splitting, as her phone number was on the information pack given to all vendors, and she anticipated a day of firefighting, dealing with the teething problems that always happened at big events like this.

The town was vibrant and full of people, as if the gusting wind had spurred everyone into action, and she couldn't remember the last time Port Karadow had been so busy, noisy and colourful. Most of the businesses along Main Street had tables outside their doors, selling their festival specials. Cornish Keepsakes had an offer on picnic hampers, and Maisie had put together a summer garden package, including garden lights and barbecue sets, which Sandy and Parker would sell while she was on festival duty. Whenever the weather got too much, they could easily bring everything inside.

'Maisie!' Meredith called from outside Cornish Keepsakes. She was standing behind her display of hampers, the wicker baskets full of cookies, bottles of local gin, packets of bunting, fudge and cutlery sets. 'How's it going?'

'It's predictably busy, but no disasters so far.' She peeled a sticker off a sheet and handed it to her friend. It read *Summer Indulgence Festival.* She'd had them made up specially, and was giving one to all the contributors. 'Here you go.'

Meredith laughed. 'You don't do things by halves, do you?'

'I can't right now – not if this is going to go well.'

As if in answer, the clanging of halyards from the boats in the harbour reached them on the wind, reminding Maisie that their biggest challenge was going to be the weather.

'It'll be great,' Meredith assured her. 'Everyone's happy and content.' She said hello to a couple who had approached her table, and Maisie left her to it, not wanting to get in the way of a sale.

She popped her head into Sea Brew, where there was already a long queue, and Max waved at her and went back to making coffees. So far, Maisie thought, as she reached the bottom of the hill, then took the lane that would lead her to the primary school, so good.

She tried not to be too smug as she reached the school doors, the building caught up in the familiar bustle and chatter of a busy event. Groups of friends walked out clutching paper bags, one woman corralled three small children, all of whom were munching on doughnuts, and a man went inside carrying large sprigs of pampas grass, which Maisie didn't even try to understand.

Penny and Lance waved from the Dainty Doughnut stall, and Maisie waited for a break in the queue to check on them.

'It's going well, then?' she asked, as she gave them each a sticker.

'Great so far,' Lance said. 'We're really well placed: the footfall's been continuous.'

'I'm so glad.' Maisie breathed a sigh of relief. 'And honestly, being out of Marcus Belrose's sightline might be a blessing.'

'He's been charming whenever we've eaten there,' Penny said.

'That's because you were paying customers. But,' Maisie added, not wanting to be unprofessional, 'when I swapped things around he was fine, and he's brought some great publicity to the festival.'

'Where's the Cornish Cream Tea Bus?' Lance asked.

'Gertie – that's the bus's name – is down by the harbour for the week,' Maisie said. 'I'm hoping it won't get blown into the water.'

'Nah.' Lance waved a hand. 'A vintage Routemaster isn't going to budge. I think we're all safe.'

'I hope you're right.' Maisie realized the queue had built up behind her, so she said goodbye and moved swiftly along.

She had made her way around most of the stalls when she saw Jeremy, looking authoritative in a crisp white shirt and grey trousers. He was surveying his kingdom, a pinched expression on his face. Maisie took a deep breath, and walked up to him.

'Hey,' she said. 'It's looking great in here.'

'Isn't it? We've been nonstop since we opened at nine.' He glanced at his watch, and she saw surprise flit across his face when he realized it was almost eleven. That was the thing about events like this: when it was busy, the time flew by before you'd had a chance to blink.

'You've got some good stalls for the school,' she went on, gesturing to one side of the hall where there was a bake sale, a bric-à-brac stand, and a jewellery stall selling bracelets made out of sea glass, manned by a couple of the older girls and their mums. 'I'm sure it'll be worthwhile for you.'

Jeremy finally looked at her. 'It will be. Mr Fielding is, as you can imagine, very glad to be a part of it. Glad that I've been able to organize all of this.'

Maisie chewed the inside of her cheek. He had done nothing more than agree to it, finally, to tell her when the doors would be unlocked, share copies of the building risk assessments and fire plans, and let her use the school tables and chairs. He'd arranged precisely three stalls that would raise money for the school wildlife area, and yet – of course – he'd organized *all of this*. But she had spent enough time arguing with him.

'That's great, Jeremy.' She gave him her brightest smile. He was managing to look put-upon and superior all at once, and she felt a spike of anger. Not quite sure how to deal with it, she peeled off a sticker and jabbed it over his breast-pocket. 'There you go. Call me if there are any issues, but with you manning the place, I'm sure it will all be perfect.'

She hurried towards the exit, keen to leave, when she noticed one last stand next to the door. She had it on her list, but it hadn't lodged firmly in her mind, because her telephone call with the organizer had been brief and, she remembered, hampered by wind, their words broken into bits.

Now she saw that it was Lizzy, and one of her teenage sons – Maisie could never remember their names – and their table was covered in a myriad of crocheted figures: crabs and octopi, avocados and cauliflowers, even a crochet wheel of camembert. Looking closer, she saw that some of the items were a bit haphazard, but they were all colourful, they all had faces, and they were – unanimously – cheerful.

Maisie walked over. 'Lizzy, hi! I had no idea . . .' And then she saw the sign, made out of wood, on the front of the table. It read: *Mrs Arthur's Crocheted Creatures*. 'What is this?' she asked. 'Mrs Arthur's not well enough to . . .?'

'No,' Lizzy said, her bright smile fading slightly. 'She's still very poorly. But that didn't mean her tradition had to end.'

'But . . . how has this happened?'

'It's happened, because when you get word out in this town, oftentimes you can muster up an entire army,' Lizzy said proudly. 'And when we learnt that there was a summer festival taking over Port Karadow, and that Mrs Arthur wouldn't be able to make any of her famous crocheted animals, we swung into action.'

'But who thought to . . . I mean, when did this all . . .?' She tried to swallow the lump in her throat, and picked up a little, sky-blue surfboard. Its crocheted body was soft, its slightly wonky smile entirely friendly.

Lizzy didn't reply immediately, and when Maisie looked up, the older woman gave her a knowing, almost smug, smile.

'Mum,' her son said, sounding slightly impatient, 'these guys want a whole fruit bowl. I don't think we've got a bag big enough.'

'We do have a bag, Simon.' Lizzy reached behind her and pulled out a large brown paper bag that contained more paper bags, all folded in half, with strong carrying handles.

Maisie recognized the customer from the school gates, though her children had never been in her class. 'Hello.'

'They're just wonderful, aren't they?' the mum said. 'And with all the money going to a cancer charity, too.'

'They're beautiful,' Maisie agreed. She was still clutching the surfboard, which she had already decided to buy. 'And it's such a worthwhile cause.'

Simon took the paper bag from his mum and – with more grace than Maisie had considered a teenage boy could have – lowered the crocheted fruit into it, peering in as he did, as if they were real apples and peaches and he didn't want to bruise them.

The mum exchanged a smile with Lizzy as she paid for her items, then handed the paper bag to her daughter and led her to the doughnut stall.

'I'd like this one please.' Maisie handed her squishy surfboard to Lizzy.

'Looks like it was made for you.' Lizzy gave it to Simon, who put it in one of the smaller bags.

'I love it,' Maisie said, as she got out her purse. 'And you haven't explained, yet, whose idea this was.'

Lizzy had a gleam in her eye. 'What if I told you,' she said, 'that this whole thing came about because Colm Caffrey came to me and said he wanted to raise money for a cancer charity, and this is how he wanted to do it, to honour Jeannie Arthur. That he had no crocheting skills himself, but he wanted to find people who did.'

'I would say,' Maisie replied, though it was quite hard to speak when she was on the verge of tears, 'what the hell? And also, are you messing with me? *Colm* did this? But how – why?'

'I'm not messing with you,' Lizzy said, her smile softening. 'He told me about Jeannie, though of course I knew she was unwell, and said he wanted to do something for her.'

'When was this?' Maisie asked.

'A few weeks ago, just after the festival was announced. Ordinarily, I would have said it couldn't be done at such short notice, but then I hadn't banked on the charm of the man, or the loyalty he inspired in some of the older women in this town, who remembered him when he was a confident, helpful teenager.'

'He hasn't . . .' But Maisie didn't know how to finish the sentence. She clutched the paper bag containing her surfboard, which had suddenly taken on a whole new level of significance.

'I think he wanted to surprise you, Maisie love,' Lizzy said gently. 'Wanted to get it done under the radar. I don't think Jeannie Arthur was the only one he was thinking of when he put his plan into action.'

'OK.' She couldn't manage anything else.

Lizzy reached over the table and put a hand on her arm. 'He said that he'd been reminded of something since he got back; something he didn't think he'd ever forget again.'

'What's that?' Maisie croaked out.

Lizzy's smile was positively gleeful, now. 'He said that someone he cared about reminded him that he was back in Port Karadow, and that he couldn't get away with living a solitary, quiet life here: that he needed to be fully invested. He said that this was one way he could think of to show that he was.'

Maisie, hearing her own flippant words repeated back to her, the ones she'd said to Colm outside Mr and Mrs Arthur's house on that warm spring afternoon all those weeks ago, couldn't think of a single thing to say in reply.

'I was convinced he was heading out of here, moving onto other things,' Lizzy said. 'I thought this was just a kind gesture he wanted to set in motion before he left. But now I'm wondering if I got it wrong, because it looks to me like he's relearning what it means to be a part of this place.'

Well, Maisie thought, as tears threatened to overwhelm her. She *definitely* didn't know what to say to that, so instead she said, 'Lizzy, Simon, do you want a dainty doughnut? I'm buying.'

They both replied in the affirmative, and Maisie went back to the doughnut stand clutching the little paper bag containing the crocheted surfboard, which felt like a talisman now, against her chest.

Chapter Thirty-Four

'I still have Mrs Arthur's cauliflower, you know.' Heather's voice sounded loud on speakerphone. 'And now you have Colm's surfboard.'

'Colm didn't *make* the surfboard,' Maisie protested, but it was half-hearted, because without him, it wouldn't exist. She had it with her now, in her compact cross-body bag, as she strode through town, on her way to drop Sprout off with her dad for the second day of the festival. The wind was stronger than yesterday, and the smell of impending rain mingled with the usual sea-salt freshness.

'Colm may as well have made the surfboard,' Heather said, echoing her own thoughts. 'Colm is, in all kinds of ways, responsible for you having that cute little woolly surfboard.'

'How are you so awake?' It was just after four in the morning in New York.

'My event finished an hour ago, and I've only just got home. It was a food-themed ball where the waiters were dressed as different dishes. Mr Macaroni Cheese was particularly handsome, if you could look past his costume.'

Maisie laughed. 'You had a waiter dressed as *macaroni cheese*?'

'He was one of the least ridiculous,' Heather said, and Maisie could hear the pride in her voice. 'But that's not what we're talking about. Colm is as charming, and as kind-hearted as ever. He's got the whole of Port Karadow under his spell, all the women making crochet cuddlies for him, and you had him in your *bed*, Maisie, and what did you do?'

'Technically, I was in *his* bed,' she said. 'We weren't together long enough for him to come to mine.'

'But he wanted to?'

Again, she thought of his shouted words as she'd left him by the Happy Shack: *I'll prove it to you, Winters! I'm not giving up on us.* 'I think so.'

'And you told him you didn't trust him?'

'He's leaving. All the signs are there.' Except she couldn't help thinking about what Lizzy had told her. 'He said he had to figure things out, and I have to figure things out, too—'

'What, exactly, do you have to figure out?' Heather's voice was sharper than Maisie could remember hearing it. She had reached the end of her parents' road, and her sister's words brought her up short.

'What I'm going to do.'

'About what?'

Maisie opened her mouth to speak, but nothing came out.

'Because, Maisie,' her sister went on, 'it seems to me that

you've always had it figured out. You've followed your own path, and you haven't let anyone stand in your way, even when there were some pretty forceful people trying to. You always loved the family business, and – OK – you gave teaching a go, but when you decided it wasn't for you, that Dad and the shop needed you more, it was like everything slotted into place.

'And even though Mum is constantly on your back, you haven't let her change your mind. You love Port Karadow, you love being involved in community projects like the calendar and this festival, and – from my perspective, which I totally get is a geographically distant one – the only thing that seemed to be missing, was having someone, a soul mate, to share it all with.'

'Women don't need men to—'

Heather growled down the phone. 'Don't you dare spout all that feminist stuff about women not needing a man to be complete. This isn't about need, it's about want. What *you* want. There's nothing wrong with wanting someone to share everything with, someone you can love and who loves you back, someone to have great sex with, to be intimate with in all kinds of ways. And you've never had that, because you've always been hung up on Colm.'

'Heather.' It came out as a groan.

'I mean it. I often thought that your past relationships haven't worked because there was a little bit of you thinking, *this isn't Colm*. And now, Maisie . . .' She laughed. 'You *have* him. Or you *had* him, anyway. He came back and he came to you, and you pushed him away.'

'But he's leaving.'

'Has he ever actually said that?'

Maisie sat on the low wall of one of the houses. She hoped the owner wouldn't come out and shout at her. Sprout sat on the pavement next to her, his warm body against her bare shin. Above her, the last bit of sunshine was blocked out by cloud, and a light drizzle started to fall.

'He said there were some things he wasn't ready to tell me,' she admitted.

'And isn't that allowed?' Heather asked gently. 'Especially after everything he lost, the way his confidence was stomped on in Sydney? Have you told him about your few hopeless dates with Jeremy?'

'I told him we went on some.'

'But does Colm know the details? Or about that cheating wanker Gavin the gardener?'

'No,' Maisie admitted. 'But we were only just starting to get to know each other again. It would have felt weird if I'd given him a full rundown of the last ten years right away. That happens over time.'

She waited for a response, but her sister's reply was silence, so Maisie was left to replay her own words back in her head. 'I asked him outright what he was doing,' she protested.

'And he's got some reservations about telling you right now, which I understand is hard. But from what you've said to me, it's because he wants to be careful. He lost his savings, his job – his whole life. Surely a bit of caution on his part isn't a reason to give him up completely?'

Maisie huffed out a breath. 'I hate it when you're so wise.'

'You must hate me all the time, then,' Heather said, and Maisie laughed. 'Seriously, though. You and Colm: on some level, I knew you were always meant to be. Just talk to him, OK? Lay it all out on the table.'

'What if it's too late?'

'If it's too late, then he was never that serious about you in the first place,' Heather said. 'But I get the feeling that you won't need to worry about that.'

'But what if I—'

'Talk to him, Maisie. This is Colm – the man of your dreams. If you don't want him to leave, if he really is planning on doing that, then you have to try and do something about it. You can't let him get away.'

By the time Maisie had dropped Sprout off and walked back to the Happy Shack, the drizzle had solidified into a downpour. There was a parade scheduled for later that day, but Charlie had planned it so everyone taking part had to have brightly coloured umbrellas as part of their costume. She had thought of all the ways the entertainment could still happen despite the weather, but Maisie was worried that, while the umbrellas would guard against the rain, they would be destroyed by the accompanying wind, especially down by the harbour where it was most exposed.

She checked the Facebook page – Charlie was using it as an up-to-date source of information, posting any plans altered by the conditions. It looked as if the parade, for the moment at least, would be going ahead.

One thing that wouldn't fall foul of strong winds was the surfing competition, and as Maisie sheltered under a shop awning while she checked for any new messages, she felt an uneasy twist in her stomach. Was Colm planning on taking part? She couldn't imagine him not being involved, but since their argument, they hadn't been on messaging terms, let alone speaking ones, so she didn't feel comfortable asking him.

Marcus's restaurant was open for breakfast as well as lunch and dinner during the summer and, as Maisie reached it, the Edison-style ceiling lamps shone out in the morning gloom, showing off how busy it already was.

She pushed open the door, aware that she was dripping everywhere, and got her first surprise when Devon gave her a warm, genuine smile.

'It's good to see you, Maisie.'

'Uhm, you too,' she said cautiously. 'Is everything OK?'

'It's great! Let me get Marcus for you.'

'All right.' She hovered by the bar, wiping her face with a tissue, and smiled at a couple who were at one of the nearby tables. The woman had sleek, shoulder-length hair dyed a beautiful lilac shade, and the man's kind eyes and unruly chestnut mop made him seem instantly friendly.

'Did I hear him say you were Maisie?' the woman asked.

'That's right. Do I know you from somewhere?'

'No, but we know about you. I'm Ellie, and this is Jago. We're friends with Charlie and Daniel, and she told us that she had someone on the inside, someone who's moved her entire festival from Porthgolow to here.'

'It's lovely to meet you.' Maisie shook their hands. 'I was able to help, because I know Port Karadow so well, but Charlie had already done the groundwork.'

'Without you, I don't think we'd be having a festival at all.' Jago gestured outside to the beach, where the waves were taller and fiercer than Maisie had seen them for years, and the rain was still coming down hard.

'I honestly think that—'

'Maisie Winters!' Marcus's voice boomed out, his arms raised to the sky, and most of the patrons turned in his direction.

Maisie straightened her spine. 'Marcus Belrose. What can I do for you today?' She prayed fervently that he wasn't about to chew her out in front of his full restaurant.

Instead, she got her second surprise when he clasped her shoulder and turned her, so she was facing the tables, then draped an arm around her. 'Everyone, this is Maisie Winters. She's one of the festival organizers, and she asked me to be a part of it, so she's indirectly responsible for this incredibly special, delicious menu you're all enjoying.'

She had to give it to him: his confidence knew absolutely no bounds.

'Maisie,' he continued, turning towards her, 'I had one of my most successful days yesterday, and last night I was contacted by a producer at the BBC.' She noticed he kept his volume up, so his words carried to the four corners of the room.

'They saw the festival coverage?' she asked.

Marcus grinned. 'And heard me on Radio Cornwall, talking about the event, the importance of community and how that fits in with my ethos.'

Maisie tried very hard not to snort. She had listened to Charlie's slot on Radio Cornwall, talking to the wonderful Tiffany Truscott, but hadn't been able to listen to Marcus, too. It sounded like she'd made the right decision: if he'd been banging on about how much community mattered to Port Karadow, when he'd made her move a start-up doughnut business because they threatened a single item on his not-even-serving-it-this-week dessert menu, she might have thrown her radio out of the window.

'And you've got a TV show as a result?' she asked.

His shrug was all nonchalance. 'They want a pilot to begin with, my agent's hashing out the details, but it looks like the Happy Shack is going to cement Port Karadow's reputation, put this place on the map.'

'It's already on the map,' she heard Jago say dryly, and offered him a quick smile of solidarity.

'Anyway, my darling,' Marcus went on, 'this wouldn't have happened without your good instincts, your understanding of what I, my food and my restaurant, could bring to the festival. It's a win for both of us.'

'As long as you paint Port Karadow in a positive light, then I'll be happy.'

'It's my home, as well as yours. But I was wondering if – when it comes to it – you would be interested in doing the segment about the town? You've been here your whole life, and it wouldn't hurt the ratings having your sunny smile on screen.'

'I . . . what?'

'Nobody better to sell Port Karadow to a national audience.' He didn't give her a chance to respond, to consider the offer or to find out what, exactly, it meant. Instead, he turned back to his customers. 'Three cheers for Maisie Winters, everyone! A shining star in Port Karadow's constellation. There is nobody more dedicated to the town than this girl.' He pulled her in for a sideways hug.

She thought she could *almost* forgive him calling her 'girl', because he might have just offered her a role on his TV show, which she couldn't even begin to think about now, but the recognition was certainly nice. And he was right about her being dedicated to the town. She'd do everything she could to see it thrive, even if that meant cooling her frustration with a certain award-winning chef who thought Cornwall's happiness revolved around him and his food.

It also helped a bit that, while the clapping and cheering – which was as much for Marcus as it was for her – went on, Jago gave her a gentle eye-roll and mouthed, 'Well done' at her. She decided that, on this occasion, she would take all the praise that was offered to her. She thought that she might, actually, deserve it.

Chapter Thirty-Five

Maisie felt buoyed by Marcus's ostentatious show of praise, and by his understanding of her loyalty to Port Karadow even if, when it came down to it, the offer of being involved in his TV show didn't come to anything. The fact that he'd recognized her part in the festival at all, and wanted to reward that in some way, made her think that he wasn't an entirely self-centred person.

The other thing she kept thinking about, as she walked through town on Wednesday, reassuring and trouble-shooting as she went, was her conversation with Heather. Sometimes, her sister being thousands of miles away, and having the perspective of being at a certain distance, had its benefits. Colm was here, and – despite the rumours she'd heard, and the evidence she'd found in Rose Cottage – he had never said that he didn't want to be with her. Whatever his future plans were, he was still in Port Karadow, and he wanted to spend time with her. All she'd done over the last few days was waste that opportunity.

She walked up Main Street, checked on Sandy and Parker at the ironmonger's stand, and discovered that they had sold most of the garden sets. Cornish Keepsakes was also busy, and Maisie popped her head in and waved to Meredith, who was wrapping a beautiful glass bowl in blue tissue paper.

The rain and wind kept up a steady assault – the stand selling waterproof ponchos must be making a killing – and Maisie had resigned herself to never quite being dry over the next few days, despite her own waterproof jacket.

As she walked and chatted, soothed and checked, she realized she hadn't seen Colm since the festival had begun. Had he stayed away from it entirely? Was he busy building websites, he and Thor sheltering from the weather in Rose Cottage? Was he psyching himself up for the surfing competition?

Her fingers itched to text him, but she was the one who had walked away. And right now, she didn't have the time to talk everything out with him. After this weekend, her days would be clearer, and then she could do what Heather had suggested: lay all her thoughts, her fears, out before him.

She dipped into the town hall, where the majority of stalls were arts and crafts. There were intricate paintings in minute frames on table-top wooden easels; delicate silver earrings studded with turquoise stones; pottery made by a local artist who had a kiln on her farm. There was a stand selling pet accessories, leather and fabric harnesses and collars in every colour and pattern imaginable, and food and water bowls that could be personalized.

'Maisie!' The woman manning the stall was Helly, a regular in the ironmonger's. 'How are you?'

'I can still feel my feet, just about,' she said with a laugh. 'Is it going well here?'

'Brilliantly,' Helly admitted. 'People want to spend a lot of money on their pets, which I fully endorse.'

'You have beautiful things.' She stroked a red, white and purple tartan jacket, the material deliciously soft against her fingers.

'Sprout would love that,' Helly said.

'Sprout would look like a little king,' Maisie admitted. 'And you're doing engraving?' She pointed to the workstation the other woman had set up behind her stall.

'Of course. It's much more personal than those machines you get in pet shops.'

'I'd love a new tag for Sprout. Could I have this one, shaped like a bone?' She picked up a silver tag, big enough for her dog's name and her mobile number to fit. His current one had been in the sea so many times it was rusting over.

'Absolutely.' Helly took it from her. 'I've just finished one for your friend.' She grinned, her deep brown eyes sparkling.

'Which friend? Ollie, Thea or Meredith? Or is it Lizzy?' She knew a lot of pooch-loving people who would happily spend money on their furry companions.

Helly picked up a small tag from her workstation, and handed it to Maisie. It was a pretty copper colour, and she felt its cool smoothness against her palm. She read the engraving, and felt something shift in her chest.

There, on the little copper oval, was the word *Thor*. It was followed by a number that she knew — because she'd put it into her phone that day outside Mr and Mrs Arthur's house, had made him repeat it to make sure she'd typed it in right – was Colm's.

She was so distracted when she walked out of the town hall that it took her a while to realize her phone was ringing. She pulled it out of her bag and pressed answer, wondering what the problem was. Maybe someone had parked their van somewhere they shouldn't, or one of the food trucks had been overcome with rain, causing their electric to short; or perhaps Marcus Belrose's good humour had subsided and he had found some fault with one of the vendors using his function room. But – no, not that last one. She was being unfair to him by even thinking it: she and Marcus had turned a corner. Maybe it was—

'Maisie? Maisie, are you there?'

'Mum!' Her voice was loud with surprise. 'How are you?'

'I'm very well, darling. What about you?'

'I'm good. Busy. The festival's in full swing, so . . .'

'I know that,' Aimee said, impatience edging into her voice. 'I'm at the shop.'

'Why?'

Her mum tutted. 'Mr and Mrs Arthur need more bird-seed, and your dad has a bee crisis on his hands. Something about them swarming, or . . . God, I don't know what it is.'

'Oh no! Poor Dad.'

'He seemed perfectly jovial when he went up there, donning that strange white uniform. It looked like he was thoroughly enjoying the drama. Anyway, as you have so much on your hands, I thought I'd do the delivery for the Arthurs.'

'Right,' Maisie said, thinking of sweet, gentle Horace. 'Do you want help?'

'To take round some sunflower hearts and a bucket of fat balls? I have done this before, you know.'

'Of course,' Maisie said, but she'd totally forgotten, until that moment, that her mum *had* been involved with the shop, doing deliveries and sometimes working behind the till, when her dad was still in charge. She'd often been there on Fridays, her day off at the council, chatting and laughing with the customers in a way that seemed almost alien to Maisie, handling problems with cool efficiency. How had she forgotten that? 'I have a bit of time free, though,' she went on. 'I could come with you?'

There was a pause, then her mum said, 'If you wish.'

'Great. I'll be there in three minutes.' She was close to Main Street, and everything seemed under control. Still, she gave Charlie a quick call, the festival matriarch sounding entirely in her element. Maisie explained that she was running a quick errand for the shop, even though she and Charlie had been doing their own thing, only checking in at the beginning and end of each day unless something critical came up.

'Do what you need to do,' Charlie said, the sounds of her busy café in the background. 'It's all going so well.'

'Thanks, Charlie.' Maisie hung up and hurried to the ironmonger's.

'Pop this in the boot,' her mum said, when Maisie stepped through the door.

Maisie took the bucket of fat balls, and Aimee, carrying a big bag of sunflower hearts and a smaller one of mealworms

– which always made Maisie shudder – followed her out. Of course, Aimee had parked her Mercedes A-Class in a side road that had been designated as *Keep Clear* for festival traffic. She looked stylish and cool, and at least ten years younger than she was, in cut-off jeans and a loose white shirt.

The boot slid open, and Maisie put the bucket inside, then took her mum's bags and put those in, too. Then she got into the passenger seat and her mum started the car, the vents puffing out a gentle heat that, despite the time of year, was very welcome.

'All going well, then?' Aimee asked, pulling away from the kerb.

'It's pretty seamless so far,' Maisie said, then worried she'd jinxed it.

'You know what Phillip says?'

'What's that?'

'That seamless only happens when behind-the-scenes teams work.'

Maisie pressed her lips together.

Her mum glanced at her, then looked back at the road. 'He's not the best at penning motivational quotes,' she admitted. 'He had the right idea, but it's not really pithy, is it?'

'No,' Maisie said, letting out the laugh she'd been holding in. 'No, it's not.'

'Bless him.' Aimee chuckled, and it soon turned into a full-blown laugh, her knuckles white on the steering wheel, Maisie experiencing the unusual thrill of a moment of camaraderie with her mum. The drive was mercifully short, and it wasn't long before they were pulling up outside the

Arthurs' house. Maisie's laughter died as quickly as it had arrived.

Her mum switched the engine off and turned in her seat. Without the gentle puff of the car's heater, the silence seemed incredibly loud.

'What I meant just now,' Aimee said, 'though I can see how it got lost, is that if the festival is a success, then it's only because the organizers have worked incredibly hard. These things don't happen without a huge amount of diligence and planning. I've organized away days for county councillors, so I know what goes into a large-scale event, and how oblivious some people are to the effort involved.' She put a hand on Maisie's arm. 'I don't want to be one of those oblivious people. I know how hard you've worked.'

'You . . . you do?'

Aimee's smile was rueful. 'I do, Maisie. I heard about Marcus Belrose's speech; I've been around the town, along the harbour. The way Sandy and Parker seem entirely at ease on that stall outside the shop – I know that's all because of you.'

'Not *all* of it,' Maisie said. 'Charlie—'

'Charlie would be submerged under water on Porthgolow beach if it wasn't for you. And another thing,' her mum said, before Maisie could reply.

'What other thing?'

'This comes from me, rather than Phillip.' Her smile softened. Her eyes were startlingly blue, her lashes always feathered in inky mascara. 'The energy you get from anguish can only keep you going for so long, and I don't want you to crash.'

Maisie frowned. 'But—'

'All I'm saying,' her mum went on, 'is that it's fine to stay distracted, keep your mind on other things, but you need to be kind to yourself, too. Don't run on the hamster wheel until you fly off and are forced to examine all your bruises.' She frowned. 'That's an awful metaphor. But, regardless, what I said to you the other day was incredibly heartless.'

'Mum—'

'No defending me, Maisie, and no heaping blame on yourself. I was stressed about work, but there was no reason for me to take it out on you. And seeing the festival, your achievements, the way it's transformed this town even when the weather is doing its best to ruin everything, it's made me realize how unfair I've been.'

Maisie shrugged. 'We have different ideas about success.'

'And that's fine,' Aimee said. 'There *are* different ways of being successful, different measures, and maybe I haven't ever truly appreciated that.'

'What's made you say all this?' Maisie asked.

Aimee tapped her fingers against the steering wheel. 'When your father said he needed me to deliver the birdseed to the Arthurs, I called Horace, just to confirm their order. Frank had told me about poor Jeannie, so I didn't go blundering in with some insensitive comment, but Horace took a few minutes to tell me how grateful he was, for your kindness and the security they have, knowing the shop is always there, that you'll deliver to them.'

'That's down to Dad,' Maisie said. 'I'm just carrying on with the service he set up.'

'There you go again, dismissing your own part. I feel as if . . . as if I've contributed, in some way, to your lack of confidence in yourself.'

Maisie rested her head against the car seat. 'I'd like to say the answer is no.'

'But you can't, I understand that. But Horace's comments, they weren't about Frank. He said that your kindness, when you delivered their logs, meant a lot to him, and that the stall with the crocheted animals, carrying on Jeannie's tradition, is just . . .'

'That *definitely* wasn't me.'

'Horace knew that, but he also knew that Colm setting up that stall, all those townsfolk crocheting those creatures and vegetables, was partly because of you. He said – and this is almost a direct quote – that your influence in this town is like a sweet, pure quality to the air, quietly making everything better.'

'I mean—'

'And he's right, isn't he?' Aimee narrowed her eyes. 'And that makes me think that it wasn't Colm who ended things between you.'

Maisie swallowed. 'It was never going to work, Mum. We're in such different places.'

Aimee scoffed. 'You think your dad and I live in harmonious accord all the time? He's chasing bees around the garden and has a steak pie in a tin saved as a special treat for his dinner; I'm due to meet my girlfriends for a spa day next weekend, and I'm banking on there being champagne and oysters. If we felt and thought the same about everything, where would the romance be? Where would the fire come from?'

'I don't want to think about the fire between you and Dad,' Maisie said faintly.

'So think about you and Colm, instead. Was there chemistry?'

'A whole lab's worth.'

'And is he still here, in Cornwall?'

'Yes, but—'

'Maisie Winters,' her mum said sharply. 'One of the things I most admire about you is your sticking power. You know what you want, what makes you happy, and you go after it. And then Colm Caffrey, the man you've adored since you were in cut-off denim shorts and Charlie body spray, comes back here, shows you that he cares as much about you as I believe you do for him, and you run away.' She slid her red-nailed fingers through her perfect hair. 'The only thing you've ever run from, and it's the one person who could make you blissfully content.'

'I'm not running away,' Maisie said.

'No?' Aimee pushed open her door and rain spattered inside, landing on the leather dashboard. 'What would you call it? Pushing *him* away? Deciding it's over before anything can get between you? Self-preservation by hot-footing it in the opposite direction, that's what it is.'

Maisie climbed out of the car, and the wind blew her curls into her eyes as she went around to the boot. 'What's got into you?'

Aimee piled the fat balls, sunflower hearts and icky mealworms into Maisie's arms. The smile she gave her seemed more genuine than any other expression Maisie had seen on her mother's face. 'I lost my job at the council,' she said. 'I'm no longer needed, after all. It's put a lot of things in perspective. Now, come on. Let's see if we can bring a little bit of sunshine – and robin food – into Horace and Jeannie's lives.'

She walked up the familiar path, and Maisie, reeling from her mother's revelation, had no option but to follow her.

Chapter Thirty-Six

It was Friday morning, and the festival was gearing up for its weekend highlights: the surfing competition on Saturday, followed by a concert on Sunday afternoon with a number of local bands, which would either be on the harbour-side stage if the weather allowed, or in the town hall if it didn't.

Charlie's meteorologist – and the national forecast – were both predicting that the worst of the weather should be gone by Sunday, so they were hoping for a glorious swan-song down by the harbour, with the Cornish Cream Tea Bus, music and dancing and food, all against the backdrop of the beautiful Cornish coast.

It sounded idyllic, and as Maisie strode through the woods close to Foxglove Farm, it was clear that today's rain was softer than it had been, even though the wind was still strong.

She couldn't quite get over the conversation she'd had with her mum, and had been left to stew on it while they

340

took the bird food to Horace, and found Jeannie on the sofa, looking small and pale wrapped in a giant dressing gown, but smiling at them over the rim of her cup of tea.

Maisie's mum had been the perfect blend of kind and authoritative, and soon had Horace helping her restock the feeders in their windswept back garden, while Jeannie moved to a chair in the conservatory to watch, and Maisie made a fresh pot of tea and found some chocolate biscuits in their neat kitchen.

'They'll need it, with this spell of weather,' Aimee had said, as she got Horace to hold the feeder steady so she could pour the seed in. 'They're expecting bugs, calm skies and sunshine, so this'll be a real shock. Any help we can give them, they'll be glad of.'

'Isn't that the truth,' Horace had said, glancing at his wife.

When Maisie sat down next to Jeannie, the older woman had said, without preamble, 'I heard about the crochet stall. You and that Colm boy, working wonders. I had thought, until that moment, that he was on the other side of the world.'

Maisie had shrugged. 'I suppose he realized the truth.'

'What's that, Maisie dear?'

'That once you've lived in Port Karadow, then nowhere else quite measures up.'

'Not even Australia, with its endless sunshine and beaches, pools in every back garden?'

'Not even there, Jeannie.'

The older woman had patted her knee, nodding as if Maisie had passed some kind of test. Maisie had taken the little surfboard out of her bag, and Jeannie's eyes had lit up as she'd examined it, laughing with delight.

341

It was a reminder, as if she needed another one, that life didn't always turn out how you wanted it to, and if you *could* go after the things that mattered, if you had that option, then you should do it, even if there was a chance that it wouldn't last. Maisie needed to take a risk, to open herself up to possibility, and see where it led her.

But today, as she reached Rose Cottage, its flowers and foliage dripping with jewelled raindrops, she wondered if the decision was no longer in her hands. Colm's car wasn't there, and when she peered through the windows, she found the whole place in darkness. Fear trickled down her spine, and she felt a huge surge of relief when, her nose pressed against the cold glass, she saw a jumper discarded on the back of the sofa, his Kindle, the cover folded back, lying next to it. He was only gone for the day, and she tried not to speculate where he was, but the words *London* and *interview* crept traitorously into her mind.

She walked back through the woods to Ollie's barn, where she had left her car, the mud splattering her sandals and her bare calves, her thoughts choppy like the sea.

She knocked on Ollie's front door and Thea opened it. 'Are you OK?' her friend asked immediately, taking Maisie's hand and pulling her over the threshold. 'You look flustered. Come inside.'

The barn smelled of incense and coffee, and there was a string of fairy lights trailed along the mantelpiece, counteracting the gloom.

'Hey.' Ollie looked up from where she was stacking piles of their teaser whiteboards, Colm's smiling face and tanned body repeated over and over on the plastic. 'These are going really well. We've already had over sixty pre-orders, and I'm going to push them over the weekend, especially at the surfing competition.'

'Let Maisie catch her breath,' Meredith said, laughing.

Ollie gave her a sheepish smile. 'Sorry. How are you? Dead on your feet?'

Maisie kept her gaze studiously away from all the Colms. 'I think if I sit down for too long, I'll stop altogether, so it's best to keep going. But it's all gone well, no disasters so far.' She tapped the solid wood of Ollie's farmhouse table. 'It was a lot busier at the beginning of the week, getting the stallholders settled.'

'Hence being able to have coffee with us today,' Thea said, pouring her a cup. 'Strawberry shortbread?'

'Oh God, yes please.' Maisie joined the others at the table. 'I'm so glad the teaser's proving popular.'

Ollie caught her eye across the piles of whiteboards. 'It was always going to draw attention. Have you spoken to him?'

Maisie shook her head. 'I just went to Rose Cottage, but he's out. His car's not there, so I think he's further afield than the beach.'

'You're going to talk to him, though?' Meredith asked.

'I am.'

'He'll be at the competition tomorrow,' Ollie said. 'I went to the bus earlier, and Charlie told me he's put his name down.'

'So that's going ahead?' Thea asked.

Maisie nodded. 'The forecast is for strong winds, but no rain. Ideal conditions, and apparently there are surfers travelling from quite a long way away to take part.' She chewed her lip. 'It's obviously a great way to finish the festival, but I'm worried it'll be extra dangerous, after those high tides have churned everything up.'

'I don't think any surfing competition is without risks,' Meredith said, 'but Colm's a pro, and he's faced shark-infested waters for the last decade, so at least it's not as scary as *that*.' She shuddered, and Thea murmured, '*Ugh*.'

'Anyway,' Ollie added, 'he's our poster boy for Cornwall's most successful charity calendar, so nothing can happen to him. But you *should* talk to him before it kicks off, because then he'll go into it knowing the love of his life is still in love with him; that you're waiting on shore for him to come home victorious.'

'Like a battling sailor returning after months at sea, a fraught, desperate voyage that he barely survived, clinging onto the knowledge that his sweetheart is desperate to hold him in her arms.' They all turned to look at Meredith, who had a dreamy expression on her face. She blinked, her cheeks flushing. 'I've been reading a historical romance,' she told them. 'It's so dramatic.'

'Hopefully the surfing competition will be boring by comparison,' Thea said, 'but I agree with Ollie – you should clear the air with Colm, be honest with him about how you feel, what you're scared of. That way you can both enjoy the end of the festival. You've worked hard enough on it, you deserve to have fun, too.'

'And if Colm wins,' Ollie added, 'you'll be like the festival king and queen. I saw a stall selling these gorgeous flower crowns: you should each get one of those.'

'Flower crowns are very *Midsommar*,' Maisie said, 'and we all know how that film turned out.'

'Basically, Maisie,' Meredith said, then swivelled 360 degrees on her stool, 'You need to talk to Colm, he needs to win the surfing competition, then we can all enjoy the last day of the festival, sing and dance at the concert, consume our own body weight in burgers, chips and churros, then spend the rest of the summer having barbecues here or picnics on the beach, all *eight* of us. A big happy family of friends.'

Maisie swallowed. She didn't think she'd wanted anything more in her entire life. She would go back to Rose Cottage this evening when she was off-duty, once the stalls had packed up for the day and it was only the food trucks and evening entertainment left down by the harbour.

'You,' she said, 'are the best friends I could have hoped for.'

'Aww.' Thea leaned in and hugged her. 'Right back at you.'

'We just want you to be happy,' Meredith added, waiting her turn for a hug.

'But also, we will only stay your friend if you update us on the group WhatsApp the moment you've spoken to him,' Ollie said, giving Maisie the tightest embrace of all. 'Now go and make this festival shine.'

'There's not a lot left to do,' Maisie said, laughing. 'But I will go and check everyone's OK, that nobody's fallen in the sea or been attacked by Dad's errant bees. Thanks for the shortbread and the pep-talk.'

'Any time!' they chorused, and Maisie walked out of the barn with a smile on her face and a spring in her step.

She wanted the rest of the summer to be just how Meredith had described it: full of barbecues and picnics, days out and nights in the pub, followed by a slow, sultry slide towards Halloween and Christmas. Port Karadow was beautiful in every season, especially when she was enjoying it with the people she loved. It could all still happen *without* Colm – of course it could – but it wouldn't be the same.

No, Maisie Winters was on a mission. She just hoped she could fulfil it before Colm got his surfboard and took to the Port Karadow seas tomorrow morning.

Chapter Thirty-Seven

When Maisie opened her eyes on Saturday morning, she could hear the wind whistling along her roof tiles and shaking the windows in their frames, but when she listened for the telltale spatter of rain against glass that had greeted her all week, she was relieved not to find it.

Her stomach twisted with nerves. She was going to speak to Colm today. Whether she managed to do it before or after the surfing competition was another matter.

Of course, having told her friends that the festival was running itself, when she'd got into town yesterday, there had been several issues for her to sort out. The last few days of rain had built up on the roof of the town hall, then chosen yesterday morning to leak through a skylight, threatening to ruin Amelie's silk tapestries. Maisie had called Ben and, hero that he was, he'd come straight away to fix the damage.

Then there had been an argument on the harbourside between the Bratwurst stand and the dirty fries stall, about their relative positions in the row of food trucks. Charlie was close by, but she was busy with her bus and, besides, Maisie didn't want her near two angry vendors when she was growing a small person inside her. Maisie knew Greg, the owner of the Bratwurst stall, because his twin girls had been in her class several years ago, and she had soon been able to defuse the situation.

Then the giant purple inflatable octopus, which sat on top of the Seafood Shack, had tried to get loose of its ties, and she had spent a good half an hour helping Colin, who ran the shack, tie it back down. Strong winds and inflatables were *not* a match made in heaven.

All of this meant she had been busy all day on Friday, and when six o'clock finally came around, she was tired and sweaty, all her brainpower had been fully used up, and the last thing she wanted to do was go and find Colm, and have an honest conversation with him that had the potential to alter the course of her life.

In any case, Ollie had called her as she was going to get Sprout from her parents' house. 'I just got back from the calendar promo stall,' she had said. 'I took Henry for a walk through the woods, and Colm's car still isn't there.'

Maisie had sent a virtual hug to her friend. 'Thank you for checking for me.'

'It's been a day, huh? Thea told me about the leak.'

'The leak was the least of it, so I'm not sure I'm in the right frame of mind to see Colm now, anyway.'

'You'll feel fresher in the morning,' Ollie had said, her tone kind but forceful, impressing a certainty about the task Maisie had ahead of her that she didn't feel herself.

But this morning, even though her nerves were there,

she was also filled with a steely determination. She had never felt this way about anyone other than Colm, even though they had barely scratched the surface of each other's likes and needs, habits and desires, and surely that was a sign that she had to try to fight for a future with him, even if there was a lot about it that scared her.

She showered, dressed in a beautiful blue dress with a peacock feather design, and spent longer than usual taming her blonde curls. She put on cheek and lip stain, glossy mascara, and a spritz of her favourite perfume, the smell like almonds and summer sunshine. She slipped on her sandals, and picked up her small cross-body bag.

'Come on, Sprout.' Her dog jumped off her armchair and padded over to his food bowl. 'We'll get breakfast out, OK?'

Sprout looked up at her, his head on one side.

'Burger,' she said, and he lifted onto his hind legs, as if he was desperate for his harness. 'Good boy.' She extracted his paws from the folds of her dress. 'You're the *best* boy.'

She walked past houses with small, colourful windmills in their front gardens, spinning like they were trying to take off. Wind chimes clanged inharmoniously, and a wheelie bin hurried down the street all by itself, coming to rest against a parked van. Maisie had seen the choppy water from her bedroom window, so she knew the conditions would be ideal for surfing: ideal if you were a crazy thrill seeker, anyway, but not if you were a beginner. *Colm is not a beginner*, she reminded herself, and she and her dog turned towards the beach.

The surfing competition wasn't being held on the busiest

stretch of Port Karadow beach, where families usually gathered on blankets, but further down, close to where they'd done Meredith and Finn's photo shoot, the section partly cut off by a stretch of rocks that acted as a natural barrier. Here, the sand was wide and flat, and the currents made it a popular surfing spot. This part also allowed dogs all year, something Maisie was thankful for. She wouldn't feel right doing this without Sprout: he was always a comfort to her, but he was also her family.

'Maisie!' She turned to see Devon, the front-of-house manager from the Happy Shack.

'Hey,' she said. 'Are you here for the competition?'

'I'm running it,' he told her. 'Charlie's man on the ground. The restaurant is my normal gig, but this is where I'm happiest. Charlie knew I was a semi-pro back in the day, and asked me to make sure everything runs smoothly.'

'That's great,' Maisie said. Other than confirming they could use the beach for the competition, and asking Marcus to open it, she hadn't had a huge hand in organizing this part of the festival, because Charlie already had the relevant contacts.

'We've got extra lifeguards,' Devon went on, pointing to three people wearing the red and yellow outfits that were so familiar over the summer, 'and our competitors are gathering.' He gestured in the opposite direction, and Maisie saw a group of men and women, most already in their wetsuits, a few chatting and stretching, limbering up before they sneaked off to a discreet part of the beach to get changed.

She peered at them, hoping to land on Colm's familiar silhouette, but she couldn't see him. She couldn't see Ollie,

Thea or Meredith either, or their other halves. They were all due to be here, but she supposed she was quite early.

'It should be brilliant,' she said to Devon. 'The waves are looking good.'

She didn't really know what made a good surfing wave, other than that it should be big, and these ones definitely were.

'Yeah.' Devon laughed. 'Couldn't have asked for a better day, really. This is going to be swell.'

'Swell,' Maisie repeated, grinning.

He frowned and then, realizing what she'd said, chuckled politely.

God, she was nervous. She needed to be around people she knew, so she could babble aimlessly without them thinking she was losing her mind. She said goodbye to Devon and wandered further down the beach, in the direction of the surfers. Perhaps Colm was here and she simply hadn't spotted him, or maybe he'd changed his mind and wasn't coming. Wherever he'd gone yesterday could have taken longer than he'd anticipated, or he could have planned to stay overnight, or . . . She took a long, deep breath.

'Get a grip, Maisie,' she told herself.

But she needed some connection with him, some kind of contact. She had expected him to be here, had prepared herself for seeing him. She pulled out her phone and scrolled to her message thread with him, not looking at their last happy, hopeful exchange before that morning next to the Happy Shack.

She typed quickly:

Good luck with the competition. I'm already here, on the beach, and I'll be watching! Mx

'At least he'll know I'm thinking about him,' she told Sprout. 'That I haven't forgotten him. That'll have to do for now, won't it?'

Her dog barked, as if in agreement.

She crouched down and ruffled his fur. 'You're a good dog, Sprout.'

His eyes were trained on the water, and he barked again, then again. Maisie followed the line of his nose, trying to see what he was looking at. His little body was vibrating, and the hairs pricked up on Maisie's neck, goosebumps travelling the length of her arms.

She kept peering, following her dog's gaze, and then – *there*. There was something in the water, out beyond the surf, being tossed about by the rough swell of the gathering waves. She couldn't see much from where she was, but it looked like a person, and they were wearing something purple – a T-shirt or a dress? It was bigger than a swimming costume, anyway. They seemed to be floating face down, and Sprout was concerned about whatever, *whoever*, it was. His barks were mixed with whines now, the sound high-pitched and frantic, as if he was in distress. She hated that sound, because it made her distressed, too.

Maisie tore her gaze away from the water. The surfers were gathered to her left, chatting and preparing their boards, laughing as if they weren't about to do battle with an unruly sea, and to her right, there were the lifeguards. They were talking less animatedly, scanning the beach at the same time. But they were still a long way away – under-standably, because the competition hadn't started yet. Who should she run to? She knew if she shouted, she wouldn't be heard over the wind and the crashing waves, and she didn't want to take her eyes off the figure in the water for more than a few seconds, in case she lost it.

'What should I do, Sprout?'

Her dog glanced up at her, and then, almost too quickly for her to realize what was happening, he raced into the shallows. The waves were rolling in from a long way away, getting progressively bigger as the water got deeper, and Sprout splashed in the foam, skittering from side to side in a way that told Maisie he was really unhappy. She thought he'd stay there – he loved the water, but never went too deep.

'I'll get . . .' she started, but her words dried out as Sprout ran deeper, his solid little body buffeting waves that were as tall as him. The purple thing floated further out, getting knocked about by the tide, and Maisie still couldn't make out what it was, but it definitely had a shape and volume: it wasn't just a discarded item of clothing. 'Sprout, come back!' she called.

He looked behind him, then padded forwards. Another wave caught him, and he stretched his neck up to stop himself being submerged. 'Sprout!' Maisie called again, but this time he didn't turn around, and soon his steps turned to paddles as he made his way out to sea, towards the purple form in the water.

Her little dog was brave, Maisie thought, as she kicked off her sandals, and checked again that the surfers, the lifeguards, were no closer to her, but he was also an idiot. She dumped her bag on her shoes and took off after him, the first laps of water against her skin almost soothing, the cold shocking her when she got up to her knees. She tried not to think about how much the days of rain, the high tides, would have affected the sea; how creatures might be coming out now, after the storms, to hunt for food in the calmer, clearer water.

Except, Maisie realized, as she waded in up to her waist, her dress already heavy around her, it wasn't calm today: that was the whole point. It was clearer, but very, very far from calm. She followed her dog, his progress surprisingly quick now that he was swimming, and the purple object was nearer.

The swell lifted her up and dumped her back down, and then she reached the first row of breakers, and one came crashingly, shockingly, over her head. She spluttered, salty water in her mouth and nose and eyes, and tried to remember the rules about doggy paddling, which was a lot easier when you weren't wearing a floaty dress that seemed to have absorbed a metric ton of water.

But she kept going, following her dog out. 'Sprout!' she shouted. 'Come back!'

The things you do for that dog, she remembered her dad saying once, when she'd had her parents round to her newly finished house for Sunday lunch, and she'd done Sprout a mini roast, complete with veggies and meat, and a couple of crispy potatoes. *The things I do for my dog*, she thought, as another wave broke over her head.

When the water had cleared from her eyes, she saw that Sprout had almost reached the purple figure, but to do it, he'd gone beyond the biggest breakers, the ones the surfers would soon be riding. Out there, the sea was much calmer. Maisie knew it was deadly.

'Sprout!' she called again, and he turned his head towards her, but he couldn't bark – he couldn't do anything but paddle. She saw a huge wave coming and, even though she was trembling with fear, she took a deep breath, and went under the surface. She swam forwards, her dress unbelievably heavy around her legs, then pushed herself up, beyond the cresting waves.

Sprout was there, and so was the shape, and she was in the endless, surreal stretch of the ocean.

She heard shouts from the beach, turned around and was shocked – and not a little horrified – to see how far out they'd swum. And she was tired now, too, her dress trying to make a beeline straight for the bottom, and dragging her down with it. Sprout finally reached the figure, grabbed it between his teeth, and pulled. Maisie took a couple of sluggish strokes towards it, then nearly gasped a whole lungful of sea water when she saw two eyes . . . two large, staring eyes, and the bulbous body of – *holy shit*, she thought. *It's the fucking octopus*.

The giant purple octopus that had donned the top of the Seafood Shack, and which she'd tried to help Colin secure the day before. Well, clearly they'd failed, and this, it seemed, was her punishment.

'Good boy, Sprout,' she panted, because even though it wasn't the world's greatest rescue, his intentions had been pure. 'Good, *good* dog.' He swam into her, nudging his little body against hers, and she realized that he was exhausted, too, wanting her to carry him and his octopus back to the shore.

But Maisie was so tired, and her dress was so heavy, and even though the tide would carry them back, they'd still have to navigate the huge waves that were, probably any minute now, about to become the stage for a hard-fought surfing competition. Her energy was gone, her limbs felt as if they were made of lead, and the swell of the water was making her drowsy.

She realized, then, that – as courageous as it had been – she and her little dog had also both been very, very stupid.

Chapter Thirty-Eight

Maisie gathered up all her remaining strength, and with Sprout held tightly against her with one arm, the ridiculous purple octopus still clamped in his teeth, she used her other arm to swim towards the beach. The people on it looked tiny, like figures in a Lowry painting, and they bobbed in and out of sight as the swell rose ahead, those huge waves – that she would have to go over – intermittently blocking her view. She tried not to think about the crash, the roar they made, as they broke.

'We'll get there,' she said to her dog, and he whimpered, clearly also regretting their brave dash into the sea. 'We *will*,' she repeated, even though talking took up energy and let water into her mouth.

She thought that if she just stayed determined, positive, then it would all be OK, but then her dress tangled around her legs and there was something else, something stringy but strong, like rope, around her right ankle. She pulled, her leg muscles straining, but it didn't let go. It held her in place, felt as if it was trying to tug her down into the murky depths.

Panic took over, threatening to overwhelm her. She dipped under the water, trying to fold herself in half to reach her ankle, tug off the seaweed she must have got caught in, but her dress was in the way and Sprout was whining and scrabbling, and fear was a thick lump in her throat.

She straightened and heaved in a lungful of air, the seaside scent she loved so much, which made her think of home but was now a part of this nightmare. *We can do this*, she thought, because she was too tired to speak, now. *We can definitely do this.*

She heard a shout, louder than the background sounds of the beach, reaching her over the cries of the seagulls. She looked towards land, the blue of the sea rising up, obscuring her view, then sliding back down. There was someone running, surfboard under their arm, towards the water. Was the competition starting? Would she have to avoid the surfers and their surfboards as well as everything else, or – no. *No.* She recognized the way he moved, his silhouette, the same way she had when she'd seen him surfing all those weeks ago.

'Colm!' she shouted, using up her remaining energy, and water flooded her mouth, making her splutter.

'Maisie!' Oh, how sweet her name sounded in his voice.

She stopped struggling then, using her free arm to stay upright, trying not to think about the seaweed, which seemed to be getting tighter and tighter around her leg.

'I'm coming!' was the next shout, and she saw him launch himself into the waves, paddling fervently as he lay, stomach down, on his board. 'Maisie,' he called again, 'I'm coming to get you!'

Tears pricked her eyes, the lump in her throat making it hard to swallow.

And then Colm was cresting the large breakers, paddling towards her, his face a mask of determination. She saw his gaze take in her and Sprout and the octopus, saw his confusion, and the way he couldn't quite hold back a smile.

'What the fuck, Maisie?' he said, but he didn't sound angry, only relieved.

'Seaweed,' she rushed. 'My leg – I don't know how . . . how long . . .'

His smile vanished. 'You don't need to.' He slid into the water, bringing his beautiful, sky-blue surfboard to her. 'Here.' He lifted Sprout from her arms, putting her soaked dog, still gripping onto the octopus for dear life, onto the board. 'Hold onto it,' he instructed, as he came up behind her, circling her body with his own, creating a comfort and warmth that threatened to shatter her last bit of resolve. Then, as if she hadn't heard, he lifted her hands, one by one, and placed them on the side of the board, his warm palms covering her fingers, making sure she was holding on tight. 'I'll have you on there in a moment,' he said. 'Once your leg is free.'

'What if you can't—' she started.

'I can,' he said into her ear.

Then he was gone, diving under the water, and she felt his hands on her hips, using her body as his guide to get to her legs, under the dress, to her feet, her bound ankle. She felt the seaweed tighten and chafe, felt him tugging it, and for a few, horrifying seconds she thought he wouldn't be able to get it free, but then there was a last, sharp *tug*, and it snapped.

She waggled her leg, relishing the freedom, the relief.

Colm popped up beside her, gasping for air, water rushing off his face.

'Thank you!' She took one hand off the board, clutched his shoulder and kissed him. Their faces were wet, salty and slippery, and they were both breathing hard, Colm catching his breath after being underwater, her completely worn out. It was short and clumsy, but also one of the best kisses of her life.

'We need to get you back,' he said.

'My dress is so heavy.'

'I know. Jesus.' He rubbed his face. 'I don't want to think . . .' He shook his head. 'Right, on the board. I'll push you in.'

She tried to haul herself onto the surfboard, to join bedraggled, shivering Sprout, but her arms were so tired. 'I can't.'

'OK,' Colm said calmly. 'Here.' He came up behind her, grabbed her hips and then, with a mixture of force and gentleness, pushed her up and onto the board, until she was splayed inelegantly across it, like an oversized starfish. When she turned her head to the side, Colm was holding onto the board with both hands. He grinned at her. 'Sorry. That wasn't the prettiest way of doing things.'

'I don't care about pretty,' she panted. 'You rescued us.'

'I wasn't going to just leave you here. I mean, I wouldn't have left *anyone* here, but you . . .' He shook his head.

'What?'

'There's time for that. Is the octopus coming with us?'

360

Maisie tried to nod. 'It would take the rest of our energy to get it away from Sprout. As far as he's concerned, he's carried out an act of impressive bravery today.'

Colm laughed as he moved the surfboard around in the water, so it was facing towards the beach and he was behind it. 'Ready to get onto dry land?'

'What about the big waves?' Maisie asked, panic creeping back into her voice.

'Don't worry,' Colm said, 'I know how to time it right.'

'Thank God.' Maisie let her head drop back against the solid blue fibreglass of his surfboard.

When they got closer to the beach, Maisie saw the lifeguard rib coming out to meet them and, behind the boat, a crowd of onlookers standing on the sand. Among them she could see Ollie, Thea and Meredith, Max, Ben and Finn, and someone, arms folded over his chest, who looked a lot like Marcus Belrose. God, she thought, embarrassment heating her cheeks, she'd caused a proper scene.

The lifeguards reached them, the rib elegantly sliding in sideways, drawing parallel to the surfboard. 'We can take it from here,' a sturdy, dark-haired man said.

'Could you take the dog?' Colm asked. 'And the octopus – he won't let it go.'

'Right.' The man looked bemused, but he scooped Sprout up, and Maisie was grateful that her dog was in safe hands. 'And you . . .?' he started, reaching a hand out to Maisie.

'We're fine,' Colm said. Maisie couldn't see his face, but whatever his expression communicated, the lifeguard nodded to Colm while he puttered alongside them both. Maisie could also see his colleagues standing in the shallows, one on a radio, the other holding a large, fleecy-looking blanket.

'We have to walk now,' Colm said, and Maisie slipped off the board, reluctant to have to move in her ten-ton dress. But before she'd taken a step she was weightless again, this time with strong arms around her, one cradling her back, the other under her knees.

'Colm.' She turned her head, and he planted a quick kiss on her lips.

'You're safe,' he said, his voice low and soothing, as another surfer hurried over and, wordlessly, took Colm's surfboard from where he'd abandoned it, and carried it back to the beach.

Maisie could hear the crowd cheering, a voice that sounded like Thea's saying, 'Thank God!' and then Colm smiled at her, tightened his grip on her and said, 'I'll keep you safe forever. Rescue you every day, if I have to.'

'You will?' Maisie croaked.

'Yup.' He splashed through the shallows, and she might have been imagining it, but she thought there was a gruffness in his voice, too. 'You, Sprout and that bloody octopus, if that's what it takes.'

She laughed, raised her gaze to the sky, then closed her eyes. She couldn't describe how good it felt to be back in Colm Caffrey's arms.

'You missed the competition,' Maisie said, her hands cupped around a large mug full to the brim with black coffee, the steam rising up to caress her lips and nose, her forehead, with another layer of heat.

'I don't care about that,' Colm said.

She turned to look at him. 'You don't?'

They were sitting on the veranda of the Happy Shack, two chairs facing the beach, where the competition was going ahead, the water peppered with sleek, shiny bodies in wetsuits, their bright, sometimes garish, surfboards beneath them, a crowd of people watching from the sand.

Maisie couldn't get over how kind, how concerned, Marcus had been when Colm had carried her onto the beach. He'd offered them his restaurant, and spare clothes – though they would, he said apologetically, be chefs' whites – food and hot drinks. Colm had insisted Maisie get checked out by the medics who'd arrived, but once they'd assured her – and him – that she was fine, that she just needed to warm up and get some rest, they'd taken Marcus up on his offer.

Colm had changed out of his wetsuit, back into the jeans and T-shirt he'd brought with him, and Maisie was in a pair of oversized chefs' pyjamas, a thick, fleecy blanket wrapped snugly around her. Her hair was drying in the dancing wind, and she felt, for the first time in days, that she had everything she needed: hot coffee, Sprout at her feet, Colm at her side.

'Nope,' he said now. 'I love surfing, but I wasn't that bothered about the competition. All I cared about was that message you sent earlier, the one that said you'd be watching me: that was my motivation. I hadn't expected you to try watching from the water, though.'

There should have been humour in his voice, but there was none.

'Shit, Maisie,' he went on. 'When I saw your sandals and bag on the beach, and no sign of you . . .' He didn't say anything else, and when she sneaked another glance, he was staring out at the sea – the sea that she'd been in, up until very recently – and rubbing a hand against his chest.

'I'm sorry,' she said. 'And I'm also so, so grateful. Sprout and his stupid heroic ambitions.'

'*You* were the heroic one, because you thought it was a person,' Colm said. 'Sprout knew it was a plastic octopus, and he wanted it for himself.' They both looked down. Her dog *still* had the deflated purple sea creature in his mouth, and she knew she would need to have a stern conversation with him soon, and then another, slightly more awkward one with Colin at the Seafood Shack. Right now, though, there was only one person she needed to talk to.

'Whatever our motivations, I don't know what would have happened if you hadn't realized where I was.'

'It would have been fine,' Colm said firmly. 'The lifeguards weren't that far behind me.'

'I should never have gone in.'

'You're safe now,' Colm said again.

Maisie turned to face him, and he turned to her.

'I needed to say—'

'I want you to know—'

They smiled at each other, Colm holding her gaze and refusing to let go.

'I should have told you what I was doing,' he said. 'What was going on with me.'

She shook her head. 'I shouldn't have demanded it. I should have let you tell me in your own time. Everyone says that I'm running away, because I've realized how important you are to me, and I'm scared of what that means.'

His shoulders lifted, dropped back down. 'What do you think?'

She sighed. 'I was worried that – that after all this time, the way I felt about you – the way I feel about you now, which is fresh and new and even more overwhelming, it was too good to be true; that there was no way I, and this place, could ever be enough for you.'

She expected him to roll his eyes, maybe laugh, gesture at the view. But there was no sign of cool, light-hearted Colm right now. 'That couldn't be further from the truth.'

He put his mug on the floor and held out his hands. Maisie copied him, putting her coffee down, and Colm took both her hands in his. His skin was warm, and familiar, and the mingling of relief, comfort and desire was almost too much.

'I wanted to show you what you mean to me,' he said. 'To show you that I want to build a life with you, here. I was hoping to, and then you decided that – that it was too much of a risk.' His smile was lopsided. 'That hurt quite a bit, if I'm honest. But I understood it, too. Trust is so important, but I . . . I didn't want to make promises when I didn't know if I could keep them.'

'What do you mean?' She licked her dry, salty lips.

'I don't want to spend my life designing websites – or not *just* that. I want to do what I did in Australia, offer the whole package. PR, events, the digital stuff too, managing whole customer accounts. I want to start my own business. But what happened with Anders, it knocked me sideways. I'd always done it with him, we were a team, and it felt so hard, even thinking about starting again. Especially on my own.'

'So, the London company—'

'London?' He frowned.

'I saw it on your laptop. Thor knocked the trackpad. And there were RSPCA leaflets, about getting stray cats rehomed, so I thought you were leaving.'

'It was research,' Colm said. 'I had a meeting with a firm in Falmouth, my first potential PR client, and I wanted to get all my ducks in a row – look at companies I thought were doing well, make sure what I was offering would stand up to the competition. I'm not interested in conquering any big markets, but having some decent clients in Cornwall and Devon would be great.'

Maisie swallowed. 'I'm so sorry. But when I asked you—'

'I didn't want to be a failure,' he said, the words coming out in a rush. 'I didn't want to tell you about this grand plan I had, and then for it to come to nothing and for you to think, *Oh well, he's useless, isn't he?* Just like . . .' He stopped.

'Like Lainey,' Maisie finished.

He nodded.

'Colm, I would *never* think that. All that matters to me is that you're here. Whatever you want to do, I'm happy, I'll support it. Your job, your career, isn't why I care about you. It's not why I . . . I love you.' There. She'd said it. Had it been the right thing to do? It *felt* right, didn't feel too scary or like she was going to pass out. From the way his hands tightened around hers, and his eyes widened, but he didn't get up and leap over the veranda railings, she thought he might be OK with it, too.

'Maisie.'

'Don't say it back,' she rushed. 'You don't have to.'

'But I . . .' His laugh was slightly incredulous. '*Maisie.*'

'Keep going. The other things.'

'Thor? The leaflets?'

'Maybe he does have an owner,' she said, but then she thought of the pet stall in the town hall, the engraved tag Helly had shown her.

'He does,' Colm said, and now he was beaming. 'Me.'

'You've adopted him?'

'I took him to the vet. He wasn't microchipped and we couldn't find any missing pet notifications about him. The vet was confident I'd done all I could to find an owner, and she thought he was maybe a farm kitten who'd got out and started adventuring too early, proving that he's tough stuff. So now, Thor is officially Thor Caffrey.'

'Oh Colm!' Maisie pulled him towards her, then let go of his hands and hugged him tightly. It felt monumental, because this man and his cat were putting down roots. She'd been wrong about so many things, and used those wrong assumptions to fuel her insecurities.

'You're building an extension on the kitchen,' she murmured into his neck.

'Ben told you?'

'He did.'

'Granddad said the cottage is mine, if I want it, and . . . fuck, Maisie, I don't deserve it, really: him or the house. But I'm so glad to have him back in my life, to have a relationship with him, and I'm going to up the rent I pay him. I'd like a bit more space, more light, too, and he's OK with me updating it. Ben says it's doable, despite how old the cottage is. We're looking into the regulations, and I was wondering if . . . I mean, you've renovated your entire house. I don't know if you'd want to be involved too, but . . .'

'I'd love to help,' Maisie said. 'I am a bit of an expert, after all.'

'You're a total pro,' Colm agreed. 'I couldn't imagine doing it without you.'

'And I can't think of anyone who won't be pleased you're staying in Port Karadow.'

She felt his chest rise and fall against hers. 'There's one other thing, though. I've sort of, over the last few weeks – or actually, if I'm honest about it, as soon as I made the decision to come home . . . I've been imagining my life here a certain way.' He pulled back so he could look at her. 'Can I go back to the thing you just said? The thing that . . .' He ran a hand down his face. 'You love me? Really?'

Maisie winced. 'I'm sorry I didn't act as if I did. When I blew up at you.' She gestured behind her, to the path where they'd had their argument. 'But I was just – I was scared. That you'd turned up here again, after all this time, that you cared about me in a way that I'd always longed for – which was a big thing for me to get my head around, anyway – but you were keeping things from me, planning on leaving again, blowing out of this pokey town.' Why had she said the last bit in a stupid American accent? She was nervous, that was the problem.

'Hey,' Colm said. 'Don't call my hometown pokey. And Winters, there's something you really need to know.'

She swallowed, bracing herself. 'OK.'

'I was in love with you ten years ago,' Colm said, his gaze steady on hers. 'I was also a teenage boy, and I didn't realize it, didn't ever say anything to you. I think part of me was

368

hoping you might feel the same and do the hard work for me, make the move. And then I was suddenly going away, with Dad, and the way I missed you . . .' He shook his head. 'But it felt so futile, impossible, when I was so far away from you. So I tried to put you behind me, not even sending you a letter or email, or a Facebook message, because it was too hard.

'I made a new life for myself, which worked for a while. I thought, eventually, that I could be happy, but then it fell apart, pretty spectacularly, and all I could think about was coming home. I'd had updates from Lissa, I knew you were still living here, that you'd done exactly what you said you would. But when I came back here I was pretty broken, and I didn't know how I was going to pick myself off the floor. Then, that rainy day, I came into the ironmonger's.'

She remembered it so well. Even through the dizziness of his confession, the emotions flooding through her, she could still remember the feel of the cobwebs in her hair; him looking soggy but so utterly, gloriously Colm; the slight wonder in his eyes which she'd put down to him rediscovering places and people he'd once known like the back of his hand; the newness of his accent.

'I fell in love with you all over again,' he said, 'and I realized I wasn't done. That things might be dented, but they weren't broken, and with you in my life, so close and fun and loving, I could be better than OK. I could be really, really happy.'

'You . . .'

'I wasn't going to let you walk away,' he said, gently. 'I just wasn't. Because I knew you cared about me, and it was the uncertainty that was making it hard for you.

369

So I was going to show you, when it was all confirmed: the extension, Thor, my business. I'm not going anywhere, Maisie. I love this town, the people in it, but I could live without them, at a push – I've done it before. But the one person I can't live without, the one part of this that is entirely non-negotiable, is you.'

Maisie felt tears slide down her cheeks. 'You love me,' she murmured. 'You're staying?'

Colm nodded. 'I love you, and I'm staying. Stay here, with me, forever?'

Maisie's smile widened, her cheeks, still damp with tears, starting to ache from the strength of it. 'Forever is a big word, Colm Caffrey.'

He returned her smile, starting slow and almost careful, then matching hers in intensity. 'Forever is what I'm after, but right now I'll settle for today, and we can see how it goes.'

Maisie laughed. 'I think that's wise. But we're in this together, and I'd really like to aim for forever, as well.'

'That's great, Winters.' Colm leaned towards her, his lips, soft and coffee-flavoured, finding hers, his strong, warm arms coming around her, until she was enclosed in her blanket, wrapped up in him. She kissed him, let the fear, sadness and disappointment of the last few days dissolve, Colm's desire fuelling her own.

When they pulled apart, the beach was as busy as ever, the surfers were still in the water, and the sun was breaking through the clouds.

Colm glanced behind him and said, 'Do you want to go to the harbour and get a hot dog?'

Maisie laughed. 'We'd better not tell Marcus. He's been so kind.'

'We'll book to come here for dinner next week, if he can wangle us a table. All the courses, the seafood platter, champagne because I know how much you like bubbles. A proper date.'

'I'd love that,' she said, grinning. 'And right now a hot dog *does* sound pretty good. I'm starving after all that unexpected exercise.' She glanced down at Sprout, who was still lying on her feet. 'What about the octopus?'

Colm laughed and rubbed his hands over his face. 'Do you think he can be bribed with his own hot dog? Made to let go of the octopus if we replace it with a prime sausage in a bun? That way we can give the inflatable back to its rightful owner, even if it is destroyed.'

Maisie nodded. 'Sprout loves hot dogs.'

'Great. We have a plan. Let's go and get some food, and then head to your place. I don't know about you, but I could do with a shower.'

Maisie thought about the sand and salt crusting her skin, the disastrous tangle of her hair, the dress that she hoped was dry now, for the walk home, but would need at least a couple of washes if it had any hopes of surviving.

'A long, hot shower at my place sounds perfect,' she said, taking Colm's outstretched hand and letting him pull her to her feet.

'That's what I thought,' he murmured, managing to communicate a whole lot with his soft voice and his lowered eyes, and Maisie felt a happy shiver move through her.

They thanked Marcus for his kindness, Maisie replaced the chef's outfit with her crumpled, but thankfully dry dress, and she and Colm walked along the beachfront path, towards the busy harbour, holding each other's hands tightly, as if they were communicating that *forever* through the touch of their palms, their entwined fingers.

Sprout trotted along beside them, the purple octopus gripped firmly between his teeth, and Maisie knew, in that moment, that she had everything she had ever wanted.

Chapter Thirty-Nine

It was Sunday afternoon and the harbour was bustling, busy with people and food stalls and music, and there were no rain clouds in the sky, which was a light, carefree blue. The sun was beginning to slip towards the horizon, an orb dipped in gold paint, dripping its excess onto the dark water in a long trail, and the breeze was almost gentle.

There were rarely waves in the curved shelter of the harbour, but Maisie could see that, along the beach beyond, the swell was a lot calmer than the one she'd swum out into. *Swum out into.* She still couldn't quite believe that the last thirty-six hours had happened, the nightmare followed by a better dream than she'd ever let herself imagine.

She squeezed Colm's hand and he turned around, his smile soft but his eyes dancing, then faced the counter again.

After their hot dog, which gave Maisie a much-needed burst of energy, Colm had driven them the short distance to her house, then stripped her dress off her, taken her into the shower and turned the water up to steaming, then slowly washed the sand and sea water off her. That shower had been the best – and hottest – of her life, for all sorts of reasons, and a combination of post-rescue attempt exhaustion and Colm had kept her in bed until nearly midday today.

But her work for the festival, Charlie had assured her yesterday, was done, and now she had a chance to enjoy the final evening, the concert down by the harbourside. It was the last hurrah of a week that had gone better than expected, and had been more eventful and dramatic than Maisie could have anticipated.

'Here.' Colm turned again, this time handing her a cold beer bottle, condensation tracking down its side. He moved them away from the bar truck, then clinked his bottle against hers. 'To us,' he said. 'And Port Karadow. And, mostly, to you and all you've done for this festival.'

'Oh, I . . .' Maisie started, the usual protests about to trip off her tongue, but then she stopped herself.

Instead, she looked at the busy stretch of concrete full of food trucks, people eating, drinking and laughing, the band warming up on the stage. The fishing boats bobbed on the water, always there regardless of what was happening, but now with their masts and cabins adorned with gold fairy lights. She hadn't made all these individual things happen, but she had been a big part of it: a founding member. 'It's gone OK, I think. Mostly because of these.' She pulled the crocheted surfboard out of her bag, and Colm flushed.

'That is not . . .' He shook his head and huffed out a breath.

She had told him what she thought of his secret project

at her house the day before, unable to stop a few tears escaping when she explained about her and her mum's visit to the Arthurs', how much Jeannie had been touched by what he'd done. She had seen the emotion in Colm's eyes, too.

'Hey,' she said now, 'if I'm taking credit for my part, then you have to take credit for yours. You have made yourself even more loved in this town, though I know that's not why you did it.'

He shrugged. 'I wanted to help.'

'You have, and it's another reason why I love you.'

Colm planted a soft, swift kiss on her nose. 'What's your surfboard called?'

Maisie turned it around, examining it from every side, then smiled up at him. 'He's called *Never Again*.'

Colm laughed, his head tipping back. 'You weren't even *on* a surfboard. Not until the end, anyway.'

'And I have no desire to be again, so—'

'Lovebirds!' The shout came from behind Colm, and Maisie peered past him to see Ollie and Max approaching, Henry on his lead. Sprout, who had stayed quietly by her side since they'd left home, strained to sniff noses with the other dog.

'Hello,' Maisie said, as they took it in turns to hug each other.

'You made it, then,' Ollie said with a grin.

'We wouldn't have missed the end of the festival,' Maisie assured her.

'No, I mean this.' She pointed her index fingers up to the sky, then brought them together, in a clumsy approximation of an embrace.

Maisie laughed. 'We did – after Colm's heroic rescue.'

'I still can't believe you went in after the Seafood Shack's *octopus*!'

'I thought it was a body.' Maisie wrinkled her nose. 'A *person*.'

'So you thought you were saving a dead person, but got a deflated octopus instead.'

'I would argue that's the better outcome,' Colm said, and Maisie felt him shudder. 'Anyway, Sprout started it. Didn't you?' He looked pointedly down at the dog, and Sprout looked up at him with adoration.

'It was a great outcome all round,' Ollie stated.

Max shook Colm's hand, and said, 'We'll have to go on that hike sometime.'

'We will. I'll need a break from the kitchen refit.'

'Are you going to work on it with Ben?' Ollie asked.

Colm shrugged. 'I'd like to be involved, but I'm not anywhere near as expert as he – or Maisie – is. I'm going to see how it goes, try not to piss either of them off too much.'

'We can give you endless jobs to do.' Maisie jumped as Ben clapped a hand on Colm's shoulder. 'Can't we, Maisie?'

'Absolutely,' she said. She hadn't noticed him and Thea, Meredith and Finn, joining them. The band was warming up, guitar chords filling the air, cutting through the chatter of the crowd.

'Looks like I'm going to be busy after all,' Colm said.

Once the others had got drinks, they joined Maisie and Colm at a spot against the barrier, looking out at the water that was glittering with the lights from the boats, and lapping gently against the harbour wall.

'Now that we're all here,' Ollie said, reaching into her handbag, 'I wanted to give you this, Maisie.' She held out a slim rectangle, and as Maisie took it, Colm puffed out a laugh beside her.

'The mini whiteboard,' she said. 'With some half-naked guy on it. Who's this poser?' She held it up, showing everyone the photo of Colm walking out of the water. There were grins and laughter from the others, and Finn wolf-whistled.

'I didn't think you had one of these,' Ollie said, 'even though I know you've got all the photos on your laptop, and your phone, and probably your bedroom wall . . .'

'OK, OK,' Maisie said, her cheeks warming. 'Thank you, it is nice to have one. Have you got many left?'

'Nope.' Ollie shook her head. 'As you can imagine, they were snapped up fairly quickly, and we've got over *two hundred* orders for the calendar, which, considering it's not even August, is incredible. I'm thinking up more marketing tactics for the rest of the year, which I will of course rope you all into.'

'Of *course*,' Meredith said, rolling her eyes.

'We could do something in the water,' Finn said. 'Surfing or swimming, maybe. And it's for the RNLI, so possibly . . .' He tapped his chin thoughtfully. 'How about rescuing something? A series of inflatable sea creatures, perhaps. I mean—'

'Finn!' Meredith gently slapped his arm. 'Maisie could have been in serious trouble.'

'I *was* in serious trouble,' she admitted, and while she stuck her tongue out at Finn to let him know she didn't mind his teasing, she felt a faint echo of unease. It could have been so different yesterday, if Colm hadn't noticed her

377

bag and sandals on the beach, if she hadn't messaged him to let him know she was already there, waiting to watch the competition.

'It sounds so scary,' Thea said, her neat brows coming together, as Colm wrapped his arm around Maisie's shoulders, pulling her in tight, bending his head to whisper, 'OK?' in her ear.

She looked up at him. 'I'm OK. Thank you.'

The *thank you* didn't feel like it was enough: not just for his concern, but for everything. For him turning out to be the man she'd always thought he was, even when he was really still a boy. She'd always felt, *known*, that behind his confidence and teenage swagger, and then the reticence, the occasional cynicism when he'd returned, that he was a wonderful, warm, good-hearted person: one of the very best.

'I'm OK,' she said, more loudly now, to reassure Thea. 'But if you *do* come up with any water-based promotion I will be staying firmly on the beach. Preferably on a towel, with suncream and a hat on, and possibly a cocktail in my hand.'

'Oh, that sounds so *good*,' Ollie said. 'We have to do that in the next two weeks. All of us, if we can manage it.' She held out her Pimm's, and everyone clinked their glasses and bottles together.

'All of us,' Maisie repeated under her breath.

The band strummed the first few chords of a Taylor Swift song, and she felt a sudden wash of contentment, like when the waves had broken over her head the day before, only a whole lot more pleasant.

'Maisie,' a voice called, and she turned to see Charlie

and Daniel, walking hand in hand towards them. 'Hey, everyone.' Charlie laughed, giving quick hugs to Meredith, Thea and Ollie, saving Maisie for last. 'I can't thank you enough for everything you've done.' She stretched her arms out wide, as if Maisie had been responsible for the entire festival.

'It wouldn't have happened at all without your suggestion,' Daniel said, as if reading her mind. 'Then all the work you did to make it a reality.'

'I'm so glad it did happen,' Maisie said. 'It's been wonderful – lots of money raised for charity, support for small businesses, footfall in the town.'

'A watery disaster averted,' Charlie added, then her smile faded. 'I heard you had your own drama yesterday. Are you OK?'

'I'm completely recovered,' Maisie assured her, 'which is more than can be said for the Seafood Shack's octopus, though I think he expired long before Sprout got his teeth into him.'

'I'm surprised we didn't have more wind-related issues,' Daniel said. 'I heard you fixed the town hall's leak,' he added, turning to Ben.

'It was an easy fix,' Ben said.

Daniel nodded. 'Do you think I could talk to you sometime, about the next round of improvements we want to make to the hotel? It's the latest stage of our sustainability project, and I'd like to use local contractors where I can.'

'That would be great,' Ben said, his expression measured, as it always was.

They swapped numbers, and Charlie said she had to get back to the bus, which was still busy, even though it was heading towards evening. She looked happy about it, though.

'Come for a cream tea,' she said to Maisie. 'All of you, if you like? We can close the bus, give you a special celebratory meal as a way of thanking you. I know you were all involved in this.'

'That's too generous,' Maisie said. 'And you don't need to give yourself more work to do over the next few months.'

Daniel slipped his arm around Charlie's waist. 'If you can get her to slow down, then I will be in your debt for life. It's like talking to a very beautiful, very determined, brick wall.'

Charlie laughed. 'I will slow down, I promise, but there's no need to right now. And this is the last night of the festival – make sure you enjoy yourselves!'

'We will,' Ollie assured her.

They said their goodbyes, and Maisie watched Charlie and Daniel stroll back to the Cornish Cream Tea Bus, which stood tall and gleaming on Port Karadow's harbour, and thought about everything they had ahead of them. Then she felt Colm's arm against hers, his warm skin setting her nerve endings alight, and thought of everything they had ahead of them, too.

'I was thinking . . .' she started, but then the band moved onto its next song, the opening notes stopping her in her tracks.

Colm's eyes widened, and he laughed. 'Did you plan this?'

'Definitely not,' she said. 'But . . . Oh my god!'

'What is it?' Meredith asked.

'It's our song,' Maisie explained. 'Well, it's Colm's karaoke song, really, but it's . . .'

'It could be our song,' Colm said. The surprise had faded from his eyes, had been replaced with something much more tender. 'It's pretty accurate, after all.' He handed Sprout's lead to Meredith, which she took without question, then pulled Maisie away from the railings, to the space in front of the band, where a few people were standing and swaying along, but where absolutely nobody was dancing.

'What are you doing?' Maisie asked.

'What do you think?' Colm said, and as the first line of 'You Got It' filled the air, he swung her around, catching her off guard so she fell into him, laughing. He held on tight, wrapping her up in his arms, and looked down at her.

'I mean it,' he said. 'This should be our song. That first kiss, the night of the lock-in . . . I thought I was more drunk than I realized, that I'd made it all up. But I hadn't, and this is real, and I want to build a life with you, Winters. Our song, our favourite pub for Sunday roast, our usual Saturday morning walk. Then, we'll decide which of our expertly renovated houses we want to live in together, and move onto his-and-hers tea towels, mugs, a doormat that says, *Maisie and Colm would like you to fuck off.*'

She laughed, giddy and delighted. 'I'd love that.'

'Even the doormat?'

'We might have to rethink the message,' she said lightly, as she trailed a finger down his chest, drawing a line against the soft cotton of his T-shirt, the hard muscle beneath. 'But I'm ruling nothing out at this stage. You're my person, Colm Caffrey. I'm pretty sure you always have been.'

'You're my person too, and I'm going to do my best to remind you of that, of how much I love you, every chance I get.'

He took her breath away with a long, lingering kiss, one that seemed to promise years of happiness and contentment, and, in the more immediate future, his touch, his passion and his certainty. And then, when their kiss finally ended, he spun her around again, in the space that wasn't really a dance floor, but had the music from the band and people standing around the edge, singing and swaying along, including all their friends.

All around them were the lights of the town she loved, winking on as the afternoon shifted towards evening, the happiness and exhaustion of a festival well-enjoyed permeating the air, the inky blue sea mirroring the amber perfection of the setting sun, the harbour and the twinkling boats and the beach beyond, all a part of it. Every place she looked seemed to be more beautiful than the last.

Colm spun her around slowly, reverently, letting her take it all in, understanding how happy she was here, what Port Karadow meant to her, and proving how much he loved her with this one, simple gesture. It was a moment she wanted to hold onto forever, pinned at the top of her thoughts like a framed photograph secured with her best-selling adhesive which, when used properly, would never come down.

This was her town and her man: her perfect slice of life. It was the forever she'd always wanted.

Acknowledgements

How is this book eight in the Cornish Cream Tea series? I can't believe that from that one spark of an idea, *I'm going to write a book set in Cornwall*, eight books have emerged: eight sets of heroines and heroes I've loved, eight stories that I've put my heart into. A whole lot of other people have also put heart, soul and hard work into making them what they are, and so here are all the thank yous.

Thank you to Kate Bradley, who has been my wing-woman – and also my editor – from the very beginning. We have worked on fourteen books together, they would all be a hot mess without her care, knowledge and guidance (and so would I be, probably) and I hope we get to work on many, many more together.

Thank you to my wonderful agent Alice Lutyens, who makes me believe absolutely anything is possible. The world feels like a ginormous oyster with you in my corner. Thank you for all the advice, support, hilarity, kindness – and that is on top of all the standard agenting jobs you do for me. You are one of the coolest, and loveliest, people I have ever known.

Thank you to the wonderful HarperFiction team who look after me and my books so well. I say this in every set of acknowledgements, but it never gets less true. To Susanna Peden, Meg Le Huquet, Lynne Drew, Kim Young, Lucy Stewart and everyone else at Harper, thank you for all the hundreds of jobs, large and small, that you do to get my books into readers' hands.

Thank you to copyeditor Penelope Isaac and proofreader Charlotte Webb for making this book make sense: for picking up inconsistencies and mistakes I was too close to notice. The work you do is mighty, and I am so grateful for it.

Thank you to Holly Macdonald and Emily Langford for the utterly stunning cover. I have judged – and bought – so many books based on their cover, and bearing that in mind, I am feeling confident that I'm going to find some new readers for this book based on its beautiful, eye-catching jacket.

Thank you to my writing friends who keep me going in all kinds of ways, who make this sometimes solitary-feeling job less lonely, and who inspire me to be better with their hard work and deserved successes. Including but not limited to Kirsty Greenwood, Shelia Crighton, Pernille

Hughes, Jane Casey, Sam Holland, Isabelle Broom and all the Bookcampers.

The biggest thank you to David. He is another of the hundreds-of-quiet-jobs people, because he brings me coffee and makes every stage of the writing process less stressful, often just by being there, sometimes by doing a silly dance that makes me laugh. He also gives world-class hugs, and is my constant and best source of romantic hero inspiration. I am so lucky I get to share my life with him.

Thank you to Mum and Dad, who are the foundations of my writing career. They brought books into my life early and often, and showed me how much stories matter. They read my books as soon as they come out, they let me ramble on endlessly about everything, they celebrate all my successes. I know I am lucky in a hundred different ways to have them as my parents.

Thank you to Lee, to Kate and Tim, Kate G and Kelly for the laughs and friendship, for helping to keep me sane and not totally, 100% obsessed with books.

A leftfield but heartfelt thanks to the BBC, Aidan Turner and Cornwall, for the recent adaptation of *Poldark*. I have to admit that Cornwall wasn't on my radar – I'd never been – until it aired. But I saw Ross Poldark riding across those magnificent cliffs and knew I had to see it for myself. As soon as I did, I was desperate to jump on the setting-my-story-in-Cornwall bandwagon. Now I've written eight books set there, it's pretty much changed my career, and I could not be more grateful to everyone involved in that programme – and to Cornwall – for being so mesmerising and moreish.

And finally, thank you to all of you – my readers. A book is a sad thing without anyone to enjoy it, and if it had only ever been me, reading my own books over and over again, I don't think Charlie and Daniel, Lila and Sam, Hannah and Noah, Ellie and Jago, Meredith and Finn, Thea and Ben, Ollie and Max, and Maisie and Colm, would feel anywhere near as real as they do. You have embraced my stories, you've emailed and messaged and DM'd me about them, and I'm so glad they've brought you happiness, escape and moments of hope. There would be no point in doing this without you, and I hope you'll stick with me for all the new things I've got coming up. Gertie forever! xxx

Cosy up with more delightful stories

from Cressida McLaughlin

All available now.